Jumping

Jumping

Dana Wildsmith

INK
BRUSH
PRESS

ISBN: 978-0-9909452-5-3
Library of Congress Control Number: 2016957128

Manufactured in the United States

Ink Brush Press
Austin and Dallas

Por Cesar y Rolando y la familia Razo, con amor

and for Mama:
Mary Grace Patten Scoates McCurley, 3/26/21- 4/14/16

Other Fiction from Ink Brush Press

Acknowledgments

Thank you to all who have helped me so generously throughout the writing of this book:

To Don Wildsmith: thank you for always supporting my writing trips when you'd always rather I'd stayed home. And my eternally grateful heart for your loving care of Mama.

To Larry Germain, my first, best reader. Thank you for employing your editor's eye and musician's ear to my manuscript. And also for loving and supporting our students.

To my colleagues at Lanier Tech's Adult Education Department: Barbara Smith, Larry Germain, Beth Magness, Sally Brown, Eleanor Green, Ann Miller, Loretta Vail, Delores Simpson, Dorothy Peppers, Lisa Prescott, and to the memory of Belinda Arrington.

To the Good Shepherd Church of Christ, and to the Green Valley Samaritans, especially Shura Wallin and Peg Bowden. I am in awe of your tireless and selfless work.

To the organizations and locations that housed and supported me during the writing of the book: The Hambidge Center for Creative Arts & Sciences, The Lillian Smith Center, the Artist-in-Residence programs of Grand Canyon National Park and Everglades National Park, Hindman Settlement School, Susie Waldrup and Georgina Deal at the Asheville Log Cabin Motor Court, Gloria Whiting at Los Cuatro Vientos, and Boyce McClung.

To Jenni and Tery Overbey for being the best travelling buddies; to Cassie Moses, Frieda Mullins and the memory of the inestimable Mike Mullins; to Jim Webb, Scott Goebel , Pauletta Hansel and the other fine members of SAWC; to my forever friends: Darnell Arnoult, Joni Caldwell and Moir Quin; to those who shared their stories: Dinora Acevedo, Miriam Duran, "Alfredo Sanchez", and Pablo; to Vivian Alford, Donna Varnadoe, and Tom Vail, for believing; to Pete and Chloe, for keeping Mama's feet warm;to Lily, for good companionship; to The Panera Bunch: Wayne Ford, Terry Kay, Wally Eberhart, Gail Karwoski, Jennifer Patrick and Cindy Farley; to Sonny Houston for singing for Mama; to Ingrid Sandez and Tara Rush for keeping Grace Farm whole; to Will Balk, for understanding.

All love to my family: Don, Snow and Barry, Gaylon, Luellen, Elizabeth, and Mac, for your support. What a long, strange trip it's been.

Other books by Dana Wildsmith

Back to Abnormal
One Good Hand
Christmas in Bethlehem
Our Bodies Remember
Annie
Alchemy

Wade in the water
Wade in the water, children,
Wade in the water,
God's a-going to trouble the water

See that host all dressed in white
God's a-going to trouble the water
Must be the children of the Israelites
God's a-going to trouble the water

See that band all dressed in red
God's a-going to trouble the water
Looks like the children that Moses led
God's a-going to trouble the water

Look over yonder, what do you see?
God's a-going to trouble the water
The Holy Ghost a-coming on me
God's a-going to trouble the water

"Hope has two beautiful daughters. Their names are anger and courage: anger at the way things are, and courage to see that things do not remain as they are."
—St. Augustine

I. Puerto Vallarta, Mexico, 1985

1
Cesar

That morning, it started the same as all the mornings.

"Buen dia, Gordita."

I stopped and turned to look back through the doorway into my casita. The buckets for the water were hanging empty from both my hands because I had just started out the doorway when I heard the big voice of my abuelo. It was not to me he spoke so loud, but to my little cousin, the chubby niña who I knew prayed each night that the Virgin might bring a miracle of thinness to her while she slept. She had been trying to slip away like a brown mouse to make her morning pee, but our grandfather saw.

Good Day, Little Fat One.

This was why she was afraid of him.

Me, he ignored. He did not want to startle me away to one of my hiding places. My granny needed the water I would bring for the cooking of his breakfast.

All the days, I went early to the well to get water for making the breakfast. I did not sleep late in the bed filled with my brothers—brothers who turned and curled to their sides and made whimpering sounds like puppies if anyone shook them awake while an hour of good sleeping coolness still hung in Mexico's summer air. I did not want to be in our bed when the waking and grumbling began. I wanted out of the bed and into the day with no one talking to me, except me to my own self.

I squeezed my toes deep into the cool dirt as I walked to the well. Every morning I cranked the well's steel handle and watched the rope wind around itself on the drilled log. Creak, creak, creak—a whole song of creaks and squonks, until finally one bucket was filled and then another filled with the cold water I tipped into my own buckets. At home, I would pour the water from these buckets into a big brown jug my granny kept near her cooking stove.

As I walked back to our casita, the water in my buckets sloshed, while the cold water I had drunk from the well sloshed in my empty belly. Those waters made a morning song with always the same two singers—my belly and my buckets.

I counted my steps to our house. Twenty. When first I became old enough to bring the water, I had to make twenty-five steps from the well to our house. The distance was now five steps closer than when I had only five years to my age. In twenty years more, would the well be no steps at all from my casita?

Ai, but in truth, my house was no casita, because it was the biggest house in the village. I called it *little house* only because it is not a good thing to boast, and, well, what right had I to boast when this house did not belong to my family alone? All the people in our village had worked together to make this house for my grandfather because he was the keeper of the village temascal, the sweat lodge. It was right that everyone should work for what everyone would use.

The temascal kept one long side of the house for itself alone. Those who came to use the temascal entered through a patio with many trees and flowers. The temascal was one side of the patio, and along the back side were the two big rooms for sleeping, and on the side opposite the temascal, one little room where my granny cooked the meals. Every day she made the fire in the stove for cooking, and my granddaddy kept the fires burning in the sweat lodge so anyone could come and use it. All the time the house smelled like smoke. Our clothes—the same, you know?

Most mornings I hurried to be outside before anyone else. I just pulled on my clothes from yesterday, still smelling like yesterday's smoke. I visited a tree to make pee before I grabbed the buckets for the water. In our house, in all the houses—no bathroom. Our grandfather, he dug a hole and when that hole was full, he covered it and then dug a new one. Some mornings early, when a person's body is out of bed and walking but the mind is not yet, we would forget where the new hole was, and stumble around looking for it like puppies when their eyes are not yet all the way open. This always made us laugh afterward.

When my granddaddy laughed it was very strong, but he was not laughing when I came again into our house. Abuelo was yelling over his shoulder while he walked to the table.

"Old Woman, bring me my breakfast."

I stopped for one moment to watch him yank out his chair. This was *his* chair only. My brothers and me would have spit on the blessed altar before we would be so foolish as to sit in his chair. I watched my grandfather swing his legs across the seat of the chair and lower his butt like he was mounting a bull. Mestizo blood had made short the legs of my grandfather, but I always believed there could be nothing so powerful as his legs. His legs were like the pistons I had seen in the engines of tractors.

Cesar, I spoke to myself then in a voice like my teacher at school when my mind was wandering again: do you forget that your granny is waiting for this water?

I grinned at what a good imitation of my teacher I had made, and then I hurried into the little room for cooking. My granny had lit the fire in the oil stove, and was heating her petate for tortillas, one tortilla after another to feed Abuelo and all my brothers and cousins, and me.

"Mijo, did you have to walk to USA for that water?"

"No, Abuelita. Perdón. Sorry."

My little granny reached up with both hands to poke another pin into her two braids of white hair to hold them where she had twisted them to a knot on the top of her head. Then she lowered her hands to shoo me from the room.

"Chilaquiles, mijo."

She talked while she moved me toward the door.

"For a wonder, you and your brothers did not eat all the tortillas from yesterday, so I will make chilaquiles if a certain boy will get out of the way."

She started flapping her blue apron at me like I was a chicken in the yard. Maybe I was a chicken; I know I wanted to peck at the tortillas she was frying and stacking with salsa and queso fresca.

"Chico. Boy."

Now my abuleo was shouting for me. I was the one he called *boy*. I could not remember that he ever said my name. Maybe he did not believe I was yet man enough to be called Cesar. Cesar was a ruler, a builder of empires. I was a boy.

"Chico. Listen to me. You will eat and then you will go with me to the wood pile to help carry the wood back for the fire. You are not much help, but you are all I have."

I followed him out to the wood pile after breakfast, before the time for school, and I sat on the dirt while he chopped. I picked up a stick and began drawing a picture in the dirt so I would not look like I was watching for the cats that lived in the wood stacks.

There. Two yellow fires flared between logs. It was a cat; I knew it was, though I could not see the body. I never saw the bodies of the cats. I saw only the eyes glowing between stacks of logs. I was not scared, not scared at all. It was right that the cats should be there. The wild cats were the keepers of my mornings with Abuelo.

I had thought many mornings about the cats and my grandfather, and I had figured it out. Cats are sly by their nature. The wild cats had to be more sly, to steal what they needed to survive. And so I believed these cats had the talent to steal a thing so big as the bad from my granddaddy's moods. It was why the cats lived where he worked. The cats waited for him each day, to take his anger from him.

Many times I had watched Abuelo as he began to do the chopping. Quieter and quieter he became—a good kind of quiet that meant the hungers of his heart were calming like the hungers that had lived in his belly before we ate my granny's chilaquiles. With all the hungers satisfied, we could be together then in the way we preferred: neither of us talking or needing to make talk. I was sure it was the cats who gave him that calm. The cats had to be there to take from Abuelo the fires consuming his heart; they stole the flames from my grandfather's heart to feed the fires in their eyes. It was for this reason I had no fear of the eyes of the cats.

Once I asked Abuelita why my grandfather was always angry. I remember she wiped her hands on the skirt of her apron and sat down on the little stool by the kitchen stove.

"He is not angry with you, niño. Listen to me: there was once another granny. Not me, the mamá of your mami, but before. Your granddaddy was made a widowed man when one time in the town it was raining too hard, for too long. He was not living up here then, you understand, but down in the town. The rains they always come in August, September—every day in those months— and heavy like altar curtains. But that year the rains forgot to leave when October came. Soon all the wells like ours filled up and spit their waters out, and the rivers ran like a drunk man's flow; all down the side of the mountain water ran like a crazy man after the children and pretty women. That water, it found your abuelo's wife and she died, floating away from him to the Malecon, to the sea."

I remember looking at my little granny while she talked, but her words made me see in my mind the waters of the Malecon swollen like a pot boiling over, and on those waters floated the body of a young woman without a face.

Abuelita laid her hand on my head.

"He left the lights of his heart down in the town and moved up this mountain so he could live as dark with dark because it was the only way he could imagine to keep living. Niño, you know how these ridges are like hands holding back the sun each day until eight or even nine in the mornings? All day the sun must keep pushing back against those hard hands of the mountain until finally it grows weary and says goodbye, good riddance, by four on each afternoon. To your grandfather, so much darkness felt the same as the night in his heart and so he came here to live as dark with dark."

She smiled, and gave my hair a tug.

"Until he met me."

"Pero, Abuelita, he still is angry too much."

"Not angry, mijo, but injured. Some hurts never heal. When he works hard, it helps him to forget his hurting."

I looked up from my remembering when my grandfather swung the ax down to split a log like it was the little stick I was still holding in my hands. One day, I would have the strong arms of my grandfather. Already, we were twins of the heart. Like me, he was most easy in himself when he was alone.

I knew he had a love for my granny, but he had not let the first granny leave his heart and go to God. My grandfather lived stuck between the wife he could not touch and the wife he could, like an ax wedged tight in a log that will not split. To him all other women were only *not her,* and other men were all men whose wives not had been taken by the waters of the Bay. This was why he did not talk, talk, talk as the other people in the village did. What could he have to say to anyone who had never had his heart split in two? And what could people say to him that would make sense or matter?

Once I had tried to say this to Carlos, but Carlos only waved his hand like I was a fly and said, "You are stupid, my brother. Abuelo is mean, that's all."

Carlos and me were not alike as brothers, inside or outside. I was always short like this, with hair curly as a donkey's back. Carlos was born to be tall from long legs, with hair as straight as his nose. And smart. Books have always loved my brother; words make patterns for him and show him the truths that move life around like wheels under a wagon. I have to beg to the words to make them come to me. It is always a long courtship and sometimes I give up and vow to live as a single man without knowledge or knowing.

So why was I, a boy with ten years and not much else to claim as his own, thinking this day about books and the teaching of books? What was the reason I was thinking about how I, Cesar, should someday be a teacher, when Carlos was the one with a head for books, and not me? Maybe Carlos was right and I was his stupid brother. But, Ai. I could not stop the thoughts that came to me. Thoughts arrive like little brothers, whether you want them or not. A good brother scoots over and makes room for the thoughts. Here in my granddaddy's wood—chopping place, the dirt was flat and wide with lots of room for many thoughts to settle in, to draw up their knees to their chin like me, and consider the reasons for their coming.

A little wind of dust blew up as two big feet stopped their walking near to my feet.

"Pues, Martín, the temascal, it will be ready for me to come at midday? Good. Good."

I looked up at the man who had spoken to Abuelo, a quick look not to be noticed. It was only Sr. Franco. Huh. He thought himself very grand for a man who bred only daughters.

Sr. Franco walked on, but the numbers of people walking near us grew more large as the heat of the morning also grew. Everyone wanted to be out taking care of their business before the day became too hot. My granddaddy raised his ax again and again to split many logs to the size of the fire they would make. I knew he wanted to be finished so he could take himself out of the sight of so many neighbors.

I watched the arms of my granddaddy while he worked. Did his arms still have the strength they had yesterday? This was a new worry for me. His legs still were as solid as logs he had not yet split, but lately I believed the ropes in his arms had to strain against the weight of his ax more than I remembered from a year ago.

Each time the rope at our well would begin to stretch instead of tighten to my pull on it each morning, I would tell my granddaddy and he wound a new rope around the shaft, tossing the old rope to the lodge fire later that day. But what could be done for the wearing away of the muscles of the arms of my grandfather? This worried at me, but I did not say it to anyone. I had the knowledge of his lessening, but I did not allow it to others.

Just then the stick I still held in my hand fell, almost, and I looked down again at the hard dirt. A new picture came to my mind and then to my hand. I drew the picture in the dirt, a picture of the way a rope winding around a shaft of wood eases the weight of a filled bucket, and how the handle I turned each morning eases the winding of the rope. Could I not figure out a system of ropes and cranks and pulleys to take the weight of the ax as Abuelo raised it after a chop? That was the key, yes. It was not in the lowering but in the raising of the ax that my

15

granddaddy had to call most to the memory of his younger strength. And does not memory fade more quickly even than muscle? I drew faster in the dirt, this angle and that, rubbing out each false possibility with my bare toe.

"Niño, are you digging for silver?"

Abuelo had stopped his chopping to look down to where I was drawing very near to his sandal. I nodded my head a little, looked up at him, and grinned while I scrubbed away the picture with the bottom of my foot.

"Oh, sí, Abuelo. And I am getting closer. By this time next year silver will be jangling in our pockets like festival music and we will all be living in a mansion in the Distrito Federal. What color would you like your new house to be?"

"Yellow, like the one I have now. Do you know the place? It is the house with no wood for the fire because a grandson has his head in the clouds and his hands in the dirt instead of his arms out for firewood to carry. "

I grinned more, and held them out, my arms strong from mornings of bringing the water home.

I was smiling because he had given me a new picture I could see in my head: a long stretch of a boy, his neck like a tree trunk rising through flocks of swallows up to a cap of clouds, while his arms like vines dangled toward earth from a belly as plump as the one I could see if I looked down, which I dared not because my granddaddy was piling fresh-chopped logs onto the platform of my two arms: eight, nine, ten logs, landing like small earth tremors, one quickly after another, but I did not let my arms shake. Maybe only a little.

Back we went to the house with our firewood, an old man and a boy not talking because there was no need for talk between us when we had nothing to say. The rest of that day—as every day—my granddaddy lived inside the house, feeding the fire, trying to be as unnoticed as the next log on the pile. I believed he did not want people to look too closely at him because they might see he was not as strong as he used to be. He was now older and more little, and he did not know how to live in the world as the man he was now, so he kept mostly out of the world, except in the mornings early when he still had strength enough to chop wood and be the Martín he once had been. People on their way to their morning places saw him working like a young man and remembered this Martín in their eyes for the whole of the day. It was a good trick.

And if a man must pass his days inside, our house made a fine place to pass those days. The adobe on the outside walls of our house showed back to the sun its own yellows and oranges, but the inside was cooled with whitewash. The windows sat so deep in the walls that I could drop my butt there like the window ledge was a bench, and lean my back against the iron bars that kept the animals from coming in.

In my granny's kitchen, a pottery jar as tall as my littlest brother made cool the water I brought each morning, and always an iguana stayed near the water jar, sleeping in the cool spot there. When I walked through the courtyard with the firewood, I saw in the kitchen my granny flapping her apron at it: "Váyase. Get." But the iguana opened its mouth in a yawn and got back to sleep.

16

I carried my load of firewood past the pool that would fill when the rains began—soon, because the summer was coming to an end. Our courtyard curved like a large bowl around this pool that was like a smaller bowl made from rocks my granny had cleared from her garden. In all the courtyard around the pool and up to the walls of the rooms there were flowers and big-leafed plants and banyan trees. A bullfrog lived under the flowers by the pond, but he had no more body than the cats in the woodpile. The cats had eyes, only, and this frog lived as only his croak, that was all, but such a loud croak as he had was more than enough. Many nights too hot for sleeping I had counted the croaks as they came every four and a half seconds. I remembered one night hearing my granddaddy in his bed swing from granny in his arms, to the gun under his bed. He was out in the courtyard aiming at the next croak by the time Abuelita stilled him with "Ai, Martín. Come back to bed. Do not be a fool."

It being ever his aim to appear not a fool, he now kept his old self unnoticed each day in a chair just behind the largest banyan in the courtyard, except when he needed to feed the temascal fires.

I walked past him. He had already stacked his load of wood and now was easing as quiet as a cat into his chair in the shade of the courtyard. I had just dropped my own firewood into its stack by the temascal door when I heard the yard dogs howl and snarl.

"Míjo. Go and see what is troubling the dogs."

"Sí, Abuelita."

My granny wanted me to go outside and watch a dog fight instead of getting dressed for school? Sí, I could do that. I stepped from the shade of the courtyard to the sun of the village yard. I had not yet put shoes on my feet for school and the sand was already hot enough to make me hop from foot to foot while I looked to see where the dogs were fighting. One yellow dog I always called Carlito because he was as nervous as was my brother, this dog ran behind me to hide and I almost stepped on him with my feet dancing from the hot sand.

The other dogs—the little red one and the two big brown ones that bit at my feet sometimes and made me kick them in the nose even though I did not want to kick any animal—were standing close together and barking but the dogs were not fighting with each other. They were all barking, but not at the other dogs. They were barking at someone I did not know. It was a woman. A white woman.

Ai, she was a turista, that was all. But, Díos, what was she doing up here where turistas never come? What I saw most plainly was what she was *not* doing. This turista was hiding something. I half-closed my eyes to see more closely. Huh. It was her camera that she did not want anyone to see. Did she think we were all banditos? No. I shook my head to myself after I watched her for a minute more. It was not because she was afraid that she held her camera so tightly to her side. Her hand was over her camera to say that she was *not* taking photos of our house, or of our donkey standing near the well, or me, because she knew she did not have the right; she was a guest in our village and knew she should leave us our privacy. That was what her hand was saying.

17

Pues. I nodded my head, once. This gringa lady was a nice lady. My granny would say she had been raised in the right way by her mami and papi. Granny. I had not told her what was happening. I turned so quickly to run to the kitchen that I stepped again on Carlito the dog, who yelped and ran off, looking back at me like he was more hurt in his feelings than in his foot.

A hand came down on my shoulder and I twisted my head sideways to look down at the fingers. I knew that hand.

"Abuelo?" But he shook his head hard at me, one time: *Do not talk.*

Talk? My words had all run away the moment I realized my granddaddy had come outside in the bright of day, with all the people milling around on their daily business. How long since he had done this? Probably some of our neighbors were as surprised as I was at the sight of Martín in the open air for all to see, and they may have stopped to stare , but if they did so, I did not notice. My neighbors were nothing to me. I turned back toward the road to watch the lady my granddaddy had come out to see.

Her hair had curls like mine, but her curls lay long on her shoulders, and loose, and were brown to my black, but, no, more red as she moved into the sun. And when she moved, it was as a person strong, someone whose body has been used for doing work. Tall. She was taller than my most tall uncle. But what I noticed most was how she had not fear of the dogs. Her other hand, the one not hiding her camera, reached out toward the yard dogs, but I believe she did not even know she was reaching, only did so in the way I once saw Sr. Franco make public his secret passion for the wife of his brother, by a gesture that could not stop itself. This turista had a deep ease with the company of dogs, and the dogs gave her welcome by stopping their barking and ignoring her.

Abuelo and I watched her pass all the way through the village. It did not take long for her to walk beyond the dozen houses that circled around our well. She would follow the road down the side of the mountain half a mile and then she would again be in the town, back to her hotel, I supposed.

I looked again at my grandfather. He, too, had narrowed his eyes like he wanted to see more better.

"Abuelo, who was she?"

"You ask too many questions."

He did not look at me, but answered so quickly I thought he must have known that she would come and I would ask.

He turned and went inside, walking like a man who has finished at last a job that had been long in the doing. *Finally,* his old back seemed to say as I watched him go back in the house, *that's done.*

I am no fool. I may be Carlos' stupid brother, but I know things he does not, or if he does, he sweeps such knowings out of his head like trash to the pile. Carlos's head will not carry what cannot be labeled. But I am a tinkerer. I find little bits of this and that and save them for later. Many times, I do not even know how to name these bits, or where they came from or what their use might be, but I know that all things can used eventually, and so I save what I find. The way

Abuelo acted when he saw the tourist lady was a bit that had broken off from a story he would not yet tell me, so I must go looking for other bits myself.

My granny was still waiting for me to tell her what had happened. I yelled over my shoulder as I ran to pull on my school pants and shirt.

"Abuelita, estaba una turista, solamente. Just a tourist."

I jammed both dusty feet into my shoes (who would see that they were dirty?) and stopped long enough to prop one foot and then the other against the well while I tied the shoes.

I ran down and down the cobbled road just far enough behind her so she would not notice. It felt good to be by myself and following my own wishes, not everyone else's . It was always: "Cesar, bring me a bucket of water." "Cesar, can you not see the fire needs feeding?" "Hey, my brother, where are you going without me?" But if anyone had seen me run out of the village on this particular morning, they did not care enough to call me back. All their eyes were still where my abuelo had stood, watching to see if he might come out a second time—as if the sun might rise twice.

The August sun rode hot on my shoulders but I did not care. It was a fine thing to be away from everyone, and walking. The busier the road became with little stores and bigger and bigger houses, the more I was only a boy the people of El Centro did not know--and I liked that. I settled down to a watching place inside my head and let my feet follow the lady while my eyes took their own travels. The closer I came to town and the bay, the less I saw dirt or fields. It was all houses now and stone stairways between rows of houses, and after another block or two there was not even any *between* between next-door houses. The houses there shared their walls so that they looked like they were hugging each other to keep from falling onto the Malecon. My granny's courtyard full of flowers would find no space along such a train of houses. A few front windows had boxes of poppies, but mostly the brightest colors of the town were in the tiles framing the doorways and in the mats of tile that greeted the feet of guests.

Oh, but I needed to pay attention to the lady again as she turned past a tall townhouse with someone's burro tied to a post outside. Left she turned, and then one block more, and then she went into the inn on Matamoros that my granddaddy helped build before floods took his wife and he climbed alone up our mountain to live. The lady was staying at the inn Los Cuatro Vientos: The Four Winds.

Ai, but it was pretty. A low wall curved smooth and white along the walkway, and plants with leaves like umbrellas grew tall from a planter in the wall, touching the pointy ferns hanging from hooks somewhere high out of sight. There was a black iron gate so heavy I wondered if I would be able to push it open, but I did, my arms stronger than I knew from so many mornings of drawing up our well bucket again and again. On the other side of the gate, the whitewashed stone wall that was half again taller than I was climbed along a little walk-up of steps with flowers set into the facing tiles, and hanging all over that wall were red and yellow hibiscus.

Inside the gate I went up the steps past a swimming pool I could see only when I had reached the tenth step. Yes. I remembered. Mi abuelo told me once how la dueña had hired the strongest men of Jalisco to dig a great hole for that pool; how for too many weeks Martín and the others had dug themselves into earth shovel by shovel until the people who stopped to watch could see only small explosions of dirt rising as if tossed by the devil himself. Tiles lined that hole now, tiles of greens and blues like the sea, and there were green trees with large leaves shading the pool's edge. No one was swimming. Who with any sense would be? The July sun was so hot as to cook a swimmer like he was a lobster caught and thrown in the pot.

My gringa lady must have known it was time to leave the sun outside to its burning because I saw her hurry through the inn's courtyard, and I believed she was not the kind of person to hurry through a place of green without stopping to be part of it for a small minute. Up the stone stairs and up again to the third floor of rooms. I kept watching until she stopped at a door and went in. Her room was the corner room. This would be the best room, I thought, with its two walls of windows and a view of the bay.

"Chico, que quieres? What do you want here?"

A man was looking at me from behind a low counter I had not noticed because my eyes were on the lady. I turned toward him. He was not tall with Spanish blood, but an indio like me, and he was fat-cheeked from no meals missed. He was maybe the age of my father but I could not say for sure for either of them. He was not smiling on the outside, but a smile was there for me; I could feel it. Very fast, I thought how to answer him.

"A job? You have some small work a boy could do?" I do not know what made me say this. I had work enough a casa—at home— where I did the work with my granddaddy and also the chores my granny needed from me.

The man tried to look more serious. He bent his head down a little and made his eyes go narrow.

"Let me see your arms. Are you strong?" His fingers measured the width of my right arm just below the shoulder and then he pulled his hand away like he was shocked. "Ai, Díos. The muscles of a man. Un gigánte. Never have I felt such power in one so young, no more than—what? Eighteen? You have maybe nineteen years?"

This man made me grin all over my face.

"No, señor, I am only eleven. Once, solamente." After such wondrous lying from him, how could I answer him back with the dull truth of my ten years?

"Pues, Senor Gorila, such great strength in one so young must be made useful. Can you be here in this courtyard tomorrow, seis a punto? No later than six, hijo. Breakfast for the guests is at seven and you must be here to help me prepare. Can you do this?"

"Si, me puedo. I can. And gracias, senor. Mil gracias."

But how, Cesar, I asked myself as I ran down the steps of the inn toward my school, are you going to bring your granny's water and slip away from your brothers and keep Abuelo from asking where you think you are going? All this will be tomorrow's troubles, I answered to myself. And tomorrow's pleasure would be to work with this kind man. And to watch the lady as she started her day. Maybe to speak to her.

2

Cesar

"Adónde vas? Where are you going, Brother?"

Ai, no. Carlos. Why was he awake so early on this morning of all mornings, the morning after the lady had come? I was awake before my brothers, like always, and I had stayed very still, listening to the breaths of the brother sleeping closest to me before I pushed Juan's arm from where it had fallen like a log across my shoulder. I was sliding my legs down and around so that both feet would touch the floor together when Carlos
whispered his question in the dark. Always Carlos had for me a question I must answer. I had ready an answer for this one.

"To the well—where do you think?"

Carlos raised up and leaned on one elbow, squinting at the dark outside the window.

"It is too early."

It must be too early for Carlos to stay awake, too, I thought, because I watched his elbow slide from under him as he curled back to his pillow. My littlest brother Juan stretched his legs into the warm space I had left

I hurried fast, but quiet, to the well to get the water for my granny. When both buckets were full all the way to the tops, I carried them back the way you must if you want to keep the water from sloshing out. I bent both elbows like door hinges to balance the weight of the water, and held my shoulders as stiff as door frames. I waddled a little, like a duck, while I walked the twenty steps back to my house; I was a boy duck waddling between two small lakes of cold water. In the kitchen, I lifted one bucket almost over my head to pour the water into the jar there. All day the clay of this jar would breathe and sweat to keep the water cool for drinking.

And then I turned to leave all the sleepers behind me. The man at the inn was waiting for me; I was in a hurry to get there and talk with him again. Usually, I wanted only to be *not* talking this early—and this man, he had talked a lot—but his words were like many small kindnesses, so I did not mind.

But Díos, the bad luck was following me: Carlos stood watching me from the doorway. He threw another question to me.

"Why are you awake this early?"

I tipped my head back a little and a little to one side the way I had sometimes seen Sr. Franco do to try to make himself seem more important than my granddaddy. I tilted my head in that same way, to put on the importance of the two years I had more than my brother because it was not possible to make myself

21

taller than him.

"And why do you ask such stupid questions? I went to get the water for Granny and now I have."

Carlos raised both eyebrows.

"Well, then, where are you going now?"

He waved his skinny arm toward the road where we stood.

" This does not look like our kitchen to me, Cesar, and you are not eating breakfast. I heard you come in and then leave. It is too early still to walk to school and yet here you are by the road. Or maybe I am still asleep and this road I think I see you standing on is actually the floor by our bed where you are climbing back in to sleep one hour more while our granny cooks?"

"You are right, Brother. Who says you are stupid as an ox? We are most certainly still in our bed and you are dreaming. Now stop talking and let me sleep.'

"Sleep, and we both will be killed by some crazy turistas who cannot drive down the mountain without burning out their brakes."

We both turned and looked up the road as if Carlos speaking aloud what too often was true might make it true at this moment. Abuelo says los americanos should always use the taxis because americanos expect even the brakes on a car to stop the car where stopping is impossible, simply because someone from America wishes this. But, no--I looked all the way up the road—at this moment we were safe from loco americanos; the road was empty.

The sunlight was crawling up the hillsides and shining down from the tops of the Papellio trees. The birds in the Papellio trees always saw the sun first and announced to the rest of us its coming, like the new day was a visitor who would make a difference in our plans for the day. When the cool winter months came we would welcome the sun to warm us, but in this month, the coming of the sun meant another day of living outside only in the morning and evening, and during the midday hiding in shadows like those who jump the border without papers.

Carlos dropped his arm around my shoulders. "Tell me, Brother. Where are you going?"

I grinned up at him, "Where I am going and what I will do there will be a story better told after than before. I will tell you, but later. Go home, and if Abuelo asks where I am, tell him your crazy brother is spending the hours before school trying to make one of his useless inventions from scraps. He will believe you."

"I should lie for you?"

"Yes."

Carlos stared at me, his slick black hair falling over his eyes as it always did, and he tossed his whole head back one shake to swing the hair out of his face. He tightened his bony arm around my neck like to choke me, then he shoved me away from him a little as he took back his arm. "Ah, what do I care where you go?" He turned and headed toward our casita, his long bare feet slapping the dirt.

This was always the way of things between me and my brother Carlos. He wished to be with me and do what I was doing, but he wished more for me not to do the things I did. Carlos was the careful brother. I was the clown who jumped into the path of the bull and headed off danger from Carlos and my other brothers while all the people laughed at how funny I was. I did not mind them laughing; I *was* funny.

One time I remember when I had maybe six or seven years only, I was squatting in the dirt watching the cars of the tourists come slow, slow down the mountain, their brake lights shining like the red night eyes of coyotes and the white-faced drivers squeezing tight to the steering wheel until their hands were white, too. And I was bored, sí. Then I had an idea that pushed the boredom away. I knew of a big Papellio tree close to the road at one curve, with limbs long and knobby like my granddaddy's arms reaching over the road. We called these trees Tourist trees because their red bark always was peeling like the skin of the tourists after too many hours on our beaches. Hard these trees were to climb, with that bark peeling away from under a heavy climber's hands, but I was a little kid so the tree didn't much notice me. I climbed up, pulled off my T-shirt and shorts and waited like a ripe coconut until a car came by. Then I dropped onto the hood of that car, grinned like a naked demon at the driver and slid easy off the hood to run away.

Carlos had watched. "You are going to be in big trouble" was all he said, but I knew he wished he could have jumped with me. Later, I heard him tell our cousins that he did.

Carlos would never have wanted to slip away from the house with me so early to work for a few centavos serving breakfast to tourists just so he could spy on one American lady.

"Abuelita will catch us, Cesar." he would have said to me, "and she will tell Abuelo to punish us."

I knew he would keep talking, talking: "What if our little brother Juan sees us leave and follows us and gets hit by one of those crazy drivers?"

And would Carlos be satisfied with only these two imagined disasters? No, not my brilliant brother. His mind is always thinking of more and more. "What if another flood comes and I am washed away like the other granny and no one knows where we went and so no one comes to help us?"

Ai, Díos. By the time he had finished thinking through all the possibles, the bells at the cathedral would be ringing us to class. That was why he must not know where I was going. I must remember exactly, like a catechism, everything I would see on this morning. Later I could tell my brother about my morning, so he could have what he could not take for himself because he thought too much.

All the way down the road and through the middle of town I watched for neighbors who might ask my granny later where I had been going so early; I watched for dogs of the sort who might bite a boy; I watched for la policia who might stop me just to have something to do with their time and their power. Always there is someone wanting to keep people to their same places. I had only ten years to my age, but already I had figured out that if you act like you are supposed to be doing whatever it is you are doing, if you act like you have the right to be wherever you are, everyone else will believe this is so.

No one stopped me or looked at me suspiciously, or even looked at me at all as I counted the many tile steps down to Los Cuatro Vientos. I jumped every other step from the gate up to the courtyard, and there was the kind man smiling at me as he brought in his fruit trays.

"Pues, aprendiz, so you are here. Bueno. I am but an old man and weak with age. I cannot by myself feed these ravenous guests. Already they have devoured like lobos all the eggs and the tortillas and just before you arrived, they began circling me, licking at my arms to see how tasty I may be. Quick. Run to the kitchen and bring out another tray of food. I will throw chunks of papaya and guava at their feet to make them slip on the tiles, but this will buy me only a little time. You must hurry."

Armando glanced at me to see what my reaction would be to this blathering. Ah. Good. He was happy I was grinning at him as a person does when he knows he's being included in a joke. Only a quick grin, though, and I was off through the kitchen door behind long tables set up on the restaurant side of the inn's courtyard.

I wanted him to know I was of the same turn of character as he was, so I hurried back, balancing in one hand a bowl of eggs cooked in their shells and in the other, a platter of tortillas covered with a cloth to keep them warm. I hoped Armando would not be ashamed of me for how I was dressed. I could hide in the kitchen and do only kitchen work, if he wanted. Like most boys from up the mountain, I was wearing a T-shirt soft from many washings and many cousins before me, and a pair of blue cotton pants. My sandals were huaraches, true huaraches with the thong braided by my abuelo during his long afternoons sitting by the lodge door. Like Armando himself, I would never have great height, and also like Armando, I supposed I would carry a rounded belly with me like a pillow even when I became a man. I have already said how my hair twisted and curled around on itself like the gnarly limbs of the Papellio tree—Armando's hair was the same—and my eyes were as dark as Armando's. He looked at me when I came out with the food.

"Gracias, Señor Aprendiz. Shall I call you by your title or is there a name I should use?"

"Cesar, Tío. My name is Cesar."

"I am not your uncle, Cesar. We are to be co-workers, it seems. Call me Armando.'

"Ai, no. I cannot call by his first name a man older than my own father might be. My grandfather would be shamed."

"Your grandfather would be proud that you would honor the request of a man older than your own father might be. I am Armando, and you are Cesar, who must be as honorable as his name. Now, Cesar, I can see that your hands are clean..."

"Sí, I have washed them twice this morning: once before I drew the water from the well, and again as the water was flowing into my buckets."

"...but your hearing is not so good, evidently, since you have started into talking before I had completed my own talking."

"Perdón, Armando."

" So. Your hands are clean enough—twice clean—for you to be the man to take the used dishes from the small round tables after the guests have eaten and then to check the tablecloths to see if a clean one is needed before the next guest arrives. Can you do that? Can you remember that you are to be polite to the guests if they speak, but you are not to start up alot of chatter with them as if you were a guest yourself?"

"Sí, me puedo. I can."

Armando's eyes watched me as I walked toward one of the tables where a couple finished eating and left to return to their room. His eyes on my back felt good, like the hand of my granddaddy when he sometimes, only sometimes, rested his hand on my shoulder while he studied one of my drawings of an idea I hoped to build into a real thing. Abuelo's hand resting on me spoke not of pushing me back toward the chores my hands should have been busy with, but of wanting for me a life where I could sit for a time with my thoughts and then work from my thoughts to my hands. And now this good man Armando dropped his attention back to the trays in front of him and left me to do the work he had asked me to do, his confidence feeling like the warm hand of my grandfather still on my back.

I gathered up the pottery cups and plates, dishes so happy, with their yellow flowers and red birds and orange and green trim. My granny had one jug and a few bowls of this good Puebla pottery such as the tourists buy, as turistas *should* because they are the craft of my people. I felt pride every time I saw such plates and bowls and cups, proud of what my people made and had made since long before the Spaniards came. Some day I would buy a whole set, all the cups and plates, for my granny. After I carried the plates back to the kitchen for washing, I brushed a few crumbs from the white tablecloth—there. It was fine, No stains; no spills. Ready for a young man and woman—maybe they were just married—who had come down from their room. I backed away, nodded toward the table.

"Gracias." The man smiled at me.

"De nada.'

And so it went, with the inn's guests sitting and eating and leaving, and me hurrying to clean for the next guest, but still I did not see the lady from yesterday. I heard the cathedral bells chime half after the eighth hour and I must be at the school by nine.

"Cesar, do you not need to leave for school soon? You have done fine work here, but a man has many demands on him and must know when to finish the one and begin the other. Almost all of the guests have come and gone. I can take care of the one or two who might still need a breakfast. But, here, before you go..."

Armando shook some centavos from the jar where the guests left tips for him. He hesitated, then also pulled out a bill, a peso note. He meant to give so much money to me? I could not look away from such money, but then, suddenly, I easily could because here at last was the lady coming down the stairs and into the courtyard. I watched her walk in, watched her sit. Armando then did put his hand on my shoulder, for the first time.

"What is it, hijo? You are too young yet for a woman's beauty to take your attention away from ready money, and yet you are staring at that lady, and not at the pay I am offering you. *Good* pay. You have a history with this Americana? Pues, there are no other guests for you to disturb and she is alone. Go. Speak to her. Wish her a good day."

He was serious? I studied Armando. Sí. He meant what he said. I thought probably this man always meant what he said, except when he was being so much the storyteller there could be no mistaking. I walked over to where she sat at the table most hidden by the courtyard's tall plants, exactly where my granddaddy would have chosen to sit. I felt like all the world was watching me walk, though no one saw except Armando.

Even she herself had no notice of me as I walked closer. Her head was bent over a book, but her back was not bent. She sat as straight as if one of the nuns from my school might just have passed by and pushed gently on the small of her back to remind her of "Posture, please." The way her head leaned forward made her long curls split into a part in the back; the curls fell in two sections on either side of her face, hiding her face. She was wearing a white T-shirt with no sleeves and a blue skirt that reached to her ankles and looked soft. The sandal on her right foot was on the floor and that foot was curled around the chair's bottom rung. Her toenails—her toenails were painted the same blue as her skirt. I had never seen such color on toes.

She was not fat nor thin. She looked of good health—that was it. She looked like her body was her friend and worked with her all the day. Right now her body was still, letting her mind do the work of the moment. I thought I could have stood there for a year and she would never notice me, she was so much a part of the words she was reading. But I did not have a year to stand there. I had to leave for school, so I spoke.

"Buenos días, Señorita."

The lady looked up from her book, but kept her finger marking her place. I liked that. The words inside the book were of equal importance to her as the people who lived outside of what she held in her mind. She smiled, nodding at me a little. "Buenos días."

Ai, and now what? My words of inglés were so few. I needed to ask her who she was, why she was here, what had made my grandfather pay attention to her.

"You are teacher, yes?"

"Yes, sí. Good lord, is it that obvious?"

Of that, I understood only her yes, but that was good enough.

"You are here long time?"

"For two weeks. Dos semanas."

"You teach me the inglés? I bring words to you?"

She laughed, a good laugh, not laughing at me.

26

"Cómo te llamas?"

"Me llamo Cesar."

"Well, Cesar, I am Trish. Me llamo Trish. And you are a trip. So, sure, why not? Tomorrow if you bring ten words to me, I will give them back to you in English. Entiendes? Diez palabras. Mañana. Está bien?"

"Está muy bien, maestra. Y gracias." I stepped back from her table just a little, smiled and bobbed my head at her. " Hasta manaña."

"Hasta manaña, Cesar."

Armando was smiling and shaking his head at me, slowly back and forth as if he could not believe the strange ways of his new apprentice. He dried his hands on the towel he was holding and gave his head a nod toward the steps and the gate.

"To the school. Cesar. You will be late. And your pay—do not forget your pay."

I took it, shaking his hand as I did, and ran down the steps. In my head already I was writing the beginning of tomorrow's list:

1. abuelo
2. cuando
3. donde...

"Hasta mañana," I yelled back to Armando, but I wanted Teacher to hear me, too. Como se dice *hasta mañana* in inglís? I stopped on the bottom step and jumped so she could see me.

"Maestra?"

3
Trish

"Maestra?"

He was still here? I scooted back my chair and stood up so I could look down the steps. Where the heck was he?

"Maestra."

A curly head bobbed into sight for a second, then was gone. Waiting. Waiting. Yup—here came the head again. The crazy kid was jumping straight up, high enough to grin at me before his chunky body thudded him back to his feet again at the bottom of the stairs.

I raised one eyebrow and lifted my chin a little toward his air space.

"Yes, Cesar?"

Another jump, another brief sighting of curls, and the grin. His message came on his way down, "I see you tomorrow."

"Yes, Cesar."

Lord help us, what a charmer. Just what I need: another irresistible man in my life. Mama's always sworn Daddy's charm made her break her hard and fast rule against dating handsome men. *The good-looking ones are too stuck on themselves to be interesting,* she'd justify her stance. Well, my daddy was sure

27

enough interesting.

And charming, too, no question about that. Many's the time I've been told about Daddy sitting down to dinner with folks of assorted skin color in way-south Georgia one evening long before I was born. Just as the biscuits were being passed, hatred in the form of a posse of Klansmen came riding up the drive. My handsome daddy headed off all that white-robed hatred by flinging the door open and giving a hearty wave, calling the hooded locals by name: *Brother Jones, it's good of you to come join us in Christian fellowship. Come on in here, son.* Sometimes, inviting the devil in is the best way to get him to leave.

It's a sure thing a girl who's had a daddy like mine stands no chance at all against charming men. I plopped back into my chair with a soft thud of resignation. The innkeeper's Siamese, Saki, levitated himself like a silky cloud onto my lap and I started stroking his handsome head. I couldn't help myself.

Was the boy gone? I stood as best I could while steadying a cat to my lap with one hand, and took a last look down the steps. Nothing but wavering greenish light reflecting from the pool to the stone steps .

He really had talked me into teaching during my vacation, hadn't he? Because I *was* on vacation, sure enough—only two days into two-weeks my mother had been willing to underwrite in hopes that a respite from the very public life of a small-town teacher would restore my hermit soul to some semblance of civil obedience. I'd ended this school year teetering right on the razor's edge of rebellion against all things community-minded. Mama said I needed taming.

Things had looked promising at first. The gods of air travel had blessed me with a seat mate who sensed how intensely I did not want to chitchat. This wondrous man honored his unspoken vow of benign avoidance until we began our descent into Puerto Vallarta, but then his good manners got the better of him.

"Can you see?"

Really, I could hardly crucify him for being thoughtful.

"Yep, thanks, I can see."

Only minimally gracious, but better than snarling at him.

"You said you're here on vacation?"

I nodded and kept my eyes on the Mexican air, not him. Maybe he'd take the hint.

There wasn't a cloud out there on the other side of our window. The sky was all blue, deep and wide. It would be hot as blazes on the ground; I'd bet money on that. A hard blue summer sky in Georgia is a merciless sky that burns all its clouds to dry puffballs of absolutely no use to our droughty late August gardens. The sky I saw outside our plane window informed me that August in Mexico would be a lot of what I already knew. I stopped looking and made an effort to give the man a polite answer.

"Yep. I really needed to get away by myself, to some place where the whole town hasn't known me since I took my first steps and therefore feel it's their right and their bounden duty to remind me on a regular basis that I would have walked a lot earlier if I hadn't been such a fat baby."

One side of his mouth lifted in a smile, so I blathered on.

" I'm hoping the entire country will ignore me for two weeks, and then will let me drift back homeward without a single Mexican having had any desire at all to discuss me over coffee. There cannot possibly be a more examined life than that of a public school teacher."

He completed his smile, slowly. He had a good face with a lot of bone, and deep dimples that showed when he smiled all the way.

"Oh, maybe there is one."

I raised both eyebrows in question.

"I'm a Methodist minister."

"My daddy was a Methodist minister, too," I told him, nodding my head a little.

"It seemed to me Daddy never got to enjoy his dinner because he was always rushing off to a seven o'clock meeting at church. And if he was two minutes late to one of those meetings because he'd stopped to buy flowers for Mama, some lady at the meeting was sure to have seen him in the checkout line and would feel it was incumbent upon her as an official of the church to advise Daddy he should have bought mums rather than roses, because the church wasn't paying him to be extravagant."

I sighed, remembering, and let my sigh out in a slow whuff, but he didn't snag that opportunity to gallop into the fray with his own story. He didn't even move from his position of listening. Truly, this man knew how to hold up his end of the silence in a conversation.

"And now I live in a town with one stop light." I glanced at him. He was waiting.

"You know, it's not like I have any real cause to worry about what my neighbors think , but every now and then I'd love to be able to—oh, I don't know—maybe sit naked in the creek behind my house, without the produce man at Publix greeting me the next day with, 'Mornin', Miz Trish. Hear the heat's been getting to you a bit.'"

The man had laughed then, a powerful crack of a laugh that flung him backwards. "Ow, ow." His head of curls—black to my reddish—whammed against the headrest and bounced off it like a soccer ball.

"Trish—it's Trish, right?"

I nodded yes as he rubbed his noggin. I could not for the life of me remember if he'd told me his name.

"Trish, I often tell myself the world could offer me no greater gift than a day in which no one is trying to catch me in a slip-up, and no one is tip-toeing around me in case I've caught them in one."

He'd grabbed my left hand when his laugh burst out, but now he gave it pastoral pat and let go. I wasn't sure, all of a sudden, that I wanted my hand back.

"But your mother? You said she had a part in this trip?"

"She did. I told her I'd kill for the chance to go away somewhere for a week or two but there was no way I could afford to. I'm a teacher. Resort vacations do not figure into my budget. I'm lucky most months if I can afford a *budget*."

Then I smiled at him, a smile honoring the wonder of mothers who'd do what she did.

"She wrote me a check."

She had. Mama had sat down to her kitchen table right then and there, and started writing me a check without asking me a single question about practicalities, while Pete the cat rested one white paw with feline formality on her checkbook ledger.

"I still had not a clue where I should go, but a friend at my church told me about an old inn in Puerto Vallarta. 'My cousin went there and showed me pictures,' she said.' It looks pretty.'.So I called the inn, found out their rates are a lot cheaper in August, and seeing as how teachers are out of school then, I took that as a sign from God that I should go."

God's employee and I grinned at each other.

"Señorita?"

Saki, not Pete, *mrrrp*ed in my lap and I looked down at him, then up to see who had spoken.

Armando. I was at the inn and Armando was speaking to me. I tried to look as if I had good sense. How long had this poor man been waiting patiently for me to come back to the here and now?

"I can take the dishes, señorita?"

"Oh, of course. I'm so sorry. I was thinking. It's such a bad habit of mine. Lo siento. Please let me help you with these."

I closed the copy of *To Kill A Mockingbird* I'd brought down to the table so I'd have an old friend to eat with. I stacked my silverware on my plate and laid my napkin across the top to make the whole pile easier to carry.

"Gracias, señorita. You are kind."

I picked up my stack of dishes to carry them to the kitchen.

But Armando was shaking his head, "No, no, señorita. I will carry."

"Oh, no—I'm happy to help."

He stopped clearing dishes and gave me what Mama would call *a significant glance.*

"You will help the boy. Será suficiente."

So I gave Saki's head a knuckle-rub and scooped him to the floor. It was hot already, too hot for a lap full of cat. I ran my fingers under my hair and lifted the whole hang of it to cool my neck. I'd write to Mama, I decided as I let my hair fall back to my shoulders, and then go for a walk around town before it got any hotter.

The writing paper I'd bought yesterday was on the desk in my room ready for me to grab and scoot with it back down to the courtyard, leaping the bottom two steps together so I wouldn't stomp on Saki, who'd lazed up the stairs behind me. Armando had already wiped my table clean and set out a pottery jar with a huge orange hibiscus bloom in it. I slipped off my sandals and curled my toes around the chair's bottom rung.

Dear Mama,

I'm writing to you before I head out sight-seeing, though I probably should do it the other way around, seeing as how only fools and tourists (which may be redundant) go out in the Mexican noonday sun. It's only my third day in Puerto Vallarta, but I've already learned this truth about the custom of the siesta: it isn't a custom at all, but a survival tool. If I wandered out onto Matamoros Street mid-afternoon, I'd likely drop dead where I stood. Of course, there could be a positive side even to my premature death: I'd provide a few street dogs with the best meal they'd had in their scrawny lives. My demise would not be a complete tragedy if it saved one or two Mexican dogs from starvation.

So, moving on from talk of death, which was probably not the wisest way to begin the story of my first journey to a foreign country, let me assure you first of all that the inn, Los Cuatro Vientos is lovelier even than it looked in the pictures Jenni showed me. There's a mammoth iron gate so intricately scrolled that it puts Savannah's famed grillwork to shame. A huge padlock straight out of a fairy tale castle hangs in an opening in the gate so the inn's guests can reach through to lock themselves in. (I'll pause briefly, so you can sigh a motherly "Thank goodness.")

Wide, curving stone steps lead up to the courtyard, past a swimming pool that was hand-dug, the owner told me, when the inn was built in 1952. And such a profusion of tropical flowers spilling down the wall behind the pool and enclosing the courtyard. It is lush, Mama—that's the only word for it. There are two floors of rooms and mine is on the second, a corner room with a sign naming it, "El Nido." The Nest. See? Your birthday gift has provided me with a nest, and a cleanly beautiful one, at that. It is all white, except for the reds and greens of the crewel work on the bedspread, and a border of red flowers running around the top of the room just below the ceiling. The wall that faces the bay is all windows, curtained with sheers that float in the breeze. I can push the sheers aside and stand looking over the tops of three layers of houses progressing down to Banderas Bay.

I've slept dreamlessly each night and waked to breakfast in the courtyard. The sweet man who prepares the food, Armando, sets out trays of hard-boiled eggs and warm tortillas and platters of papaya, pineapple, and guava. While I load up my plate shamefully, Armando brings a cup of manzanilla tea to my table, and I read (okay: re-read) *To Kill A Mockingbird* and fortify myself for a morning of walking.

I've been doing a lot of walking. Well, you probably assumed that already. But I did take a really interesting walk yesterday. And before you ask—no, I'm not using "interesting" as a euphemism for "potentially threatening of life and limb." I set out on a major road, or as major as they get in this part of town, not some dingy back alley. As the road and I went higher, everything started to look less like city, more like country. I felt right at home. And you know I love to walk alone—I wasn't at all nervous or lonely. As a matter of fact, I was keeping myself pretty good company, chatting up a storm with my own self. The only thing I was missing was one of your guidebooks for trees and flowers. I really wanted to know the names of the trees I started to see as the houses thinned out.

Uh oh. I can hear you now: "The houses thinned out? You were out alone in the middle of foreign nowhere without even a house you could run to in case of sudden political insurrection?" No, no. Calm down (says the daughter with all respect to her sainted mother). The pretty, photo-op houses that line the hillsides in El Centro were gone, but before I knew it, I was walking right through a little village.

To tell you the truth (which I always have and always will, of course), I would have turned around right there if I could have. I felt a little weird walking right through the middle of such a teeny community, like an uninvited guest in someone's home.

I flipped the paper over to write on the back.

But I was already in the center of town, so to speak, and some of the people had noticed me. It would have been just rude to turn tail and backtrack, as if their homes had horrified me.

I lifted my pen from the paper and leaned back in my chair, smiling to myself, remembering a sort of similar time from a vacation when I was little.

Mama—remember the summer we went to the New York World's Fair on vacation, and we made a side trip to New York City? Daddy wanted to see Harlem, but this was during all the Civil Rights unrest and you—wise protector of your children—vetoed his whim. So Daddy proceeded to get "lost" and wound up right in the heart of Harlem. He pulled the car over and—I can still see this in my head—started chatting with a man walking by, asking him for directions. I remember the startled look on that middle-aged black man's face, and then how the man's face eased as he realized Daddy saw no racial divide or danger in that man or his neighborhood. All Daddy saw was a nice man who might help him out. The man was nice, and he did help us out.

I had to write "help us out" sort of curved around the Oaxaca design at the bottom of the stationery because I was out of room , so I started a second sheet.

Sorry, Mama. Ran out of room. So my point was that I decided if I could not in good grace back out of my intrusion on these people, at least I could present myself as not having any sort of agenda—just a walker passing through by mistake. I put my camera down close to my side and closed my hand over it so they'd know I had no intention of using their homes as the source of a "what I did on my summer vacation" slide show when I went home.

I couldn't help but look, though. I've always had a lust for seeing how other people live. There were maybe twenty or thirty houses lining both sides of the road. The houses were low and flat-roofed, mostly adobe with a kind of white-wash on them, but one was bright crayon yellow. Most of the houses were little and square, and a few had no front door, just a heavy cloth hanging over the opening. The yellow house, though, was a good bit larger than all the others. It was built in kind of an open U, with a room on either end, joined by—I guess-a long room or rooms along the back wall. I'm just assuming, since I couldn't see the back of the house. What I saw was an open courtyard in the middle of the house, with lots of trees and plantings there.

And, no, Mama, I was not staring. I'm a teacher; teachers can see one thing while seeming for all the world to be looking at something else entirely. I did figure it was okay for me to look at the well right in the center of the village, and I mean right in the center: the road actually split to curve around either side of the well.

I was looking at the well and remembering all the times on farms in south Georgia when I've poured a gallon of water down a well pump to prime it, and how I like the idea of giving a little of what you want to receive. This well didn't have a pump, though—just a bucket on a rope. I've done my share of hauling water up in a bucket, too.

I turned the page over. Okay. I'll write to the bottom if this page and then quit for now. I can mail it when I go out to explore around town.

There was a donkey tied to a tree over by that big house, so when something moved and caused me to look over that way, I thought it was the donkey that had moved, but, no; it was a boy. This boy looked ten or so, exactly the age of my students, Mama. He stood there staring for a second and then he started to smile at me. Before he even had a whole smile on his face, I could tell what kind of kid he was. If this boy was in my class, I thought, I'd both adore him and tear my hair out over him. I know, because I had a boy just like him last year, remember? I called him my Tom Sawyer. When I passed him along to his sixth-grade teacher, I said, "He's yours now, you lucky dog. And may God have mercy on your soul."

This Mexican boy's smile got stopped before it made it all the way out to his ears, though, when an old man came out of the courtyard of the big house, and stood behind him. The man laid his hand on the boy's shoulder—I got the idea then that maybe he was the boy's grandfather— and the boy jerked his head around and the smile dropped right off his face. I wonder what that was all about?

It came to me even as I wrote that line, that what I had seen on that boy's face was not fear, but astonishment, profound astonishment.

The rest was pretty anti-climatic. I passed through the village in about thirty seconds and followed the road back down to the inn. I collapsed into bed and prayed that I would not simmer to a slow death in my own sweat while I napped.

Just kidding, Mama. I'm perfectly comfortable here. Really.

Love you,

Trish

I sat for a minute resting my hands on the paper until my palms started leaving little sweat marks. I folded the letter and slipped it into an envelope addressed to Mama, licked the flap, and then gave the flap a wham with the side of my hand to seal it against the humidity.

The bells of the church rang nine times. Nine o'clock. I should get out and walk before the morning heated up any more. Other people were doing the same; I could hear them talking down on the street. A few Spanish words drifted up to me like clues.

On my way back upstairs to grab my hat, I stopped Armando to ask him a question. Might as well make a total pest of myself.

"Señor, could you tell me how to get to Cesar's school? I'd love to see his school. I'd like to see how his school is different from the one where I teach."

That was a bald-faced lie, of course, or at least nine-tenths a lie. I truly was curious about the local schools, but mainly I wanted to spy on Cesar, who was the most interesting soul I'd met in many a month.

Armando was smiling at me like it hadn't yet dawned on him what a pest I was. What a nice man.

"Sí, Señorita, It is only a little walk on Matamoras, maybe two streets, or maybe three if you want to go more far. Any time, you can to turn and walk the steps more low until you go on the street of la iglesia. The school it is on this street, a little more far."

"Thank you, Armando."

I think.

Saki didn't even make a try for my lap as I zipped through the courtyard and down the steps, running my hand through the cool water of the swimming pool where it sat level with the topmost step.

It was a beautiful day in the neighborhood. Tiles patterned in deep greens and yellows and reds and blues framed the doorways of nearly every house I passed along Matamoros. I walked Armando's "little walk." then turned by a small, oval landing perched over steps that led me down one set of eight or ten steps after another, with a small landing separating each flight. On every landing, there was an ironwork bench chained by one leg, potted hibiscus in full bloom behind the bench, and an unhealthy scattering of cigarette butts across the cobbled paving.

A woman stepped out the door of one of the houses, a broom in her hand. She set in to sweep her tiled entryway as if the very possibility of untidiness were a sin against Heaven.

"Buenos dias."

She looked halfway up from her sweeping when I spoke, nodded, then

34

dismissed me. I would dismiss me, too, given a choice between looking at me or down at that glorious mosaic entryway. She was sweeping a flower garden of tiles, a Monet welcome mat. It came to me that my fellow Americans would likely feel a lot less stressed if we walked across tiled flowers when we came home every evening.

I kept stepping down and down, keeping my eyes on my feet so I wouldn't catch my sandals on the lip of a step, so that I almost smacked right into another lady doing her morning sweeping.

"Perdón, Señora."

She smiled slightly and fluttered her fingers at me, murmuring something gracious-sounding, and I did the same, both of us paddling furiously toward the other side of an unintended social moment.

One landing more, and then I could see the onion-domed Catholic church about a block more to my left. Cesar's school was just on the other side of the church, if I had interpreted Armando's surprisingly instructive directions correctly.

4
Cesar

I had not a long walk from the inn to my school, not nearly so long as from my home to the school every morning—only three blocks—and on this morning with the happy singing of the coins in my pocket, but when I heard bells strike the hour, I ran. Only one block more to the Cathedral, and then my school would be there on the other side.

When I ran past the front of the church, though, I stopped. There sat Carlos and my other brothers on the steps. Why did they not stand up and run with me? We were late. Carlos had his elbows propped on his knees and his chin in his hands, looking like he was waiting for a train ride to sorrow, and he was to be the only passenger. He straightened up when he saw me, and gave his head a quick jerk to shake the hair from his eyes before he spoke.

"Abuelo asked where you were."

"And what did you tell him?"

"That you were off somewhere following the clouds in your head. He asked me if one of those clouds had the shape of an American lady. I told him I did not l know. That was true; I do not know of any American. Digame, tell me, brother, are you chasing American women? Do you think yourself such a man already?"

"Claro que sí. Like a bull, I am. Can you not see?" I grinned as I grabbed Carlos in a choke hold, but only for play, knuckling his head with my free hand. This made Carlos laugh one quick laugh like a cough, then he punched me easy in my belly. Our little brothers Jose and Juan tried to join in, boxing our legs and pulling at us. That did it. The nuns had noticed us. Two black skirts moved up the stone steps towards us like storm clouds pushed by a wind.

"Cesar. Carlos. Again? And, mira. Cesar, your uniform is still in your bag and not yet on your body. Why is this? Rapidamente al baño to change, and then off to school with you where you must try to remember how God would have you behave."

"Sí, Sister. Perdőn."

I liked Sister Maria Terese and truly did not want to make her angry. She had not the age of most of the other nuns and so she must not have been the nun to teach the catechism to my father when he was a boy, but somehow she had known him, and liked him, it seemed to me. Sometimes she would say to me: *Ah, Cesar, you are just like your father.* She said this not when I was once again in trouble for making clown faces at the little boys and causing them to laugh until they peed their acolyte robes, or (I did this once only, I swear) when I held my cousin by his feet upside-down from the sanctuary's high balcony. No, she would speak to me in a way almost like a mother proud when I alone among all the boys asked a question I had noticed hiding underneath the words of the doctrine we were learning by heart.

Half a minute was all I needed to pull off the clothes I had worked in, and to mostly pull on my uniform. I ran from the bathroom back to the cathedral's front steps, tucking my white shirt into the grey pants which Sister seemed to think would please God more than my T-shirt and shorts. My hair and face were still wet from a quick splash of soap and water at the bathroom sink. Sister was waiting there in the doorway. I looked at her to see if she was angry with me, but when she saw me looking, she smiled and laid her hand soft on my head for a moment.

This made me to wonder if she loved me the more for being just like my father as she said. How was I like my father? I needed to ask her. Someday I would ask her, but just then I could not imagine a way to begin such a conversation with a nun. She gave me a little a shove toward the school and turned to walk back into the cathedral.

I ran around the corner to where my brothers were waiting by the iron front gate of our school, by the date in gold numbers: 1936. Our school had been new when our grandfather was a boy, built during the *sexenio* of el Presidente Cardenas. Abuelo had often told us this, and told us how el Presidente spent his six years giving much Mexican land back to the people whose indio ancestors—*my* ancestors—had worked all land together, sharing the use of it. Abuelo always said Cardenas was a smart one: he kept alive Zapata's cry of "land to the tiller" like it was a sacred song, and he used his power of office to make the *ejidos,* the communal lands, like almost a sacrament for most of us. Zapata put a dream into the hearts of poor people, Abuelo said, and this dream of having land of our own came true only because of Cardenas, who believed.

All this I was thinking, but my thoughts sounded in my head in my grandfather's voice, as they always did, so often had I heard him talk of such matters late of an evening. He had told me many times how when our grandfathers' grandfathers came of the age to marry, each novio had the right by culture and tradition to claim a plot of land for himself and his bride. As his family grew, more land was given to him, and then when his children married and left home, his share of the land was cut smaller because he did not need so much. That was fair. It was not fair when the Spaniards came to steal our lands to build their giant haciendas. Because of this unfairness, Zapata rose up from his little village in Morelos and with his revolution turned upside down what had been so unfair, and after that Cardenas gave us our *ejidos*.

The only problem—Ai, Díos, my mind always finds the problem—is that thepeople keep having babies and those babies will need their own land to till. There will always be more and more babies to share the land, while the land stays just as much as it always has been. In our barrio, my grandfather still had the right to more of the *ejido* land than others, even others much younger and with children, because he needed to gather wood to burn in the lodge and the lodge served all the *ejidatários*. But even so, sometimes I have heard Sr. Franco mutter to his wife that he should have more of the land to use, with so many daughters to feed.

And what of my brothers and me? Would there be enough land for us? If I had to, I could find other some way in life, but I would have to take Carlos with me. His head was so much in his books that without me he could be killed some day by people who fight with sharper knives than knowledge.

"Cesar, hermano."

There was Carlos now.

"Cesar, you are stupid and your face helps you out. Why are you standing there with your mouth like a trap for flies while the late bell has already rung? Hurry."

My classroom and that of Carlos were next to each other on the far side of the hot, roofless courtyard. Carlos leaned near to me as he went into his class:

"Abuelo said you must see him when you get home from school. I think you are in trouble, my brother."

But I did not think so. Our grandfather did not bother himself with the discipline of children. When we misbehaved he would walk away as if we were not worth noticing, leaving our granny to flap at us like a hen.

Abuelo was a man who poured out words like the coins of a poor man. He would not waste words on bad children. There were times, though, when he would call us all to sit with him around a fire he had built not for the lodge but in a clearing in front of our house, and then his words would come as stories, stories that were like movies of the people who had come before us. On nights like that, the stories my granddaddy told were like another knot in the rope tying us to who we were. Sometimes in my mind I could see Quetzalcoatl—Kukulkan, my people called him—far at the other end of that rope, nodding to me like he was telling me it was right for me to use my hands to use my head, because my hands were so much smarter than my head.

Again the problem of the weakening of the arms of my Abuelo came back to me from where I had left it lying when the American lady walked through our village—maybe I could mount the ax somehow with a tight spring to take the weight from his arms… but, no, then he would have to pull against the spring in raising the ax…

"Cesar, did you hear what I asked you?"

I blinked my eyes back to my classroom and grinned at Maestra. I always gave a smile first and then an excuse when I was caught with my head in the clouds. Sometimes it worked.

"Sí, Maestra."

"And what did I ask?"

"You asked if I would like to choose the subject we will study first today. Sí, gracias. I choose Science."

I liked Science well enough, but also I knew that Ana Franco loved Science best of all the subjects. And Ana was pretty.

Sra. Murillo studied me for a minute. I knew she was fighting inside her head between punishing me for lying to her about daydreaming , or wanting to laugh.

"Ah, Cesar. I cannot be angry with you." She smiled as she would have at her own son.

"Bien. We will deal first with the science this morning."

Ana Franco smiled at me from across the aisle, a shy smile, like she was not certain I had chosen the subject because of her, but she hoped I had. And I had, but she did not need to believe that. Later today when I saw her with her sisters playing around the well, I would call her *snotnose*.

"And for homework, everyone will answer the question I had asked Sr. Cesar before he came back to us from his dreaming. Cesar, your homework is to try to find out from your more diligent classmates what that question was. Now, everyone open your science books to page 42. It is late summer and the trees are well leafed out, cleaning our air for us. Let us talk about that process."

I could see the top of one tree from my classroom's high windows, a large oak with a good deep fork just higher than my shoulders when I stood next to it. I could wedge my left hand into that fork, put my right foot against the trunk and pull myself up. As soon as I was in the crotch of the tree I could crawl along that big limb stretching out toward Los Cuatro Vientos and lie on my belly with my arms and legs hanging down like strange fruit. I had done so many times. If I climbed there during our break for lunch today, maybe I could see if the American teacher was reading and eating, still.

Eating. Díos. I had not eaten yet this day.

5

Cesar

Por seguro, for sure if I had climbed out on the limb of that tree instead of sitting hungry in my classroom I would have seen how, as soon as the back of my head had disappeared around the corner in my hurry to make it to school on time, Sister Maria Therese let out a sigh and rested her little weight against Jesus the Carpenter for a moment while she thought such thoughts as a nun should never think. I did not understand about her thoughts until many years had passed, and, truly, never yet have I grown to feel comfortable in the knowing of such feelings in her.

A plaster Jesus half the size of my father had been standing there in our cathedral, holding a large plaster hammer in His hand, since the day some artist made Him—perhaps somehow knowing there would be a need on this very morning for Jesus to knock impure thoughts out of a certain nun's head.

That nun was thinking about my father, and about herself before she became Sister Maria Therese. *Twelve.* She had been only twelve years old the first time she saw him. He had three years more than her twelve, and he had grown too fast in those years, too fast for his bones to catch up with each other. When he walked, he looked like his leg bones were floating around inside his skin trying to grab hold of his ankles and knees. And his arms. His arms hung down past his knobby knees, swinging like pendulums that were marking time until the whole of him could grow together into the tall man he would become. His hair was blacker even than hers, and in the front it swooped back from his forehead in curls as deep and as high as early morning waves in the waters of Banderas Bay. His eyes were black, too. Maria ached from the beauty of him.

But Francisco was three years older—fifteen—too close to being a man grown to notice a girl as young as Maria, right? Wrong. Sister Maria Therese smiled a slow smile to herself at the memory of tall, skinny Francisco one Sunday morning folding himself like a wooden marionette onto the pew next to her just after the start of mass, too far into the quiet of the service for her mama to whisper for Maria to change seats with her. All through the mass, Maria was as aware of his body as if he had been wired to send electricity through her. She half-believed the awareness between them could be seen by everyone in the church, but this must not have been, because no one paid them any mind, except for her mama who scowled a bit to let them both know she thought Francisco too old for Maria and too much of a firebrand, which he was. Francisco's father passed his days building and stoking fires in their barrio's sweat lodge, but Francisco's fires all burned within his handsome head.

Ai. As she stood there remembering, Sister Maria Therese pulled herself up straight again and began a little lecture to herself. What a very good thing it was that she was standing right then in the narthex, which was the gate of the penitents. You are in great need of penance for these thoughts of yours, Maria. Remember that you are a Bride of Christ. You do not moon after an old boyfriend, no matter how lovely a male he was. Well, obviously, I do, she answered herself back. I have never claimed to be a good Bride. All I can do is to give God my best effort, and in this case that must involve going along with God's fine sense of irony, because (Sister raised her head higher just then to see who was easing open the Cathedral's heavy front door) here comes another American for me to deal with.

Isn't it enough that America was the death of Francisco and me? And yet not a day goes by that I am not called away from my duties because of some Americano wanting something from me. Perdőn, Señor, but sometimes I wish all Americans would fall into the bottom of their Grand Canyon. This lady probably will ask if it is okay for her to take flash photos of the Stations of the Cross even while Sra. Franco is at this moment kneeling at her family's pew praying her new baby will be a boy, finally. Or perhaps the turista is wondering how much a souvenir bottle of Holy Water costs, and if we accept Master Card. Yes, I know; I know (Sister Marie Therese looked heavenward for a brief instant). Penitential thoughts should not include sarcasm. Sorry, Señor.

Sister decided the best way to make right with God would be to speak to the turista, politely:

"Buenos Dias."

6
Trish

That is one pretty nun. I stopped halfway up the Cathedral steps and just gawked at her. Who knew a nun could be so pretty? She's what? maybe 30? Five foot two and eyes of black. Doesn't rhyme, but it sure works on her. I realized I was grinning at her like we were long-lost cousins, because who could *not* smile at someone so lovely?

The tiny nun was standing as still as the statue of the Virgin behind her, studying me exactly the way cats do, like they're assessing whether you're worth their effort or not. Evidently, I passed muster, because she nodded her wimpled head at me just enough for its slight movement to qualify as a nod. And then she spoke.

"Buenos Dias."

Sheesh, she even *spoke* lovely. She had an alto voice, like me, but with that sort of velvety huskiness I've always wished I had. When this nun lifted her voice in prayer, God must be a happy deity.

"Buenos Dias." It killed me to have to follow her Billie Holiday voice with anything at all in my work-a-day alto, but I needed to get a conversation going with someone who might be able to help me learn more about Cesar. "Do you speak English?"

"Yes, a little."

She didn't offer to prove her fluency further, though; she just waited for me to state my purpose. It was quickly evident to me she would wait until the Second Coming, if need be, for me to say what was on my mind, so I dove right into that pool of receptivity with the first thing that plopped from my subconscious to my tongue.

"I'm a writer, writing a book about this area."

Lying to a nun. May the Lord have mercy on my immortal soul.

"I met a boy this morning at the inn where I am staying, Los Cuatro Vientos. He is probably ten or eleven years old. He asked me to teach him English. He said his name is Cesar, but I don't know his last name. Do you know him? I'd like to get his family's permission to help him with his English. And I thought maybe getting to know him would help me with my book."

"You want to use Cesar for the book you are writing?"

Yikes. That seemed a bit paranoid, especially from a nun. Obviously I'd hit on a sore spot. I reached my hand out toward her, shaking my head so hard a couple of curls whapped against my nose.

"No, Sister. Perdón. I only meant that perhaps in spending time with this boy I might gain a better understanding of the Mexican people. But mostly I would just like to teach him, because he asked me if I would help him learn some English. He is very smart, I think."

The nun studied me for such a long moment that I began to wonder if she might be silently summoning God as back-up against yet another conniving American. But then Sister's face—God, I'd kill for her skin— relaxed a teensy bit and she answered me.

"He is Cesar Ramirez, and, sí, I know him. He is very smart, sí. He knows much English already. Why does he need more? He is mejicano."

"Well, maybe it's *because* he is so smart that he wants to learn even more. I am a teacher, besides being a writer, and I believe an intelligent mind is always a hungry mind. Learning English will not make him less Mexican; nothing could ever do that. It will just make him a Mexican with more mental tools to use."

"Tools?"

"Um...herramientos."

"Ah. Tools. Cesar is good with tools. Señorita, what is your name?"

"Me llamo Trish. Y usted?"

"I am Sister Maria Therese."

Having said her say, the nun's face settled into a meditative repose. I wasn't sure if she was thinking or praying. Maybe for nuns it was one and the same. What I could tell for sure was that some sort of judgment was being reached concerning my trustworthiness, and seeing as she had God in her huddle, this didn't take long.

"Trish, I think you must not talk with the family of Cesar. I give you permission to teach him the English. You stay where?"

"Los Cuatro Vientos."

She nodded. Yes, she knew the inn.

" You teach your lessons at the inn . Mañana, sí? After school I see Cesar and tell him to go there tomorrow at his lunch. Al mediodía. Señorita."

Sister Maria Therese slid her hands into invisible pockets in the sides of her habit exactly like the Mother Superior in the Sound of Music, then turned and walked inside toward some nun's inner sanctum where such as I could not follow. Well, now, wouldn't it be great to have holy carte blanche to remove yourself so absolutely from any conversation you considered completed? I was briefly envious, until I remembered that the contract for such a solitary retreat included a chastity clause. Okay, well, never mind.

So now what? No law against walking over to the school and seeing what a Mexican school was like, right?

A lady was sitting on the topmost of the church's twelve steps, selling little cloth dolls. I stood and watched as she braided a doll's yarn hair, then tied a narrow strip of yellow ribbon around each braid to make a teeny bow. Imagine doing that every day, one doll after another. Did she make dolls for her own daughters? Or did she have to save her materials for making the dolls she sold here on the steps of the Cathedral to tourists like me?

"Cuál es el precio?"

She told me and I paid. Who knew if she'd upped the price a peso when she saw me, an americana? I truly did not care. I'd already tested my bartering skills and failed, with the guy who'd sold me my hat. He'd looked at me, not smiling at all, and asked, *Señorita, you have the money to pay what I ask, yes?* I had nodded and given up bartering as an anathema to my soul and spirit. *We do not have the money,* he had continued softly as I handed him the amount he'd asked.

And he was right.

Besides, the doll was pretty. I slid her into my skirt pocket as I skipped down the steps, avoiding eye contact with the sweets seller across the street. I did not want to have sticky candy in my pocket while the morning temps climbed relentlessly toward hellishness.

The school's back wall butted up against the side wall of the Cathedral, the two buildings almost, but not quite, touching each other. That's appropriate, whispered my American subconscious mind: separation of church and state. I followed the school wall to the end of the block, running my left hand along the rough white stucco as I walked, until I turned the corner and had to drop my hand to my side to keep from catching my fingers in the open iron grillwork of the school's ten-or twelve-foot wide double gates. Gates so massive seemed somehow less of an enclosure than smaller gates might have—more of a frame for the children inside than a barrier.

Other than those impressive gates, Cesar's school struck me at first assessment as pretty much like any grammar school in the U.S., especially judging by the sounds I had heard even before I rounded the corner. I can name that noise in one word, I thought: recess. The school's inner courtyard was open to the sky, with a swept dirt floor and a couple of huge, wispy palo verde trees shading thirty or forty adorably uniformed kids who were trying to sling off as much pent-up energy during recess as possible. A great deal of running was going on, but not as part of any particular game that I could recognize. Every time any boy got close to any girl, the scream decibels sky-rocketed. Yep: exactly like recess at my school.

Three recess-duty teachers were yelling randomly at token miscreants so as to make it appear the adults had a prayer of keeping control. Oh, I could so totally identify. One of the harried teachers, bless her heart, was standing guard close enough to the gates for me to call out to her with what I desperately hoped was an air of professional fellowship:

"Señora, I need to speak with someone in the office, please."

I wanted to head off from the get-go any suspicions that I might be some sort of American pervert peering in at the children with nefarious intent. Surely, a fellow teacher would understand that only a person of crystal-clear conscience would offer herself freely into the clutches of a school's Office Lady. Sure enough, the very sweet-faced young teacher opened the gates and nodded me in the direction of the office, where a woman of indeterminable age was guarding the sanctity of primary education from behind a massive wooden desk. She looked eerily like every Office Lady the world over.

Office Lady looked up from her wooden desk and tilted her head suspiciously at me, as if ascertaining what manner of misdeed I might be trying to pull off. I folded my hands in front of me before I spoke, defaulting to a third-grade protocol I had had no idea still lingered intact in my unconscious. I offered her my excuse for being there.

"Señora, I am a teacher from Georgia, in los estados unidos, and I would like very much to see the inside of your school, to see what a Mexican school is like."

Office Lady focused on me more intently. I could feel her stare boring through my unworthy skull in search of past offenses involving tardiness, note-passing, or faked illness. Finally, she nodded me to a chair, my criminal record having been found acceptably puny.

"Sientése."

I sat. I sat while a mother retrieved a queasy-looking small girl, the mailman in shorts and a crisp white shirt (did these people never sweat?) popped in with the mail, various adults came and went through the office and nodded politely but guardedly in my direction. I sat, feeling extremely white and increasingly ready to apologize for any xenophobic act ever perpetrated by my country's government. After an awkward eternity of the sort I'd not experienced since my eighth-grade prom, a tall, deep-voiced woman came in to the office, smiled and spoke firmly to me—thus rescuing me from committing social suicide through some wildly inappropriate gesture of liberality fueled by societal guilt.

"Hola. I am Polly, the English teacher." Polly was taller than my five-nine, and lanky. She wore a pretty flowered skirt and recess-sturdy shoes. "You come teach my next class."

Blessings on you, Polly for saving me. I hoped the quick smile I gave her somehow conveyed eternal gratitude and hearty camaraderie.

"Bienvenido, Polly. I'm Trish. I'm a teacher from Georgia."

She nodded, tossing a follow-me jerk of her head as she strode out of the office and across the courtyard.

Well, all right then. I hitched my purse strap higher on my shoulder, swiping a thick ribbon of sweat from my neck as I hustled in her wake.

Polly led me up and up three flights of open cement stairs, the sort that are easy to mop. At each landing, a huge pane-less window had been made safe for young stair-climbers by a cage of bars on the street side, just like the windows in my room at the inn. Classrooms on each floor opened onto mezzanines, keeping the school's center open to the sky.

It was a fifth-grade class, Polly told me as we reached her classroom door. "We are working from the syllabus, the same one you have in the U.S.A. Today we are reading about the Pied Piper."

The Pied Piper?A Germanic cautionary tale with a fairly harsh ending, if their texts hadn't sugared it up. I raised a mental eyebrow at the thought of diving into such gloomy literary seas with the ten-year-old faces now watching me, but Polly was plowing authoritatively onward.

"This is Teacher Trish, from Georgia in the USA."

Smiling my hello's gave me an excuse to look around the room. Polly's classroom was a teeny bit smaller than mine at home; a boxy room with four long rows of double desks, two children at each desk. One, two, three... I counted six desks in each row. So, twelve in each row... lordy, that's forty-eight students. This lady spends her days with forty-eight ten-year-olds. And yet the room was quiet; the two girls closest to me were both wearing long brown braids plaited just behind their ears, blue-and-white checked uniforms, and the kind of comfortable stillness that comes from someone having explained to them the reasons for good manners.

It was a hot stillness, though. The only breath of air came from windows set above a ten-year-old's height, inches deep into thick walls painted dark red. stirring a slightflapping of the long string of soccer pennants reaching from one high corner of the room to the opposite corner. How in the world could Polly teach in such heavy heat, and how could these children possibly learn, much less stay so well-behaved?I'd thought I had misheard earlier when Armando shooed Cesar off to school. It was August. Why was he in school? Armando told me schools here took the monsoon month of July off, but otherwise went year-round, bless their sturdy souls.

Polly picked up her copy of the text and all the kids immediately, without being told, pulled out their own books and turned to the day's lesson. Jealousy seared through my teacher heart like hot knife.

"Today we read page 2. Trish, already we know the Pied Piper came to the town of Hamlin. It is a town in Texas, yes?"

Not exactly, but somehow perpetuating that small bit of geographic misapprehension seemed to me a much lesser evil than correcting a teacher in front of her students.

"Yes, I think so, Polly."

Forty-five minutes passed—no time at all, or all the time that mattered. I could just as easily have been teaching a class on chaos theory or Eastern European economics or the migration patterns of hummingbirds; the feeling of timelessness would have been the same. It continually surprised me how I could walk into a classroom feeling sleep-starved or hormonal or pulled in a million bureaucratic directions, yet as soon as I entered into the lesson itself, my students and I no longer existed in a place or a time, but within a sort of boundlessly intriguing process. Teaching seemed to me not so much a handing-over of facts, as it was a knitting together of what I already knew with what I learned through finding a way to pass it along clearly to one ten-year-old brain and then another and then another.

The only tricky side to teaching Polly's class was avoiding eye contact with young Señor Cesar. As soon as I walked in the room I'd spied him two tables back in the third row from the door. And as soon as he saw me, he winked.

I had to consciously push his needy brain away so it wouldn't distract me from the rest of the students. That boy is on fire with something,, I was thinking after I'd taught my lesson and said my thanks to Polly. He's either going to burn a bright path through life, or self-immolate.

Two of Polly's girls dashed out the door after me and shoved drawings into my hand. That tickled me, as it always did when my own students gave me something from their hearts, by way of their hands. I rolled up the drawings like a tube to keep them from getting wrinkled while I followed the student Polly had assigned to lead me back down to the office. Apparently, elementary school administrators the whole world over gave children the right and authority to officially escort adults from their school buildings.

I wasn't ready to settle back into my room at the inn; I was too wired from teaching, so I took the long way back. It was blasting hot already. I kept to the shady sides of the streets, admiring the tile work framing one doorway after another, and trying to translate hand-written menus posted at the entrances to three-table taquerías. I didn't have to watch my feet on the blocks near the cathedral because the sidewalks there were unbroken and level and swept clean every morning by congregants, but as I made my way up flights of stairs and along side streets in the direction of the inn, I had to sidestep broken Dos Equis botttles and crumpled Bimbo bread wrappers. Even on the trashiest streets, though, yellow and orange and red flowers trailed along the edges of the steps, and at every landing where I stopped to suck air into my laboring lungs and to calm the fires in my calf muscles, there was a blessed tree or two to shade me. It being ever my goal to not appear pathetic in public, I tried to convey to the few passersby an air of having stopped only to admire their trees. I waited until they had moved on down the street before I wheezed and gasped as covertly as possible.

The gates of Los Cuatro Vientos were standing open when I finally made it home, and Armando had obviously scooped the pool clean of fallen hibiscus blooms just before he left for the day. I trailed my hand through the cool water as I walked up the steps, and it tempted me, but that sun was telling me to *get inside, fool, before you fry*.

I wrote one letter and then turned my room's fan to Turbo while I took a nap.

45

Sweet Man O'Mine,

Except of course you aren't mine, are you? You aren't anyone's man, really, but your own, and that's alright, that's okay, I'm gonna love you anyway. Besides, we're enough birds of a feather that I'd probably get to feeling all itchy if you clung to me the way some men cling to their women. I am your woman, you know.

But enough of that. I need to confess that I've found a summer love. He's short and a little bit of a chunk, with curly black hair. You know I'm a sucker for curly black hair. His name is Cesar. Oh, and he's ten years old. He's a whiz brain with a wit and a tongue to match his mind. About two minutes after I met him he gave me a grin that curved all the way up to his interestingly slanted brown eyes (wonder who in his ancestry hooked up with an oriental?), and I found myself saying sure, I'd be happy to spend part of my vacation giving English lessons to a ten-year-old.

Actually, though, I'm kind of looking forward to it. Nothing suits me better than to have a project, even when I'm supposed to be loafing. Yeah, yeah, I can hear you: "Loafing??? Sweetheart, you couldn't loaf if you tried. You'd just start thinking about all the things you could accomplish while you were loafing." Well, true enough. But at least this project is right up my vocational alley. And it will give me the chance to get to know a very adorable young Mexican man.

There's a mystery involving Señor Cesar, though, or I think there may be. I took a walk up the mountain yesterday and found myself embarrassingly in the middle of a tiny, poor village, grossly invading the villagers' privacy. While I was trying to make as graceful an exit as possible, this kid caught my eye because he was watching me and grinning at me. I know, I know—you say any male with eyes in his head would grin at me, and I love you for believing that. But the thing is, when I met Cesar at the inn, I was sure he was the same boy I'd seen up the mountain, even though he acted like we were meeting for the first time. Not that it matters; it's just curious.

Another thing that has me intrigued is finding out from some pamphlets I picked up that Puerto Vallarta was a mining town. I had no idea. Well, why would I? It's not as if a preacher's kid from Georgia would have had a lot of exposure to the history of mining in coastal Mexico. To me, mining has always meant Kentucky and Kentucky means a place my granddaddy had to leave because his land was mined right out from under him.

But you've heard all that. I'll fill you in on this place's mining stories as I learn them, and also Cesar's story. Oh, I almost forgot to tell you I got to teach Cesar's class today. It was so neat. I'd tell you how that came about, but the heat is singing a naptime song to me. I wish you were here to make it even hotter.
Sweet hugs to you,
Me

I shoved that last category of musings away as I folded the letter and sealed it in the envelope. Pointless to think along those lines.

With the huge fan set a bare two inches from my head, the air it was blasting felt almost cool. I was growing to love that fan. By the end of my vacation, I might want to marry it and have its little fan babies.

7
Trish

At some blessed moment while I was napping the early afternoon hours away, I stopped sweating. Don't move, Trish, I warned my waking self. You'll blow it. I raised my head just a little and squinted so I could read my watch without having to lift my arm and chance breaking into a new sweat. Four o'clock. The sun was now aligned with my front windows overlooking the Bay; bits of conversation drifted up from the courtyard along with the dusky afternoon light. The life of coastal Mexico was back in session.

I needed a shower. It had taken me only one day in Mexico to figure out it made no sense to wash *before* the sweat started pouring. Post-siesta was the logical time to get rid of a morning's worth of sweat and grime. I stretched, let my arms go limp by my side, and then stretched again, all the way down to my starting-to-tan toes. The tile floor felt righteously cool under my feet when I stepped into the black-and-white shower stall, turned the water to lukewarm and let it pour over me for a long while, not bathing, just being pleasantly sluiced as I watched my iguana raise his head to catch the mist. Well, okay, he wasn't *my* iguana, but he had sauntered in through my shower window during the hottest part of the day every afternoon so far. I figure if a guy showers with you, he's yours.

I liked my reptilian shower buddy. His craggy face reminded me of some of the regulars I saw on Friday nights at my church's homeless shelter. Most of the guys there were Viet Nam vets who were too cracked open by war to hold down any employment except addiction, but somehow they'd not lost their gentleness. Or maybe gentleness was all they had left after they'd burned up a lifetime's worth of anger in Southeast Asia. All I know is, they never spoke above a murmur when I checked them in to the shelter for the night, and they were always gracious: "Evenin', Ma'am. Thank you for letting me stay."

"Which is exactly what you'd say, if you spoke English, right?"

My iguana bobbed his knobby head once up and once down while I turned off the water and grabbed one of the thick orange towels. He blinked at me very slowly, but did not deign to speak a reply. I do like an inscrutable man.

So what to wear? I squeezed the water from my hair and shook my head, hard, to break the curls free from each other. Mama says one day I'm going to knock myself permanently silly, doing that. I tell her it's too late to warn me. I pulled my long denim skirt from the wooden wardrobe, reached in the bottom dresser drawer for a blue T-shirt, and while I was already bent over, groped around under the bed for my sandals. The ankle-length skirt and the sleeved top added up to a whole lot more material than I'd normally wear for a walk on a hot August evening, but I was in Catholic country now, so it couldn't hurt to err on the side of modesty. Besides, a skirt allows the breezes up and under like a personal wind tunnel.

I grabbed my purse, locked the door and started down the stairs to test my skirt-as-cooling—station contention, but then I had to quickly grab a big handful of skirt to keep from billowing over two fellow guests.

"Hi."

The retired couple from Arizona who were staying in the room next to mine smiled at me in tandem as they spoke. I smiled back, but I didn't stop to chat. This was my vacation; I was exempt from having to chat.

Matamoras Street was busy with families. Absolutely gorgeous children were walking home from school with their moms and their little brothers and sisters, or sometimes, their very machismo Papa holding a small hand on either side and leaning down to listen as one or the other child told him about their day.It was all about family up here in this neighborhood five streets and five terrace levels higher than the Malecon.   I wanted to visit that little kiosk I'd noticed across the street from the Cathedral, the one that sold religious....things? I had no idea what to call the stuff for sale there—souvenirs? icons? relics? indulgences? I needed to buy a first communion gift for a friend's little girl, and wouldn't Emily and her mom be tickled if her present came from a Mexican church store?

The tiny corner shop stood open to the sidewalk, with the wedge of inside floor space taken up mostly by a glass display case that seemed to be filled solely with white lacey goods. Even the crucifixes looked frilly. A fortyish woman behind the counter was changing the tape in a boxy tape player perched on one edge of her wooden desk.

"Perdón?"

The lady clicked the tape cover in place and then looked up as sacred-sounding music began to play, but the little girl sitting on the floor next to her ignored me and kept reading. Wise choice, honey.

"Necesito un regalo por ...um..." Was there some special name for First Communion? Who knew? "... primera comunión." Betcha I just butchered that. But, no. She smiled and reached into the open back of the case.

One exquisite silver bangle bracelet, two folding church fans trimmed in white feathers and a couple of postcards later, I headed out of the store and three blocks over to the post office where the folks in line for stamps were happy to ignore me while I bungled my way through buying ten stamps, apologizing in bad Spanish for my bad Spanish.

I grabbed the free end of the long steel counter top to write out the first of my cards:

La Iglesia
Nuestra Señora de Guadalupe
Calle Hidalgo, Puerto Vallarta
August 28

Mama,
This is the church. Don't you love its pink stone walls
and lacy onion dome? I can see the dome from my room,
but I like to sit on the inn's rooftop and
look at that gold onion
as a part of the whole skyline,
like it's the tallest plant in a stone garden.
If Daddy were here,
he'd have the parish priest deep in theology talk,
despite not knowing a lick of Spanish.
Miss you,
Trish

And then the second card:

Los Cuatro Vientos
Built in 1952 of local stone

Mi amor,
This inn is almost perfect.
It needs you.
Every place I am needs you.
I know this most when I'm someplace without you.
Knowing how I need you is the sole gift of absence.
Tu Querida

Out of the postcard-writing mood after writing to my guy, out of the mood to do anything but think moony thoughts or eat, I started climbing steps, because the café I wanted to try was three streets up the mountain.

The sidewalk leveled out on Calle Miramar so that I was walking the ridge line, as we say at home; I could breathe without making a flat-lander spectacle of myself. And a good thing that was, because there were so many police cruising around as afternoon progressed toward evening that the last thing this lone American wanted was to draw attention to herself due to odd behavior. A white truck emblazoned with Policia Federal Preventia in black and red letters crept slowly past me. One policeman in blue-and black fatigues sat rigidly behind the wheel and his two compadres leaned out of the truck's open bed with machine guns resting on their knees.

Now there's the way to cut down on crime in the streets.

I half-smiled at them as they crept past. They did not even nod.

49

I had to say, their method of law-enforcement seemed pretty effective to me. There's something about strolling past a cocked automatic rifle on your way to dinner that focuses your intentions wonderfully on eating rather than on crime.

I stopped for a second to tilt my head back and crane up at the long stretch of the mountain. I was too far down to see Cesar's village, but I knew it was up there. And I knew there must be small farms and family compounds even higher up on the mountain, though they'd be so hidden by the dips and folds of the mountainside that a hiker wouldn't know a house was there until the dogs came running out barking in Spanish.

Just because I was a Georgia girl, that didn't mean I didn't know a thing or two about mountains. My family's roots ran about as high as they could go—all the way up to the coal seams of Kentucky's Black Mountain and Pine Mountain. It was coal that drove my great-granddaddy down from those mountains eighty years before. He was cursed by coal, he and all his neighbors, whether they had coal on their land, or not. No coal meant you worked for the coal company, mining someone else's land until the coal ran out. Or if you had a seam of coal under your land, as like as not you couldn't mine it yourself because *your* daddy or granddaddy had signed away the mineral rights years before on a tricky contract known as The Broad Form Deed, It gave the coal company the legal right to come and take that coal any way they saw fit, even gouging out a man's tobacco fields and cow pastures, and not a blamed thing the farmer could do to stop them.

After the coal company tripped the coal veins as bare as those farms, they'd take their mining operation to blacker pastures. No coal company meant: no jobs, no stores, no schools. My great-granddaddy hadn't been willing to stay and watch his land raped, so he sold out and moved as far south as his money would take him, down to the swamps of the Okefenokee where he felled cypress until a load of those logs slipped from their railcar and buried him. The grandson he didn't live to know got his education at Emory, in Atlanta, and that's how I came to be a Georgia girl.

I was still a block or so from the corner of Miramar and Guerrero where I'd been told there was a café I'd probably like. The café was just a little ways west of the river, but north of the touristy section. There'd been almost no one walking on the street with me for the past block, and now there was no one at all, but I was okay with that. There was still plenty of daylight left for me to find some supper and then make it back to the inn before dark.

Then I stepped on something that gave a little under my foot, and then jerked away. A quick sharp pain hit my right foot at the arch where the opening of my sandal was—like a shard of glass cutting me.

"What was that?"

I don't know who I was asking.

I twisted my foot up to look down at it and saw the snake. It was just a little snake, but it had raised itself up as stiff as a spear, its tongue flicking in and out, its rattles rattling.

A snake had bitten me. It didn't make sense that I 'd been bitten by a rattlesnake, but I had.

I sat down hard on the sidewalk. I shouldn't move; I knew I should keep my blood flowing as slowly as I could until help arrived. Help from where?

If the snake was still there beside me, I didn't notice, didn't even look around to see. It had emptied all its guns into my foot. It couldn't do me any more damage.

"Teacher? You okay?"

Two small dirty feet in sandals stepped even with my eyes. I looked up as far as I could without raising my head: gray pants, black belt, white shirt, then two Chinese-looking eyes in a worried face. It didn't make sense, either, that Cesar should be here, but, Lordy, I was glad he was. I dropped my eyes back to the foot I was holding in both hands while I rocked back and forth just a little.

"Un vibór. A snake, Cesar. A snake bit me."

He hunkered down on one knee, rested his hand on the other knee. He had chubby fingers.

"Ai, Teacher, this not good."

He straightened up just a little and made a quick scan of the houses around us, then he sprinted straight from his squat to the second house down, where he pounded the door with both fists, yelling:

"Pronto."

A woman opened the door, listened to Cesar for a couple of words, and called over her shoulder, "Viejo." Cesar kept talking. Her husband stepped around her to stare at me, hitching up one suspender strap. Cesar pulled at the man's arm and kept talking. The man shook off Cesar's hand, grabbed something from his wife and took off running down the street.

Cesar came back and squatted by me again.

"He get the truck, Teacher."

"Cesar, why are you here?"

What did it matter why he was here? But I needed the answer.

"Why aren't you at home?"

The way he shook his head, it could have weighed a hundred pounds. I hated it that he looked so burdened, and that I was the burden.

"I talk to Sister after school, Teacher. She say tomorrow I go to the inn and you teach me English. Then she say I need go now. I say, 'Okay, I go home, Sister.', but she say, 'No, no go home, You *go, go.*'"

He lifted his hand from his knee and ran his fingers through his hair, catching a thick handful of curls in his fingers and squeezing tight.

"I no understand, Teacher. Go where? So I just walk and walk one hour, maybe two. And then I see you. Now I know."

He raised his head enough that he could look at me, his fingers still knotted in his curls.

"It you and me, Teacher. Sister saying I need go to *you.*"

I pulled away from him a little, scrunching up my face again. Too much here didn't make sense.

"How could she know I needed help? That's impossible."

"Sister say Impossible just another name for God."

We both heard it then: truck tires on cobblestones. I knew that sound. *Whup-bump. Whup-bump.* Front tires and then the back. Up and over, up and over. Savannah's cobblestones or Mexico's: it was the same sound. Cesar stood up to look; I didn't. The man was gunning and jerking his truck up a maze of one-way cobbled streets from where he'd parked it somewhere down nearer town.

Then he was in sight, backing the truck to where I sat. I heard the emergency brake squawk when he gave it a yank so it'd hold the pickup nose-down the mountain with the tailgate open and facing me. He threw the driver's door open so hard it kept swinging while he ran to where his wife had laid a blanket on the sidewalk next to me. The man nodded to me and then toward the blanket: *Lie on the blanket so I can lift you into the truck.* Bless his heart. Like five-foot-five him could hoist five-foot-nine me into the truck bed.

I smiled and shook my head—I could climb in by myself. *I'm not that bad off, Señor.* Was I? Maybe a little bit queasy, nothing else. My foot didn't even hurt. It just felt odd. I felt odd. To play it safe when I stood up, though, I bounced my weight on my left foot and held my snake-bit foot in the air like I was playing hopscotch. I hoisted myself left-side-first over the rusty tailgate and scooted so I could lean my back against the side of the truck bed. His wife tucked her blanket over me. I wanted to cry.

The man jumped back behind the wheel and let off the emergency brake. His truck lifted from the cobblestones and clawed air all the way down the mountain. Its worn-out shocks let forth a long, piteous *squawnk* each time the truck hit ground for a spine-jolting second before achieving airborne status again.

"Lord God." I hadn't mean it as a prayer, but I was holding that option open. Bruises began blossoming all over my butt.

He spun the truck to a merciful stop by a low, block hospital building's Emergency Room that turned out to be pretty much like all emergency rooms; walls that looked cold, a gurney with cold white sheets, nurses sweeter than I would be, a heated blanket over me, an IV in my left arm. It was all so embarrassing. I wanted to apologize for being so much trouble. So I did. "Sorry. Lo siento. Estoy bien." Idiot. They can see good and well that you're not fine. But I couldn't help myself. Southern Hostess Mode held me fast to good manners even though the little bit of queasy feeling I'd had before was now rocketing up to a whole lotta hurting going on.

"You must to make a decision soon, Señorita." The doctor crooked his left arm up around my chart and folded it to his chest as he laid his other hand on my shoulder and patted me while he talked. "We keep the anti-venom on stock because Jalisco's hills hide many snakes. I can use it now, but you must to know there are many dangers with the anti-venom. Maybe you have a reaction of the allergies and you die. Maybe only we must cut off the leg."

Oh, so there's an upside. What a relief.

"And you must to decide very soon. Six hours only, you have for the anti-venom."

I looked at the clock. Oops, no, only five hours now, Doc.

He gave me one more pat and left as a nurse walked in with a syringe in her hand.

"What are you giving me?"

She had started to inject something into my IV line.

"For the pain."

"No, gracias. I must be awake. I need to listen to my body. Entiendes?"

The nurse tipped her head to one side and studied me for a long minute before she nodded once and put the syringe away. I felt honored.

"Gracias."

She nodded again and left the room.

It made it easier that she was okay with my choice, but I would have stuck by my guns even if she'd given me a fight. I needed to be able to hear what was happening inside me, to listen for the sounds of anything happening for better or for worse. It was the only way I could decide wisely what my next step should be. And I had to be absolutely alert to do this. No morphine.

I rode through the next couple of hours on waves of pain, actually riding the pain like I was surfing the poison, trying to ride it to some other shore than the death of my leg. It was hard work. The clattery world of the ER faded into background noise, like a TV left on.

And then around nine o'clock, something shifted. As surely as if I had heard a door slam, I knew the venom had stopped its coursing. No matter how much the venom had messed up my veins over the past couple of hours, I knew it would not now get any worse. They could keep their anti-venom.

"Señora?"

The nurse at the desk just outside my cubicle raised her head from her paperwork.

"I need to see the doctor, please. Necesito el doctór."

He was pleased, bless him.

"Ah, bueno. It is good that you decide this. The anti-venom it is very dangerous. Pero, we must keep you here tonight, maybe two nights. You need much Benadryl, and much saline to wash the poison away. After that, who knows? Each person reacts much different to the venom. We must wait to see. You must not travel. You have a place to stay, yes?"

Well, sure, assuming my room hasn't been promised to some other tourist next week and assuming the inn is okay with a gimp-legged American staying on for an extra week or two, and assuming I suddenly come into an inheritance to pay my bill, then, yes, I have a place to stay.

Oh, and I get the added pleasure of telling my principal. I'll be needing a sub for the first week of school. Dios mio. What hath God wrought?

8
Trish

Dear Mama,

First of all, I'm okay.

It was a terrible thing to have to call and tell you I'd been bitten by a rattlesnake, more terrible than if I'd broken my leg at a street dance or had my heart broken by a Latin lover, because I'm pretty sure news like mine instantly shut down your option of playing the empathy card with your friends. I mean, how many mothers have gotten such a phone call from their daughters? It's not like you know somebody who can say, "Oh, honey, I know just what you mean. My daughter had the exact same thing happen to her."

But I'm okay, Mama, really. It could have been a lot worse. Everyone has been so good to me—starting with the man and his wife who got me to the hospital without sailing us and the truck off the side of the mountain, to the nurses who treated me so sweetly that if they were secretly thinking of me as a serpent-marked pariah they surely didn't show it, to the doctor who actually encouraged me to be a partner with him in the whole tricky process of deciding if I should allow the anti-venom and possibly die or not allow it and possibly die, to the blessed woman who owns the inn and told me of course I should stay on in my room for as long as I needed to and not to worry about the cost because we'd work something out, to Armando, who's made a point of having a chair pulled out for me to fall into after I hop down to breakfast, plus, he pushes up another chair all nicely padded with a cushion for my swollen leg.

Not that the swelling is anything to worry about, Mama. Just a normal response to the veins sloughing off the rest of the snake poison and getting themselves back to normal, that's all.

I stopped writing and looked for a long minute at my right leg. Since the swelling began, I had zealously avoided looking at that hideous bloated log of a leg, as if acknowledging it might somehow encourage it to stay swollen longer.

By day three, yesterday, my foot was a black balloon of pain with no discernible toes or ankle, and how it felt was beyond bearing, literally. Any time I absolutely had to lower my football foot to the ground so I could hobble to the bathroom or make my way down the stairs to eat, my blown-out veins tried their darnedest to pump blood to and fro as per usual, but it was like trying to shove toothpaste back into the tube. My poor veins were valiant, but ineffectual. My nerve endings worked like champs.

There was no way I was going to tell all this truth to Mama.

"And if this is to be a truth-telling day." I leaned over to Saki curled in my lap, and whispered into his black-tipped ear, "I reckon I should own up to what's scared me the most, huh?"

True to his breed, Saki twitched his ear as sign that he was singularly unconcerned with my problems. It was his nap time.

So, all right, I wouldn't tell this cat and I couldn't tell Mama and I mustn't tell my guy how the hardest part was not knowing what to expect next. I was okay while I was in the hospital because I could ask questions that had answers: How long before I have to make a decision about the anti-venom? Six hours. What are you giving me now? Benadryl, steroids, saline solution. Do I have to stay in the hospital? Just overnight so we can observe you. Can I call my mother? Tu madre? Por seguro. Of course. Can I leave the hospital this morning? Yes.

Ah, but then the good gods were done with helping me, it seemed, because all the satisfying answers went away. What should I do now? Rest. Wait to see if the swelling goes down. If? You mean you don't know? My answer was a very Latin shoulder shrug from the nice doctor: No one knows, Señorita. Usually, with the bites this bad, the person does not live.

So sorry I stepped outside the norm.

I truly *was* sorry. I was good with boundaries, limits, explanations, narratives, endings. It was why I love ballads and hate jazz—I needed the story line I can't find in jazz's meanderings. And so far I couldn't find the next page in this story I was unintentionally living out in a tourist town in Mexico. How could I tell my mama I was scared? I loved her too much to drag her down to the same powerless place I was hobbling around in.

And how could I ever tell my man I didn't know what to do next? He loved me for my strength: You don't ever just say "Screw it" and look for a shot glass instead of a solution, do you? He'd said that to me once as he'd swung my legs up over his legs stretched out straight on the bed, and he'd run his hands down my thighs as far as he could reach, over and over, as if the skin of his hands could soak up through the skin of my legs the strength that lived in me but not in him. God, you have gorgeous legs, he'd said, and he'd meant it, but he also meant he needed me.

What if my leg was never gorgeous again?

Shake it off, Trish; shake it off. I shook my head as if I could literally shake away that unknowable. Armando noticed my head shake; he suddenly glanced up from wiping down the breakfast tables and furrowed his forehead as he looked hard at me to see if I needed some sort of help I wasn't admitting to. I gave the sweet man a quick smile and little wave of my fingers to say: No, no. I'm fine. Don't worry about me. I picked up my pen and started writing again as visible proof of my okay-ness.

In fact, Mama, my main problem is in keeping the folks around here from fussing over me too much. I get the feeling that Armando, for instance, works way harder than any person should have to, and I don't want to add to his load.

Oh, Lordy, and I've forgotten to tell you the reason I was rescued in the first place was thanks to my young friend Cesar, who happened to find me and run for help, and the reason it's only just now popped into my head that I forgot to tell you this is because I've only just this second remembered that I've completely forgotten to ask anyone what happened to Cesar after they zoomed me off to the hospital. Did any of that last run-on sentence make any sense at all?

This boy is the main reason I'm okay, Mama, and I just left him standing on the sidewalk without so much as a fare-the-well. And have I asked about him since I got back to the inn? No. Have I tried to find him to thank him? No. But your daughter is not one to let failures lie flaccid, Mama. I'm going to ask Armando right now how I can get word to Cesar that I am in his debt and would love to see him so I can say thank you. I'll mail this letter and write again tomorrow to let you know how it turns out.

Love and hugs,
Me

"Shoo, Saki. I need to stand up now."

Siamese cats do not shoo. I gave the handsome cat a teeny nudge of encouragement, just as someone spoke from an inch behind me, "Yo tengo las palabras."

I jumped, making Saki jump, too, so my lap was finally free. Well done, whoever just scared the life out of me.

It was Cesar, clutching a notebook in his hand down by his left side. Typical. I'd gotten so lost in Mama's letter and my own thoughts and the paths those thoughts led me along, that I'd not noticed him walking up the steps from the street to the courtyard. But then, maybe it was a *good* sign that I'd been able to forget about my leg long enough to succumb to the familiar seduction of words.

"The words, Teacher. I have the words."

That's what I thought he'd said.

Cesar handed his notebook to me and I leaned forward to take it just the way he was handing it, opened to a written list. A list. Right. I'd asked him to make a list of ten words for our first English lesson and here it was. This boy had an uncanny way of showing up just when I needed him most, carrying exactly the right sort of aid in his chubby hands. Or maybe Sister was right, and Cesar 's hands were simply doing the work of her Great Impossible God.

I waved toward the chair across from me, "Sit. Sit." took one deep breath, and settled my foot more comfortably onto the pillow.

"We'd better get to work. We're three days behind schedule."

An hour later, neither of us heard or noticed as Sister Maria Therese stepped softly up the stairs and stood behind Cesar and me, his notebook open on the table in front of us and our shoulders almost touching. We must have looked like old friends working on a puzzle together. Actually, I guess that was exactly what we were.

"No, like this, Cesar. Watch me: put the tip of your tongue between your front teeth, then pull it quickly back. Thhh. Thhh. Think. Now you try: think, think. *Pensar*. Think. I think I can, I think I can. Creo que puedo."

What I was thinking was that *The Little Engine That Could* would not flow nearly so trippingly in Spanish, when I realized someone else was with us. I looked up and over my shoulder. It was the nun, Cesar's friend. Cesar's bodyguard?

Whatever.

"Sister, hello. Please, sit with us."

" No, gracias. It is time for Cesar to return to school. He is late for his afternoon classes."

"Oh, no. I am so sorry. We were forgot the time."

Cesar grabbed his notebook and ran for the steps, turning around long enough to call *gracias* over his shoulder. And also, "Mañana, maestra?"

"Yes, tomorrow, Cesar. Ten more words, bien?"

"Okay, teacher."

Both of us watched the charming kid dash away to the class he was missing. Then the nun sat.

Sister Maria Therese smoothed the fabric of her habit over her lap.

Do nuns have laps? I wondered. Saki sauntered over from the corner of the courtyard, stretched, and transferred his fickle self to the nun's lap, thus neatly providing me answer to that mystery.

"I am sorry for your accident." Sister Maria Therese nodded slightly in the direction of my leg, gently dismissing my black and green log of soggy flesh as worthy of nothing more than token polite concern. Her obvious belief that my leg was speeding along toward being whole again was the very best sort of get-well wish. I warmed toward her as to a long- lost cousin.

"Oh, thank you. And I need to tell you how wonderfully everyone here has treated me. I couldn't have chosen a better place to be bitten by a poisonous snake."

"In Mexico, we help each other." She lifted one eyebrow and gave a head a little tilt. "You needed help. And now you help Cesar. This is good. I was not sure. I did not know if you would take from Cesar more than you gave. He must not be hurt because of his hungers."

I leaned forward to put my hand on her knee, wherever a knee might be under all that fabric. I didn't know if touching nuns was verboten, but I couldn't help myself; I'm Southern, we're touchers.

"I would never hurt him, please believe me. I am a teacher, Sister. I teach, and he wants to be taught. Besides, there is something very special about that boy. He is smart, yes, but there are lots of smart children. You must see this, too, because it is obvious you care about him."

I took my hand away and leaned back against my chair, smiling at her the way I smile at my friend Jenni, back home, when we're telling each other things we already know.

"Maybe he lives just a bit closer to your heart than the other children in the parish?"

The nun lifted Saki from her lap to the courtyard floor, and stood.
She nodded as she gathered her skirts up just a little in her hands and stepped down the first step.

"Thank you for teach Cesar. He will return tomorrow, at the same time."

Then she left, floating down the stairs just like The Flying Nun.

And thank the good lord, Cesar *did* return, each day at noon, never mentioning my fright show of a leg, but always making sure I didn't have to stand unnecessarily. This boy, I thought over and over, has the soul of a gentleman.

My only normal times on those days following the bite happened from noon until a few minutes before one, when Cesar and I explored English together. Every tutoring session began the same way: Cesar would time his stepping into the courtyard to that exact moment when I was deepest in thought, and as soon as he was sure I was far gone to the world around me, he'd leap up the last two steps and plant his landing right in front of me, grinning like a boy possessed. "Hello, teacher." Once I got over my heart attack, for the next hour I could be myself again. When I was alone with my leg, my normal optimism kept threatening to leave me for a more hospitable host, but working with Cesar shushed the threats for an hour each day.

He knew more English than he'd let on at first, so our word-for-a-word exchanges quickly progressed to daily Socratic debates about the structure of English grammar.

"Teacher, scuse me, but that don't make sense."

"Maybe not, Cesar, because English is a mongrel language, like a street dog with spots from his mother and a curved tail from his father and floppy ears from who knows where. That street dog may not be pretty, but he is what he is. You can't rip off his legs just because they look too short for his body. And if those legs get him where he needs to go, then they do make sense, in their own way."

"So you telling me, Teacher, that your language is ugly and don't fit right, but it the language the whole world need to learn?"

"Must be, Cesar. You asked me to teach it to you, didn't you?"

"I got reasons, Teacher."

"What reasons, Cesar?"

"Ask Sister. She knows."

Having thus defended the honor of his native language, Cesar bent his head back to the necessary work of learning this bastard language. But why was it so necessary to him? I made a mental note to ask Sister.

My chance came three days later, Monday of my second week in Mexico, the first week of September. My leg was still bad, very bad, and when I went for my appointment with the sweet doctor, he had cupped my right hand inside both of his while he told me I could not, I must not even think about flying home for another week or two.

"The veins they are still too weak, bonita. They would to rupture, if you fly."

But he didn't tell me not to walk, and, Lord God, I needed to be outside moving in the fresh air and sunshine. I figured out a system of easing into walking by setting my bad foot down, gritting my teeth as long as I could against the agony (truly there was no other word for it of blood trying to squeeze into the vessels of my foot, then lifting my foot just high enough to take the pressure off for a moment, then lowering it again before the blood had a chance to relax. Over and over, I'd do this macabre little foot bob until at last the teensiest trickle of circulation came into my foot and I could hobble on it for a bit.

I would wait until Armando had left for the day so I wouldn't have to see him wrinkle his forehead in worry over me, and then I'd hobble down the steps from the courtyard to walk along Matamoros's row of tall block houses the color of sand, each with their flowered tile entryway and second-floor balconies with scrolled railings. Street-level windows were burglar-proofed by cut-away terracotta screens built in as part of the window, but most houses allowed me a glimpse through an open kitchen entry around the side, where dish towels hung drying over old red linoleum-topped tables and trash piled up in one corner. Parked cars, nine out of ten of them Volkswagen Bugs, stood nose-to-bumper the lengths of both curbs.

Halfway to the river, I started down the two flights of steps to Juarez Street and had just made it off the last step when my traitor leg forced me to sit and recoup, my arms resting on my knees and my head drooping down.

"Trish?"

I raised my head to a swirl of dark fabric near my nose. "Sister?"

"Trish, you are okay, yes?"

"No. No, Sister, I'm not. I truly don't think I can make it back to the inn by myself. Do you think you could find someone to help me?"

"I will help." Sister Maria Therese held her hand out to me.

"Thank you, Sister, but you are so small. I'm afraid I need someone I can lean my weight on."

"You can lean. I am small in body only."

Finding it impossible to argue with logic I didn't quite understand, I decided to just go with what was being offered, and it worked. I was tall enough and the nun was short enough that her shoulder fit perfectly under my armpit as a kind of human crutch. This arrangement got us back to the inn with no one giving us a second glance. Nuns, apparently, are expected to be seen lifting up the fallen.

Saki greeted us at the top of the stairs, swishing and *mrrping* to encourage us in the direction of his favorite corner table as if his having been deprived of a lap all afternoon had been the greater of our combined struggles.

For a good ten minutes or more I did nothing at all except sit and sweat and think cooling thoughts. The Sister sat across from me looking like God didn't allow her to sweat, while Saki translated his thoughts into a loud continual purr.

When Sister spoke, it wasn't at all what I thought she might say.

"Trish, where you were going?"

"Anywhere."

The nun nodded. "Yes, I have many times tried to go there."

"Really? Verdad? Why? Sister. Tell me. I need to think about someone else's story right now; anyone's story but my own."

Sister Maria Therese stopped stroking Saki and studied me.

"You would like to hear a story? Perhaps the story of the father of Cesar?"

"Yes. Please. Claro que sí."

I settled back in my chair, shifted my foot a little, and relaxed as the Sister begin talking mostly in Spanish because she was telling a story of her culture—how could she tell it in English? My high school Spanish kindly came back to me well enough that, if I let the words flow over me without trying to translate each one, I could basically follow her story, whichever language it arrived in. She told her tale like a lover describing her beloved. They'd adore her at home, especially up in the mountains, I thought as I listened. She understands how the wealth of a people lives in its stories.

Saki even stopped chirruping and playing for attention as Sister began to speak.

Everything was no so bad after Zapata's revolution gave back to us the lands of our ancestors, land that was taken from us two times. You know the history? You have gone up into the Sierra Madres and seen the old silver mines? No? Pues, the mines are still there, but most of their silver is not. Our people have always known of the silver in our hills, but we took only what we needed and left the rest to the hills. For many generations, that was how it was. A man would dig out a little silver for to pay his taxes and then go back to his farming until the next year.

I was nodding at her: "Yes, yes, I know exactly. That's just what my grandfather and his father did with the coal under their land in Kentucky. They'd dig a little now and then, but it never occurred to them to dig it all out and sell it away. That'd be foolish, like draining all the water from their wells."

She smiled at me, a slow smile.

Ai, but when one of your Americans heard of the silver, he thought this all must be his. He was a man of great wealth and therefore of great influence, so our government said to him, "Yes, of course you must mine the silver. Here, we will give you this little village of Las Peñas—that was the name for Puerto Vallarta then. It will be for the convenience of you and your workers." And our government did this. The farmers up in these hills were poor and without power already because the Spaniards had seized the land for their large haciendas, many years past. Can you see how it was? Our people had no land of their own to farm and now even their businesses down in town had been given like a dowry to the mining company. Our men left their mountain villages to work in the mines, or they ran the stores in town that now belonged to the mining company. What else could they do? And of course when one day the silver was no more, the company left. And what did Union de Cuale leave behind for our grandparents? Poverty and no hope.

Then Zapata came out of his small village to be our voice to the government. "Yes." el Presidente answered to Zapata's demands, knowing he and his administration were standing in a corner with no door, "You are right. Our good people of Mexico must have their land." Cardenas drew official circles around many thousands of hectares of land—dozens of such circles in Jalisco alone—and announced that these allotments of land would be called ejidos, and that each ejido would be owned and worked and governed by the people who lived there, los ejidatários. Perhaps Cardenas' intentions were good—only God knows, but the results were good, at least for a while.

Because, mira. Many of the men in power after Cardenas so hated the ejidos that they even allowed the assassinations of populist peasant leaders. This is so, Trish. I am a Bride of Christ, I do not speak lies. Worse and worse the corruption grew, and greater and greater grew the anger among the young, until the anger and the frustration all burst into flame during that decade of wildfires, the 1960's. Your American young people were not unique in the world in their protests during that time. Here in Mexico, also.

Francisco was eighteen in 1968. Sí, Cesar's father. Is that not whose story this is? Francisco was in his first year at the University, the first from his family to go. You believe Cesar is intelligent? You did not know Francisco. Such power his brain had as could change the world, but fires of anger were burning away that power, reducing possibility to coals of hatred. Francisco had heard how your American president was coming to Mexico before the start of the Olympic Games, and the Games themselves were coming very soon. The eyes of the world were to be on Mexico. What better time to put injustice out on display than when all the world is watching?

The students gathered at the Plaza of the Three Cultures in Mexico City. Noplace could be more appropriate for championing the rights of all Mexicans. Thousands of young people gathered; most were students from the University. They were all young, all very intelligent and full of love for their culture and their people. Five thousand of them died there when la Policia came in to that plaza and began firing. The young students fell where they stood, dying dozens at a time, as if they were birds over a field.

No, Francisco did not die that day. You think Cesar is the son of a ghost? Francisco fell among the bodies, but only so that he would not become one of the dead himself. He lay as a person dead for a time, until he realized the police had begun tossing bodies like firewood into the backs of trucks, then covering the murdered young with blankets and tarps. I have told you how smart Francisco was; it took him only an instant to understand that these killings were meant to appear as if they had never happened. In less than hour, there would be no bodies littering the plaza and no words about those bodies from the mouth of the government.

Francisco allowed himself to be one of the tossed, and then as the truck began its slow progression away from the plaza—slow, because the unhurt and the merely injured were blocking the roads as some were running away, or in protest some were with great courage not moving from the road—he slid from the truck bed to the sidewalk, then rolled out of sight behind a parked car. As I have said, it did not take long at all for the police to remove all evidence of the protest and of those lives that were no more. When the troops had finished their clean-up work, they drove away as if their shift was over at the factory, no more than that.

Francisco was free to go back to class, or go home. But where now was home for him in this country that killed its best children in order to kill their ideas? He could see no way to stay, so he left. He rode a bus that night headed to the border and then at the border, he boarded another bus, a U.S. bus. It was so easy at that time to go back and forth. In those years Mexicans who lived in border towns would cross each Sunday to shop in the United States. Francisco did not go there to the U.S. to shop, but to look for his soul, which he had not been able to find in his body since the shooting began.

I waited for her to go on, but she had lowered her head to nuzzle Saki's head, and seemed to be done with talking. I couldn't stand it.

"Sister? What happened then? Did he stay in America? Was Cesar born in America? Who did Francisco marry? Where is he now?"

Sister Maria Therese smiled and laid her hand on my hurt leg. "You must to rest. The story will not vanish. Tomorrow. Before Cesar comes for his lesson tomorrow, I will come here to the inn. I will help you walk for the sake of your leg and then it will again be time for the story."

Great, I thought while I watched her leave. Now I've been given a little mental torture to balance out the physical. She's one smart lady, that nun is.

But I did rest, a long, dreamless nap before dinner, and later that night a sleep so deep that when I woke to the sun starting to turn hot where it streamed in the back window, I felt normal for a full thirty seconds before I woke up enough to remember about my leg.

True to her word, Sister Maria Therese was back at the inn by ten, ready for her stint as volunteer physical therapist. Around and around the courtyard with Saki turning his handsome head away in mortification, I gave walking my best shot, telling myself I was limping my way toward my reward: the rest of Francisco's story.

The rest of the story has not such much drama as the first...

Sister began with a shrug of one shoulder after we had sat down to our table with cold water in those tall green crinkled glasses you could buy everywhere in Mexico,

...but perhaps has more sad. Francisco was four years in America. He worked. He lived with cousins for a while in Texas, then in California. He was always smart with his hands—this is how Cesar comes of his talent, and it was easy for him to find work as a carpenter, as a hanger of drywall, even for a while as a mechanic. It was honest work and he was able because of the work to send much money home to his Mama, but his mind was restless, always. He decided to come home, to go back to the University. He was beginning to think he might like to teach.

The same as how a bus had taken him out of his country, a bus brought him home, truly home, here to visit his family for a week or two. Then he went back to the city to enroll again and finish his education. The problem, as he soon found out, was that Francisco Ramirez did not exist, at least not as a former student. He had been killed in the student uprising so far as anyone at the University knew, and because that uprising had not happened, Francisco had therefore never been a student. This does not make sense to you? It did not have to make sense. It was a government edict passed down to the University officials, which made the University's position more binding than common sense. Oh, and they were so sorry, but the University was not accepting first-time students at that moment.

What was there left for a man such as that but to return home and fall in love? Passion must find a focus, any focus. The girl he focused on because he had long loved her, had also long loved him, as he well knew, and so all should have been well, but her father would not allow his angel of a daughter to associate with this hothead, this known enemy of the government. Such a marriage could not be, and it was not. Francisco married another and though he had no passion for this one, he cared for her, so all should have been well, but God kept his back turned to Francisco. There were no babies for three years.

Sister Marie Therese stopped talking just as Cesar stepped into the courtyard. She smiled at him and patted the chair next to me, for him to sit down there.

"We will work again tomorrow, senorita."

I watched her walk away. Oh, sister, I was thinking as Cesar got out his notebook, I *so* know who that angel of a daughter was.

9
Trish

Late afternoons were the cruelest time, I'd decided over the past couple of days, despite Mama always having claimed Sunday evenings were the worst time to be by yourself: "Everyone has been to church and gone out for dinner and now they're all at home together doing quiet, family things. You feel like you're the only person in the universe sitting in a house by yourself."

I spent every late afternoon sitting in the hotel room by myself, a room still holding onto the heavy heat that had built up during the day. My deceptively white and window-filled room stayed so oppressive in the afternoons that if my spine had been the Appalachian Trail, the sweat rolling in rivers down either side of the spinal ridge could have filled Lake Chatuge on my east and Blue Ridge Lake on my west. My face felt permanently slimy, and I couldn't seem to wipe my hands all the way dry. I put off taking my shower until right before I went out in search of supper, in hopes I'd arrive at a restaurant relatively stink-free.

And that was the other thing—I was thoroughly sick of eating alone. When you live the public life of a small-town teacher, it's a novelty and a blessed relief, at first, to wander around browsing for a restaurant of your own choosing, and for a while it's fun to people-watch from the solitude of your own table without having to listen to your best friend's opinion of the high heels all the women were wearing, or have your sister whisper way too loudly for you to look at how that sad-looking woman with the graying braid down her back was trying to hide in the shadows of her booth near the kitchen doorway. After two weeks on my own in Mexico, though, *I* was that sad-looking woman. My social options consisted of giving English lessons to the world's cutest ten-year-old, or taking history lessons from the world's prettiest nun.

I rolled my eyes at myself, which is not easy to do.

Get a grip, Trish. The ten-year-old and the nun both meant more to me now than some folks I've known back home all my life. Connections like that have a reason, even if I don't know what the reason is. I don't need to know. Meeting people who fill a hole in your life you hadn't even known was there until you met them should be cause for profound gratitude, not a pity party. Count your blessings. Write a letter to the dearest of those blessings and then go find some dinner.

Good idea. I could mail the letter at the post office down by city hall. Then I could walk along the Malecon to Los Palomas and get there early enough to grab a seat by the sidewalk. Good. Now I had a plan. The longer you stay alone, the more you need a plan.

I grabbed the my paper and pen and the biggest book in my room to use as a lap desk. No question about who I needed to write to.

My Handsome,

It shouldn't shock you greatly to hear that a neato highlight of my day was learning some of Cesar's family history. The nun I told you about gave me a story-telling time right before Cesar's lesson.

Did you know there was a mining history to this part of Mexico? Call me a clueless American, but I had no idea. It was eerie, hearing the Sister talk about how the locals had no choice but to go to work for the mining company and then had no choices at all left to them once the silver had played out and the company moved on. I'd heard that story before; she could have been talking about Kentucky and my family.

Or yours, because I can't really claim my family's mountain heritage, can I? My great-granddaddy packed up and headed south when he saw how things were starting to go sour in the mountains; he left for good and all, never even drove back of a weekend to tend the family graves. And me? I grew up in the flattest of flatlands, south Georgia. Where did I get off talking about heritage? I know good and well most people in eastern Kentucky think my claim to their region is all wind and shadow. The fact that I had absolutely no say in where I was born, or that my heart sings its truest song only when I'm in Hindman or Whitesburg or Blacky doesn't count for squat with them.

64

But you are my mountain man, no question. Your family got off their boat from England and hunkered right down in Pound Gap, never to set foot much beyond. I'll bet some great-grand of yours knew Davy Crockett by sight. Who could argue your claim to be of those mountains? Not me—I have traveled your personal hills and hollers many a night—I know them well. Your body is the mountain heritage I can claim without challenge.

And if a claim to place is based on time spent there, I'd say the time I've spent with you should count twice: once in the moment of being there with you, and once in remembering.

Remember that late afternoon we drove past Blacky and back again, over and over, trying to find the road up the mountain to Carcasonne? I'd never been to the monthly square dance there and it was a famous one. Take me?I'd tipped my head and asked you with a smile that said I knew you'd take me to the moon and back if I asked. (And you have, my sweet; many times, you have.) You know I don't dance, you'd answered me, as if that made any difference. I'll dance for both of us, I'd answered back as if more dancing were a sacrifice for me.

But we could not find the turn-off; there's only one road that runs through Blacky but somehow we couldn't see the side road that should wind us up to Carcasonne. You'd slow the car and prop your elbow in the window opening, nodding with a slow smile to a lady rocking on her porch. "Carcasonne?" she'd ponder a bit. "I allus goes that way." She'd point and we'd "thank you kindly" and off we'd go the way she'd pointed, which would turn out to be no more the right way than the last "that way" we'd been offered. Dusk was moving in to the holler by way of shadows cast by the rise of the ridge. Hon, I said, don't worry about it. We can try another month. It's getting dark.

But you just laid your hand on my leg and squeezed—Look there— nodding to a store built long and skinny to fit the teeny ledge of flatness between road and ridge. I know that store. We can ask for directions.

If anyone had asked me before that evening, I'd have sworn on my great-grandmother's grave (which is in Neon, Kentucky, by the way) that such things as sliding panels set into doors at eye-level were the stuff of Al Capone or the Wizard of Oz, but this store claimed one. You knocked, the panel slid aside, and the barrel of a shotgun poked through the opening alongside a pair of dark brown eyes narrowed in warning.

"Yeah?"

A voice somewhere below the eyes and the gun asked you what your name was, and when you answered, the voice growled, "Yeah, I know who you are. Who's she?"

"I know Mike Mullins." I blurted out. It's not always a wise move to share the first words that pop into your mouth during a moment teetering between a happy ending and a messy one, but that time it worked.

The voice grunted, the panel slid shut and the door opened.

Turned out, the store owner was being hunted by the EPA to testify against some mine owners, and also by the mine owners who were hoping to weaken his ability to testify.

I know; I know-I can see you holding this letter with a bemused look on your craggy face and shaking your head. Lord God, why is she wasting time and ink and paper writing all this down just to send it to me? I was there.

I'm writing it down, love, because you were there, but you aren't here. There is no "us" here, except as I create it by writing our past with these words on paper, words that I can see and touch and believe in. Why do you think I write? I write to save what I love.

But also, too, this story always shows me clearly how enduringly I am the outsider: a preacher's kid packed from parsonage to parsonage; a Georgia girl two states and two generations removed from any roots I could claim, having to claim someone else's good name and history as my right of entry; and now, here I am a tourist all by my lonesome in a family-centered community. Wherever I am, I'm from somewhere else.

Except when I'm with you.

I'm beginning to think maybe my young Cesar is an outsider, too, despite that his roots have never been yanked out of Jalisco soil. It's his craving for words that makes me believe this. It's obvious both of us need to be able to "talk in everlasting words" because—" words are all we have." Just ask the Bee Gees. They understand.

And, yes, sweet, you do try to understand. It's just that when I talk about being a woman without a place, it's like trying to explain drought to the rain forest. Oh, but I'm rambling. If you were only here, you'd shush my rambling, fold my hands in yours, and lead me home.

I'm sending you the kisses I'd rather give to you,

Me

The room had cooled down while I was writing, and so had I. I still had to go out alone in search of supper, but at least now I felt peacefully lonely, instead of frantically lonely. Writing always worked that miracle for me. By the time I worked my way to the end of a letter or a poem or a page of an essay, I felt shriven, to use an ancient word. I liked ancient words. Sometimes I felt they were my only heritage.

10
Cesar

"Again you are late, my brother."

Carlos stood waiting for me by our school's iron gate, making himself late along with me. He was right. I *was* late, so why was Carlos still standing there?

"For sure, Cesar, your greatest talent is stupidity."

Of course. He had waited so he could use his good insult on me. Always my brother's words were sharp, but kind were his actions. I prefer it this way from any person.

I was late, but I was not stupid. Most noon times I stayed with the teacher as long as I could because I liked how we studied the language in the same way I might take apart a motor that was still working well, but I wanted to understand the working of it. I needed to know how the English worked and she knew how to tell me.

This day, though, I had stayed even a moment or two longer because of what I heard Sister say when I walked up the steps to the courtyard. She had said my father's name and now I could not stop thinking about him.

I turned my head to look at Carlos. It was four in the afternoon and we were walking home from school.

"Carlos, what do you remember about our father?"

"I remember that he left us."

"You do not remember that; you were too young. I had only five years when he left."

"Well, maybe I do not remember his leaving, but all I can remember is our father being gone." Carlos let his long legs put him ahead of me and my questions, but I threw one more question to him.

"Do you know why he left?"

Carlos stopped, pulled his face up tight on one side the way you would for a bad smell, and said, "Nothing matters less than 'why'."

We did not talk the rest of the way up the road. It was so hot even the birds had stopped talking to each other. I saw one lizard run from the shade of a barrel cactus to the shade of a palo verde so fast his feet left no little scratches in the sand. I wondered if I could run so fast I would leave no footprints behind.

As soon as we were home I changed from my school clothes and helped my granddaddy for a while, bringing in more wood for the temascal fire, scrubbing the small lodge with a rag and sand to clean it from the people who had used it that day. I did not mind; it felt good to work after so much sitting at school. It felt good to use my body and let my mind take a siesta. It felt good to not talk with Abuelo, who also liked to not talk. This day, though, there were words tugging at me like a little brother wanting to be noticed. I finished wiping water from the inside of the door of the lodge and closed it behind me, drying my hands on my T-shirt and pulling up the neck of my shirt to wipe sweat from my face while I walked to where Abuleo was sitting under his tree. His sandals lay on the dirt of the courtyard near his chair and he had folded one leg under the other one so only the tough bottom of his foot showed. His heel had cracks in it as deep as an arroyo where no rains have come. I wanted my feet to be so hard.

"Abuelo, I know the name of my father was Francisco."

He raised his eyes but not his head, making three rows of lines come across his forehead.

"Ah, who says you are not a genius?"

"No, but that is all I know. What is the story of Francisco? Will you give me his story?"

He flicked his hand at me, like at a fly.

"You are his story, Cesar, you and your brothers. Francisco began his own story; you will finish it. I cannot tell you the story that is yours to make."

While he talked, he got up from his chair and kicked his sandals right-side-up with his toes so he could slip his feet back into them. He waved his hand—come—and then hooked his thumbs under his suspenders to pull them onto his shoulders from where they had fallen to his elbows while he rested. He walked us away from our house, away from my granny who might call us to bring her more water, away from my brothers who would not listen but would scramble the story with their interruptions, and away from our neighbors whose ears always hoped for gossip. Abuelo sat down on the stump he used for chopping wood and looked hard at me when he spoke.

"But I will tell you another story that is like a cousin to your story."

I dropped to the dirt at his feet and crossed my legs, leaning forward to rest my elbows on my knees. The yellow dog belly-crawled towards us, but Abuelo flung his arm out like a whip and with a loud *hiahh,* sent the dog running. I waited. Abuelo sighed, deep, and began.

Everything that happens is a circle, like the earth, like the sun, like the belly of a woman soon to bring life. If a good thing happens, so must a bad thing, because each is only half of the circle.

There once was a year when all the round world took notice of Mexico. The Olympics were coming here, to our country. The American President had come to stay in a house by the Bay—here. In our Jalisco with our Presidente. And just there—Grandfather nodded toward where our road traveled down the mountain to meet another road I had never walked, a road climbing high into the Sierra Madre along the cliffs above the Bay—two leaders ate and drank and talked like equals. In Mexico City every plaza and street was being made clean and hung with banners. Pride rose each morning like a second sun.

But one morning just before the Games were to begin, a great hole opened in the Plaza of the Three Cultures like a doorway to the devil, and many hundreds of las que protesta muy jovenes fell through that hole before it silently, silently was covered over, as if it had never been there at all.

"A hole, Abuelo? A hole in the street?"

Grandfather put his hand up to me: *silencio*.

"Listen, mijo. Close your mouth, open your mind, and listen."

The people who saw what happened closed their mouths, as well. Some of the young protestors who survived ran silently for the border, as if they were competing in their own Olympic event. The Opening Ceremony of the Olympic Games was held soon after, with all the color and festivity of an event that is wholly good. But this was a lie. The other half of that circle—the dark half where lay the bodies of those young ones—was real and could not be kept hidden.

Those who were there that day say the shadow of a black dog ran across the air over the stadium before the start of the Opening Ceremonies and again before each event, each day after. As the families of the athletes, dignitaries, and visitors from across the world waited for the time of the competition, one spectator would suddenly start to shudder, and then the man beside him, also, as if a cloud had blocked the sun's warmth, and soon everyone there wouldlook up to see passing over them a black cloud like a dog running, each time exactly like a running black dog.

Abuleo stopped, pushing with his fists against the small of his back to stretch the muscles there. He shook his head and rubbed his eyes like he was tired. Was he finished with talking? No. How could he be?

"Grandfather. This story is sad, but I do not understand what happened. And what does it have to do with me? I want to hear my own sad story; I am a boy whose father left him."

Abuelo stood. "He did not leave you, Cesar. He was never with you. He left with the black dog before you were born."

I raised up on my knees and grabbed Abuelo's shirt to hold him a moment longer. A rock dug into my right knee. "What do you mean? Is my father not alive?"

My granddaddy put his hand over mine, "Only his body is alive." Gently, for him, he pulled my hand from his shirt. " The black dog came from the old gods to carry away the souls ofones like your father who died, though they were not killed. Why do you think I hate dogs?"

I knew I would get nothing more from my grandfather, so I vowed to do the next day what any good Catholic would do when he has no one to help him: I would ask God to help me. Well, not God Himself, but I would speak to the person who speaks to God. Tomorrow I would skip my last class of the morning to meet with Sister at the inn and ask her to finish the story for me. Skipping class for ask God's bride for a favor? Well, what can you expect from a boy born from the ghost of a dog?

I worked very hard for Armando the next morning and said nothing to him of my plans. When the last guest had finished eating and I had carried the plates to the kitchen, I changed to my uniform and left for class the same time as I always did. I should just have skipped the whole morning at school for all the attention

I gave to my lessons. As soon as the ten o'clock bells played in the cathedral tower, I raised my hand for permission to use the bathroom and then slipped out the front gate while the señora in the office was busy with a girl who felt sick, and so the señora did not notice me.

I felt a little sick, myself, from fear someone would stop me while I was walking back to the inn. I made myself walk slowly, trying to look like I was *supposed* to be out on the street at a time when all children are in school. *Act like you have the right and people will believe you*—that's what I was always telling Carlos. It worked for me, but not for Carlos. His face was always a sign that read "Guilty."

When I stepped from the street up into the courtyard, Sister was just sitting down at one of the little round tables with Teacher. I made no sound, but they both turned to look at me as if a band had announced that I was coming. I believe God has given ears of a different sort to women than he gave to men.

"Cesar. Why aren't you in school? Did you leave your homework here? Is everything alright?"

I wasn't sure which one asked me; both women talked at once, and both sounded like my teacher, or my mother.

"No, no, gracias. I am fine. I just need a story."

Sister Maria Therese's bowed her head toward her lap, as if she'd been seized by a sudden need for prayer. It must have been a need quickly met, though, because she snapped her head back up in an instant and shook it slowly back and forth as she looked me through in the way only a nun can.

"You are, for certain, your father's son."

"Am I? Please, Sister, I need to know what is the same between me and my father. How can I be what I have never known?"

Sister shook her head again, but more gently this time. "You knew him, Cesar. You had five years with him before he left. Do you not remember?"

What I remembered, of a sudden, was that we were speaking Spanish and Teacher could not understand us. When I turned to her to apologize I saw her legs stretched out from under her skirt to catch the cool air and I noticed at once how the swelling and the dark color in her hurt leg were not so bad today as yesterday. I did not mean to stare, but the difference was so large that I could not help but see. Her leg was beginning to look less like something dead and rotting and more like a thing that is healing from inside. I should have been happy for her because I did not want her to be in pain, but all I could think was that as soon as she was well she would leave.

I would not think of that. I would think of the English.

"Teacher, today you teach me the English word for papi?"

"Cesar, you know that word."

"Teacher, I know, but I do not understand. Yo conozco, pero no me entiendo."

Sister had been watching me while I talked; she pulled out the table's other chair and tipped it so the cat slid from the seat where he had been sleeping, and then she nodded to me to sit down. I sat.

"Trish, con su permiso, we will continue this morning the story of Francisco."

Teacher nodded and I nodded along with her. Neither of us spoke one word. Sister's voice was soft and sweet, like chocolate. I sometimes imagined her hair must be, too. Her skin that I could see was the color of a peach. Ai, I was hungry.

Francisco married Sonia. She was pretty and they had known each other all their lives. Her father talked too much of empty things and he valued power more than people, but what of that? Francisco was not married to Sonia's father. Also, the mother-in-law fretted about the marriage and spoke to me of her worries: "What do we know of this boy while he was in America?" She told me she had asked her husband over and over before the marriage: "He was at Universidad and then he was not. Why?" But Sonia's father would only flick his hand at her: "Woman, he earned much money and sent it home to his mama. What more do we need to know? It is possible he saw an opportunity in America and took it. He will do as well by our daughter."And so the marriage took place, a big wedding at the Cathedral, and all was well for a while. For a while, but not forever, because no babies came to fill Sonia's arms and heart. From nothing, only nothing can come. Francisco's spirit was barren; so, too was Sonia's womb.

The father-in-law found a good job for Francisco as a clerk at the city offices, even though Francisco was not of the family name to have such a job. One year passed, then two years, years of "Sí, Señor" from Francisco to all who were born of the right names; years of Francisco's palm greased so that Francisco might grease the palm of another so that a necessary form might magically be approved and stamped. The little that was left of Francisco's soul shriveled until it rattled around in his chest like the last coin in a child's bank.

One morning early as Francisco walked down the hill to the city offices by the Plaza, that single centavo of a soul clinked, once only, but enough to remind him of its presence. Ah, what is the good of one coin so small? He asked himself. I will stop off at la iglesia and drop it in the poor box. But as he entered and knelt and genuflected, a nun stepped up to greet him, and like a song remembered there rose within Francisco the need to talk, truly talk. For an hour, as his father-in-law two blocks down the mountain worried and stormed and made excuses for Francisco's absence at the job, Francisco told the nun about his life that was no life at all but for his wife's goodness to him. From the nun's ears to God's ears; God heard, and then He remembered Francisco.

Where have you been? God asked in a relieved-sounding voice. I've been looking everywhere for you.

Francisco looked through the nun to God. Sorry, Father, I thought I was dead for a while, but the good Sister seems to believe I am still living. I'm not sure why she thinks this, but if it is true, what should I do next?

The Sister was smiling at him. Go to work, Francisco. And then go home; give your wife babies.

Can I?

Yes.

But what if the making of sons is all that is left in me to give? Who will raise those babies if the last bit of my soul goes into the making of them? Who will teach my sons to be men?

You have two fathers, the nun told him. One of them is the Father of the church. The other has beenup in your village waiting for someone to fill the love-shaped hole in his heart that has been there since the floods took his beloved.

Sister stopped talking and lifted her hand to her face, resting her chin against her thumb the same way my grandfather sometimes did. When Abuleo sat this way, it always meant he was finished with the story he was telling. But, Ai, no. How could Sister stop talking when there was still so much I did not know? I knew for a fact that Francisco had fathered four sons because was I not the first of them? And I knew well and good he had lived with us no more after my littlest brother was born, but I still did not know the why or the where of my father's leaving. I raised my own hand, like I was in school.

"Y entonces ? And then, Sister?"

"And then he went back to America."

This was not the answer I had expected; any answer but this one. "To America? Is he still alive? Where does he live?"

"This I do not know, Cesar, because he does not want anyone to know."

"Not even the nun he had talked to?"

"Especially not the nun he had talked to."

"But why not?"

Sister Maria Therese looked at me for a long moment in a way she never had before, like we were not nun and boy, but partners in some way I did not yet understand.

"Because he was right, your father was. The small part of Francisco that was left alive after Mexico City was too wounded to survive many demands on himself. Four strong sons drain a man's strengths, more so when the first of those sons has a mind that will not stop questioning." She smiled, then, and touched my knee just barely, so that I would know she spoke with love.

Sister stood, as if to leave, but spoke one more time. "Your father would not leave you comfortless. Before he left, Francisco made a bargain with his father, your abuelo. Martín agreed to what Francisco asked of him because he knew Francisco would do more harm than good to you and your brothers if he stayed. The agreement was this: if Martín would protect Francisco's sons and see to their education and their needs while they were children, Francisco would send someone to help them when they were ready to become men."

"Send someone? Send who? From where? How will I know this person?"

But instead of giving me an answer, Sister turned toward Teacher, who

72

had been sitting all this time without speaking. I had forgotten she was there. Sister and I had been speaking Spanish again.

"Trish, It is fine that you are feeling better, but your leg needs more good blood. You must walk. Give this one his lesson and then walk to the Cathedral . You can buy for yourself sweets from the man who sells dulces every day at the steps of the church. He needs the money, and you need to walk."

Sister started once more to leave, but stopped to give Teacher one more direction. "And there is a dance in the Plaza Sunday evening. You will come this Sunday? You should come." Then she turned away from us to walk down the inn's steps to the street.

I stared after her for a moment, then I looked at Teacher.

Teacher looked at me. She smiled and shrugged—*what can we do?* Teacher patted the table where our books waited.

"Cesar. It is past time for our lesson. Today I want you to practice your writing. Describe this dance it seems I will be attending. And then tell me how you feel about it.'

I opened my notebook and I wrote.

11
Trish

Cesar was sighing dramatically, but I ignored him for a moment to watch as Sister Maria seemed to float leglessly down the stairs. We women are all the same inside, I realized, whether we wear habits or have habits. We are a mystery to men but we're an open book to each other. A woman's silences are packed tighter with truths than all the talking we'll do in a lifetime.

I turned back from watching Sister to look at Cesar as he was let out another long, loud sigh . Sister had left without giving him a hint of what he so desperately wanted to know. Bless his heart, only ten years old and already he'd mastered that exasperation of men everywhere who don't have a clue why their women won't give them a straight answer.

I couldn't help but smile as I watched my frustrated young student sink to a slouch in his chair and shove his short legs straight out in front of him. Wasn't he the very picture of a disgruntled male? He crossed his black-socked feet at the ankles and sighed again. His right foot knocked against one of the shoes he'd kicked off earlier, but the other shoe lay like a flung fish under the next table. His shoulders were slumped so far forward that his belly pooched up under his white shirt; he folded his square hands together over the mound of his belly.

Slowly, he leaned forward to open his notebook, moving like he was hauling on his back the weight of the mountain he lived on. He laboriously wrote his title, "The Dance." and then he just sat there flipping his pencil back and forth between two fingers, scowling at the paper like it was to blame for its own vast blankness .

73

I knew how to make the writing easier for him.

"Cesar?"

One eye and one eyebrow raised in my direction. "Teacher?"

"Sometimes when I have trouble writing it is because my brain is afraid of that word, 'writing'. What I do is, I try to trick my brain: I say out loud what I want to write and then I write down what I'm saying so that my brain thinks it isn't really writing, but it is just recording what someone has said. Easy, right? Just say the words and then write them down. Let's try that. Tell me about this dance Sister wants me to go to. You talk and I'll write your words. After it is all written down, we'll go back and take a look at the grammar."

I reached across the table for his notebook and slid it over so that it was in front of me instead of him.

Cesar grinned, and pulled himself back up straight, tipping his chair back on two legs. He was a man restored, mightily relieved to turn this task over to me.

"Not much to tell, Teacher. Most Sundays 'round five all the peoples come to the Plaza for a dance. On Sundays, most everybody they not work, you know? After they go to the mass, all the peoples walk up and down the Malecon, just walk and talk about all the other peoples. You know, the womens got to say some things about what the other womens wear? And the guys look at the girls and the girls act like they not see the guys look. Then when everybody tired from walk, they go to the Plaza so they can dance. Ha. Too tired to walk, but nobody ever too tired to dance, right, Teacher?"

"Right, Cesar." Well, that was true for me, anyway.

"All the peoples dance, even the little kids and the abuelas. That about it, Teacher. Just a lotta music and everybody dance."

"And you, Cesar? Do you dance?"

"Claro que sí, Teacher. How you say?"

"'Sure thing', Cesar, 'Sure thing'."

"Sure thing, Teacher."

Exactly how the heck I was supposed to dance with this gimpy leg, I had no earthly idea, but I'd figure something out by Sunday. The thought of *not* dancing was just heinous. If there's music, you dance. One moonshine-sweetened Kentucky night the summer before , six of us had thrown down a sheet of plywood on a rocky ridge and danced an entire reel across the level slickness of the board's short length while Sonny fiddled and Chris called.

But you just hunkered off to one side and smoked, and watched us, didn't you, Love? Never have been able to drag you out on a dance floor of any sort.

Remembering, even though I'd vowed not to think on matters of my heart while I was on vacation, I felt pretty much like Cesar had felt a few minutes before: ready and willing to sell my soul for a straight answer from the guy who owed me at least that.

"Teacher? You need more words?"

Cesar 's head was tilted toward his shoulder and he was looking at me like he'd had about all the confusing women he could take for one day.

74

More words are exactly what I need, Cesar, you sweet little guy, but you can't give them to me.

"Go back to school, Cesar." I closed his notebook and handed it to him, smiling to let him know he wasn't to blame for not being able to figure out the workings of women's minds. "I'll see you Sunday at the dance."

"Sí, Teacher. At the dance."

Come Sunday evening, I had walked almost all the way down to the Plaza before it popped into my head that it would likely be pitch dark when I would be walking home alone, and now there was not an earthly thing I could do about that except take my chances with the demons of a city night, once night came.

But then I heard the music, and suddenly nothing in my world seemed worth fretting over. I stepped into the Plaza and followed the wail of an alto sax to the municipal building just across the gazebo, toward the Malecon.

Four older men were hanging cloth-fronted speakers way up high on opposite corners of the block building, and even as they yanked each speaker with both hands to make sure it was seated safely on its hook, a couple of younger men on the ground were already slapping a tape into the tape deck and cranking up the volume. I needed to be closer to that music, so I con-su-permiso-ed myself to the closest edge of the dance area. I couldn't help myself. As soon as the musical scent of a dance wafted my way, I was a like junkie to the pipeline, a Deadhead to Shakedown Street.

I wasn't alone in my surrender—a twenty-ish couple had swung into a salsa practically under my stinky armpit, close enough for me to be astounded and hotly jealous of how they weren't even sweating as they danced like Satan was lead fiddler. Oh, but to call what they were doing "dancing" was like calling the Bible an overview of an ancient cultural movement. There was so much more going on than just the steps. These lovely young dancers were two copper ribbons curling and uncurling in constantly varying swirls, as if a fitful wind kept changing direction all around them. The lithe latina was desire and her novio was desire fulfilled; the song was the wind that teased them together. I yearned to dance like them.

"Bonita? You dance?"

A man in cowboy boots and a plaid shirt was smiling at me from a couple of inches below me, an indio like Cesar, holding out his right hand as he bowed just slightly. I smiled back, a little bit startled out of the cave of my thoughts but tickled that he had asked.

"Oh, no, gracias," I shook my head while I made my smile bigger, warmer. I didn't want to hurt his feelings, but I really wanted to just watch a while longer before I dishonored the salsa by making a complete fool of myself trying to dance it.

It truly was a community dance, just as Cesar had said it would be. The tiled Plaza had become a ballroom with all generations of Jalisco families slapping the floor with slippered or sandaled or booted feet. Off on the far opposite side from where I was standing, a tiny abuela was dancing with her husband. I moved

75

a little to th left so I could see around the young couple, almost stepping on a little girl with braids like I used to wear. I laid my hand on her head for a second and smiled at her when she looked up at me.

The small man *had* to be the husband of the tiny older woman. The bodies of those two obviously long-marrieds answered each other in movements that appeared as intuitive as the steps of the young dancers had looked practiced and polished. The old couple's back and forth of move and respond had been learned through years and years of babies and work and love-making. I was charmed by them by how the abuelita's shoulder turned in answer to the slightest touch of her husband's finger tips, and how as the husband's right foot moved forward, the abuela's left foot stepped exactly backward. There was no stuttering there. Dancing gave them back a grace which in other ways had long ago slipped from their aging bodies.

"Baile, señorita?"

Another man, this one also in cowboy boots and with grey tingeing his mustache and temples in the Latino way that seemed not old, but sexy, was smiling and waiting for me to say yes. *Oh, why not?* I gave him my hand and he wriggled us through the maze of dancers to a teeny open spot. I had not a clue what I was supposed to do, but it didn't matter, because el hombre knew. Ah, the delight of an accomplished partner. All I needed to do was follow the clues he gave me.

And then it really didn't matter if I had been taught all the steps or not, because dancing isn't about thinking; it's about feeling. When my buddy Mike was struggling to turn me into a halfway decent waltzer a couple of years back, he stopped one night right in the middle of the Kentucky Waltz, grabbed me by both shoulders and whispered into my right ear, "Stop thinking. Feel. Feel. Feel." Well, Mike would sure enough have been proud of me, because there was no longer a thought in my head. Most of my brain cells had apparently devolved to a charming mixture of sweat and snot that was now streaming from my nose, but, Lordy, I was having fun.

Even the ending of a shared dance is delightful. The gentleman (and he was) bowed to me, I offered a curtsy back to him, and we stepped away from each other pleased to have swum through that hot ocean of music together, and yet fine now with leaving each other to partner up with someone new. All of society should be like this. I'd never known any dance anywhere to be other than a pleasurable equalizer.

But, sadly ,all that dancing was more than I'd asked of my poor leg since the day I was bitten, and my muscle and blood were starting to whine at me some. *Okay, okay,* I conceded to my leg. I'd just watch the next dance, maybe two. No more dancing; I'd just watch and then I'd head back up the hill to Los Cuatro Vientos. Maybe I'd even make it back before dark. That would be sensible.

"Teacher?"

Cesar was all of a sudden right next to me, looking so gussied-up in his school uniform pants and a boy-sized version of the plaid western shirt on the backs of every male there in the Plaza that it turned my heart inside-out. He'd obviously slicked his curls down with a wet comb. Won't do any good, I could have told him from the perspective of a fellow curly head—those black coils are going to *boing* right back up again as soon as your hair dries.

He was smirking at me, a good sort of smirk.

"May I have pleasure of next dance? I say that right, Teacher?"

"You did. And you may."

A slow dance, waltz tempo, was just starting. Apparently it was God's turn to pick the song, because the devil would have opted for making me try to salsa with my student. Cesar's smirk had turned to a courtly smile. He offered me his left hand; I met it with my right hand, palm to palm. He placed the very tips of the fingers of his right hand at my waist; I reached down with my left hand to touch his neck with the tips of my thumb and first finger. He counted, "UNO, dos, tres; ONE, two, three."

And we waltzed.

"Cesar, where did you learn to dance?"

"Dance not something you learn, Teacher; it something you do."

And we did it well, my young student and me. I was so deeply into the step and swirl that it took me a minute to realize there was suddenly a great deal of talking going on around me-only one word at first, "Mira," and then a growing rumble from some of the dancers and even more from people standing around the edges watching the dance. Except now they weren't watching the dance, I noticed.

Most of the people around us were staring toward the Cathedral, so I did, too, but, to my great relief, I couldn't for the life of me see anything more threatening than a man talking to a nun, a man who looked harmless enough to me. In fact, he looked less than harmless; he looked beaten down. I knew defeat when I saw it, thanks to my volunteer time at the homeless shelter, and this man could have put the D in Defeated. He was tall, but his height gave him no claim to substance. He was right on the edge of scrawny, and he looked kind of sunken at the middle like a loblolly pine crumpled with pine beetle rot. This man looked like he'd been waiting a long while for somebody to cut him down and get it over with.

"Teacher, what you see? What happening?"

"Nothing, Cesar. I don't see anything."

"Maybe that because you not looking with Mexican eyes. 'Scuse me, Teacher."

And he was gone, my suave young dance partner now ducking and dodging his way toward the Cathedral like any normal ten-year-old boy hoping to see the fight before some grownup breaks it up. I hesitated maybe half a second, then: Oh, what the heck? I tailed Cesar as best I could but I made poor time, dragging my throbbing leg like a female Quasimodo, and doubly hindered by the mandates of my Southern upbringing to never knock strangers flat in your hurry to get past them without at least offering up an *I'm so sorry*. There must have been two hundred people in the Plaza, which made for a lot of time-consuming genteel mumbles on my part, but I made it there. Cesar had stopped a few feet away from the couple, and was standing behind the man, his arms crossed over his chest and his face as hard as Judgement Day.

And, well. It *wasn't* a nun standing next to the man; it was Sister Maria Therese. Okay, yes, of course, Sister was a nun, but not a Nun. She was my friend. She evidently was that man's friend, too, because the two of them were standing in each other's air the way two people do when they have at some point in their past considered themselves to *be* each other's air.

My goodness, was all I could think. My goodness me.

"Teacher, I walk you home now."

Cesar had passed by me and was heading up the block as he spoke, walking toward the inn and away from the Cathedral steps, away from Sister and her friend.

"Cesar, wait. I want to speak to Sister."

"You no want to speak to her right now, Teacher. She with bad company.

Bad Company, I noticed, had just caught sight of Cesar. The man looked at Cesar for a long moment, then placed his hand lightly, so lightly on Sister's shoulder and leaned in to say something close to her ear. The two men standing near him leaned in, too, exactly mirroring his movement toward the nun. It was almost like a dance figure, but this was the sort of dance step I knew intimately from my childhood in the segregated South. Sister's friend was a man who had broken the rules, and those men were ready to break him if he tried it again.

Maybe this *was* a good night for companionship on my walk home, after all. I fell into step with Cesar.

"Cesar, do you know the man who was talking with Sister Maria Therese?

"No, Sister. I not know him for nothing."

We covered the two blocks along Juarez Street without saying anything more, but that was okay, that was alright. The afternoon's swelter had backed off and I was lost in the bliss of wearing skin that felt dry for the first time in twelve hours. My skin was crusted with a day's and a dance's worth of dried sweat, but at least my sweat glands had stopped adding more layers of sticky stink.

I didn't even break a new sweat when we started the climb up the hillside toward Matamoros and the inn. Maybe I could actually acclimatize to this sauna of a country. Maybe if I spent my whole summer vacation here next year. I'd ask for my same room at the inn, set up a writing corner and figure out some way to keep the room's cyclone fan from blowing every sheet of paper out of my word processor while I wrote. Some kind of clamp system might work...

"Teacher."

"Hmmm?"

"Teacher, he behind us."

I came back into the moment with a start.

"He? Who? He, who?" Good Lord, I sounded like one of the Seven Dwarves singing their off-to-work song.

"That man, The one what bother the Sister."

I turned and looked.

Sure enough, he was a half block or so behind us, which probably should have made me nervous, but nope, I was fine. Not scared at all. Blame it on all those midnights at the homeless where I volunteered back home. My main job there was to collect everyone's weapons and lock them in the shelter's safe for the night. The men willingly gave up their knives and scissors and box cutters (box cutters were definitely the homeless population's weapon of choice) without a fuss because this was the price of a warm meal and a warm bed for the night. The men knew, too, that for the next ten hours of so they wouldn't be needing to protect themselves from anything more than their own demons, and I did what I could to help with those. The men with the most persistent demons often could not sleep at all, so I'd sit with them in the darkened lobby while they talked in low murmurs through the night, trying not to wake the more fortunate guests. It didn't seem to matter what they talked about during those hours around midnight and after; they just needed to talk and they needed me to listen. Volunteering at the shelter had given me the skill of recognizing right off which men might be dangerous and which were a danger only to themselves.

The man walking behind us along Matamoros Street was one of the latter.

"Cesar, it didn't look to me like he was bothering the Sister. He doesn't look dangerous. Maybe he's just walking home, same as us."

"Dangerous sometimes wear a quiet face, Teacher. And, anyway, he got no home."

"How do you know? I thought you said you didn't know him?"

I got no answer from my somber companion, but just as we reached the inn's gate, an owl added his own question to a night of questions: whoo? whoo? I flung a silent answer his way: I wish I could tell you, Sir Owl. Should I have thought that in Spanish, I wondered? And did owls say "who" to Spanish ears? I'd have to ask Cesar, but later. He was obviously not in a linguistic mood right then.

He hadn't even smiled since he saw the man behind us talking with Sister, and now he wouldn't look at me when he did speak. That was not like my Cesar. His whole body had gone robotic, like someone who's walked a long way in the cold with no coat.

"I maybe not come to my lesson tomorrow, Teacher. I got things I need do."

"Oh. Okay. But Tuesday? Martes? You'll be there on Tuesday?"

"Sure thing, Teacher, Sure thing."

Cesar helped me unlock the weighty padlock on the inn's front gate, and handed the lock in to me through the bars once I was inside. I locked myself in and Cesar out, keeping hold of the bars with both hands and slotting as much of my face through the bars as would fit, to watch him head up the hillside to his barrio. The man kept walking behind Cesar. It was odd, but that actually made me feel better about Cesar walking the dark road alone. Maybe it shouldn't have, but it did.

I padded as softly as i could up the stairs to my room. Saki padded behind me.

Before I was even all the way awake the next morning, I was aware of my foot whining at me for dancing that second dance. I told my foot to shut up, and got out of bed, deciding to view the aching as a sign of healing, Something that is dying doesn't whine.

My mission for the day, as soon as I'd done justice to Armando's breakfast buffet, would be to find Sister Maria Therese and get the scoop on last night's mystery man and how he was related to Cesar and why so many people at the dance had reacted to the sight of him like homeowners discovering termites.

But breakfast wasn't ready. That was odd. Armando came hustling out f the kitchen juggling cups and dishes, grumbling as he set the eggs down to cool and put out the cups for coffee. He was doing Cesar's jobs. I craned around to peer into the kitchen, but as best I could tell, Cesar wasn't there. I looked at my watch. Twenty minutes past the time he usually arrived to help Armando, and he wasn't there.

"Missing in action" later proved to be the theme for the day, because Sister Maria was nowhere to be seen when I stepped into the narthex of the Cathedral half an hour after I finished breakfast. I dropped a few centavos into the box for the poor, then stood around getting in the way of tourists and their cameras until I finally felt too awkward to keep just standing there. But I had no idea what to do, instead. How could I start my day with no Cesar to teach and no nun to sit around and chat with after?

I clomped down the church steps in high dudgeon, one by one by one. The dulces seller was down there at the bottom of the steps as he always was. Figuring I had nothing to lose by sounding nosey, I asked him flat-out why he worked seven days a week.

"Because I eat seven days a week."

This made me smile, finally. I'd needed an answer that made sense.

"Por favor," I pointed to my choices, "uno, no, dos de esos."

I would eat his coconut bars so that he could also eat, which was a laudatory-sounding way of fighting my pity party with a sugar rush.

As he handed me candy and change, he touched my finger for a moment. I looked at him tilting my head a little in surprise: *yes?*

"The Sister, she say tell you come to the school."

"Oh. gracias. Gracias."

It seemed that in my time of need I would have both candy and company for solace.

12

Sister Maria

While Sister Maria was waiting for Trish to finish buying the sweets, she was thinking what a good thing it was that Francisco would never set foot in a school or a church, and so he would not interrupt her talking with Trish. Of this fact, she was as certain as if it were holy doctrine. For seventeen years, Francisco had made it a rule of his life not to enter churches or schools, and Francisco did not break his own rules. That was why the nun had chosen the courtyard of the school as her place for talking with Trish. She could just as well have asked Trish to meet her at the Cathedral, but schools were where Trish's spirit lived, not churches. Besides, at the Cathedral, Sister would have been able to avoid the man, but she could not have avoided God, and she wanted this talk to be between her and Trish, alone.

Maria wasn't staying away from Francisco because she was afraid being around him might threaten her vows to God. Love, even the kind of bone-deep love that had once drawn Francisco and Maria together as if they had been cleaved from one body in some previous life and in this life were healing toward each other like opposite edges of a wound, even a love so foregone could alter—not lessen, but alter. Her love for Francisco, which had been the whole of her heart, now pulsed like blood through the heart of her love for God. But desire redirected remains desire, nonetheless. And what is a woman if not a creature ruled by her blood? Blood quickens every woman for the passing of blood to a new heart, or blood passes from a woman to mark the moment of a new heart not ready to start its way toward life. Francisco was now not all of Maria's heart, but was yet within the blood of her heart, so did this fact not mean her blood might still be quickened by his presence? She and God had had many talks about this.

This morning, though, she needed to talk with Trish, not God. She had asked the candy seller to pass her message for Trish to meet her here at the school where Sister needed fear only the wrath of the school's office administrator, Sra. Sanchez, who was a much lesser god. Sister knew Trish had seen Francisco and her talking at the dance. The dance! A dance was a place where you could be sure to find Francisco. That man would walk five hours to dance for an hour, so Sister had not been at all surprised to see him there, only surprised to discover that he was in Jalisco at all, because no one had warned her this time. Usually, at least two or three women trampled all over each other to be first to tell her he was back—only because they "thought Sister might want to pray for his poor family," of course. Certainly they were not hoping their news might cause the holy sister's cheeks to flame, and toss a new log onto the fires of their gossip.

But this time Francisco had not taken care to remain as a ghost to Cesar. This fact worried Sister the most. For all of the five years since his first leaving of his sons, Francisco had slipped into and slipped out of town like a cloud, not to be noticed by Cesar and his brothers. What small boy pays attention to a cloud? Clouds come and they go and little boys pay them no mind unless the clouds darken and rumble of rain. So what did it mean that this cloud was now rumbling? What was Francisco intending to do?

It had been just after Sunday evening prayers when he stepped out of the crowd and walked over to her as if they had made plans to meet there at the foot of the Cathedral steps. Probably some of the people standing nearby believed they *had*. Her vows to God and his vows to his wife had never been able to conquer the way even a chance meeting between Francisco and Maria looked for all the world as if they had planned to meet, the draw between them was so easily seen. Sister was well aware of this. Whenever Francisco was near her, she always needed to take a moment to push away the guilt she had no cause to feel. When she saw him heading her way Sunday evening, she took that necessary moment and had just put on a nun-like smile to greet him with, when she realized he was no longer looking at her because he had seen Cesar. He studied his son for a long moment, and then he leaned in toward her, resting his fingers on her shoulder just as he had done so many times when they were dancing into the opening strains of a salsa. The men standing near saw him touch her, and they leaned in, too, ready to pull Francisco away if Sister gave the sign. But he only whispered, "I have to." and then he was gone, following after his son.

For the long length of a fitful night, Sister Maria Therese tried to let go of the moment of Francisco's turning away from her toward his son. Even now, she was too lost in the night before—and in the many nights long before—to notice when she no longer sat alone on the bench because Trish had come to sit with her.

13
Trish

"Sister? Sister, I brought the sweets. You did still want me to meet you here. right?"

The nun looked at me like she would look at someone who'd waked her up from a deep sleep. It was pretty obvious she hadn't heard me walk into the courtyard, and she didn't look good, not good at all. I knew that look. Every teacher knows that kind of face—it was the face of a kid who is truly sick, not trying to fake being sick so she can go home early. It took me only one flu season as a teacher to be able to determine precisely how much time I have before a child throws up on my desk. I was pretty sure Sister wasn't going to throw up on me, but there was something going on with her.

"Sister, are you all right?"

"Sí, yes, I was thinking, that is all."

"Are you sure you were just thinking?" I asked, readying myself to struck by lightning for cross-examining a nun. "I didn't interrupt you while you were praying, did I?"

"It is teachers who pray at school, Trish, not nuns. Dígame, tell me, you have care for Cesar, yes?"

"I like him very much, yes, if that's what you mean. He's a rare bird."

"I need you to tell me what happened when you and Cesar left from the dance."

I relaxed back against the metal bench, remembering.

"Well, Cesar walked me back to the inn, young gentleman that he is. The only thing was, he was very solemn. He hardly talked and he didn't smile at all. It was so out of character for him that it worried me."

"You saw a man walk on the street near to you?"

I leaned away from Sister a little, surprised, but she didn't notice. Hmm, I thought. Now we're getting down to brass tacks.

"Yes," I kept my voice casual, as if I had no inkling we might now be talking about a man she had a non-nun history with. "The man who was talking with you by the Cathedral. I asked Cesar who he was, but Cesar claimed he didn't know him."

"The man, he talk to you?"

"No, he just walked a ways behind us, all the way to the inn. Why?"

A tiny girl had come up behind us while we were talking, and was waiting for the nun's attention. Sister Maria Therese reached back with her left arm to pull the little girl in close for a hug. She turned her attention back to me only after she'd given the little girl a good long moment. I liked that.

"You remember the story of Francisco and how the police not kill him because he ran from them?"

I nodded.

"This niña one day will know that story, too. All the schools now teach that story. It is right for the schools to teach this history, but also it is smart for the government because the bad histories, they grow more weak when they are history, only. The school not teach all of the story, though."

"What do they leave out?"

"They leave out the end that does not end."

"I don't understand."

The nun looked away from me and back to the little girl she still held close to her side. Sister Maria smiled, and wrinkled her nose at the girl, then gave her a small shove back toward her classroom. The child grinned and skipped away, the pleats of her short uniform skirt swirling out like leaves caught up by a wind.

"You can stay for some minutes more, Trish? You have no hurry?"

"Well, there was my ten o'clock with the mayor and city councilmen, but I'm sure they'll understand."

Now she was the one who looked startled.

I laid my hand on my best guess of where her knee might be. "I'm kidding, Sister. My time is your time.'

Children who had been running off a morning's worth of energy during their recess were now being shepherded back to their classrooms. The late morning sun blazed straight down into the open courtyard like a searchlight. The nun and I scooted back tight against the cool stone wall of the courtyard entrance into the shade from a lip of a classroom overhang. Sra. Sanchez leaned around from her desk not four feet away to frown at us, not at all certain but what this American teacher and the holy sister might try something subversive if she didn't maintain constant vigil over us. Sister Maria Therese studied her hands clasped in her lap, as if Francisco's story were hidden there.

The shootings on 2 de octubre began with the fireworks. A crowd of ten

83

thousand men, women and children, and, of course, students, had assembled in the Plaza. A student had just stood to announce that the planned march on the Santo Thomas campus—which the army had occupied the month before and where many killings had already happened—would not take place because of the fear of more violence. A flare, then another, shot into the sky and the people looked up, naturally, thinking to see the fireworks. As they watched the sky, machine gun bullets began to slice them down: men, women, children, and students. Francisco had been leaning against a wall of the ancient church of Santiago Tlateloco. Gracias a Dios, he thought as soon as he realized what was happening—the church will give us shelter. He threw his arm around a young woman holding a little boy with only two or three years, and he half-carried, half-dragged them to the church's front doors, but the doors were closed and locked. The Fathers had locked the church doors against the dying, and would not open them. Within half an hour, the street in front of the church ran slick with blood.

Francisco found an open doorway to an apartment and pushed the mother and child inside, but it was as if he had saved two fish from becoming a shark's dinner by tossing them into the bucket of a hungry fisherman. Even as the soldiers continued to shoot, other soldiers lined people up to search them and send them to jail, or sometimes to shoot them, one after one, while they stood in their obedient lines. Meanwhile, the police were searching houses, apartments and schools, imprisoning everyone they found. Francisco soon realized he could do nothing to help anyone, perhaps not even himself.

This was why he fell to the ground like a person dead and allowed himself to be tossed into a truck with the bodies of the truly dead; it was the only chance left to him. It is when we have no choices left that we either begin to die, or we begin to realize for the first time how very little we need in order to stay alive. Francisco was not yet ready to die, so a space among the dead and dying was good and sufficient for his needs. His ride in the truck was also the reason he rejected the church from that day, but did not reject God. The church locked its doors against good souls dying in the Plaza, but God sent an open truck for Francisco. It is important that this truck was open, Trish, because just a few hours after the shooting began, by the time the sun sent down on dos de octubre, the government sent sanitation workers to toss bodies into covered trucks and compact the bodies of young students like they were sacks of garbage.

I sat straight up on the bench and interrupted her.

"Oh, no, Sister. Are you sure that really happened? Maybe it is just a myth that has grown out of the craziness of that day."

"Sister Maria Therese unfolded her clasped hands and held her right one u to shush me, the folds of her sleeve following her hand's movement like a white flag. I shushed.

It happened. Even our great poet Octavio Paz has written about this:

84

The municipal sanitation workers
Are washing away the blood
On the Plaza of sacrifices.

I slumped back against the wall.

"I'm sorry, Sister. Please, go on."

And I was, indeed, sorry, sorry to realize my country could match her country sorrow for sorrow, injustice for injustice, poet of the powerless for poet of the powerless. She had her Octavio Paz; we had our Zora Neal Hurston: *I have been in Sorrow's kitchen and licked out all the pans.*

Go on? This is what they cannot do, Trish, the people who were there at Tlateloco that day cannot go on. A mother who lost her son asked a government official to please tell her what she should do with all the free time she would have for the rest of her life. Many of the hundreds who were imprisoned spent years in jail—years. Even the ones who died outright were not allowed the prayers of the church to speed them on their passage to heaven. "I'm sorry," one priest after another told the families and the groups of students who asked them to say a special mass for the souls of the murdered one, "our schedule is full that day. Also the next day. And the next." Finally, one kind priest mentioned that prayers were offered by the church each day for the poor—perhaps the murdered ones could be included in prayers for the poor.

The young ones like Francisco who lived because they were able to slip away into to the night of that day of killing, even they never really lived again after 2 de octubre. Francisco made his way to America—I have told you this—where he found work, but was never able to do the work of the intellect he was born for because he had no papers. He had not even his Mexican passport—why would he carry his passport with him to attend a public meeting in the town where he lived? And now he could not return for his passport because he would have been questioned and probably imprisoned. The questionings and imprisoning continued for a long time; even in 1971 I heard of a cousin of mine who was in jail, still.

Why did Francisco not go to the USA government for help? Ah, Trish, your President was a supporter of the Olympics, and the Olympics began as scheduled, one week after the massacre. No one in American would say that the killings had happened, because no official in Mexico would say the killings had happened. Only Octavio paz made his voice heard by submitting his resignation as Mexican Ambassador to India. But who of an sense pays attention to the actions of poets?

No, Trish, Francisco was caught, bound into a braid that would not let him move. Did you notice the niña who was here by me a few minutes ago? Did you see the long braids of her hair? The lives of the students who escaped became the same as those braids. The life of Francisco after 2 de octubre was a life made of three strands woven together: Francisco was one strand; the

Mexican government was the second; the USA government was the third. Francisco could not wiggle his way free from that braid, but he also could do nothing within that braid. This was the life as it always is when a government takes control over the person's life. Francisco had two governments controlling them and each of them wanted him to do nothing.

A mind as quick as that of Francisco must have a purpose, a project. If such a mind is forced to do nothing year after year, it will die or it will become violent. Francisco had already shown that he was not willing to die, and so all these years since then he has fought to keep the violence from escaping from his mind to his hands. For a while, he was so busy with his young wife and little sons that his mind did not have time to escape to the dark places, but then when his wife died while giving him his fourth son, Francisco knew he must leave, because his mind had begin to whisper to him of violence.

I drew in a deep breath, then let it out. It didn't help. I took another. It didn't help. The sun was now so hot in the mid-day sky that even under the shade of the school's mezzanine, sweat was layering on my skin like piled-on clothes, but for once I wasn't jumping at a chance to whine about the heat. Sister was waiting to see what i would say.

"And so...that's why he has kept his visits home a secret from his children? Because he's afraid he might hurt them?"

The nun shook her head.

"I do not believe Francisco could hurt his sons' bodies, but he knows he cannot live with them as a father should. He must exchange one hurt for another. His absence hurts Cesar as much as a beating would. When Cesar Francisco left the first time, only Cesar had years enough to feel the deepest anger at his father's leaving. Never until you came have I heard Cesar talk about his father, or ask questions about him."

"But why would I cause Cesar to wonder about his father?"

She shrugged.

"El Señor sabe. I only know that you have shown great kindness to Cesar, and kindness makes a person brave."

I wasn't so sure it was a mark of kindness to pry into other people's lives, but I needed to know of the hunch I had was right.

"Sister, the man you were talking to at the dance, the one who followed Cesar and me—that was Francisco?"

"Sí."

"Then why did Cesar tell me he didn't know the man?"

"Because this is true? He does not know his father at all."

"And why did Francisco show himself to Cesar after all this time? What does he want?"

"No se, Trish. I do not know. Do you know if Francisco talked with Cesar after Cesar left you at the inn?"

"No, I don't know. I think he followed Cesar home, though. Cesar told me he could not come to the inn for his lesson today, but he promised to come tomorrow. I'll talk to him then and see what I can find out. And I'll let you know."

"Gracias, Trish."

Good southerner that I am, I know when I'm being politely dismissed, so I stood, stretched, swiped another tributary of sweat from my face and walked out the school gates toward the inn and a nap.

Sister sat there a few minutes more until Sra. Sanchez came out of he office to ask if she could possibly assist the good sister with anything? Sister smiled, shook her head, and walked back to the church.

14
Cesar

One thing I got to remember to remember befor eall the bad makes me forget, is how the teacher, she danced with me like I was as tall as she is, not like I was some kid. I don't want to forget how she made me feel like I was Cesar—like I was my name and not my years. She made me feel like a man, not just some boy that not have a father. that was why when some people started to whisper and point, I stopped dancing and ran over to the Cathedral to what was happening. A man watches for trouble.

There *was* trouble, por seguro, right there with his face in Sister's face. Sí, I knew who he was. Sister thinks I do not know he sneaks into town like bad weather every year or two, but I know. Only difference was, this time he looked at me. Always before, it was like he thought if he did not look at me, I could not see him, just like when I was a real little kid I would close my eyes when I wanted to be by myself because I believed if I could not see the people, they could not see me. That always made my mama laugh at me, laugh with him, at me. My mama told me that when they laughed, I always laughed, too.

Not this time, though. I did not feel like laughing when he turned from Sister to look at me. I felt cold inside of me. For five years he had been like a shadow in my life. It is easy to ignore a shadow—you just walk on the other side of the street so you stay in the light, but I could not walk around this man watching me like he had a right to. I could walk away, though, and was what I did. Ai, but then I saw Teacher come up behind me, so I changed my walking away into walking her home.

Teacher did not ask me why I was in such a hurry, and she asked me only one necessary question about him. She is the most kind person I have ever known.

He walked after me all the way up the road, but he never spoke and he never came close enough for me to need to speak to him. He just walked.

It was not yet very late when I reached my house after I left Teacher at the inn, but it was late enough and dark enough that all the people were still down at the dance or they were inside their houses for the night, all except my granddaddy. Abuelo was standing by the well, leaning against the well's round wall of stones, waiting for me. When he saw me, his face went soft, but then it changed again when he saw my father walking behind me. I did not like how my granddaddy's eyes looked all of a sudden tired, or how Abuelito sat hard down hard on the edge of the well like he could not longer stay standing. He did not even first catch up the back of his long short as he always did to keep it from pulling tight at his neck when he sat. I wanted to yank his shirt loose from under him, but I could not move. He smiled at my father. This I could not believe. He smiled?

"Pues, you are here."

It was not to me that Abuelo had spoken the obvious. I turned around then, and I watched how my father looked at his father.

"Papí."

That was all that my father said, but it must have been all that he needed to say, because Abuelo pushed himself up from the well, waved with his right hand for my father to follow him, and they went together into the house, leaving me alone in the dark but for one bullfrog croaking from inside the well.

Hola? Hello? And what of me? Was I to spend the night standing alone by the well? Sí, pues, why not? I would not then have to rise so early to come for my granny's cooking water in the morning if I stood here all night, verdad? Híjole. Sometimes adults disgusted me. There was nothing for me to do but go into the house by myself and crawl into bed with my brothers. Carlos, of course, woke up.

"Brother?" He pushed up on one elbow and shook back the hair from in front of his eyes only because it was his habit; it was too dark for him to need to see. "Tell me of the dance."

"Go back to sleep, my brother." I kicked with both feet to shove Jose to someone else's part of the bed. "I cannot tell you of the dance because it is not yet over."

In the morning, it was as if my father had become a shadow again. He was not in the house at breakfast and Abuelo did not speak of him to the family. I had no appetite for food; I rolled up a tortilla into a tight pencil, unrolled it, rolled it up again. Granny slapped my hand as she walked by with another plate of tortillas. "Go, go. Do not sit playing with the good food I have cooked." I went.

It was still too early to walk to the inn, but I thought maybe if I walked very slowly I might not arrive before Armando was there to unlock the gate. I walked toward the road, kicking every small rock.

"Mijo."

I turned around. Abuelo stood near the well just behind me, waiting for me to answer him, Words had abandoned me on this day as surely as my father had, so I just raised my eyebrows: *yes?*

"We will talk for a minute. You have the time."

I followed him to his wood-chopping spot and sat down on the dirt with my legs crossed, but I did not look up at him.

Abuleo sat down on the edge of his chopping block.

"When you were very little, mijo, sometimes you would tell me, or your mami, or your papi things we did not know how you knew, things we had not taught you. We would ask you: *where did you learn this?* And always you answered us: they told me before I came here. Do you remember this?"

I shrugged one shoulder.

"Maybe."

"Ah, so the boy can speak. I wondered if perhaps your American lady was charging you one Spanish word for every English word she gives you, and so your Spanish was growing as bare as this old man's head?"

I had to smile. Abuleo's head was covered ear to ear with grey curls as thick as my balck ones. I shook my head, still smiling.

"No, Abuelito. She charges me nothing. She only gives."

"And why do you think this is?"

Again I shrugged, but with both shoulders this time.

"She is a teacher. Teachers teach. Abuelo, how is it that you know Teacher?"

I had wanted to ask this since the day she first walked through our village and Abuelo came out of our house to watch her go by, but the time for asking had never seemed right. This day I did not care if the time was right, or not.

"Niño, why do you think I know her? I do not."

"But when she came here that day you looked at her like you had been waiting for her."

It was his turn to smile. Abuelo almost never smiled. His face was long, with a wide nose and many freckles across the mud-colored skin of his cheeks. When he smiled,those freckles came close together in bunches along the two deep grooves on both sides of his mouth, like stars around the moon that is growing thin. Many times when I go for water in the early morning dark, I see the stars around the moon exactly like this. Abuleo leaned forward a little to put his hand on my shoulder.

"It is possible to wait without knowing what you are waiting for."

"But when you see it, how do you know that it is what you waited for?"

"You know."

I thought the next question I wanted to ask might make him raise his hand from my shoulder to slap me for being rude, for forgetting that he was the grandfather and I was a child who had no right to question him, but I asked, anyway.

"What were *you* waiting for?"

He smiled, still.

"Someone to teach you, of course."

"To teach me what? Abuelo, I go to school."

"And it is a fine school, but you are a boy who will need more than your school can teach you. I believe you will one day again listen to the voices of the ones who taught you before you came here to us. When I saw your American teacher I did not know her name or her face or anything about her except that she, too, is a person who listens for voices."

Voices. On this day I did not want to hear talk of any voices except my father's. Why was he here? What had he and Abuelo talked about? I wanted to ask but I would not, not now. I had never known Abuelo to give as much attention to one of his grandchildren as he had to me this morning. I would not push him more. Carlos was the brother with great intelligence, but I had the most sense.

"Abuelo, I must go. Armando will be waiting for my help."

In truth, Armando had only just begun to prepare the breakfast foods for the guests when I came up the inn's steps three at a time. I was early yet, but there was work for me to do. That was the good thing about work—you could always count on it to be there. I put the eggs on to boil.

" Señor Aprendiz, your face is solemn this morning."

Armando had paused with a tray of fruits in his hands.

"Did your American lady reject your offer of marriage? Ai, the women, they have no sense, they have no pity. She has turned away a handsome man of great promise simply because of a small difference of age. Have faith, my friend; there will be others. "

So I was not to be allowed to feel sorry for myself this day? Very well. I nodded my head, grinning.

"Sí, Armando, it is her loss, but I am a gentleman. See if I do not treat her with great courtesy when she comes to eat."

"A true Don Quixote, you are. And here comes your Dulcinea now."

He was right; Teacher was coming down the last flight of steps from her room, looking at the open book in her hands. She was walking almost normally again; her leg must be nearly well. I stepped backwards into the kitchen, quickly before she saw me. I realized I was not yet ready to talk with her. I knew nothing about what had happened with my father last night, so nothing would be all I could tell her. Too many people talk all the time about nothing; I would not be one of them.

Armando saw in my face what I was feeling. He handed me a dish cloth and nodded me toward the sink.

"I need your help most back here this morning, hijo. Many dishes to wash."

I looked at the sink: three cups, one pot and a spoon. I looked up, but Armando had already left the kitchen.

I heard Teacher at the food table fixing her breakfast plate.

"Armando, where is Cesar this morning?"

I stepped further back into the kitchen, almost out the back door.

"Señor Cesar is a man with many demands on him, Senorita. He is at this moment taking care of one of those demands."

"Well, please tell him I will miss seeing him today and that I will look forward to our lesson tomorrow."

Ai, I felt bad that I had to hide from Teacher, and that Armando had to almost lie for me. It was my father's fault. My father's greatest talent was his ease in making me feel bad. Armando's hand was suddenly on my shoulder.

"Señor Aprendiz, I want you to run to the market for me. We will need more papaya before tomorrow. Here is the money. No, no—out the back door, please. It is a quicker route, so you can go there and back before time for school."

Armando shooed me out the door with small shoves at my back. This way to the market was no faster than by the front gate. He knew that. I knew that.

I looked down at the money in my hand, counting to make sure I knew how much Armando had given me before the seller in the market could confuse me with a lot of talk. I almost stepped on the man sitting by the kitchen door, his back against the inn's back wall, his arms resting easy on his propped-up knees.

"Cesar.'

Again he looked at me—the second time he had looked his son in the eyes in five years. At least he remembered my name. He had not said my name as a question, though, so I did not answer.

He pushed himself up from the sidewalk. He was very tall.

"I will walk with you."

This man was quite good at assuming his company would be welcomed—first by the Sister, then my grandfather, and now me. We walked down the hill to Matamoros and turned toward the market before he spoke again.

"I want you to stay out of school this morning, Cesar. Buy what the man at the inn sent you for and return it to him as quickly as you can. Then meet me at the bridge over the Rio Cuale. I will wait on one of the benches there."

And then he turned and walked away. Claro que sí. Of course he did. Walking away was another of his best talents.

When I slipped back in to the inn's kitchen, Armando was washing the dishes for real. I took the cloth from him and fished under the suds for dirty plates and cups my eyes could not see.

"Hijo?"

Armando was waiting for me to return from my mind's travels. The courtyard was quiet. The guests must all have finished their breakfasts because Saki was rubbing around my ankles; he had lost his morning audience. I dried my hands and knuckled the cat's head the way he liked.

"Hijo, you must go soon. You will be late for school."

"Sí, Armando. Gracias."

I ran down the steps to the Malecon and hid myself by walking among the groups of tourists. I did not want the mothers of my friends to see me and ask why I was not in school. How could I answer them when I could not answer that question for myself?

He was sitting on the bench at the highest part of the bridge, where you can look back toward the restaurants and shops on the Isla Cuala, or you can stare—as my father was doing—out into Bahia de Banderas. He was not watching the men fishing on the beach under the bridge, and he was not watching the pretty young American woman walking her little dog. He was not watching for me. He was not, I thought, watching anything.

"Cesar?"

Oh, so my name was a question this time. Perhaps he was testing to see

91

if he remembered correctly? Or perhaps he has had many sons in American and wanted to remind himself that this was the son with a Mexican name? Or perhaps..."

"Cesar, there are worse things than dying."

The young American woman leashed her fuzzy dog and walked toward the condo village, talking to the dog and smiling at him. Once she picked up the ugly little guy and hugged him to her neck. When I could not see her any longer, I sat down on the corner of the bench, right on the edge where a line of decoration like small endless waves had been carved so that it continued the whole way around the bench, under my father's knees and back to me.

"I could write a list for you of those things that are the same as dying: watching your wife die, watching your friends bleed to death on the street, hearing the thin, wailing sounds that come from the throat of a mother whose son has just been murdered by her government. But these are only as bad as dying, not worse."

I could not help it:

"Then what is worse?"

"Worse is to be alive, but to never again have the right to live as other people live."

"What other people?"

My father turned, finally, and looked at me. That was the third time.

"Cesar, I ran away when the massacre happened at Tlatelolco, but that was the right thing to do. It was the only thing to do. If I had stayed there a moment longer on the street by the church where I was standing when the shootings began, I would have been killed along with the others. I ran, and lived. I lived to come back here and become your father, and the father of Carlos and Jose and Juan. That was also the right thing to do. And when your mama died, I ran away because if I had stayed here you would have had a father who was alive only in his body, not in his spirit. I knew my father possessed the spirit of ten men and would share his spirit with you—especially with you, Cesar."

"Why especially me?

"Because you were born with the soul of the ancients."

Ai, this made me squirm. I was not special. Carlos was the smart brother, and he and Juan were both growing tall like our father and handsome like the Spaniards. I was short and round as an *indio*. I kept looking at him straight in his eyes, but it was hard to do.

"And do you now have the spirit to be our father? Is this why you have come back?"

My father shook his head as if it weighed more than a head should. A thick wave of his hair fell down across his forehead and he tossed it back away from his eyes, exactly like Carlos.

"Not yet, Not yet. It is hard to stop running, once you start. I have come to believe the only way I will ever be able to stop running is if I go back to where the running began. I am leaving today to return to Mexico City. The mother of one of my friends who died in the massacre has called me. Our government has never admitted to the killing of her son or even that he died that day. She needs my help to petition for a death certificate for her son. This is the only way her grandson can receive permission from the U.S. government to enter a college where he has been accepted in California. Her grandson must prove his father is dead and not a guerilla in hiding from his own government. Because I have lived many years in the U.S. and have learned much about legal dealings there, she has asked for my help. If I am able to do this thing for her and her grandson, I believe I will then be able to stop running. I cannot explain why I believe this to be true. Some things must be done, not explained."

"And will you then come home?"

"I think that I will. And will you then want me here, Cesar?"

I got up from the bench. The sun was now so hot even the oldest fishermen had left the beach.

"I am very late for school, Father."

In truth, when I finally arrived at school I was so late that the office lady had already sent word to my grandfather that I was not there, because she was worried something might have happened to me on my way to school. When I met Carlos in the courtyard at lunch he said Grandfather had told Sra. Sanchez I was taking care of family business, and then he apologized for not letting her know. Carlos still could not believe this:

"Abuelo apologized."

Carlos grabbed a handful of my shirt at the neck.

"Where were you, really? And why are you here now? Why are you not studying with your American teacher?"

"I will study with her tomorrow. Today I must spend my lunch time doing the work I missed this morning."

I yanked my shoulder back, pulling my shirt loose from his hand, but then I rested my hand on his shoulder and we walked together to find a place to sit.

15
Trish

Dear Mama,

If you could see me now, your kinky-headed child...

I just woke up from a typically sweat-drenched afternoon nap and I obviously slept the whole time on my right side because my head looks like a mountain halfway through being strip-mined: the curls on the left side of my head are all standing as upright as Baptists, but every single curl on the right side is a toppled tree.

Actually, Mama, it really won't be much longer now until you see your baby girl again. Hopefully, my hair will look better then than it does now. It's for sure my leg will look better than it has for the past couple of weeks. In fact, my leg is looking better and that's the reason I'm suddenly starting to think of this trip in terms of its ending. And it's about time— after all, I came here the first week of August intending to spend two weeks lazing and sightseeing (you know I'm a sucker for sightseeing) and then be back home with a week to spare before I had to report for teacher planning week the end of the month. Now here it is September ninth. Sheesh.

My leg is mostly back to its original size and freckled appearance, and when I saw the good doctor first thing this morning, he gave me the go-ahead to fly. I'll call the airline tomorrow and set up my flight home. It's time, I reckon. My students need me to set them free from their sub; you need to see me in the (somewhat bruised and battered) flesh; I need to stop having adventures and start writing down all the adventures that have come my way in Mexico, before it all fades into the Writers' Limbo of Good Intentions.

And I need to stop sweating. Even in Georgia, please God, it has to be cooler than Puerto Vallarta.

I set the pen down to run a napkin between my sweaty fingers. The doctor really had declared me fit for travel: "If you stretch and move your leg always during flight. Señorita, you must keep the blood flowing all the time." I promised him I would be a veritable Whirling Dervish of circulation exercises.

I'll finish your letter later, Mama.

Right now the best exercise for me would be to go in search of a big plate of huevos rancheros.

When Cesar bounded up the steps to the courtyard the next morning, Tuesday, for his first lesson since the night of the dance, I was still pretty psyched from making my flight reservation a few minutes before, but as soon as I saw the grin that had been so achingly missing from his face the last time I saw him, it wrenched my heart to know I was going to have to tell him I'd be leaving soon. If he'd come in looking as somber as when he left me at gate Sunday night, it would have been hard enough, but, now? Lordy.

"Guess you missed me big yesterday, right, Teacher? Guess you was lonely at lunch?"

"Actually, I did miss you, Cesar. And it's: 'guess you *were*', not *was*."

"Ahhh, Teacher."

We sat, and he slapped his notebook onto the table, making Saki jump and move to another sleeping spot in disgust. Cesar reached to open his notebook, but I laid my hand over his.

"Cesar, I have to go home this week. I'll be leaving on Friday. We can still have our lessons today and tomorrow and Thursday, but since we have only a few days left, I thought I'd let you choose what we talk about this morning. Is there anything special you'd like to work on today?"

Cesar's smile dropped like smiling had just that minute been declared illegal. He leaned forward a little and pulled his hand from underneath mine to rest both his arms on the table and braid his fingers together.

94

"Teacher."

He blew a small breath out through his nose, breathed another one in. Evidently he'd decided if their time together was now limited, he wasn't going to waste any more of it on grammar rules.

"Teacher, in America, the government is good to the people, fair to the people, yes?"

I took a personal moment before I answered to squelch a hundred sardonic responses fighting like little demons to be released into a self-serving speech. Cesar deserved an objective answer. I thought for a second, then gingerly swam into those waters.

"I believe the U.S. government has been set up in a way that easily allows for fairness when good people are in charge, and also that our form of government makes it difficult for truly bad people to stay in power for very long. That's more than many countries can claim. The loophole—"loophole" means a weak spot, Cesar, where dangers can find a way inside—the loophole is in how easily a system of government like ours with its many layers of rights and responsibilities can choose to do nothing, simply by allowing each branch to pass authority or blame to one of the other branches. It's true there have been shameful times in our history when the government has harmed through legislation—through the deliberate making of laws—but there have been many more times when harm was allowed to happen because the government did nothing."

I was talking way over his head, of course, I realized that, but it was the only way I could puzzle out for myself the truest answer to what he had asked me. While I was talking, Saki jumped back onto the table, ready to offer us a chance to show proper homage. The cat *mrrumphed* and head-butted me, then Cesar, and then settled himself into a cream-colored lump of purr between us. Cesar relaxed enough to sit back in his chair. It was like Saki had plumped a little cushion of feline serenity under our discussion. Cesar hooked his sandals on his chair's bottom rung and tipped the chair and himself backwards, rocking while he thought about what I'd said.

"Teacher, I believe maybe it easier to forgive somebody who do something to hurt you, than to forgive somebody who hurt you by doing nothing, 'cause doing nothing got no end to it."

Lordy, I was going to miss this boy.

"I agree."

"Teacher, maybe I can have a lesson of listening today. Maybe you can tell a story and I listen? A story about some time when your government not do nothing to stop people from being hurt?"

Oh, good idea because I wanted my legacy as a teacher to this wise young Mexican to be that I was the one who taught him about America's failures to itself.

I reached toward the middle of the table to scratch Saki's ears. Cesar rubbed the cat's back. Saki lay between our hands, purring, a furry dichotomy of gratitude and entitlement.

"My grandparents are from eastern Kentucky, Cesar, where the mountains are full of coal. The state that's right next to Kentucky is West Virginia, and there's coal there, too. In just the same way that miners dig for the silver in your Sierra Madres, the miners of Kentucky dig for the coal people need for heating their houses and running their factories. You know how dangerous mining is, don't you?"

Cesar just nodded his head.

"Back when my grandparents were young, some people came to West Virginia to help the miners organize into unions. They told the miners the Union would work with them to set up a system to protect the miners' rights, and also keep them healthy and safe. This sounded good to the miners; no one had ever talked with them before as man to man instead of boss to worker. No one had ever offered to work with them.

But, now, the mine owners didn't like this kind of talk one bit. Hold on a minute, the mine owners said to the miners. You work for me. I give you your jobs. I give you the houses you live in. I give you schools for your children. I give you stores where you can shop, and credit there when your money runs short. What kind of rights are you talking about? I give you the right to do honest work and get paid for doing it.

There was truth on both sides; there always is. Truth went out the window, though, when a third group got involved. A group of men from a detective agency came to town to investigate what was going on, to see if there were miners who were supporting the union and still living in the houses owned by the mining company, because that would be against the law. The houses belonged to the mine, so only miners employed by the mine had the right to live in them with their families. These detectives decided there *were* families living in the coal company houses illegally, so they threw them out. They made the women and children get out of the houses and they threw all their furniture out onto the road."

Cesar was shaking his head.

"Yeah, but they could do that, right, Teacher? It was the law."

I nodded and smiled, falling a little more in love with this boy each second. I adored a brain that could keep an argument balanced. Before I went back to the story, I had to shift in my chair a bit to keep my leg from being still for too long, doctor's orders. I flapped the hem of my skirt to let cooler air reach my knees.

"Well, yes, the law said the company had the right to evict people once they were no longer working for the coal company, but probably those men from the detective agency didn't have the right to do the evictions. Their job was to find out what was happening, not to force women and children out of their homes by pointing guns at them."

"The detectives had guns?"

"They did. And this made the miners very angry. It also made the Chief of Police in the nearest town very angry, so when the detectives drove back in to town, the Police Chief charged them with acting illegally at the coal camp. Well, actually, he tried to arrest them but someone fired a gun and then a lot of people fired their guns. When the shooting stopped, seven of the detectives were dead, the

96

mayor of Matewan was dead, and two miners were dead."

"Matewan?"

"That was the name of the town: Matewan, West Virginia."

"And the USA government, they not do nothing to fix the problem?"

"The state government did do something. The Governor of West Virginia ordered the entire state police force to take control of Matewan."

"But why he not help the womens and children? They got no place to live."

"I think he was scared, Cesar. Already, the newspapers were calling what had happened 'The Massacre of Matewan,' The Governor just wanted to stop everything that was happening, to stop the violence by using the threat of violence to force it to stop."

"And that work, Teacher?"

I was already shaking my head, no.

"No, it just got worse. There was another murder, and then thousands of miners joined together in a march against the coal companies, against the killings, against a government that would stand by and watch while this sort of thing happened. The march ended in another battle."

"Teacher, some of your family dead in those massacre?"

I eased back in her chair, letting my hand fall from Saki's back. I thought of my granddaddy.

"Not directly, no, but my grandfather left his family home in the mountains partly because of what happened there. A piece of his heart died when he had to leave the mountains. There are some people who just can't uproot themselves. My grandfather told me that years later he talked to a woman who had been a little girl living in the coal camp when the killings happened. She told him, 'I will never forget it for as long as I live...all those shots being fired. I never, well it just...it just seemed like the end of the world to me.' I know my grandfather felt the same way. He knew it was the end of what had been the world of the mountain people, in a way. A trust had been broken. No one in power ever blamed anyone for the killings, so there was no end to the story."

Suddenly I heard what I'd just said. Hadn't Sister said the very same thing to me? Hadn't she used those same words?

"Cesar, my grandfather knew there was no future for him in a place where bad things were not fixed, but only hidden. He knew someday he would need to speak out because he was a man of conscience, but he knew that when he did speak, the government would aim their guns at him. It is always easier to blame one person than to blame many."

I'd talked enough. This was a heavy story and that poor kid was dealing with enough heaviness right now.His face had gone somber again.

"Teacher, my father was killed in a massacre."

I shook my head.

"No, he wasn't. That was your father talking to Sister at the dance Sunday night, the man who followed us home, wasn't it?"

"Si. But his heart die in the Massacre at Tletalolco. That why he go back

97

to Mexico City yesterday. He think maybe he found a way to make himself be alive again."

The teacher in me said it was time for a break. I stood and stretched, pushing my hands against the small of my back. Saki jumped down from the table, knowing full well his time of being worshiped had come to an end for now.

"Cesar, I'll walk you back to school. The doctor says I need to keep the blood pumping in my hurt leg. Have you eaten? Are you hungry?"

Cesar grinned.

"Teacher, I always have hunger."

"Good. We'll stop on the way and get tortas. Deal?"

"Sure thing, Teacher. Sure thing. Teacher, you tell me your plane leave on Friday?"

"Yes, this Friday."

"That the thirteenth, right?"

"Yes. Why?"

I stopped walking for a minute so I could see his face when he answered. Something was going on in his head.

"But you tell me one time how Americans think that a bad luck day. Why you fly on a day you believe bring bad luck? And, if you fly back on this Friday, you gonna miss all the fun. Next Monday is la Dia de Independencia. You want to stay for that?"

"True, Cesar-Friday the thirteenth is supposed to be a bad luck day, but September 13th has always been a special day in my family because my father was born on Friday, September 13th. It seemed like it might be a lucky day for me to fly home. Sometimes it's good to step into the history of your father."

"And sometimes it is bad. Right, Teacher?"

"Right, Cesar."

Cesar thought for a minute before he spoke again.

"My father, he got struck in the middle of two countries and now he not belong to either of them. I think I might go to US someday, too, but not get stuck there. Maybe someday I go visit with you. I come live in your mountains because all mountains, they are the same to people who love mountains. I can study more English?"

I nodded. Sure thing.

"But then I come back here for stay because I am Mexican."

"Yes, you are. I think it's very likely you may someday leave your country, but your country will never leave you, Cesar. Inside, you will always be Mexican. Oh, and the reason I am leaving before all the Independence Day parties is because I might have so much fun I would decide never to go home, and then what would my students do? They would weep and cry and stop eating because they missed their teacher so much."

Cesar gave me a little shove with his shoulder.

'Yeah, yeah, Teacher. But *I* not stop eating."

He was pointing to the small café across from the Cathedral where they made the best tortas in town.

"Tortas?"

I inclined my head, slightly, in formal agreement with my gentleman escort.

"Tortas."

Back at the inn, I finished my letter before I got busy packing.

Back again, Mama, a quick note before I get so busy with my last few days in Mexico that I beat this letter home. I'll have lessons with Cesar for the next two days and then we've decided to celebrate our last class with a real sit-down restaurant meal. I have a gift for him: a little pocket-sized leather journal. I think he'll be tickled.

Okay. I'll be home before you know it.

Love you,

Trish

On Thursday, I handed the journal to him as soon we'd finished our meal. He turned it over and over in his hands, running one finger along the satiny grain.

"I wrote my name and my address and my phone number on the inside, Cesar. Even if I move from where I live now, you will know where I *was,* and someone there can help you find where I went in case you ever need to find me. I hope you can use this journal to write down anything you don't want to forget."

We had finished eating and I was nursing a cup of manzanilla tea, dreading having this time with Cesar come to an end.

"Thank you, Teacher. Mil gracias. Y gracias a Dios, thanks to God for you."

He took hold of my right hand and he bowed. It was our last dance.

It wasn't until my plane taxied in to Mexico City's airport for my connecting flight on Friday that I relaxed enough to wonder about Francisco and his own trip to Mexico City. *I hope his body gets back together with his spirit soon,* I thought. Or maybe that was a prayer. Then I raced through the terminal toward my flight home.

The Earthquake
September 19, 1985

Puerto Vallarta

Morning Mass had ended. The tourists who had been politely waiting outside were now drifting in to tour the sanctuary. Sister Maria Therese was standing in the Narthex, watching Sra. Franco walk down the steps to the sidewalk with her daughters. They were pretty little girls. The oldest one was sweet on Cesar. Knowing this made Sister smile every time she saw Ana Franco.

Sister put her hand against the wall of the Narthex for balance. Why? She was not dizzy; she had not stumbled. Her hand had simply known of the far-off earthquake before her mind knew. Now the floor of the Narthex was trembling. The steps shuddered—once, twice—and then the walls, in sympathy. Sra. Franco fell to the sidewalk, her arms across her girls. In the sanctuary, a chalice fell from the altar.

Mexico City

Francisco was whistling. He was whistling. When had he last whistled? He could have sworn his lips had lost the talent for making bird music simply by blowing air, but no. No, here he was walking down a street in Mexico City whistling, and all because he was holding in his hand a Certificate of Death. Ai, this would make him appear to be heartless, if this document were not a certificate of life for young Alfredo. Francisco was on his way to deliver the Certificate to Alfredo and his abuela. Francisco had done it. He had made the very government that had taken his youth from him agree to let another young man own the promise of his youth.

The document trembled in Francisco's hand. A breeze, he thought. I will put the paper inside my coat for safekeeping. And then as he was passing the building of the Ministry of Communication and Transport, the building, too, began to tremble, then to shake. When the building began to break apart, Francisco heard the noise as the sound of a thousand guns being fired. He fell to the ground, shielding the document with his body.

II. 2010
Nogales, Sonora, Mexico

16
Cesar

"Eh, my brother. Who you think you are?"

There he was, my brother Carlos. I jerked my chin up once to let him know I saw him there, grinning like he had a right to. He was waiting for me to ask him again, so I did.

"Who you think you are?"

Might as well give him the question he wanted. He grinned bigger; I knew he would.

"I am the Liberator." Carlos turned to face the mural of Don Miguel Hidalgo and flung his long skinny arms out like they were wings spreading across that picture covering the whole side of the municipal building. He reached with his fingers on his left hand to touch the black paint of Padre Hidalgo's cassock while he stretched his right hand toward the head of the highest of the Mexicans the artist had painted in a long line shrinking down to a dot of brown paint at the farthest corner of the mural. I knew the artist had meant his work to represent my proud ancestors rising up taller and taller as they moved closer in time to Hidalgo, the village priest who would one day grow angry enough at injustices from our Spanish oppressors to clang the church bells while he proclaimed, "Viva Maria," and "Viva la Virgen de Guadalupe." Through his brave cries, Don Hidalgo claimed for us all our identity as Mexicans.

Ai, and he also started our ten-year war for independence. Always, the road to justice runs slick with the blood of the poor.

I was tired. When I looked at the painting's line of Mexicans behind my brother, I saw only some long-ago abuelo of ours pushed down to the bottom and flattened there like a stepped-on ant. On this day, I had been the ant at the end of every line in Nogales.

I shook my head.

"La Migra gonna liberate your butt to jail, you not shut up."

Carlos dropped his arms and his smile.

Ai, and now I felt bad. It was me should shut up and let Carlos have his good mood. We had been in Nogales for a week and our money for food and other things we needed was short. We must not touch the rest of the money. Carlos stepped off the memorial's platform and walked over to me, but he did not look at me.

He mumbled at me in English, "We done nothing wrong. Border cops not gonna notice us."

Both of us were speaking the English, practicing while nobody that mattered was near to hear us.

"We done nothing wrong *yet,* Carlos. And La Migra notice everybody."

We stepped across the narrow street to the little park with its fountain and benches where old men sat in the shade. We let them have their benches, and squatted way down to sit on the curb. Carlos's knees almost touched his chin; he wrapped his long arms around his legs and lowered head an inch more to rest his chin between those two bony pillows. I looked at him. Just like our father, he was: as tall and skinny as a Spaniard, but as dark as an Indio. The hair on my head had always curled tight like the loops on a rug, but on Carlos, the hair waved thick and long, always falling into his eyes and making las chicas want to brush it back. The señoritas had an eye for him, por seguro, but Carlos loved only his wife and his little one, Carlito.

Ha. I sat up and laughed. It seemed not only las jovenas, but even the señoras noticed my brother because there was one now. A beauty with more years than me had seen my brother and was trying to look like she was not looking at him. I whacked Carlos's shoulder with the back of my hand, and I pointed.

"Maybe you right, brother. Why the police gonna look at us when they got a sight like that to make their eyes happy?

Carlos tipped his head up to see , and he laughed, too, but then he said, "Why you look at the women? Seem like I remember you got a wife?"

"Claro que sí. Sure, and my wife more beautiful , but I can look, right?"

"Right, until Ana see you looking. Then you wish la Chota drag you off, save your sorry butt from Ana."

We both laughed at that, because my Ana had the sweetest soul, una alma mas dulce. It was for Ana I was sitting here in Nogales with my brother. Always, it was me and my brother, me and Carlos. Sometimes I wondered if when I went to die, Carlos would run behind me wanting to go, too. But, no. I should not talk about the dying in this place.

"Cesar?"

My brother was asking me a question again. Always he was asking me the questions. He was like a well deep with questions instead of water, Carlos was. Every time he pulled one question out, more seeped in to fill him up again.

"Cesar, you think Elena okay while we here?"

Carlos was looking down, not lifting his head from where it was propped on his knees. He kept reaching between his knees to pick up little rocks near the curb and throw them right back at the road like the road was to blame for his worry. Maybe it was. I felt proud of my brother, though, because he was still speaking in English. Even in the middle of his worry, he did not allow himself the comfort of his own language.

I threw my head back and looked at him like I was shocked.

"You kidding me? Right now Elena's mamá and her madrina and my Ana all hangin' around her saying, 'Oh, Elena, you look tired. We watch Carlito for a little minute. Go and rest. Go. Go. We take care of everything.'"

Carlos grinned. I knew he saw in his head now those women like a bunch of hens clucking, flapping their wings to shoo Elena to the cool of her room for a nap. It did not matter if this picture was true or not—I gave the picture to Carlos to make him look at that world and not at the one walking all around us wondering how to take our money or take our life. Carlos unfolded his tall self from the curb and stretched. He nodded his head to the nearest table of old men, letting los viejos know he knew they had been listening to us. Maybe more people than these old men were wondering about two Mexicanos speaking en la inglés. Carlos slapped his arm around my shoulder.

"Una cervesa, my brother. It is time for a beer."

The old men looked back to their cards.

There was not money for beer and food, too, but this was one of those times when beer *was* food.

I stretched, too, and looked around. Nogales had one time been a pretty border town; I could see that. Little square houses of blue and yellow and pink walked up the hillside behind us, standing in rows like the crayons Carlito had worn down flat on top from pushing so hard when he colored his pictures; the brown dirt holding the houses with their flat roofs to the hillside looked to me like the cardboard inside my nephew's crayon box. Just before I turned to go find a beer, I thought I noticed maybe the paint was peeling away from the walls of a lot of those houses, like the crayon labels Carlito picked at when he was bored. I almost turned back around to look closer, but, no–it was always more smart to never turn around, especially if you might see something more bad, the second time.

Besides, I was happy to have a reason not to have to look any more in the direction of the Wall. There it was at the bottom of that hill with the crayola houses: a long concrete wall winding like some snake between the U.S. and Mexico.

In the time when our father was a child, there was no Wall. The border then was more like a gate between two houses. Nogales, Mexico blended then with Nogales, Arizona, into one loud mix of taquerías and mercados and American shops. I knew this because my father had told me about it one time when I was real little, before he started leaving us. He said the Mexican town's motto had been perfect then: *Juntos por amor a Nogales,* "United by the love of Nogales." Sundays after Mass, Mexican families like his walked over to the U.S. side to shop for American products, and American tourists wandered the streets of the Mexican town until evening when they went back to their cars carrying the sombreros, rebozos, and bottles of vanilla they had bought. Our father had seen all this when he traveled north once from our home in Jalisco with his father to settle some business in the U.S.

Now the biggest business I could see was the selling of machismo and root canals. Any gringo—and I had not seen very many Americanos since Carlos and I arrived—could not walk along the sidewalk more than a minute before vendors jumped into his face:

"Hey, Mister, you want Viagra? You need Viagra, right? Cheap. Right here, Mister."

103

"We give you root canal? $100 only. You come in, yes?"

Me and Carlos, they ignored. Why waste the breath on a couple more poor Mexicans? Let the rest of our teeth rot out, let our manhood hang limp as an old man's—what did the vendors care? There were plenty more where we came from and not one of us with dollars in our pockets for their drugs.

Drugs. Drugs were why the towns had changed; that's what I was thinking, and what I was thinking was the reason why I looked up then over the tops of the town's stores and houses to where I knew I should not look—to one of the hillsides where men with guns were keeping lookout over both towns of Nogales. Quick, I jerked my eyes back and lowered my head. Estupido. I shook my head hard. Don't look at them. Don't let them know you notice.

That wall and those men—snakes, and more snakes. They made me think of the snake that bit Teacher when I was a kid. But no. I shook my head at myself. That snake kept Teacher and me together, not apart.

Ai, but while I was looking at the Wall and thinking about Teacher, Carlos was walking fast toward some place where we could buy a beer—I had to almost run to catch up with him. I put the Wall behind us and the beer ahead of us.

Carlos was already sitting down at a tortas stand with just three tables and a counter set into the open corner of a block-long building that had dentist offices and cigar shops. I smelled the pork cooking and my stomach talked to me in Spanish. *Perfecto.* I ordered tortas and beer for my brother and me. All stomachs must have food, and men must have beer to fill the hole in their bellies and their spirits at the end of a day. The hole in my pocket this purchase made would find a way to fill itself, I told myself. A true result always answers true need, and our need for tortas and beer was true enough.

Carlos ran his finger around the wet lip of his Dos Equis.

"Brother, tell me again about this man we are to meet. We can trust him right?"

The beer that was now half in the bottle and half in Carlos's belly had relaxed him into speaking Spanish without knowing he had switched. I shrugged, and joined him in our language.

"I trust in my buddy from work, and my buddy told me about this guy."

"Work?" Carlos smirked at me. "What work? You got no work. That is why we are here, right? No jobs for us in Mexico, but all those American jobs are just waiting for us to come get them. Listen. Can you hear them? *Carlos, Cesar, come here. Hurry. We need you. We cannot go on without you.*"

My brother joked, but under the joking he sounded bitter. I knew why. Carlos was my smart brother; always books had been friends to him, and numbers, also. After he graduated the high school, he worked hard for one year and saved all his money to pay for an accounting course, and then he worked hard to learn all his teachers taught him there. Ai, I say he worked hard, but he loved it. Carlos and knowledge back then were like Carlos and anger now: a man with the food of his spirit. Now the only times I saw his face not look angry was when he was with his Elena and Carlito.

Carlos loved learning, that is true, but he also loved Elena; since we were kids he had the eye for her, just as her sister Ana had always had the eye for me. Claro que sí. And why should Ana not want me? Was I not the dream of every woman? I leaned back in my chair, enjoying my own braggadocio, but thinking what a good thing it was that Carlos could not hear my thoughts at this moment.

I put my thoughts back on Carlos at the time before his marriage— he had studied hard, studying for the love of learning and also because of his goal of getting his certification for Elena. He would finish the studies for her, he told me again and again, and for their future together; this was a point of pride for him. And he did this. He graduated; then he was hired to work in a bank in Puerto Vallarta. With a paycheck in his pocket every Friday, he soon asked Elena to marry with him.

I looked at my brother now as he relaxed with his beer. Carlos leaned back in his chair and watched a young American couple take photos of each in front of a tray of cigars for sale under a sign reading: *Cuban Cigars/ No Bullshit for sale here*. I took my first long swallow of my own beer and remembered Carlos' wedding day.

Carlos and Elena were married during Sunday mass, the third Sunday of May five years before this May. Carlos said he would not be married in the autumn—too many bad memories came with September. Our youngest brother Juan was born in September, and then the dying of our mother followed the birth of Juan. Soon after, our father began his own leaving of us. The year I had ten years and Juan, just five, our father went to Mexico City to find his soul again. He told me he had lost it there during the Massacres many years before when he was a student. He told me there was a job he needed to do and if he could do this job, his spirit would come back into his body just as it had abandoned him on the streets of Mexico City. Then he would be whole again. Then he could at last come home to stay, but the earthquake found him, instead, so there was no father, no mother at the wedding of my brother and Elena, but Gracias a Dios our abuelo was there to see his grandson marry. And also, Sister Maria Therese.

Sister. Me olvido. I had forgotten to give Carlos the message Sister had asked me to give to him before we jumped the border. The time was soon enough now; I should tell him before my stupid brain forgot again. I looked up from my beer to tell Carlos, but when I did, I saw the sign across the street, and said something else. instead. Carlos was sitting with his back to the open street side of the tortas shop so that I could see behind him a long white building with a cross and a flame on it:*Iglesia Metodista*. The Methodist Church. I sat up and nodded at the building, pointing like it was on fire.

"Carlos, Teacher was a Methodist."

Carlos let his eyes roll slow back in their sockets. He took another drink of his beer, set it down and then spoke to me sounding like I had the same age as Carlito:

"And?"

"I just remembered, that's all."

"You better be remember what this guy look like, this buddy of your buddy from work. He the one gonna help us to America, not some Americana you knew when you was a kid. Where your teacher now? What she ever do to help us except keep you dreaming about America?"

Carlos was speaking English again. That was a bad sign. It meant he was starting to feel desperate, but also it was bad because nothing would make people around us more suspicious than to hear two mexicanos talking to each other en inglés. We needed to practice, but we needed more not to get noticed by the wrong people, and we had pushed our luck with that enough for one day. I waved my hand at the man making the tortas, pointed down to our beers and nodded my head: two more. Carlos saw.

"Are you crazy? We have no money for another beer."

Well, I thought, at least if we starved to death tomorrow, we would starve in our own language because Carlos had switched back to Spanish to comment on my mental health. This was good. This was the way it should be with us. I flicked my hand in my brother's direction, shooing his worries away like a bug, same as I had all our lives.

"Nah, we have plenty of cousins in the U.S. All we promised up front is $500. When we get to the other side of the river, the guide can call our cousin and say, 'Is this your friend, Cesar? Are you going to pay for him? Good, do it. I will meet you at the Safeway store and give you the guy, you give me the money. That is it, okay? I will be driving a Honda Accord, blue.' Then la guida will just take the money and drive away, just go. We will say Hi to our cousin and he will say, 'Hey, my friend, what happened?' And we will tell him, 'Oh, everything is okay.' And it will be, my brother; it will be."

Carlos shook his head, but he was beginning to let himself believe me. He was always nervous, my brother. Always, he made a big thing out of everything. I could tell he had more questions in him that he was ready for me to make go away, so I waited for them.

"Then why did you tell me we had to bring so much money with us, Cesar? And where is the money I gave you for my share? Why have we slept in our car every night like homeless people, if we did not to need to save all that money for our guides? I don't see much money in your pocket when you pay for our food."

"Dios, Carlos, why don't you just stand out on the street and shout our business to the world?"

I shifted my right foot back under my chair, as if everyone walking past now knew I had hidden our money in that shoe. Before we left home, I took the heel from my shoe, cut a little hole up into the padding of the shoe and stuffed our pesos there. Then I pulled the padding back into place and fastened the heel back on. Not even Carlos knew about this because, well, because he was a nervous type; he was. It is always best to not give nervous people any more to be nervous about because they will find some way to get rid of whatever is making them nervous, and usually their way leads to trouble.

I told Carlos we needed the money but I had not told him about hiding it, because I knew we would need that money when we got to the other side, but I also knew there would be many people between here and there who would try to rob us. The less he knew, the better—either about our money or about the many ways we might lose it. Even the police, or maybe especially the police, would try to get any money they could. My cousin in the U.S, had told me to come to Nogales dressed for working, not in social clothes. If the police see you in dirty old clothes, sleeping in your truck, my cousin said to me, they will think: This man does not have anything. But if they see you clean, staying in hotels, they will grab you for some stupid thing. They are supposed to put you in jail, but if they know you are not from Nogales, that you have no family to help you, they will shake out your pockets and throw you back on the street. All this I did not say to Carlos because he was nervous enough.

The man came just then with our beers. I popped the cap off mine and raised my bottle to Carlos.

"Trust me, my brother. Have I ever let you down?"

Carlos opened his mouth to answer, but I cut him off quick before he could muddy up our Dos Equis moment with unpleasant truths.

I leaned forward in my chair and laid my hand on my brother's shoulder. The cloth of his old T-shirt was as soft as Carlito's diapers.

"Carlos, let me tell you why I noticed that church sign and why it made me think of Teacher. Relax, my brother. Enjoy your beer, and listen. "

I took another swallow, to wet my throat. It was a hot day, and the desert would be even hotter when we got there. But I would not think of that yet.

"Before we left Puerto Vallarta, Sister asked me to come by the Cathedral and see her when I had a little time. A little time? She knew you and me both had more time than money because we were not working then at any job. I said this to her the afternoon I went to see her; I asked her if she had forgotten how you were called in to the office of the bank manager the week before and told that your job was no longer available for you. "Not available." because some son of somebody from the right family wanted the job you had studied hard to get, and there was nothing you could do about it. Even if you had kept that job for five more years, as soon as you had maybe thirty-five years of age, the bank manager would have fired you then, anyway. They call you in and tell you to go home so someone younger and cheaper can have the job. There is no law against that in Mexico; at least, no law that anyone cares to enforce.

So while I was saying all this to Sister, maybe even bitching at her some just like I am now, not caring that God might strike me down for bitching at a Holy Sister, she was listening, just waiting for me to say what I had been needing to say.

When I stopped bitching, she asked me, "Cesar, don't you know how your father was caught in that same web of the rich staying rich and the poor staying poor when he had his job with the city government.?"

"Yes, Sister." I told her, "and look how that turned out. He left his job and ran away. We lost him those years he would not live with us and then we lost him to the earthquake. He left us because of government graft and he died with a government document in his hand. Our government killed him just like it is going to kill us, only it will kill us slower by starving us to death."

"Then Sister, she looked at me and she told me I would not starve, that *we* would not starve, Carlos. She said the journey we were starting began for us when we lost our father , but it had been in the mind of God since the day I was born. She said Teacher had been sent by God to help me with the English when I was a kid because El Señor knew I would need this knowledge when I was a man grown."

I raised my beer bottle to Carlos and tipped it toward him like a toast.

"Sister said I should tell you all this, but I should wait until we were very close to the dangerous part of our journey when you were starting to worry and maybe be a little scared. She knows you well, my brother. She told me only at this time should I tell you no harm will come to us because she and God have agreed on this."

At that, Carlos actually grinned, the first time since I made black his mood at the mural of Don Hidalgo.

"That sounds just like her."

And then my nervous brother truly relaxed into the enjoyment of his beer on a fine afternoon in Nogales.

Not me, though. Only my body dressed in dirty work clothes still sat in Nogales with my brother, because inside my head I was back in that time with Sister, thinking about the whole of what she had said to me. I had not told everything to my brother.

Sister and I sat on a bench in the courtyard of the school while we talked that day—the same school where I took classes when I was a boy. As far back as I could remember, Sister always came to the school when she wanted to be away from the ears of the church. At the school, the teachers and even the office lady had such respect for Sister that they would not try to listen in as they would have with any other person, hoping for some gossip to spice up the day.

"Cesar, your father once told you that you were born with the soul of the ancients."

I had been looking into the courtyard, remembering playing there when I was a kid, but when she said this, I jerked my head around to stare at her. How could she know this? I was so shocked I forgot to speak to Sister with the manners due to a nun.

"How do you know this?"

She did not answer, only shook her head a little and smiled and spoke again.

"I am not your mother, but I know much about you a mother would know."

Now I was also a little embarrassed. A nun talking of being my mother. If Sister noticed my embarrassment, though, she did not show that she did, and continued to speak.

"I could not be your mother because my family would not allow it. My family could not allow it because God wanted me. Of course, my family believed they made this decision themselves, for my good; it was not for them to know the actual reason they refused Francisco my hand was because God had led them to do so. God directs us toward action; he does not always choose to open our eyes to the reasons for our actions, and so we believe our choices to be ours alone."

By this time, I was only half listening to Sister because I was deep into my own conversation with God, asking Him politely (just to be safe) if everything Sister was telling me was His idea of playing a joke on a jokester. Had my father truly asked a nun to marry him? But Sister either did not know I was busy having words with God or she felt it best to keep my attention on her so I would not say something stupid to Him, because she kept talking.

"I could not be your teacher, either, Cesar, other than for matters of the soul. The paths of the intellect sometimes run counter to the paths of faith and mine is a life of faith. Faith is the belief in things not seen; it is the unquestioning assurance of the existence of that which cannot be proven, and it must be accompanied by a willingness to let go of the need to establish proof. But your mind, Cesar, is a mind that has a great thirst to question. You question so that you can prove to yourself what seems logical and what does not. You then make use of what you have proven. Knowledge, for you, is a tool. You needed a wise teacher who could give you that tool."

Before she had finished speaking, I was already shaking my head. No.

"No, Sister. I am not the smart one. My brother Carlos, he is smart."

Sister put her hand on my knee, stopping me.

"Carlos has a fine ability to quickly take in information and to organize it in his head. This is not the same as intellect. An intellectual mind takes that information one step farther, to create something new from what the mind has taken in. Your mind is one of these, Cesar. Your mind solves problems. You are a man who must always have a problem to chew on like a dog his bone-not to worry and fret over the problem as Carlos would, but to work your way through to the marrow."

"And what is the marrow in this bone Carlos and I are chewing on now, Sister?" She rose from the bench, and after I quickly did the same, she hugged me. She hugged me? Only once before in my life had Sister done this, and that was when she had come to tell me the body of my father had been found in Mexico City. Her hug felt all cloth and no flesh. How thin she was, though taller than I am.

"The marrow is what God has given you, not what God has taken from you. You have not been with your father in the way of most sons and fathers, and your mother was with you for too few years, but they loved you; both of them loved you. God knows, though, that love from a body you cannot see or touch seems only like the shadow of love, so God gave me to you to be the mother of your soul—a mother you could see and talk to—and He brought Teacher from America to be the guide of your mind."

I waited for more, watching her face. She looked like she wanted to say more, but knew she must not. She began to walk back to the cathedral, turning around only for a second to say,

"Vaya con Dios, hijo."

How could I not go with God? He had an agreement with Sister.

17
Cesar

All this remembering flew away like a dream when my phone rang in my pocket. I answered without looking first to see who was calling because I did not want to give myself a chance to decide if I wanted to answer, or not. What I wanted did not matter now. I mostly listened, saying only *sí, sí,* once or twice, and then I put the phone back into my pocket slowly, as if everything I did after this moment should be done with great care. For the second time in my life I was amazed by how few words are needed to change the life of a person forever.

My brother, of course, was watching me. I had to tell him something.

"Carlos, he said we are to bring only a small bag with socks, toothpaste and toothbrush, a blanket, a jug of water, a couple of cans of tuna and some cans of beans in case we need extra food, but he said they will get food for us while we are traveling."

Carlos was staring at me like I had started speaking Chinese.

"Socks?"

I shrugged. "He said we need to keep our feet from getting blistered. He said we have to be able to keep up with the others."

I drank down the last of my beer, got up from the little table and jerked my head toward the street.

"Vámonos, Carlos. It is time to go."

"Now? But we are not ready."

Carlos was starting to panic; I knew. I turned back to him and put my right hand on his left shoulder, looking hard into his eyes.

"When Carlito was coming to be born, did your Elena say she needed time to get ready? No. She had passed nine months getting ready. When the day for his birth came, she just got busy and brought your son to you. Pues, Carlos, it is time for us get busy. Elena is waiting for you to bring a future to her."

It worked. Carlos sighed, deep, like he was steadying his insides, before he spoke again.

"Where? When?"

"He said to meet him in front of the cigar store in one hour. He will have a car waiting for us and the others; he will drive us to Agua Prieta and we will cross from there. Agua Prieta is close to the border, but with not so many Border Patrol as in Nogales."

Carlos shook his head once and snapped at me like he was angry.

"He? Him? Does this 'he' not have a name?"

"His name is 'Do As I Say', Carlos. His name is 'Do Not Ask Questions.' When we get to the other side, his last name will be 'I Never Saw You Before'."

We walked to where our truck was parked out of sight on a side street and began to pack the things we would need. But right away I saw there was a problem: how would we carry our water? We had some plastic liter bottles of water ready for our trip, but they were heavy and hard to hold on to. I stood there for a minute, letting my mind look at the problem. Ah. Yes. I picked up a couple of the old T-shirts we had brought with us and put one water bottle inside each T-shirt like I was dressing Carlito, leaving the neck and mouth of the bottle sticking out through the neck of the shirt. The T-shirts were bigger than the bottles, of course, so I wrapped the extra cloth around and around the bottles, like wrapping a new baby in a blanket. Then I tied the arms of the T-shirts together into a knot to keep the shirts tight around the bottles. This was good; I nodded my head to myself. This would help keep the water from getting so hot, and the cloth would pad the bottles so they would not hit so hard against our ribs when we carried them. And next I jammed a thick stick through the middle of each knot, letting the ends of the stick poke out on both sides, and then I tied each end of a short piece of rope into a looping knot around each stick-handle so that the rope joined the two drinking bottles. We could sling the rope across the back of our neck and over our shoulders, and let the T-shirt-padded bottles hang on either side. We would be two runaway oxen wearing our yokes.

Carlos glanced my way once to see what I was doing, but then went back to his packing. He was used to my inventions, and he knew they worked. It did not take much time to pack so few possessions; we were on our way to the meeting place half an hour after the call came. As soon as we started walking, Carlos started asking questions. I knew he would.

"Cesar, who are the others who will go with us?"

I stopped walking and I threw my hands to my face.

"Ai, no, Carlos. La guida, he forgot to show me the guest list. How will we know where we are to sit for dinner?"

Carlos froze when he heard my voice so high and panicked. After a lifetime together, I could still trick him, at least for a second. But then he rolled his eyes and slapped me on the back of my head.

"You are crazy."

"Sí, you are right. But look, my brother."

I pointed to the other side of the street we were crossing.

"There are our fellow party guests."

We saw four men standing on the sidewalk, waiting, trying very hard to look like they were not standing on a sidewalk, waiting. All of the men had indio blood like me and it showed; none of them had the height of my brother. They looked like they had about the same age as Carlos and me-between twenty-five years and thirty-five years. But one of the men was not a man; he was just a kid. And, Dios, there were two women sitting on the sidewalk behind the men, leaning their backs against the wall of the cigar store. One of them was very pretty. I had not thought there might be women,

Carlos and I stepped onto the sidewalk with the rest of the men and I nodded to them but I did not speak. I hoped we looked like just a bunch of guys who had worked in the same factory for many years and were waiting for our ride to the night shift. I did not look at the women at all, letting them keep their privacy, but I promised to myself that I would have care for their safety.

Very soon, a man who looked no different from any of us stepped out of the cigar store and nodded his head once toward a van parked a little way down the street. We all got in.

Our trip to el norte started with the van heading south down Highway 15 until we reached Highway 2 at Muris, then northeast to Agua Prieta. This route was our only way through Mexico unless we followed dirt roads and washes through open desert, and I believed none of us wanted to do that if we did not have to. We wanted to avoid the American Border Patrol because they held the law in their hands, but la migra Mexicana were criminals who had no souls, and they were as thick as greasewood along the desert lands just south of the border.

The drive required three hours, maybe four. I did not have a watch and I spent much of the ride so deep into my own thoughts that I had no thought at all of time.

Carlos has always said that I daydream too much. He says I should pay attention to what is going on around me. I *do* pay attention, but my attention does not like to hurry. It is most comfortable for me to watch what is happening on the outside while I take a little time to make room on the inside for what I am seeing. For me, each day is like a new chair you have bought. You would not bring a new chair to your house, set it on the front step and leave it there. If Carlos did that at his house, Elena would not let him rest until that chair was inside and in the exact place where she thought it would best fit in with the rest of the chairs. So it is with my mind. I need some time to figure out how everything I see and hear fits in with what I have already seen and heard. I guess that makes it seem like I am not paying attention, while the truth is that I am paying twice as much attention as most people.

Riding in that van with my brother and seven strangers, I was not giving any attention to the men who crowded in with me because to have someone's leg crammed against mine was no different from sleeping in a bed full of brothers and cousins all the nights when I was a boy. And also, the leg crowding mine on my right side was my brother's leg. Had not that same skinny leg flopped over my leg during a childhood of nights in our bed at home?

No, I was not looking at all those legs and arms and heads in the van with me, but at the desert passing us outside the van's windows. I had not before seen the desert in the springtime. The afternoon was becoming late but there was light for most of the trip, so I could see how the desert was pretty with flowers. The ones I liked best almost did not look like flowers at all, but like small fuzzy orange birds. These blooms sat right at the tops of long brown stalks, so that it looked like some kid had stuck a bunch of sticks in the sand and caught a bird on the tip of each stick.

One of the women with us shifted a little in her seat in front of me and pulled my attention away from the flowers, to her. La guida had told the two women to sit in the front with him and he had put the pretty bird right next to himself.

I watched the driver to see if both his hands stayed on the wheel, but soon it was too dark to see. We arrived in Agua Prieta just as the last of the day's light left. The man parked by the curb, then turned around and told us to wait in the van while he bought food to us. I ate the food he brought a few minutes later without noticing what I was eating. I ate because I knew I would need strength for that night. I looked at Carlos. Carlos, too, did not care what he was eating; he ate because he was too scared to think, so his stomach was telling him what to do.

It was not far to the river, but to the other side—Ai, Dios. We all got out of the van and stood looking across the water. Here was Mexico; there was the USA. I walked over to where the guide was saying something to the chica bonita. Just as he reached out to put his hand on her arm, I spoke to him.

"Pues, I have a little problem. I cannot swim. I have this belly, though." I patted my round stomach, blowing it out like a balloon. "Maybe I can float across on it?"

He looked like he might be going to be angry, but then he kind of smiled and jerked his head for me to follow him. I thought that he was not really a bad man; he was in a bad business, that was all. He led me around to the back of the van.

"Pull out that box."

There was a big cardboard box at the back of the storage area of the van, behind all our bags. I shoved the bags and backpacks out of the way and dragged the box to me. I looked at him; he nodded, so I opened it and pulled out a heavy sack of folded-up rubbery orange plastic. Ah. It was a float, a big round float with a floor in the middle, the kind of float you have to inflate. A life raft. Una balsa salvavidas.

"You can float across in that." he said. "You can lie in it with all the bags."

I looked at the float, and then at the river, It was night, but still I could see how far across was the water. You had to be a good swimmer to make it.

The man showed me how to use a kind of foot pedal to fill the raft with air. He told me to sit in the middle of the raft while everyone dumped their clothes and stuff all around me. They pushed me and the raft into the water and then Carlos and the rest of the men and the two women started to swim. Everyone was swimming and pushing the raft with me in it.

A little water splashed in and my butt got wet, but that was the only water I touched, and I could not see the river. I saw the heads of the people swimming. It was black night and I was lying in an orange plastic bed with dark heads all around me like the heads of my sleeping brothers when we were kids. The arms of the swimmers were looped over the sides of the raft the way my brothers used to throw an arm across my chest while they slept. My brother Carlos was swimming near my right shoulder. I put my arm over his and held on.

After a while all the heads rose higher because we were coming to shore and the swimmers could touch bottom with their feet. My butt bounced when the raft hit sand.

In that moment, we were illegal.

We ran to hide in the bushes. We all grabbed our stuff and ran for the bushes. Someone would come and pick us up, the man had told us before we jumped the river. He told us to hide in the bushes until someone came to give us a ride. We waited for maybe five minutes—who knows?— then someone yelled, "Come over. Jump in the van."

They took us to a hotel room. We were six men and two women in a little hotel room. Two beds. They said, "We will call you tomorrow and let you know what is going to happen." That was all. They left us.

I looked around the room at the men until they looked back at me.

"I call the bathroom first." I grinned really big to let them know it was a joke. I was the only dry person in the room. Carlos rolled his eyes and hooked his arm around my neck like to choke me.

"My brother is an idiot." he told the others.

The men relaxed a little, nodded their heads—they all had idiot brothers, too.

I pulled Carlos's arm away and bowed to the two women. "No, no. Las primas, our lady cousins must have the first baths."

The young pretty one smiled, only a little, but enough. While the women were in the bathroom, the oldest of the men said we must let the ladies have the beds. We would sleep on the floor.

It seemed to me everyone fell asleep at the same time, like we were jumping into another river, but in this river of night we were all swimming from the fear that had brought us to this crossing, a fear we could not see the face of, or give a name to.

A knock on the door woke us at noon. The man slipped in sideways before I could even open the door all the way and he pushed it tight closed behind him. He handed us bags of hamburgers and told us we would travel again when it was dark. We must be ready to leave by six. They would drive us to Tucson. That was all he said. The man opened the door just barely and slipped back out. I locked it.

No one spoke for a minute. Then the one of us who had offered the beds to the women the night before shook his head a little and looked at the rest of us.

"And then...what?"

I laid my arm around his shoulder.

"And then we are Americans, paisano."

He shook his head harder, like I had said nonsense.

"We are migrantes, migrants. We are not Americanos."

I gave his shoulder a squeeze before I took my arm away.

"All Americans are migrantes, my friend. We are just arriving to their house later in the evening than most of the guests; that is all. But are not Latinos always late to the party?"

I sat on the floor where I had slept and I took a hamburger from one of the bags. I held the bag out to the man who had been speaking.

"Here, my friend; have something to eat and then tell me your story. We have many hours to pass in this room together before we leave."

But the man only shook his head one last time and slid down to the floor

114

to eat his burger.

"I have no story," he said. "That is why I am here."

The young pretty one had been listening to us while she ate. She moved to the edge of the bed near where I was sitting.

"I have a story."

I smiled at her. "Sí, por seguro. Of course you have a story. We all do. He is just worried and a little scared. Sometimes when you are scared, it helps to hold tight to what you love most, and what could we love more than our own stories?"

But she was already shaking her head: *No.*

"I have a story to tell, but it is not mine. My story has never been my own; that is why *I* am here."

Carlos had come to sit by me; he was waiting for her to begin. Whoever this girl was, I loved her right then for giving my brother something other than fear to hold his attention.

"What is your name, bonita?"

"I can tell you the name I was given, but I do not know if it was the name my mother wanted for me."

I nodded, but did not ask any questions. A person should not speak once a storyteller has begun. My grandfather always told me you must honor a storyteller with your silence. I leaned back against the hotel room wall to listen.

"They called me Ruth. The nurses gave me my name because the earthquake took my mother before she had time to name me, or at least before anyone knew what she had wanted to name me."

"Earthquake?" I sat straight up and leaned toward the girl. I was wrong to speak after she had begun to her story but I could not stop myself—I interrupted her. "How old are you? You were born during the great earthquake?"

"Sí. Yes, the earthquake of 1985 shook me out of my mother and then shook the hospital down around us both. She died; I lived. I lived for a week under the rubble and bricks before the searchers found me and five others buried under the hospital. They say we survived because newborn babies are really nothing more than bags of water. We fasted and slept, and most of us lost almost no weight. Our newborn skin kept the water in our bodies, and the dark, warm spaces where we lay buried must have seemed to us just like the wombs where we had been living until moments before the earthquake struck. It was really no miracle that we survived, but the world called us the Miracle Babies. I think the people of Mexico needed this name for us more than we did."

I watched her as she said all this. She told this like a story learned in school, like a tale that had nothing to do with her.

"In the years after the earthquake, we became known as "los niños del sismo." the children of the earthquake. So many names, and yet none of the names were truly mine.

"A team of nurses and doctors and some social workers took on the care of us, but we were nobody's children. We were not even truly Mexican because the money to pay for our needs was not all Mexican money; a lot of people in the U.S.

sent money to the hospital after they heard about us. Please understand—I am happy for my life, and I give thanks to all the people who never stopped being responsible for me, but I cannot help but to feel that the person I really am lies buried somewhere under the streets of Mexico City."

"I do not belong to anyone in Mexico. The nurses have given me love and care, but I was not born to their families. I do not belong to anyone in America, though many Americans have given money for my support. I need to find out where I do belong. I need to live in America for a while so I can get to know Americans and maybe begin to understand why they spent so many years sending their money to me, but when I asked for legal permission to do this, our government would not give me a visa. To the Mexican government, I am a symbol of Mexican strength at a time when the world honored Mexico for how we lived through our tragedy so bravely. A symbol can be owned, you know, and governments do not like to let go of anything they own. I had to leave without the permission that never would have come."

Carlos spoke first.

"And the woman with you?" He nodded to the other woman as he asked. She was stretched out on the second bed, napping.

"She is not with me, except in the way that women are always together among men they do not know."

Ai. I should be ashamed. This young woman had shared her story with us and we had not even given her our names.

"Perdón, señorita; I am Cesar. And this scarecrow is my brother, Carlos."

Carlos rolled his eyes at me, but bowed a little to the girl, then asked another question. With Carlos, there is always another question. Sometimes I think the questions line up inside his head like niños waiting for the toilet: as soon as one has its turn, another is there.

"If the other lady is not someone you know, then why are you traveling together?"

Ruth kept her voice low as she answered, so the woman would not wake and hear us.

"She is a cousin to one of the nurses. She came to visit the nurse last week in case she did not see her cousin again after she jumped the border. I heard the two of them talking—pues, arguing, actually, because my nurse, my madrina—did not want her cousin to cross. Later I went to the woman and asked her to take me with her. I told her I had money saved so I could pay what the guides would charge."

"This woman did not think it strange that a person who had been given such fine care by so many people would want to leave such a life?" This question came from me.

Ruth looked at me like I had wasted a question on what I should already know.

"Fine care does not keep a soul from weeping."

I held my hand out to her and she took it, for a moment only.

116

"You should rest, Ruth, as your companion is resting. We should all rest. It will be six o'clock very soon."

18
Cesar

One loud knock at the door jerked us all awake. Only one knock. Were we not paying enough money for the man to waste any more knocks on us? We grabbed our stuff and went outside. Nobody bothered to shut the door to the room.

The man opened the doors on a big King Cab truck.

"You." He pointed to the women, ""You're going to be in front. You, you, you, you." He pointed to four of us, "You go in the back. Lie down—one the head, the next the feet, one the head, one the feet. Like that."

Carlos and me and two of the men got in like he said. They took out the back seat so we could lie straight and I thought it might not be so bad, but then he told the other men to lie on top of us and he covered us all with a black cover, a kind of heavy cover like you put over a load of dirt. I could not see nothing. It was hot and I was very tired. The truck started. We passed maybe an hour that way and sometimes I could not breathe very well, but I had to handle it,

The truck stopped. When the man pulled that cover away it was like when the waves had splashed over me in the river, but the water was air this time. I pushed my hands against the back of the man on top of me to make him get off faster and I rolled out of the truck onto sand. Sand? I grabbed la guida's arm before he could walk away.

"Hey, man, why we are not in Tucson?"

He looked at me like he forgot I could speak. Then he shook his head.

"We got a call. They caught us on the heat sensors so we had to drive back fast, before the Border Patrol could catch up with us."

I had a bad feeling about what he just said. Carlos came over and stood next to me. Madre de Dios. I knew then my bad feeling was true because Carlos could smell bad news like one of Abuelo's cats sniffing out a rat in the woodpile.

"Drive back? Back where?"

The man lifted his shoulder like this was no big deal.

"Over there is the border. We will try again tomorrow. Don't worry, you don't have to pay your money until you make it for real."

We were back in Mexico? We were back in Mexico.

By then the man had seen our faces enough to make him remember we were all people, Mexican people like him, so he felt a little bad and started talking real fast to keep the women from crying.

"We are about a quarter mile from the checkpoint. See that house? You go there and you wait there tonight; you wait on the roof."

Carlos had a question that would not stay inside.

"Why do we have to be on the roof?"

117

The man pointed to a fence a little way beyond the house. When he raised his arm, I could see the man's sleeve had a patch at the elbow. The sewing looked very neat. I wondered where the wife of the man was.

"See that fence?" The man was still pointing.

We all looked. The fence was maybe twelve, maybe fourteen feet tall.

"When you are on the roof, obviously you can see the fence; you can see the patrols. There is a McDonalds on the other side of the fence. You have to watch for the shift change in the morning. When the people start to change the shift, you run, jump over the fence, then run to that creek and go in the culvert. You have to get through that culvert to the other side while all the people are changing the shift. Make like you are just another person leaving your shift and go out to the road. We will pick you up."

He left us standing in the dark.

I never knew who were the people who lived in the house; we did not see them. We climbed a ladder we found against the back of the house, letting the ladies go last so we could give them a courtesy hand up instead of embarrassing them by following close to their rumps. I think I was not the only one of us who went to sleep right away on that roof. The sun was gone by then and the roof tiles had cooled enough to feel nice under our backs. There is always a time deep in the night, in Mexico, when the heat from the day lets go like it is tired, too. All my life, I can remember waking at that time—three o'clock, three-thirty—just for the pleasure of settling back to sleep in a cooler world.

Ai, but later I woke to sweat, like always. And still we had to wait. The sun was high, but we had trees and a shadow to protect us from the worst of it while we waited. I kept jumping a little every time I saw more than two people enter the McDonalds. How many people were in a shift?

"Hey. We are going to make it." The man was standing on the ground in front of the house, calling up to us. "Now. Now is the time."

I do not remember getting down from the roof. We ran. We ran, we ran between the bushes to the ditch of the creek and we ran through the culvert, all bent over like old men running.

There were two immigration officers at the end of the pipe. They just said, "We got you. Don't make it hard; just come with us."

They were pretty nice, those guys. They were doing their job. I felt more stupid than mad. While we were up on that roof watching McDonalds, they were down on the ground watching us. You know, I thought there would be a lot of bushes or trees to hide us, but there were only those couple of bushes we ran between. All around, it was clear for miles. If some guy stopped to smoke, you could see the smoke. As soon as we came down off that roof, those patrol guys saw us, and they waited for us to do what we were going to do. The immigration saw us jump from the roof and jump over the fence. They knew we would keep jumping, so they just waited.

Both the immigration guys were young, not as old as me. Their hair was short and their shoulders were big. I thought that they probably played American football when they were in school. Both of them wore wedding rings. One of them waved his hand for us to follow him to the van. When I reached for my pack I had set down after they stopped me, they told me I could not pick it up—*Sorry, man. It's the rule*—but Carlos could bring his pack because it was still on his back. I owed them for that. I did not want to think how Carlos could survive if he lost his notebook he scribbled in every night.

They drove us to the center, the detention center. I thought it might be like a prison, but it was just a building, like an office building where you go to pay your taxes or see your dentist. The prison was in my mind; I was thinking on how what they are doing was changing me from my abuelo's *mijo* to an illegal. They took our fingerprints, our photos. After maybe half an hour, they drove us back to the checkpoint and let us out on the Mexican side.

The guy who told me I could not bring my pack, said, "You can go. Better luck next time."

After they drove away, I turned around to say something to the other *migrantes*, but the men were already gone. Only Ruth and her companion were still standing with me and Carlos where the patrol guys had left us.

"Todo se acaba." I said, and grinned so Ruth would relax a little. "Everything comes to an end. Sometimes it is a different end than we were planning, that is all. Today's ending is the ending for this day only. Ladies, we will find shelter for you for this night and try again tomorrow. Did not the patrol boys wish us luck? We are bound by good wishes not to give up now."

Ruth smiled. Carlos saw her smile and his shoulders let loose just a little. He knew already that she did not often smile. Smiling makes a person vulnerable. Carlos obviously believed if Ruth was smiling, then our situation must not be totally hopeless. I wondered yet again why some people are born convinced the world is their enemy. Pues, okay, maybe Ruth had good reason to be suspicious: being buried under a couple of tons of brick just as you are sucking in your first breath of life could make you believe life might not be such a prize. I let out a snort of a laugh at my thoughts, and Carlos rolled his eyes. Bueno. I slapped my arm around his neck and turned to our lady companions.

"Señorita Ruth y señora: Let us go visit the Methodists."

Ruth ran her fingers through her hair. I remembered that she did that before, when the guy in the van got too friendly. Ruth's hair was short and kind of spiked, like a young guy, but on her it looked good. When she combed her hair with her fingers it made it softer, and that made her face look soft. Her face was small, like a little girl.

I kept my arm around my brother and waited like there was no place I needed to go. Ruth stopped bothering her hair and looked at me with her head leaning a little bit toward her shoulder. I could tell she was starting to trust me enough to also trust my suggestions, but belief does not rule out confusion,

"Cesar, are you not Catholic?" Ruth asked, just barely touching my arm with one finger like she was ready to apologize if her question was too personal.

Carlos answered for me. "We *are* Catholic, señorita, but my brother thinks

Methodists are always on their feet getting things done while we Catholics are on our knees praying our days away. My brother likes to get things done."

Hmm. That was closer to the truth than I would ever have thought, if Carlos had not put it into words for me. He was a wizard with words, my brother.

I nodded my head.

"There was a time, ladies, when I was a fat little boy who thought himself stupider than his brothers, and so useless that he could not keep his own father from leaving their family."

We walked as I talked, heading in the direction of the Methodist church I had seen before we left... was it really only the day before? I stopped and put my hand out like the women had been about to say, *Oh, no. A man such as yourself could never be fat or stupid*—which they had not.

"Oh, si, Bonitas, I know. You find such an idea impossible to believe, seeing me now so handsome and so accomplished."

Ruth smiled again, and shook her head slowly the way a woman does when a man she likes is talking nonsense for her pleasure.

I bowed my acceptance of the protests the ladies had not spoken.

"But it is true enough. I was ten years old the day an American teacher walked through my village and my abuelo came out of the house to watch her pass by. Ruth, you must understand: my grandfather never gave any person his attention, his whole attention. Even with me, the grandchild whose company annoyed him least, his hands and his eyes always were busy with work while he gave his ears to my chatter. But this turista held him as still as a watched rabbit with her passing. I had to know why. Abuelo told me later he had been waiting and looking for her, or maybe just for someone like her, to teach me. To teach *me*, Cesar, not my smarter brothers."

Carlos, when he heard me say that about my smarter brothers, brushed his heavy hair back with one hand and posed like a movie star. I smacked him in the chest.

"Ruth, I did not know why my grandfather thought I must have this extra teacher or how he knew someone would come to be that teacher, but I did not need to know. I needed only to meet this lady Abuelo had found for me, in case she was my only chance."

"Your only chance for what, Cesar?"

I shrugged my shoulders.

"I did not know, then."

I stopped for a second, remembering. Carlos and the ladies stopped when I did, and a family walking just behind us on the sidewalk parted like the Red Sea to pass around our little army, then came back together again in front of us.

"My smarter brother, there," and as I spoke, Carlos bowed again, "is always giving me books to read. In one of those books I found a line I liked: Antonio Machado said, 'You make the road by walking.' Roads, roads, roads. All my life, people have walked away from me on roads I could not follow, but when I was a boy with ten years, a teacher walked *to* me and my grandfather came out of his hiding to meet her there."

I looked at Ruth, at her only.

"This teacher came to help me find the road I needed to walk."

Ruth nodded, slowly. "And she was a Methodist? That is the reason we are to see the Methodists now?"

"Not the reason, no." I wanted to make her understand, but there are things that can only be believed, not explained.

"We will stop for a few minutes while we eat, Ruth, and I will tell you the story."

19
Cesar

"But the American teacher went back to los estados unidos, so she did not help you find the road you were looking for."

I had finished the telling of my story when Ruth's companion spoke for the first time. Ai, it was the first time she had said *anything* since we all left with the guide the day before, and then we all came back in the arms of la migra.

I smiled, but not at her, remembering all the roads Teacher and I had walked together. Then I turned my smile to the ladies and waved my hand toward the road under our feet as if I were offering it to them.

"Have we not been walking a road together for the past day and night, mis primas? Are we not walking still ?

"But we have gone nowhere." she argued.

I saw then how tired this woman looked. I would not say so to her, though. Being married had taught me that if you tell a woman she looks tired, what she hears is that she looks ugly. My new companion needed food, and a moment to sit in peace before I delivered her and Ruth to strangers for the night. I remembered the tortas stand where Carlos and I had eaten before we crossed the first time. It was right across from the Methodist church. We would go there,

I smiled again to let her know I was not arguing with her, and said, "Teacher was given to me to *show* me the road I needed, not to be my companion to my destination. There can be many detours along a road, señora, but detours only keep the destination from sight for a bit longer. The destination is still there. Today is a detour for us; let us make it a satisfying one."

I nodded my head toward the tortas stand, which was now just ahead of us.

"It would be my great honor to buy a small dinner for all of us."

Before I even looked over at Carlos I could feel his face twisting into his worried look. I said nothing, but gave a little head jerk in his direction because I knew he would know this gesture meant not to worry, that I had it all taken care of. Ai, Dios, sometimes Carlos and I communicated more like an old married pair with each other than we did with our wives.

I found a table for four and then excused myself to the bathroom, which was to be an ATM for me, No one was using the urinal. Good. I went in the one stall and closed the door. I sat on the edge of the toilet, carefully, for how would I explain if I fell in and came back to the table with wet pants? Carlos would joke about that until we were old men.

I did not want to touch the money in my shoe because that was for paying la guida when we finally made it over the line, but I also had a small bit of money that I had pushed in to the waist of my pants through a tiny tear. I worked a few pesos out through this opening, thanking God the whole time for keeping me from hiding the money in my pack, which would now be lying in the sand for some snake to find. This money in my pants was for unexpected emergencies. The need to feed Ruth and her companion was for sure something I could not have expected. I shoved the money in my pocket and was back at our table before Carlos could begin to wonder what I was up to. And my pants were dry.

Our food came quickly and it was good. Good because we were hungry and good because we were choosing it and buying it for ourselves instead being fed like babies or prisoners.

"Ai, I am sorry to say this, my friends," I leaned back in my chair and wiped the last of the tortas from my hands with a servilleta, then tossed the napkin to the table, "but the afternoon is passing by and we must get you two ladies to the church before the pastor leaves his office for the night."

The women and Carlos turned to look at the church when I waved my hand toward it, an ordinary building just across the street. It did not look like a church, or at least not like one of our beautiful Catholic churches. Two arched windows and the arch above the doorway were the only signs that this was not another office building. The church's flat front wall facing us was painted a dark brown on the lower half and a lighter brown starting about halfway up the windows. There were a couple of merchant stalls on the sidewalk to the right side of the door, and above them, a painted black cross with a red flame swirling around it. I knew this was the symbol of the Methodists, but I was not sure why. The words over the cross read, "Iglesia Metodista." That was the place.

Carlos and I walked on the outside of the ladies to protect them from cars and merchants: one step down from sidewalk to street, a few quick steps across the street and one step onto the sidewalk in front of the church. *A short walk to destiny, eh, Señor?* I shook my head at my stupid self. Who was I to talk to God like we had made this plan together?

But when I knocked on the tall door, I knew already we were welcome there.

The tall man who answered our knock looked American, but he spoke very good Spanish. I let him continue in Spanish as we spoke. It might be better if no one heard that I could speak some English.

"Señora, señorita, señores, you did not need to knock," the man said when he opened the door to us. "This is a church. All are welcome."

"Gracias, Padre," I answered him with a very small nod. It was hard not to bow my head and bend my knee when I entered a church, even a Methodist church. "We are in need of a favor."

"There are no favors in the house of God," he said with a nice smile. "Only gifts of grace."

I liked this man.

"Pues, entonces, well, then, Padre, my young cousin and her companion are in need of the grace waiting for them."

"Of course. Please, come with me to my office." The Padre turned and walked toward a door at the side of the sanctuary, waving his hand for us to follow him. "We will sit and have a cup of coffee while I hear your story."

Carlos and Ruth both shot me a worried look. *What story?*

I gave my head a little shake: *do not worry.*

I liked the Father even more when I saw his office. The chair he sat in was a simple wooden chair with boards across the back, the kind of chair a person uses when he gives all his thoughts and energies to others, and only when he goes to sit down at his desk does he realize—*Oh, I never bought a chair for my desk. No es importante. I'll just grab one of the chairs from the vestry.* The chairs he offered to his guests, though, had padded seats and flower-printed cushions for our backs. The office walls might have once been painted to match the cushions, but who could tell? Every wall was floor-to-ceiling with books. I glanced over at my brother. Carlos was staring at the walls of books with just the same expression our drunkard uncle Simon used to have on his face at family weddings when he saw the bar well-stocked with local tequila.

Well, I would not have to worry that Carlos or one of the ladies would say something to mess up the story I was about to tell: Carlos was too drunk with desire for the books to tell me I was stupid, Ruth's companion was too scared to speak at all, and Ruth had evidently decided to let me make the decisions. I was not sure if she trusted me that much to keep her safe, or if she was just curious to hear what I might say next. I was curious, too.

"Padre, you are familiar with *los niños del sismo* ?"

Huh? Who knew *that* was what I was going to say next? Not me, por seguro.

The Father nodded his head. "Yes, of course, the babies who survived the earthquake of 1985. Truly, their survival was a miracle of God."

"Well, Father, here is one of those miracles." With a swoop of my arm, I presented Ruth like she was the top prize at bingo. "And la señora, her companion, is cousin to one of the nurses who helped raise those babies. La doña and Ruth have been traveling together in search of any of Ruth's birth family who might still be living. They had received word of a possible connection here in Nogales, but arrived too late to meet him—he had passed recently."

Sí, I was playing with the truth a little. I was playing in Carlos's field of the different meanings of words. The "connection" I mentioned was not a family member, but la guida, and no one had passed into death, but we had certainly passed into another world yesterday, even if our time there was short. A kind of

Purgatory: that was what the past twenty-four hours had been.

The Padre interrupted my ramblings inside my head to say what I should have said before I distracted myself.

"And now the ladies need a safe place to pass a night or two until they can complete their plans for travel?"

"Yes, if you know of such a place."

The good man stood up, came around to our side of his desk and put his hand on my shoulder. "We keep a room here in the church for people who have an immediate need for someplace to stay. Ladies, you are welcome. I will show you to your room as soon as I escort your gentlemen friends on their way."

When I leaned toward Ruth to receive her goodbye kiss on the cheek, I slipped my cell number into her hand and whispered that I would call them after Carlos and I had jumped successfully. We would not forget that she, too, wanted to be on the other side.

We walked back to the front door of the church, the three of us men. The Pastor shook Carlos's hand, then shook my hand. He did not let go of my hand right away.

"Sir, what is your name?"

"Mil perdones, Padre; I am Cesar. And this is my brother, Carlos."

"Cesar, I don't know if you know there is a humanitarian center near here run by the Jesuits. They are always there to help migrantes."

I did not let him let go of my hand as I answered him, "No, padre, I did not know, but it would not have mattered. I would still have brought the ladies here."

He smiled, and shook his head like he was confused.

"Why? If I may ask? I mean, I assume you are Catholic, not Methodist."

"Sí, yo soy, but because a Methodist gave me the path I am walking. I believe I must keep to that path. I am a builder. I like to keep things balanced."

The pastor stood and watched us as we walked away, but his watching did not cause me to worry. It was a good kind of watching.

On the street again, Carlos was quiet for a time, but as the spell of the pastor's book wealth wore off, he began once more to think of problems, which meant that he expected me to find answers for those probems.

"And what of us, my generous brother? Where will we sleep tonight?"

"Right there." I pointed to our truck, which by some true miracle was still where we had left it parked. "Mi automobile es tu automobile."

I curled up behind the steering wheel because I was the smaller brother and Carlos stretched his legs sideways across his side of the truck and onto mine. It was the same as when we shared a bed when we were kids: always the feet of Carlos in my face. I pulled my jacket over my ears and tried to sleep. An owl called out in the darkness, once, but then his wife must have told him to go back to sleep.

My phone woke us both, early. I was stiff from lying in the truck of the coyotes under the other migrantes, and now I was double stiff from sleeping in our truck. It was hard to move, but the man was calling to tell us we had to move, right then.

We were already so close to the border there in Nogales that when we met him, he drove me and Carlos and a couple of new pilgrims to a place only five minutes away from the town, a place thick with bushes, and there he told us to hide until he returned.

"I'll be back in two hours." He told us. "We are going to make it, okay?"

The man told us he was just going to go look. He said, "Let me see the way. I want to check..."But then he did not come back. He said was going to make the way for us, but he did not. He just went away. We waited for a long time, then we walked back to Nogales, to our truck. We walked maybe ten minutes to go back. I still had our money in my shoe.

That night we called our wives. We told them we had not made it yet. We did not tell them we had tried twice already. We just told them, "We are waiting and we haven't gone over yet." because if we told them we had tried, they would have said, "No, no. Stop it. You come home."

So we stayed that day in Nogales and the man called to say, "You can make it in a car tomorrow."

But that was what he told us before. Long time after that day, we added up all those times we tried: we tried seven times. The first time was with Ruth and her friend. The second was when we hid like Moses in the bushes and then walked back. The third time, they caught us.

That time the patrol guys did not drive us back over the border and wish us good luck. That time they took us to the big detention.

20
Trish

With one finger, I flipped the hot water taps over two of the deep, white-enameled sinks, squirted soap into the first sink and disinfectant into the second, and then while the sinks were filling, I entertained myself by building towers of cups, skyscrapers of plates and high, rolling silverware hills all the kitchen's scarred wooden drainboard.

My bare feet made soft padding slaps on the cool brown tiles as I walked back and forth between the sinks and the long wooden table where the pastor of this Nogales Methodist church and I had piled the dirty dishes the night before. We'd decided to let ourselves be lured away from the straight and narrow path of good housekeeping by the siren call of songs remembered. He'd started it, belting out a song I'd learned at summer youth camp too many years before to comfortably own up to, but I did.

"I can't believe you know *Methodist Pie*. No one knows that."

I'd reeled backwards and grabbed my chest in cartoon shock, making him grin.

"Well, Trish, I only know enough to sing out lustily for about forty-five seconds and then trail away to pitiful silence after the third line. Sort of like how all of us know exactly one and half verses of every Beatles song."

By *all of us,* he'd meant all of us born to the Beatles generation, though I was pretty sure he owned at least ten years more than my forty-five. I'd gotten to Nogales only three days before to spend two volunteer weeks in his church, so we weren't exactly at the stage of sharing birthdates and zodiac signs yet, but I'd have bet money he was more than just a couple of years older than me—not that that made either of us ready for the rocking chair. I had some silver strands among the copper in my curls I refused to cut no matter how many decades I racked up, but I was handling the long days of work here without having to take naps, wasn't I? And a good thing, too, because neither this church building nor its pastor were either one built for lazing around.

Singing isn't lazing, though, so the Right Reverend Freeman and I had signed off on dish detail until morning in favor of perching on two wooden stools in the kitchen to make a little music. I sang while he played his guitar, leaning in toward his chords with my elbows propped on my knees, my toes curling and uncurling around the top rung of the stool.

I shook my head, but the rest of the song refused to fall into place."Okay, well, I give up; I can't remember the next verse, either, but let's at least end big with the last line."

And we did, in loud unison: *I'm a Methodist 'til I die.*

"Why just the last line?" he'd threaded his question around a deep volley of laughing that had started with the last word we'd bellowed.

"Because I'm an alto. I love how the verse soars up in the middle but then resolves to a nice low note. I'm a big fan of low notes."

"Fair enough. Then let's do 'Dark as a Dungeon' next. It's mostly a bunch of low notes and the whole song is about a low place."

"Preacher, you have no idea how much you're preaching to the choir about coal mining..."

But the front bell had chimed, then, before I had a chance to launch into chapter and verse about the history of coal mining in Kentucky. My singing buddy quickly, but tenderly, laid his guitar on the table and dashed off to see who needed him more than I did.

I heard talking from the front hallway, and the sound of doors opening and shutting, but he didn't come back. Evidently, wayfaring strangers had arrived.

Those strangers would be hungry for breakfast after their late-night arrival, so I needed to get the neglected dishes washed in short order, and that was okay by me—I've always liked washing dishes. It's the kind of job where you can see what you've done. My hands went still in the sudsy water,and the Rev's dimpled face came into my head. I'd bet money he hardly ever got to see the good he was doing in Nogales, bless his generous soul. One thing I'd realized after just a couple of days into my two weeks on volunteer duty was that the best results of good work are all too often the least visible. If Rev was lucky enough to be able to fix a situation in the best way for the people involved, that fix usually allowed both situation and people to disappear: poof; gone. But *gone* was a good thing when staying meant a choice between quick death or slow death. This good man met his people's needs without obvious reward for himself and, I suspected, often without keeping strictly to what was legal. "I know the law, Trish," he'd said to me on my first night here, "but God and I often chat about how the law should be understood."

It had been twenty-five years since my last time in Mexico. Twenty-five school years of fifth-graders stacking up in my memory like presents or punishments, and living at the heart of those years had been one good man—not this Nogales preacher man, but a different good man—but he was now five years gone and consigned to my memories alone. The kids I'd taught the year I came to Puerto Vallarta were also now kids only in my memories. They'd be half-way through their thirties now; Cesar would be halfway through his thirties. I shook my head a little, remembering him. Lordy, I was so young then and such a cocky new teacher, I hope I did right by that boy.

Now here I was back in Mexico again, at long last. I couldn't tell you what had made me say yes to my church's mission team leader this year after a couple of decades of always telling him *thanks, but no thanks* because I'm a staunch non-believer when it comes to proselytizing, but I'd signed on the dotted line. Maybe I felt I owed a debt to a small buy who'd saved my life and won my affection, Whatever my reason, the team members were so stunned by my apparent agreement to do the Lord's work in a foreign land that they hadn't argued for one second when I claimed for myself the plum job of being helper to a Methodist minister in Nogales over hauling bricks or digging wells.

And just maybe it was the good memory of my brief meeting with another Methodist minister that inclined me toward this volunteer job. I was a wee bit edgy, though, when the team dropped me and my suitcase off at the downtown church of this unknown pastor. What if the fates were in a sly mood and had thrown me in with the sort of man of the cloth who'd feel honor-bound to save my immortal soul? I knew nothing about this man other than that he was an American by birth, and his name was Rev. Freeman. But then he'd opened the door and greeted me with a dimpled grin. Some things don't alter with time: I was still a sucker for dimples.

"Welcome. Bienvenido. Let me take your bag. Come in, come in, I guess you're feeling rode-hard and put away wet."

Okay, there was no way a man who talked like that could be the sanctimonious sort. And, to add to the plus side, he was tall. And handsome. The fates had been friendly, after all.

He had stopped halfway through the door with my lone suitcase hanging from his left hand, turned around and looked at me oddly. *Uh oh.*

"They told me your name, but I'm sorry, I've forgotten."

"It's Trish. Trish Tierney."

"And you're a teacher? From Georgia?"

"I am."

"Señora?"

A woman's voice jerked me back to today.

Lordy. I swung around to the kitchen door, startled witless, long curtains of soap suds draping from my arms like lace. A tiny young woman in jeans and a *Mexico City.* T-shirt was hovering in the doorway, obviously at the ready to fade back into the hallway if I gave off any unwelcoming vibes. She was lovely. She'd have been gorgeous, if she'd let herself relax. Even with her face so pinched and wary, she was mighty pretty, but she looked weary, too, which was not surprising, in light of what the Rev. had told me about her right before I'd finally gone to bed.

"She claims to be looking for family here in Nogales, Trish, and that could be true, but I have my suspicions she has a deeper agenda. I generally know a migrant when I see one. I'd bet you money she and her friend are trying to jump the border."

Then he'd shrugged, with a half-grin.

"Of course, I can't bet—it's against rules of my trade—but if I could, I'd win this one, I betcha."

"Señora?"

The girl hadn't moved from her perch in the doorway while I 'd slipped back into my own head again. I grabbed a towel to wipe my hands and arms while I gave her the smile I should have greeted her with.

She nodded toward the sinks, still holding her to her spot.

"I can wash the dishes for you?"

Bless her heart. It wasn't even dawn yet and this girl had not gone to bed before eleven. I knew, because I'd been up past midnight. I'd heard her and her companion making soft settling-in sounds in the room next to mine after Rev. Freeman had talked with them for a while and shown them their room. Then he'd tapped on my door.

"Trish?"

"I'm awake."

I'd jumped to open the door to my room, knowing he wouldn't.

"Sorry to disturb you, but would you mind heating up some leftovers for our guests? I need to talk for a minute with the men who brought them in, and then I'll fetch the food and drop it off at their room."

"Happy to."

And I was. I'm always willing to re-heat meals that someone else has cooked. It's the original cooking that I can't abide. Seems like such a waste of time, two hours of chopping and mixing and steaming just to eat it all in fifteen minutes. What was the point?

Now here it was only a couple of hours after the two women had gone to bed and one of them was up already, and offering to help me with my work. There was no way I was going to tell such a sweet person that one of the reasons I was washing dishes pre-dawn was because I craved some time alone before diving into another communal day in the life of the church.

I waved my dish towel at her in a girly way and motioned for her to join me at the sink..

"Sí, of course. Gracias."

The kitchen's two deep sinks sat side by side along a long windowless wall: one sink was for washing and the other was for dipping the dishes in a rinse solution to sterilize them. I was quite certain the rinse disinfectant was aging the skin on my hands at the rate of one year per dish-washing. I held out the first dripping plate to her.

"Me llamo Trish. Como te llamas?"

"Me llamo Ruth. I speak a little English."

"Oh? Where did you learn English? In school?"

I fished around in the deep sink for another plate, trying to avoid grabbing onto a knife blade. The sun was just beginning to whisper in through the open back door and streak along the white kitchen walls. Every kitchen I'd seen in Mexico had been white, and almost starkly plain, but always with a heavy wooden door opening on to a courtyard lush with flowers of deep oranges and yellows and reds. The early sun was softly highlighting this kitchen's back door flowers , zinnia-like flowers I could see from the corner of my eye, and the light was edging indoors across the brown tile floor. I looked down at the pale river of light as it neared myfeet and Ruth's feet next to mine. Ruth was as barefoot as I was. I was starting to like this woman, for sure.

Ruth nodded her head slightly, matching her answer to my question.

"Sí, I learned a little English in school, but also where I lived."

Now that was odd. I would have said "at home." not "where I lived." I turned away from the sink to look at her when I spoke, holding my hands up in front of me, dripping suds.

"And I learned a little Spanish in *my* school, Ruth. Well, actually, I learned a lot, but it's hard to keep it in your head ready for conversation if you don't practice speaking it. And it's hard to have a chance to practice speaking Spanish when you spend your days teaching English."

"You are a teacher?"

"Guilty as charged."

Ruth raised her eyebrows just enough to let me know she didn't have a clue what I meant.

"Sorry, Ruth. That's an American idiom. It means yes."

Ruth looked up from under her eyebrows and smiled the first true smile I'd seen from her.

"You *talk* like a teacher, Trish. I think you must love the teaching."

"Again: guilty as charged."

We both grinned, and I leaned sideways to give Ruth a friendly shoulder-bump. We didn't say anything else while we did the dishes, but now our silence was the good stillness of two women at home in each other's company. Reverend Freeman stepped in to the kitchen just as we were finishing up.

He stopped for a minute, just looking. He told me later he was thinking to himself as he watched us: *This is what Christian community is. Nothing more than this.*

"Ladies. Good morning."

The big-shouldered pastor had a way of booming rather than speaking his words. It was oddly comforting. He was a good height, six-two at least, with a head of thick black curls, and a strong back that spoke of a long history with two-by-fours and bags of cement. Every time I'd sat down to confer with him since I arrived, I'd felt like I was sitting on the floor of my grandparents' house leaning back against my daddy's knees while my tall Daddy and all my taller uncles rumbled with deep laughter. This guy had that same kind of easy manliness about him. Ruth and I turned as one to smile at him.

"Trish, I see you have some fine help in making the galley shipshape this morning." He turned toward Ruth. "Ruth, perhaps you could get things going for breakfast while Trish and I chat for a minute?"

"Sí, Padre, of course." Ruth laid her towel on the counter and moved toward the stove to start water boiling for breakfast eggs.

I picked up the towel Ruth had just laid down and dried my hands with it. Then I wrinkled my nose at her and gave her another small shoulder-bump before I followed the Rev down the long hallway to his office. Plopping like a teenager into the chair closest to his desk, I stretched my legs out in front of me and crossed my right foot over my left. Hmm. I really did need to re-do the polish on my toenails.

A bus rumbling past the window behind Rev. Freeman's desk made me look up from my toenail critique just as he spoke.

"Trish we have a little problem this morning."

I sat forward, pulling my chipped-polish toes underneath my chair.

"Already? It isn't even seven o'clock."

"Problems don't keep time tables. Or maybe they do, seeing as they seem to consistently come at awkward hours. Do you know about the Casa?" I pinched her lips together and thought for a second. I shook my head slowly.

"I don't think so. What is it?"

"It's a place for recent deportees to go for a two meals a day, or basic medical help, clothes to replace the ones they may have left behind when the Border Patrol got them—such as that. It's run by a tough-as-nails nun and a bunch of fiercely loyal volunteers. Some of the volunteers are deportees themselves, living here in Nogales on hold until they can find some way to move forward or to go back."

Rev. Freeman stretched his shoulders and rolled his head until his neck gave a little crack. I wondered if he had been to bed at all.

"Well, anyway, usually every weekday at least one humanitarian group walks across from Nogales, Arizona, to help with everything but cooking the meals, which frees the nun and her helpers to tend to the food. Sometime last night, though, there was a bit of trouble with a couple of drug cartel guys—they exchanged words with one of the volunteers, and I assure you these were not words of support for the Casa's mission. The sister called me, early, to tell me she had called the woman in charge of today's volunteer group from Green Valley to ask them not to come today; it's just too volatile this morning. Sister says she needs time to figure out what to do. But, Trish, there are ninety migrants lined up at the Casa right now, waiting for breakfast and attention. Many of them need their feet looked at. Some of them need clothing. Sister is sure at least two or three will need help buying a bus ticket home, because any money they had was stolen from them."

I put her hand up to stop his talking. I needed to get things straight.

"Who gives them money for these bus tickets? Do *you* buy the tickets for them?"

I wasn't against arranging a way home for these tired and discouraged folks, but I was not about to blithely agree to Rev. Freeman spending any more of his own meager salary. I'd been working with him only a couple of days, but that was long enough for me to know good and well he gave away a hefty chunk of his paycheck every month. I knew all about giving in to the temptation to use my own money to buy supplies for my students, so far be it from me to judge, but I'd learned the hard way there had to be a cut-off point. Not even pastors can live on faith alone.

"No, Trish, I don't diminish my munificent pay at the bus station. There's a fund. A grant-based organization provides funds to help buy bus tickets for deportees. The volunteers at the Casa do the legwork and the paperwork, that's all."

"Well, okay, then. Let's go doctor some feet and spend some granted monies."

Rev. Freeman started toward the door, but then stopped and looked down.

"Feet, Trish, look at your own feet."

I looked down, then up, and grinned at him.

"Be right back with shoes on."

It was quick three-block walk to the Casa. At first glance, the Casa looked like another of the open-air restaurants in any tourist town where the weather tends toward hot or hotter, with the wall nearest the sidewalk being only a half-wall open from table level to ceiling so the diners could see the scenery and catch a breeze, and a wide overhanging roof to shade the diners while they ate. Diners in this particular establishment, though, had to look out through a screen of chain-link fencing running from sidewalk to roof level. A few trees and some climbing flowers softened the prison yard look.

Out on the sidewalk, the Casa's half-wall was almost completely covered over by a throng of men, women and children standing and sitting, waiting to be allowed in for breakfast. Most of the people waiting wore backpacks, and every single adult had a grey woolen rolled-up blanket under an arm or laid down somewhere nearby. Almost no one was moving, and even the smallest children were not talking at all. The long, still row of migrants looked to me like a living mural. I felt shy, all of a sudden. I also felt tall, and exceedingly white.

The quickest fix for awkwardness, I've found, is to get to work, and the reverend had promised me there would be work a'plenty inside.

A middle-aged Mexican woman was stacking just-cooked tortillas onto paper plates. I grabbed two of the plates and set them at the ends of the nearest table. Then I went back for two more and two more and two more. Today apparently, was to be my day for fixing breakfast, yet never actually eating any. The cook handed me two big bowls of eggs and chiles to pass around the three long tables.

"Señora?"

A young girl I'd smiled at on the steps had come in with her little brother—I guessed he was her brother—balanced on one hip. I smiled at them both and the little boy ducked his head into the hollow of his sister's thin shoulder.

"Buenos dias. Quieres a comer?"

The girl gave her head a half shake. No, food was not what she wanted.

"Ma'am. I speak English. I live in Phoenix, or I did until they catch us."

I handed over the bowls of food in my hands to a man at the end of the table, so I could put my hand on the girl's shoulder.

"Let's sit down over there until breakfast is ready, and pet the cat."

Because there *was* a cat, a calico, standing hopefully behind the cook, wearing the cautious air of an animal who has been taught what its boundaries should be. The three of us and the cat sat on the top step of dining area. The girl shifted her brother to her lap. He was maybe three, and shy in the way of toddlers with strangers, but he was already warming up to a bit of eye flirting with me, so I did a Harpo Marx with my eyebrows at him while I ran my fingertips along the cat's spine. Boy and cat both seemed delighted.

"What is your name?"

"Amalia. Señora, you are American?"

"Yes, I am, Amalia. I am here in Nogales for a couple of weeks helping the padre."I nodded toward Rev. Freeman, "in his church. You said you live in Phoenix?"

"I did."

"Amalia, do you want to tell me what happened?"

Amalia looked at me and in the way of all pre-teens everywhere, launched right into her story with no fanfare or drama because to the pre-teen mind, anything that happens in their world is dramatic and inherently accompanied by fanfare. In Amalia's case, she was right.

"Um, I live in Arizona eleven years, but my grandpa was too sick and I never met him and I wanted to met him. And my grandma had cancer and I wanted to met her, too. So I went to Mexico with my parents and then my grandpa died so when we came here we tried to cross the border again and we couldn't. And they got us."

"When was this? How long ago?"

"Um, like Sunday. In the morning."

And now it was Wednesday. It doesn't take long for your world to change. I could say Amen to that.

"Amalia, you said they got you—how did they get you?"

"We were in the place called Ajo and we were gonna get to the reserve for the Indians. When it got dark, we were gonna try. I was laying down. I was laid down under the trees. We were sleeping and then we woked up and then when we saw them we just laid down again."

"Saw them? You mean the Border Patrol?"

"Yeah. I just saw them and thought everything was over."

I was still petting the cat and peek-a-booing with the toddler, but inside, my head was shaking itself and protesting that no child not yet twelve years old should ever have to say such a thing about her life: *I just thought everything was over.*

"Where are you going to go, Amalia?"

Amalia shrugged one shoulder. Her long fine black hair flopped forward when she shrugged. She was wearing dangly silver earrings with a tiny cross at the bottom of each earring.

"To Michoacan. My mom is from there. Ma'am? If you talk to any kids like me when you get back to America, tell them not to try it. Tell them it isn't worth it."

"Not even to see your grandpa?"

Amalia hugged her brother and leaned her head down to rest against the top of his head. He shook his head to make her move—he was having fun with the lady.

"No. Tell them just don't do it. It's too hard."

I should have said something wise and wonderful then. I'm a teacher. I should have been able to give Amalia the words to help her find where to go next.

"Should don't always come, Teacher," Cesar would say.

I stood up, brushed the dirt from the seat of my pants, and walked away.

21

Trish

The first thing I wanted to do when I got back to the church around noon was wash my face. Not that the work had been hard. All they'd asked me to do was pass food along the tables, clear the dishes and put out new dishes for the second wave of polite, hungry people waiting down on the sidewalk. I'd cleared the tables after that second seating and laid out donated clothing for the guests to take what they needed, which was kind of fun. At the toiletries table, though, I found myself having to tell one young woman after another: *no, lo siento, no tenemos tampons,* while I smiled apologetically. Every time I paused for a second, I had to push away the dawning certainty that a plate of food and a pair of used jeans would make little difference in the long run. By the end of the morning, I believed in my weary bones that my best effort had added nothing more to these people's lives than one thread in the ragged selvedge of nothing at all.

Shake it off, Trish. It did no one any good at all for me to feel sorry for myself. Standing there at my room's tiny white porcelain sink, I dried my face and then made a conscious point of grinning inanely at my reflection in the mirrorbecause when I was fourteen and taking myself way too seriously, Mama used to tell me to do that, and she was right— making a face at myself always knocked any self-absorption right out the bedroom window.

Mama. I flung my hand into the air. Sheesh, I hadn't written a letter to Mama yet. This afternoon I would, for sure. Right after I got some food in my stomach.

"Ruth?" I knocked on their door. Maybe they hadn't eaten, either. We could go together.

"Ruth? Are you there? Want to grab some lunch with me?"

Where the heck were they?

Double-stepping down the long hallway to the kitchen, I stuck my head in and scanned the room, a big square room with two tables down the middle.

Nope, no Ruth there, obviously. I took it a little slower going back down the hallway, keeping my left hand flat against the left wall and my right hand against the right wall to use my hands as pivots when I leaned a little ways into each doorway, peering into one room after another for Ruth and her friend.

I really, really wanted to tell Ruth about my morning. Where the heck was she? And—here's a though—why did I care? That stopped me for a minute. I mean, I'm the kind of solitary soul who hugs any alone moment to myself like a blessing, but apparently something about being in Mexico was making me hungry for friends.

A door opened and I jumped, but it was the custodian, not Ruth. This was weird. I mean, how many places can you hide in a church? I swung in for a peek into yet another room that did not have Ruth in it, and then another, until I was all out of rooms to look in, except for Rev. Freeman's office and the bathroom tucked between my bedroom and the room where Ruth and her friend had slept the night before.

Our sleeping area's layout was clever, if potentially tricky: the two bedrooms flanked a shared bathroom, so each bedroom had its own door into the bathroom, with slide bolts inside and outside. The idea was that I could slide the inside bolt on Ruth's door for privacy while I used the facilities and then I'd unbolt the lock so Ruth could get in to use the bathroom when she needed to. This plan worked well so long as no sleep-befuddled bathroom buddy (that would be me) forgot the final step, thus leaving her neighbor locked out of toilet usage until morning.

I was pretty sure Ruth wasn't in the bathroom because I'd not heard any noises while I was washing my face, but maybe we'd somehow missed passing each other in the hall and she was in there now. I leaned against my side of the bathroom door with my ear against the wood, listening for washing or flushing noises.

Nope. Nothing.

I eased my doorknob around, leaning the weight of my hand against it just enough that it opened. No one was in the bathroom. I stepped inside and turned the knob on Ruth's door, ready to jump back with apologies, knocking softly with my left hand as I called out.

"Ruth?"

No answer. I looked in. Her room was exceedingly neat and empty. I whipped my head around toward the hall.

"Rev. Freeman?"

Now I was yelling, but there was no one else to ask.

"In my office, Trish."

His voice carried like a thunder clap down the hallway.

I started talking to him a good ten steps before I reached the door to his office.

"Do you know where Ruth and her friend went?." ending my question at the exact moment I plopped so hard into the chair across from his desk that the word *went* whooshed from my chest sounding like *huh-whent*. I curled one leg up under the other and settled into waiting for him to make things right.

"Ah, I'm sorry, Trish, but they left a little while ago. I tried to get them to stay until you came back, but they said they couldn't."

My hands dropped from the arms of the chair onto my lap and lay there, palms up, like I was waiting for communion bread. I shook my head just a little. This couldn't be right.

"They left? You mean, for good? Where did they go?"

"They're adults, Trish. It's none of my business where they go or what they do. They did tell me they had gotten a call from a friend who could take them where they needed to go. Oh, and Ruth wanted me to tell you she was sorry she couldn't talk with you more. You are a kind woman, she said."

He smiled at me, the sort of smile you give someone when there's nothing else you can offer.

"I think they must have gone with the two men who brought them here, " he continued while he fiddled with the papers, and then he looked at me from under his eyebrows. "They were good men, Trish, I could tell, so I'm sure the ladies are in safe hands. We should just pray for traveling mercies for them all, and hope they find some way to let us know when they get to where they want to be."

Very judiciously worded, I thought.

"I can't claim praying as my forte, Rev, but I'll take a stab at talking to God if it'll keep Ruth safe. I like her."

"I know you do."

The big guy stood and started toward the door, flapping his hand in my direction as he walked.

"It's lunchtime, Maestra. Follow me to the kitchen. I make a mean peanut butter sandwich. You can tell me what you thought of the Casa while I slap some sandwiches together."

Ha. It was funny how here in Mexico, Americans called me Maestra, while the Spanish-speakers called me Teacher. I loved that quirky kind of stuff– like the fact that I was about to be fed peanut butter and jelly, the staff of my Georgia childhood, by a good-hearted American Methodist minister in a Mexican border town.

I pulled out a stool at the long wooden table and sat, hooking my toes on the chair rung. Still hadn't re-polished those toenails, had I?

While the good reverend slapped some sandwiches together in a very male manner, I told him about Amalia and her brother, and about how very American that pre-teen had been.

"But how will she make it in Mexico, Rev? She isn't the least bit Mexican."

He didn't even try to answer, which made me like him all the more, so I switched to telling about the man born in Puebla who'd left his Alabama home of twenty years to visit his aging parents. He'd tried four times to cross back over and was ready to quit trying. He talked about his work as a cook in a Mexican restaurant in Montgomery and about his wife and daughter waiting for him there. He might never see them again, he believed.

"But your daughter was born in the States," I'd reasoned with him, "so she could come to Puebla to visit you."

"She is American." The man had looked at me as I had no common sense. "Why would she do that?"

I stopped for a minute, remembering.

"But the neat part of the morning—and this is what I wanted to tell Ruth about—was the cows."

Rev. Freeman raised one dark, bushy eyebrow, Mr. Spock-like.

"Four cows broke loose from a truck that was taking them to an American slaughter house. All four roamed back and forth through the checkpoint for fifteen or twenty minutes while the border patrol guys got madder and madder and everybody watching cheered them on. We weren't really sure if we were rooting for the cows to make it to America—I mean, after all, whoopee, they all gonna die there—or for them to stay in Mexico, or for them to just keep crossing back and forth without passports. It was a cow version of thumbing their noses at border regulations: *nanny, nanny boo-boo* in cow talk."

Rev. Freeman honored the story with a long moment, then pushed with his left arm against the slatted wooden arm of the chair to tiltback the chair and himself ,and rocked there, resting his weight on his left elbow. His right hand was up at his chin with his thumb tucked just under his jaw and the first finger curled over his upper lip. I was starting to know this was how he always sat when he when he didn't have to think about how he was sitting.

A hot patch of sunshine from the open back door moved cross my legs, my dark blue cotton skirt soaking up the morning's first warmth like it was thirsty for sun. I glanced toward the door. It must be getting on towards one or one-thirty; time to close the door to keep out the afternoon heat. I scooted my chair back and abandoned my sandals so I could walk barefoot across the cool tiles. My feet were getting really brown from Mexican sun and Mexican dust and my neglected toenails still carried some patches of polish as deeply blue as that April Mexican sky.

There was a man sitting just outside the kitchen door on one of the flat terrace stones that paved the courtyard, leaning his back against the wall. I saw the top of his head first, a head thick with glossy black curls. My daddy had had hair exactly like that. The curly head's owner turned toward the movement of my stepping into the courtyard and then down toward my feet which were just inches from his eyes, slouched low as he was against the kitchen wall. He didn't look like he was sitting that way because he was tired, though; he just looked at ease. He struck me on first glance as a man who was almost always at ease. He stared for a few seconds at my toes and then he looked up as a grin started on the left side of his face and spread all the way across, lifting his cheeks up toward eyes that were slightly slanted, as if a Chinaman had snuck into his family tree some long-ago night.

"Hello, Teacher."

What the heck? I hadn't been in Nogales long enough for anyone outside of the people in the church and maybe a couple of people at the Casa to even know I was here, much less know how I earned my keep back home. Or at least, I'd been assuming no one here knew much about me, but maybe the small town grapevine worked even faster in Mexico than in Georgia.

"Hola, señor. Si, I *am* a teacher. My name is Trish. Como estás?"

The man stood, brushing the dust from his grey work pants with a couple of big, swiping slaps, and then scrubbing his hands together to clean the dust from them before he held out his right hand.

"I am fine, Teacher. And I know your name. You not remember me? I am Cesar. I was your student when I was a kid. You taught me English, but I probably not talk so good now so maybe you not want people to know you taught me? That why you act like you not know me?"

His grin grew even bigger as he said this, a grin proclaiming what nonsense it was that someone might not want to know Cesar.

I needed to give this man an answer, but I'd been struck still and dumb. How do you respond to impossibility?

"Cesar? Oh, no, but that doesn't make sense."

"Sense don't always win, Teacher."

"*Doesn't*, Cesar. Not *don't*. And how did you know it was me? Do I still look that much the same?"

Cesar nodded his head toward my feet.

"I never know nobody else with blue toes, Teacher."

"*Anybody* else, Cesar, not *nobody*."

He hadn't answered the question about my looks, I noticed. As to how Cesar had changed, now that he was standing up where I could really look at him, I recognized a lot of the little boy he'd been. His hair was the same bed of tight coils and he had grown up only tall enough to be as compact as his indio grandfather. I wondered if the grandfather was still alive.

"Cesar, what are you doing here? Oh, I'm sorry—it's so good to see you. But what are you doing here? Can you come in?"

"Sure, Teacher. I can come in and tell you what's up, but I gotta wait a minute for my stupid brother. He out on the street smoking."

Now I knew for good and all that this was my Cesar. I smiled a conspiratorial smile.

"Oh, is your brother still stupid?"

"Yeah, yeah, Teacher. He never got no better."

Cesar scratched his head, looking at me from under his eyebrows, still grinning, and corrected himself.

"He never got *any* better."

I smelled a smoker behind me, turned, and came face to chest with Carlos. He stood taller than my five-nine: six foot-two, at least. His face and his body were as long and bony as his little boy self had been, but it had all come together well—he was a handsome man. When I gave him a quick hug around his waist, he froze.

"Hey, my brother, this is Teacher. You remember her from when we was kids?"

Carlos relaxed, smiled a slow smile.

"Oh, yeah. How you doin', Teacher? You here on the vacation?"

I shook my head.

"No. but come on inside and I can tell you what I'm doing here and you can tell me the same."

Rev, Freeman was standing in the kitchen doorway when I turned, his white-shirted shoulders nearly touching either side of the door frame. I almost smacked into him, which would not have been a bad thing.

"Trish, I see you've met Ruth's friends. Everyone come in, come in. Have some coffee."

"Rev, what are you talking about?"

But now he was waving his hand vaguely in the direction of the kitchen, his attention focused on ushering Cesar and his brother to the table. While all three men took their first couple of swallows of good Columbian coffee, which to judge by the looks of bliss on their faces, was settling as smooth as sorghum into their bellies, I started water boiling to make myself a cup of manzanilla tea. I'd as soon drink swamp water as drink coffee, but I needed something.

The Rev hadn't spoken a word since he'd greeted the guys. The good pastor's body language was telling me not to say anything until he did, so I stirred three spoons of sugar into my tea and waited, content with my drink. Ridiculously sweet tea was my greatest vice, or at least the greatest sin I was willing to own up to publicly.

Besides, the waiting gave me time to study my former student. Cesar's hands around his coffee cup were still small and square, muscled in the way of someone who has long made use of his hands for hard work. While I looked at him, he looked at his brother, and then across the rough wood of the table to where Rev. Freeman was sitting so much at ease with his coffee and with the moment that you'd have thought time was an inheritance he'd just come into. The pastor's stillness was an open door Cesar walked right through.

"Padre, are Ruth and her friend okay? We just came to check on them and then while I was waiting for my brother to smoke his cigarette, Teacher came outside. She tell you we know each other when I was a kid?"

I whirled around and spit a question at poor Cesar.

"What do you mean, are they okay? Don't you know? And how do you know them, anyway?"

So much for my life-long reputation as the calmest port in any storm.

Rev. Freeman reached over and touched me, just barely, on my hand. He looked first at Cesar, then at Carlos.

"Are the ladies not with you? They told us they had friends who were taking them to where they needed to go. I assumed Ruth was referring to the two of you."

He kept his finger lightly against my skin while he talked—an infuriatingly effective restraint.

But then I couldn't help but flap away a little of my righteous indignation, because Cesar was looking as serious as I ever remembered seeing him. Even when I'd been bitten by the snake, his face had been not so much worried, as animated with purpose. Just now, though, it looked burdened, with a dark undertone of hopelessness ready to jump up and take top billing.

"Padre, Teacher, I don't know where they are. Carlos and me, we tell them we gonna come back today to see them. They supposed to wait for us 'cause they don't know nobody else but us. You tellin' me they left with somebody?"

Rev. Freeman nodded his head. Cesar shook his own head somberly.

"This not good, Padre. This not good."

I looked around the room at all of us sitting there, just sitting, because we hadn't a clue where we should go once we stood up.

"They're for sure not here," I told the others, mostly just to say something that would move us into the next moment. Rev. Freeman nodded.

"Maybe we should start to widen our circle of places where we know the women are not."

Cesar nodded, too, and slapped his arm around his brother's shoulders.

"Me and Carlos hit the streets to ask but not ask, you know what I mean?"

"Trish, get your shoes on and walk with me to the Casa,"

Rev. Freeman stopped on our way out the door to whisper a quick word to the church custodian who threw a look toward our little search party, narrowed his eyes, gave a sharp nod, and then went to sweeping as if the floor had offended him.

When we got to The Casa, all was quiet. The morning meal had long since ended, the dishes cleared away, and it was not yet time to start preparing the second meal they offered each day to deportees. A few men dozed on the sidewalk with their backs against the wall of the Casa exactly the same way I'd found Cesar at the church, except these men had shoved grey blanket rolls between the small of their backs and the wall, to cushion their spines. Amalia had told me one humanitarian group gave these blankets to each and every migrant who came through the center, and that when any of the aid groups found someone's stuff dropped in the desert because the border patrol had picked them up or because "something else happen to them." the volunteers would take the blankets home to wash them and pass along to the next person who got picked up.

I sat down on the step where Amalia had told me her story and waited while Rev. Freeman talked with the nun who kept the center running. The Casa's cat roused herself from an afternoon nap and stretched her way over to greet me, slooooowly extending her front legs out as far as they would go, opening her mouth in a wide cat yawn, then stretching her hind legs nearly flat to the floor, giving off a little foot quiver at the end of each stretch. She repeated the whole dance figure three times until it brought her to my side, where I gave her head a good scratch, mindful of the honor bestowed on me.

"No, Padre."

I jerked up my head when one of the nuns spoke.

Near the sink where volunteers washed dishes, a nun was shaking her head. Rev. Freeman said something else to her, but I couldn't hear. Another negative head shake from the nun. Rev. Freeman let out a very soft sigh, then laid his hand on the nun's shoulder for a moment. She reached up and placed her hand on top of his. No heads were bowed and nothing more was said by either of them, but I knew a prayer when I saw one happening. I watched Rev. Freeman give the nun's shoulder a fierce squeeze before he took his hand away. It was a squeeze that meant: *Okay, now to get to work.* The nun nodded and walked back to her office at the rear of the Casa.

If walking could be considered work, then I'd spoken right. We walked miles and miles and miles that afternoon. By the time the Cathedral bells rang for evening mass, I could have given directions like a native: to the bus station, to every church, and to any of several million small cafés and street-side stalls where evidently more than food or tourist trinkets were provided to those who had the need and the knowledge and the dinero.

We'd looped past the small park near the mural of Don Hidalgo so many times the old men sitting in the shade around the fountain finally stopped looking up from their chess boards when we passed by, and the aguas frescas vendor handed each of us a free cup ofhorchata.

The year might have been only halfway into April, but as we walked the afternoon heat grew and grew until I could have drawn a picture of it. I would have used a grey crayon for my drawing, not red, with only some orange highlights, because the heat seemed to me more likea shroud than a fire. It was a grey veil that drifted down with the advancing day and slowly smothered me as I trudged. The orange highlights in my drawing would have been the Nogales sun licking at my exposed skin with little tongues that seared flesh away with each lick.

Or maybe I was just a pampered American weenie. No, to be fair to myself,

I was in no way pampered. And the heat *was* an enemy, a real one, even though the Mexican people had learned to live with it in the same way we all learn to live with our environmental foes. I wondered, though, how anyone would fight against such deadly heat if they had no weapons of clothing or shade? If Ruth were out in the desert with no way to escape the sun, what would she do?

"Trish? Trish?"

Rev. Freeman had stopped walking and was waving both hands in front of my face.

"Trish, where are you?"

I focused on his easy-to-look-at face.

"Sorry, just fighting incipient heat stroke. Don't mind me. If I collapse in a puddle of melted flesh and bone, step over me and keep looking for the ladies. The street cleaner will sweep my remains to the curb in the morning."

"Will do. Or as an alternative." the preacher nodded his head in the direction of the tortas stand, "we could get something to eat before we head back to the church. Maybe some food and a sit in the shade will knit your flesh and bone together."

"We can't quit. We have to keep looking."

But the pastor was already pulling out a chair for me at the tortas stand, and, good southern girl that I was, I fell into step with his gentlemanly gesture. We leaned back in our chairs to shout our orders to the cook on the other side of the counter, and then we turned back around to face each other again.

He shook his head at me in just the same way I've been known to shake mine at a stormy ten-year-old.

"Trish, we're certainly not quitting, but we've done all we can do right now. We've asked around; we've eliminated the likely spots they might have gone; we've left word on the street that we're looking for Ruth and her friend. If anyone we've spoken to today knows anything, they will find a way to tell us. Or someone else will tell us for them."

"So what's next?"

The cook set our tortas before us, swaddled in wax paper and nestled in red plastic baskets, and we paused our conversation briefly to pay proper respect. I was so hungry I decided those tortas in their beds might be the most seductive sight ever presented to me, with the possible exception of one memorable afternoon involving a guy in cut-off Levis and bare feet.

Rev. Freeman ate half of his first torta in two bites before he answered me.

"What's next is to go back to the church for the evening. It's late, I have some work in my office that must be finished today, and we're both tired. And besides, Cesar and Carlos will be coming there at some point to tell us what they've found out. I'll make a phone call to a lady I know, too. She's the point of contact for one of the humanitarian aid groups that comes to work at the Casa each week, the Good Shepherds. You'll like Joy. If our ladies haven't shown up by tomorrow, I'll ask Joy to arrange for you to ride along on a desert search with the Shepherds."

"A desert search? Why the desert?"

Rev. Freeman wiped his mouth.

"Trish, if they aren't here in Nogales, I'd bet money they've jumped the border and are somewhere in the desert. If they had decided simply to take a bus back home, they would have told me so."

He was right, of course. I hated it when what was right was the answer you most wanted to be wrong.

The custodian was still there when we got back to the church. He rose from the pew where he'd been sitting and stood looking at Rev. Freeman, waiting. The pastor shook his head, *no*. The custodian sat down again and stared across the sanctuary to the cross behind the pulpit. His lips began to move. I was glad not to be God that night. I would not have wanted to hear the questions this man was asking his God.

22
Trish

Dear Mama,

I may have to stop writing mid-sentence if the power goes out. We're having a wham-doozy of a storm, but I'm all snuggled in safe and sound inside this big stone building. I'm tired, but it's a justified tired. I spent the morning helping at a deportee center run by a drill sergeant of a nun. The center is actually a mission of a chapter of Benedictines out of New York, but it's the nun and her crew of volunteers who lay down the elbow grease. In fact, the main reason I was there this morning was because of a snafu that left the Casa without their usual Tuesday morning volunteers from a retirement community up the road a ways in Arizona. The nun has a couple of locals who help with the cooking and the dishes, but she needed help setting out the food and such as that, so the good reverend and I walked over first thing—it's only a couple of blocks away.

I can't really call what I did this morning "'work": playing with the Casa's cat, giving food to hungry people (you'll notice they did NOT ask me to help with the cooking), and talking with a couple of the guests, including a young girl who was ethereally lovely in the way of many girls on the cusp of turning into teenagers. How-some-ever, I did manage to work up enough of a sweat that I took a spit bath as soon as I got back to the church and I've just now had a much-needed shower after spending the afternoon helping the pastor run an errand that involved intimate association with the afternoon heat (no, I am not sunburned). Showering in my bathroom's pre-fab shower stall is a lot like bathing inside a Pringles can.

So now I'm clean and wearing a tie-dyed T-shirt and jeans. I doubt this will come as a news flash to you, seeing as how my not-in-school attire almost always consists of a tie-dyed shirt and jeans. You know me—I like to feel comfortable in what I put on of a morning, and then I like to forget about how I look for the rest of the day. The only hazard associated with this attitude is the very real danger of forgetting to wear something vital for propriety, simply because I feel so comfortable without it.

I stopped writing and gave myself a quick propriety check. Yep. Good to go.

And then the lights went out.

Fumbling for my flashlight among the books and lip gloss and coins on the desk, I finally wrapped my fingers around its cold metal handle, clicked the ON button, and set off down the hall to find another human. I'd brought my flashlight with me to Mexico not because I thought they didn't have flashlights south of the border, but because I never travel anywhere without a flashlight and tea bags. I'd brought tea bags, too, but they wouldn't light my way down the hall.

Rev. Freeman met me walking up to the hall toward his office as he was walking down to the kitchen. I twirled in a 180 degree turn and fell into step with him.

"Good," he said . "I don't have to come find you. It may be a while before the power comes back on. Let's make a fire in the fireplace and wait for the guys to come back."

I held the flashlight under my chin so he could see the wry face I was making.

"A fire. You know, Rev, this afternoon I would have said a roaring fire sounded about as appealing as a Novocain-less root canal, but now I can't think of anything nicer."

Well, I could, but not anything I'd confess to this man of the cloth. In the kitchen, we plundered around for altar candles and matches, lit the candles and held them dripping over paper plates until there was a puddle of hot wax we could anchor the candles in. Voila: candlestick holders. Thusly, we lit our way to the community room and set up a small circle of pairs of folding chairs: one chair to sit in and a facing one to plop our weary feet onto. We left two sets of chairs empty for when Cesar and Carlos would join us.

We left. Join us. I snuck an assessing glance over toward Rev. Freeman. When had this man and me become a *we*, an *us*?

"Reverend, tell me what I'll be doing on this search tomorrow, if it comes to that."

Rev. Freeman reached down for the cup of coffee he'd brought in with him and set it on the floor beside his chair. I wished I'd thought to make myself a cup of Earl Grey before the power went out.

"Well, let's see, Trish. What do you know about the humanitarian groups that work with deportees?"

"Little or nothing. Just the name of one militaristic-sounding group that makes the news sometimes."

He rolled his eyes—I'd swear he did. So... the good pastor had biases like the rest of us. But then he shook his head one quick shake, as if he could shake himself free of failings.

"The group you'll go with tomorrow is nothing like that. These folks are mostly retirees who live in a somewhat upscale retirement community half an hour or so north of here. A lot of them, maybe as many as half of them, are snowbirds who'll be leaving at the end of this month for their summer homes. They're a mixed bag, but I'd say the majority of them are retired professionals of one sort or another. They are well-fixed enough not to have to worry about working part-time to supplement their Social Security checks, and they're well-educated and deep-thinking enough to care about putting their time and income to a worthwhile end.

"Joy, the woman I mentioned who unofficially heads up the group, is going to meet us at Starbucks so she can introduce you to the two or three Shepherds you'll be going on the search with. They always leave from this shopping center, I think partly so they can indulge in some good coffee before they leave on a mission of mercy."

He held up his now-empty cup in a virtual toast to their good sense.

"So, the people you'll be riding with will have a van there. They generally take along some basic medical supplies and some jugs of water in the back of the van. Oh, and a satellite phone. The phone has a sort of GPS locator on it so they can use it if they get confused about where they are in the desert."

I noticed he avoided using the word "lost."

"And it will email the van's location to a designated address so someone else can know where you are."

I interrupted him.

"But why don't they just use their cell phones? No signal?"

Rev. Freeman gave his head a tilt to one side, raised his eyebrows a little.

"Probably not, but that's a moot point because you can't take your cell phone into the desert. If the drug cartel sees someone talking on a cell phone, they tend to shoot the talker through the window of the vehicle."

Ah. I made a mental note to myself: yet another thing not to mention to Mama when I finished writing that letter to her. If this keeps up, she's going to think I spent my whole time here doing nothing but sweating and bathing, with the occasional cute cat episode thrown in.

"That reminds me, Trish: You should leave your purse here tomorrow. They recommend that you not bring anything with you except your driver's license and some money for lunch. Wear something loose-fitting; it's cooler. And take a hat and a long-sleeved shirt."

"For protection from the sun?"

"The hat, yes, and that's partly the reason for the shirt, but it's mainly to protect your arms from being ripped to shreds by cactus."

Ripped to shreds: now that's the kind of words a girl truly loves to hear in regards to her plans for the next day.

"So, Rev. How long will I be gone?"

"As long as it takes, Trish. Or until it gets dark, whichever comes first."

We sat staring at the fire, not talking. The rest of the cavernous church building was deep in dark, and the rain was a ceaseless roar at every window, but our little clustering of chairs was tight enough to fit within the half-circle of light the fire gave out.

"Rev?"

"Hmmm?"

"What about the Border Patrol? How do they feel about groups like this and what they're doing?"

He drew in a long breath and let it out as a soft sigh that made me realize how tired he must be. I felt bad about making him talk, and I found myself reaching over through the near-dark to rest my hand on his knee, but I caught myself, stretched both arms wide and yawned loudly, as if a having good stretch had been all I'd set out to do.

He sat forward and gave his spine a little crack before he answered. A log in the fire crackled in response.

"It depends on the group. The Shepherds have a good working relationship with the Border Patrol, in general, partly because they don't break the rules. They'll tell you all this tomorrow, I'm sure, but basically the people who work as part of the Good Shepherds agree to not give illegal aid or assistance of any sort. For example, if they find a migrant who needs water or medical attention, they will provide that, but then they notify the Border Patrol that they have an undocumented migrant in their presence. "

This was probably going to make me sound naïve, but I had to ask it anyway:

"Doesn't it just kill the volunteers to have to turn people over to the law? I mean, once you've given someone water and doctored their feet and talked with them and seen how defeated they look, wouldn't everything in you want to help them reach their goal? Wouldn't you just ache to give them at least that much, knowing that you could?"

Rev. Freeman sat up in his chair, set his feet on the floor and leaned close enough for me to smell his coffee breath.

"The first and most vital lesson to learn about humanitarian work, Trish, is the difference between *need*, and *want*. There are a lot of wanderers out there in the desert who need the life-saving help groups like the Shepherds provide. Sure, the Shepherds may want to give more than is required for basic sustenance, but they need to obey the law so the law will allow them to keep doing the work they do. Would you have them help two or three migrants make it into the U.S. only to have the Shepherds be shut down for illegal activity? Who could they help then?

I was already shaking my head. Of course not.

"But it must be so hard sometimes, Rev. Hard for the aid groups and maybe even for the Border Patrol."

A whoosh of cold from the hall hit the backs of our necks just before a welcome voice came out the of dark.

"Teacher, Teacher, why you talking about la migra?"

Both of us whipped around in our chairs, smiling even before Cesar and

Carlos reached the circle of light near the fireplace where we could see them, soaked to the skin.

"It not bad enough the whole town black with no lights like the inside of a mine and my brother and me got rained on so we look like we forget to take our clothes off before we get a shower, but now we gotta hear talk about Border Patrol? What you gonna talk about next, Teacher, roaches?"

Sure enough, water was streaming from Cesar's hair like someone had just dumped a bucket over him, and his T-shirt was tight to his chest in bunchy folds. Carlos looked the same, only there was a foot of height more to drip.

"Hang on, hang on—I'll go get some towels."

I was off down the hall with my flashlight before I heard what Rev. Freeman was saying to the guys, but it sounded an awful lot like he was laughing.

To my bathroom and back in under thirty seconds. I threw a towel at Cesar.

"Here, smart-aleck boy. Dry yourself and then dry the floor."

"Teacher, I no been a boy for a long time."

Rev. Freeman took a towel from my hands and handed it to Carlos while he answered for me.

"Face it, Cesar—to a teacher, every student is forever a child."

Carlos had leaned over to mop up the floor, even before he finished drying himself. The long knotty rope of his spine was curved like a frown and his arms dangled loose in their sockets as he swiped this way and that with the towel in his hand, not really accomplishing anything except to look so desolate I wanted to snatch back the towel and dry his hair for him, but that would have mortified him. I wanted to sit him down in one of these chairs while I brought him hot coffee with good brandy in it. And after that, I wanted to run to my room where I could rock back and forth and mourn over such a floppy, wet rag of utter defeat as this man had obviously become since four or five hours before. Was it any wonder the Rev felt he had to chat with me about the importance of keeping things balanced?

Cesar saw me watching Carlos.

"Hey, Teacher. It night time and we got a fire. When we was kids, our abuleo he tell us stories when we sit by the fire at night. You got a story to tell? Or maybe nothing happen to you in twenty years since you go back home? Maybe not. Probably your life real boring. See? My brother, he look bored already."

I was starting to remember one of the traits that had made Cesar such an endearing little boy. He was a clown. Not a buffoon, but the truest sort of clown in that he had a knack for turning sorrow into an act. He could put on despair like it was an overcoat, andthen strut around in it until you had to laugh. Who could be hurt by sadness that had been turned silly?

"Actually, it's been twenty-*five* years, Mr. Smart Aleck, and a whole lot has happened to me. Which would you like to hear: the good, the bad, or the ugly? You pick."

Cesar sat down in the chair at my right side and put his feet up in the facing chair, wrapped the towel around his neck and let the damp corners hang over his shoulders. He opened his mouth to answer, but for once Carlos spoke first.

"We got the bad already, Teacher. We come back without the womens, didn't we? Nobody know nothing about them except this one guy who tell us maybe he saw them talking to a Coyote. We need good, Teacher. Give us a good story."

Cesar nodded.

"And then the ugly. I always like to hear about ugly because I am so beautiful."

He raised his chin high and tilted his head in the firelight, preening like a stubbly-cheeked beauty queen.

I groaned and rolled my eyes at him, and then I looked around at the little group that was my family on this April evening Mexican border town. It was weird, the things that tether a family. I began a good story, to tether Carlos to us.

"The good thing, the best thing is that I have learned to sing and I have learned to dance."

Cesar grinned.

"Yeah, Teacher, I remember you don't dance so good that night in Puerto Vallarta."

He gave a gracious shrug.

"But you try."

"I did. And I kept trying for a long time, with the dancing, I mean. Singing has always been easy for me; I just had to find the right place to sing. Turns out it was the same place where I finally caught on to how to dance."

Carlos spoke from the chair where he'd finally slumped into a long stretch of despondency.

"Pues, tell us about this place, Teacher."

Hallelujah-Carlos was coming out of his cave. Cesar and the pastor and I all smiled, but we didn't let it show on our faces.

"Okay. There was a time in the mountains of the southern United States where I come from when it was hard or pretty much impossible for most children to go to school more than a couple of months each year. When the snows came, the children had no way of getting out of their hollers—their valleys—or down from the tops of the mountains. The snow was too deep for little children to walk on the mountain paths back and forth every day, and a lot of villages were too poor to build schools for them to walk to, anyway. Some ladies from a state up north heard about this problem and decided God wanted them to build schools where the children could live all winter. The children could go to class, but they'd also do some sort of work like farming or weaving or woodworking that would help support the school and teach the children a trade. They called these schools Settlement Schools, and they were the only school many families had, for a long time.

"After World War II, though, the U.S. was a poor country and our government needed to do something to get our economy working again, so they decided to start building roads that would connect all the parts of the country that had been hard to get to, places like the Kentucky and West Virginia. They blasted through the mountains in those states to make tunnels for cars to drive through, and they sliced off the sides of some mountains to build roads wide enough for cars and trucks."

"This was good for businesses and it made easy for tourists to come to the mountains with their money, but bad for the Settlement Schools. Once the roads were in, schools could be built in every community and children could travel those roads to school whether it was winter or fall or spring. Now that there were roads all through the mountains, children didn't need to live at the Settlement Schools, so a lot of them closed, but some just changed the kinds of things they taught."

"A couple of years after I met you, Cesar, I went to a concert where I picked up a brochure about a music week that would be happening at one of those old Settlement Schools in eastern Kentucky. I decided to go. It turns out this particular school had decided the best way to save the old culture of the mountains was to teach it. This Settlement School's Folk Week was their way of teaching the mountain culture, especially the music. I've gone there every summer since then."

"What do you do during those weeks, Trish?"

Unlikely as it might seem, I'd almost forgotten Rev. Freeman was in the room until he spoke.

We indulge, I thought. We steep ourselves in the luxury of making music with fellow music addicts. But that wasn't what I said out loud.

"Well, we start the day with an hour of group singing. We sing a lot of church songs, and old ballads, and what the mountain people call play-party songs, which are songs for the children. Then we spend the day in dance classes or musical instrument classes. After supper there's a concert and a dance and then most of us go up to the barn for a jam."

"What's a jam, Teacher?"

"It just means playing music without any program or plan. People can play and sing for the fun of it, whatever they want. We sing a lot of songs about death. It's fun."

Cesar was nodding his head.

"We sing songs about death, too. They the best songs 'cause when you sing about death, death stay away."

"Then we better sing," Carlos muttered.

"Yeah, Teacher," Cesar said, like he didn't know what Carlos had meant. "Sing a song. Sing one of your Kentucky songs."

I cocked my head at Rev. Freeman and raised one eyebrow. I couldn't do the eyebrow thing nearly as well as he could, He nodded his go-ahead.

"I'll sing a folk song that an American wrote, but he wrote it about your people."

I hummed around for a good alto note to start on, then I gave them Woody's words:

The crops are all in and the peaches are rotting
The oranges are piled in their creosote dumps
They're flying you back to the Mexican border
To pay all your money and wade back again

My father's own father, he waded that river
They took all the money he made in his life
My brothers and sisters came working the fruit trees
They rode on that truck till they lay down and died

As I started on the chorus the first time it came around, I almost stopped singing—the Rev was singing with me. A good solid baritone to my alto:

Good-bye to my Juan, good-bye Rosalita
Adios mis amigos, Jesus y Maria
You won't have a name when you ride the big airplane
And all they will call you will be deportees.

On through the verses the two of us carried the story of migrants who died when the plane deporting them to Mexico crashed, only to have a radio station announce their deaths as "just deportees."

Cesar was the first to speak after the last chorus.

"Some of us are illegal and others not wanted, alright. Some of us, both. Teacher, how a song can be so sad, but you want to sing it again?'

"Because in this case, feeling sad doesn't mean you're defeated, Cesar. It means singing the song gives you a way to grab hold of what caused the sadness, so now you can fight against it. We keep singing sad stories because that's how we tell the world we won't let those stories happen again."

Carlos sat up and stretched in a long, slow way that reminded me of the Casa's cat.

"Okay, Teacher." Carlos reached out his hand to pull Cesar to his feet. "Maybe we use your flashlight to find some food in the kitchen and then you tell us your story about the ugly. My brother likes ugly because it make him think about himself.'

Like a little band of robbers, we crept along the dark hallway to the kitchen with our candles and my flashlight. The guys heated coffee on the gas stove top and I boiled water in a saucepan for my tea. Rev found some left-over empanadas that would be almost as good cold as hot, some papaya, and a tray of *pan dulces*. Not bad for a late night snack on a rainy night in Nogales. And then I really wished I hadn't thought that, because it triggered the jukebox in my head to click on a steamy Brook Benton version of *A Rainy Night in Georgia*.

"Okay, Teacher." Cesar began to instruct me back in the community room as we all sat and put our feet up and set our mugs on the floor or rested them on our laps. "Now you tell us something ugly, but not too ugly."

"Sorry, Cesar, but the ugly story from my life is about something truly and literally ugly. I have to tell it, though, because it's the other half of the good story I told you. They can't be separated."

Cesar nodded, and raised his right hand in the air as assent and royal command.

"Then give us the history, Teacher."

"Well, just like the mountains around your home in Jalisco have hearts full of silver, the mountains of Kentucky and West Virginia have hearts of made of coal, thousands of years of coal. People like my grandparents who grew up in eastern Kentucky have always known the coal was there. Mountain families would dig into the sides of hills to get a little coal to burn in their stoves, and later, some people even made a business of selling coal to factories that needed it for powering their plants. But they never took very much coal, just what was under some corner of their farm where it was too steep to plow. What could it hurt to dig out a little coal from under those hillsides where they couldn't grow corn?

"Then about a hundred years ago, people started building more and more factories, and those factories needed more and more coal. Pretty soon, men from the cities were going into the mountains to pay families for the right to take the coal under their land. Companies needed that coal, lots of coal, more coal than a family in Harlan or Mingo or Letcher County could ever use in their lifetime. Those families didn't have much cash. Families like the Stampers—the Stampers were my family, Cesar—needed cash to buy shoes and mules and whatever else they couldn't make or grow. A handful of ready cash in trade for coal buried under a barn or a field seemed like a good deal. It made sense to trade the rights to dig up a man's coal for a bit of money, and it really was a good deal for everybody until it popped into some engineer's clever brain that it would be a whole lot easier to just scoop up the dirt that's over the coal and haul it away, instead of tunneling into the ground."

I stopped myself. I was sounding way too much like a textbook, and when was anyone's heart ever moved by a textbook? I shifted my butt in the hard chair, and shifted my story toward pictures, not words.

"It's called strip mining, and that's just what the people who had bought the mineral rights from people like my cousins began to do: they stripped away everything that was between them and the coal they wanted. Imagine it, guys: the mining company would come in with a bulldozer and dig up your wife's garden, the cow pastures, the tree your kids' swing hung from, the grove of apple trees. Every bush and tree and rock would be shoved over to some far corner of your land to sit there in a big hill of what used to be your life, and not a thing you could do about it except stand on your porch and watch. You still had your house and your porch, but they could take everything up to ten feet from your doorstep. They came onto my cousin's land just like that, 'with the world's largest shovel and stripped all the timber and tortured the land'."

Okay, now I'd gone to preaching, not to mention stealing John Prine's words. I needed to find a middle road between facts and family. Cesar didn't seem to notice.

"Your cousin, he let those men take his land?"

"Well, actually it was his daddy's land when this happened. He was still a little boy. His daddy didn't have any choice but to stand by and watch, because *his* daddy had signed a deed."

Carlos and Cesar sat as still as truth, honoring my family's story with their silence. I plowed on into the stormy night with the rest of my cousin's story.

"My cousin's name is Ken. When Ken's granddaddy sold the mineral rights a long time ago, he signed what was called The Broad Form Deed. It said the mining companies weren't responsible for any damage done to a man's land when that damage was "convenient or necessary" for the mining operation. It was all legal. The mine companies had a deed that let them to get the coal out any way they wanted. All Ken's daddy had was a piece of paper his daddy had been paid a hundred dollars for."

Cesar had been listening with his head tilted to one side. Orange light from the fire tinted the skin on that side of his face the color of a my favorite childhood crayon color: Burnt Sienna. Probably I'd liked it as much for the sound of the name as for the shade of the crayon.

"'Scuse me. Teacher. You know, me and my brother, we just the opposite of that."

"Of what, Cesar?"

" Convenient and necessary. We not convenient and not necessary. That why both countries keep giving us back. The USA say we not convenient 'cause we not legal, and Mexico say we not necessary 'cause our families not the right families."

Carlos whacked Cesar on the shoulder.

"Shut up, brother. I want to hear Teacher's story. I know our history."

"This history, Carlos, was about thirty years long for my cousin and his family. All the years of Ken's childhood and until he was a man with a family of his own, there was a coal mine in his Mama and Daddy's yard. A big pile of mined coal—sometimes they called it the gob—sat like a black mountain twenty feet from their house. There was a mine entrance on a rise behind the house and all the coal passed over the house through the tipple, a sort of pipeline made of steel. The rattle of coal through the tipple and the clanging of coal cars never stopped, Monday through Sunday, The work went on day and night. At night, giant floodlights would light up the mine, and light up Ken's house. Coal dust seeped in through every door and window and crack. Ken's mama would cry over her black laundry, her black floors, her black furniture. Sometimes the coal trucks would run over the chickens or dogs. Children learned to get out of the way."

"So, after thirty years, there was not no more coal, Teacher?"

"Well, partly, Carlos, but also there was something good that happened. A lot of people began fighting against the Broad Form Deed and a couple of years ago, the courts said it wasn't legal to do what the mining companies had been doing. Ken's family could tell the mining companies to leave their land alone. It's a pretty place now. Mighty pretty."

"Pretty? I thought this was a story about ugly?"

"It is, Cesar. The ugly is what's happening now. Now the mining companies are buying land, all the land, not just what's under it, so they can own the land and the mineral rights free and clear. Then they go in and cut the tops off the mountains and scoop the coal out like ice cream."

"But they put it back, right, Teacher? So everything good this way."

"You can't put it back, Cesar. They cut down all the trees. They push all the earth from the top of the mountain off into the valleys and the streams running through those valleys, or they haul the top of the mountain away in trucks. A lot of Ken's neighbors have to bring water in to drink because the overburden—that's what they call the top of the mountain after it's pushed into valleys—kills their creeks and poisons their wells."

"But why the people not fight this? Why they not fight for their land?"

"Some do, Cesar, but clean land is a luxury. Feeding your family comes first. There aren't many jobs in the mountains, and the mines pay good money."

Cesar was nodding his head.

"Me cajó la veinte, Teacher. I get it. Your story about something ugly, but it not about ugly mountains. It about the ugly that people gotta do to keep alive. Your mountains, my country—it the same story."

I nodded; I could feel my face moving in and out of the warm light of the dying fire. "And my mountains, my country: son los mismos," I answered him. " They are the same story."

The last log Rev. Freeman had laid in the fireplace cracked down the middle and slumped to the hearth. Dark rain still curtained the windows.

23
Trish

The rain stopped around three, just a couple of hours after the Rev and I finally convinced Cesar and Carlos to sleep at the church instead of in their truck, and we all trundled off to our beds. I woke once to the sound of no rain and pushed the little Indiglo button on my watch to see what time it was, then dropped into a profound sleep until the sun woke me just after six.

I had a lot to do before I met the Shepherds for the search. Not that I was eager to be diving into this particular day, but here it was, and I needed to make ready. I pulled the cord on the bedside lamp. Yep, the power was back on. Too bad. Our little power-outage fireside chat the night before had almost let me forget about all that had happened yesterday and all that could happen today.

Making up my bed as I got out of it (a handy skill taught me by my ex-Navy daddy), I stepped over to the sink and studied my face in the black-framed mirror. The state of my spirit always shows in my eyes, Mama says. *Today, Mama, my eyes look brown and tired.* They jumped over into Irish green when I was rested and happy. My hair looked about the same as always: loose curls down past my shoulders, and bangs that tended to separate into Shirley Temple ringlets. The handy thing about curly hair was that it *always* looked a little wild, so I was seldom dismayed by my morning hair. This morning, though, my hair needed to be gotten out of the way of the heat I'd be riding and walking through all day. I ripped through the worst of the tangles and braided the length of it into a French braid that hung even with the top knuckles of my spine. When I turned my back to the sink mirror to hold up a hand mirror so I could see if the braid was even, the deep dimples at the back of my shoulders winked in and out each time I shifted the mirror. For the thousandth time, I wished Daddy had left his cheek dimples to me in my cheeks, instead of where no one could them. Almost no one.

Looking at my shoulders also made me wish I could wear just a tank top all day. It would be hot, hot, I knew it would be, but there were those cactus spines to think about, so I pulled on the worn-out dress shirt Rev had tossed my way the night before, a white shirt soft from age and many washings, and I rolled the sleeves up to my elbows. I was tall, but even with my arms as long as they were, the sleeves hung past my fingertips. He was one big man. And not just physically, either.

No jeans, I decided. I'd swelter in jeans. I pulled on a pair of loose brown cotton slacks that tied at the waist. There. That would do. I'd put on my socks and sneakers at the last minute. Oh, I'd need a hat. Right. And a bandana. I laid my straw hat next to my black bandana with the white yin/yang symbols printed on it, then added my shoes to the pile and padded barefoot down the hall to the kitchen to find some breakfast.

Before I forgot to, I grabbed a bottle of water from the fridge. The Shepherds would have water in the van, the Rev had said, but what if there wasn't enough? And maybe I should take some fruit. I gathered my little survival stash into a plastic bag, ate a quick bowl of cereal and dashed back to my room to brush my teeth and put on my shoes and socks before time to meet Rev at six-thirty. He was going to drive me across the border to hook up with the Shepherds at a coffee shop in the other Nogales on the U.S. side. Sure enough, I heard his Reveille while I was spitting out my toothpaste.

"Trish. This ship's about to sail."

I grinned, loving how he sounded just like my daddy bellowing the household awake every morning of my childhood. Daddy would march up and down the parsonage hallway, singing out in his deep bass:

"Rise and shine. Hit the deck. Avast the mainsails."

Maybe they taught it in seminary: *Loud Metaphoric Nautical Greetings, 101.* I'd learned my response by the age of four:

"Present and accounted for, Sir."

We could have walked to the border crossing—it was that close—but the coffee shop meeting place was several blocks north of the border gates and across some busy roads, so it was safer to go by car. I got my passport out of my pocket ready to show to the guard. I made a mental note to hand it to the Rev as soon as

I'd shown it, since I couldn't take it with me. We inched up to our turn to be validated, and Rev rolled down all the car's windows. One ridiculously young guy peered at us, then at our passports, then back at us, is if the picture or the person might pull a switcheroo after a single perusal. Another agent speed-walked a leashed drug dog around the car. The dog sniffed the tires and under the car; the agent gave a quick scan of our seats and floor through the open windows.

"Trish," Rev hissed in a loud whisper, "do *not* pet the dog."

"Am I that transparent?" I whispered back. It's hard to sound indignant in a whisper.

" Yeah, when it comes to dogs, you are."

I stuck out my tongue.

The Starbucks was just inside a fairly upscale grocery store. Rev waved to a man and two women sipping their coffees at one of the round café tables, sixty-somethings who looked every bit as if they were about to head to the Club for nine holes before lunch. Everything about them said: well-fixed retirees. And that's exactly what they were. One of the men set his coffee down on the little table and got up from his chair to come greet us.

"Rev, hi." The man stood and held his hand out to Rev. Freeman, who held the man's hand hard between his own big hands for a few seconds before he turned to introduce me.

"Trish, this is Glenn. And that's Pat."

He nodded in the direction of a pleasant-faced woman who had probably taught first grade for thirty-five years—she had that look about her.

"And this is Joy."

I turned my attention to the Christmas elf scurrying towards us with a cup in her child-sized hand. Joy was five-feet-nothing and weighed negative pounds. Her white hair stood up in a longish crew cut with a proud cow-lick over her forehead. Her face was, well, elfin. She wore baggy jeans that she must have borrowed from a fourteen-year-old grandson, work boots, and a T-shirt that read, "Humanitarian aid is not a crime."

Joy grabbed my arm and held on as if I might try to escape. No worries—this woman had me enthralled.

"Okay, Hon, I can't ride with you guys today." she was saying as she steered me toward the parking lot, "so I want to make sure you understand how things will go."

She speed-talked her way through a sketch of a typical search day, all the while inspecting my clothing choices, scanning my pockets for the bulge of a contraband cell phone, and sneaking a peek inside my eyes for evidence of lack of resolve. Finally, Joy gave an almost imperceptible nod and guided me through the parking lot by my still-captured arm.

Apparently,I'd passed muster. I felt unaccountably proud.

"Joy's amazing," Glenn said as we buckled up and he got the van started. I'd been picked to ride shotgun, though Glenn kindly didn't phrase it that way.

"Everyone knows Joy and they all love her. Or they're scared to death of her. Or both."

Glenn headed the van and us west along a frontage road with the four-lane highway to our left and an expanse of desert scrub to our right. We hadn't gone far enough to even lose sight of the Nogales McDonald's before Pat announced, "Plastic by that shrine." She was out of the van almost before Glenn could pull over to stop.

The shrine looked to me like a white, two-foot-tall clam shell standing on end. It was made of heavy wire bent to the form of an open shell and then sprayed with that foam that stiffens as it dries. I couldn't remember what the stuff was called, but I'd once spent an evening in a Chapel Hill bar called The Cave where the interior was aptly sculpted entirely from that same sort of foam. The bar popped into my head partly because of the foam but also because this shrine gave second place of honor—just below the Virgin—to six (I counted) Dos Equis bottles.

We should all be memorialized by what we hold dear, I thought, and I meant it.

"Nothing of note except a couple of old water bottles. They don't look fresh. Don't know how we missed them on Tuesday." Pat climbed back into the van and shoved the black plastic jugs into a trash bag behind her.

"Why are they black?" I'd expected to see clear containers, like milk jugs.

"Migrants believe black jugs can't be seen by the night vision cameras, so they've all switched to using the black ones," Glenn answered me, looking over his left shoulder to ease us back onto the frontage road.. "There are stores in Nogales that outfit people just for the intention of jumping the border. What migrants don't realize is that the desert is studded with ground sensors. They trip these sensors into action as soon as they walk over them. That lets Border Patrol know the general path they're taking, and then heat-sensing devices can keep tracking them even at night. Those heat sensor babies can zero in on anything living that's out there, snap a photo and send an alert to Border Patrol automatically. I've heard the camera can get a clear image of a single person a half-mile away, night or day. I'll point one out to you when we get further down in the desert. Not that you could miss them—they're huge, sit way up on the tops of ridges and look like props from a Star Wars movie."

Glenn got the van up to speed on Arivaca Road and I turned back to look at the shrine one more time. On the ground in front of the shrine lay some cattle bones, bleached white. I hadn't noticed them before.

"Trish, look at the water towers over there," Glenn pulled my attention away from the bones as he pointed to a hill just off Arivaca Road. "Migrants use them as guideposts when they're starting out from west of Nogales, from the Tumacacori Mountains. They sight along the water towers to help them stay west of the freeway. Their idea is to head up through the open desert toward the Sawtooth Mountains—they say they're going to see El Serrucho, "the saw"—and then through the farming country past El Pichaco and on to Phoenix. They truly have no idea what that walk will entail."

Pat leaned up from the back seat.

"Are we going to stop at the mileposts?" she asked Glenn.

"Yep." He glanced over at me. "Mileposts 12 and 18 are major crossing points right now. We'll get out and do a foot search for any signs of recent activity. We'll probably check both places on our way back this afternoon, too."

"And, Trish, don't forget." Pat reached across the seat back and placed her hand on my shoulder for a second, "to keep sweeping your eyes along the road side. This is a search, after all. I'll take the left side; you take the right side."

And I'll get to Scotland afore ye, my brain silently sang.

I'd never been to Scotland, but I'd bet good money it looked nothing like what I was seeing though the van window. I'd never been to Arizona, either, until this trip, so I was happy to have Glenn fill me in on the names of the desert flowers and shrubs coloring the desert floor like a tapestry as we turned off the frontage road and headed down the long hilly two-lane toward Arivaca.

"That's bottlebrush over with the yellow blossoms at the tip ends of the stalks. You're lucky you're seeing the desert in April. Look at the wild heliotrope— they're the ones with the tiny blue flowers. And the dark orange ones are poppies, and that's Indian Mallow over there.

"The sort of buttery yellow ones?

"Yep. Oh, and hey—we're about to pass by my favorite cactus." He slowed the van to a crawl and leaned an arm out the window to point."Look—right here. That's the biggest barrel cactus I've ever seen. I watch for it every time we do a search over this way."

The human psyche is an amazing thing, I thought for the millionth or so time. Even on a desert search for the dead or dying, we look for something pleasurable to rest our thoughts on.

He sped up again and the next low dip gave my stomach a carnival-ride lurch. Who knew the desert would be so up and down-ish? I'd envisioned nothing but flat and more flat, but I was beginning to see firsthand that we were, indeed, in the foothills of those mountains I could see ahead of us.

You're was *supposed* to be looking at what's close by, Trish, not at the distant mountains. This is a search, after all. Yes'm, I answered myself.

"But it's all so pretty," I said out loud to neither traveling companion in particular. "I feel bad about enjoying what I'm looking at."

Pat answered me, "Might as well enjoy the pretty part while you can. It's not like the ugly will stay away forever. See that path off to the right?"

I swiveled in my seat to look where Pat was pointing to a trail that looked exactly like the deer paths I'd spent my whole life following through my north Georgia woods, a footpath worn bare of vegetation by generations of deer hooves as well as the feet of me and my neighbors and the neighbors' kids and uncounted poachers. Here, though, the path was trodden-down sand, not black dirt, and it wove not through mountain laurel but through clumps of cactus with here and there a tall, spiky plant I hadn't noticed before.

Glenn stopped the van. "Here's milepost 12. Let's get out and do a walk-around. Don't let your arms get caught by the cactus."

Walking gave everything a whole different perspective. It was hotter, much hotter than I would have guessed from inside the van. The sun felt evil and the desert vegetation were the minions of evil. I had to constantly duck and twist to avoid being pricked or snagged by cactus spines. I did a rattlesnake check before every step I took; I figured I'd earned the right to skittishness in regard to vipers under my feet. And, besides, the sand had a slickness to it that could easily wrench my ankle or slide my foot from under me to send me sprawling on something pointy or deadly.

I passed by another of those tall plants I'd noticed from the road.

"Pat, what's that plant?"

"It's ocotillo." Glenn answered. "Ocotillo is interesting. See the little green leaves all along the branches?"

" Uh huh."

"They aren't there during most of the year. The leaves pop out after rain comes. Then a week or two after a rain, all the leaves fall off again. It's a pretty smart way of adapting to the desert climate."

Pat caught up with us on the path.

"Trish; what I started to tell you is that this a migrant path. The fact that the path is so worn down and clear of any wildflowers or cactus means it's still being used as a pretty major thoroughfare. We may see some activity around."

Pat put her hand on my shoulder to stop me for a minute.

"Look, Trish: the ocotillo along this path have leaves on them. See? Okay, now look off to the left about hundred yards. There's another patch of ocotillo. See any leaves?"

I studied the farther patch. "No."

"What does that tell you?"

"That there's more moisture along this path than over there?"

"Yup." Pat stepped in front of me and started walking again. "There might even be a water source along the path, maybe an arroyo that keeps its rainwater longer than most. It's a smart route to take when you're walking."

"And the migrants would know this?"

"Some would. The ones who grew up near the desert probably would."

I didn't want to ask my next question. "But not if they grew up in the city?"

Glenn shifted his eyes from his search for a minute to lock eyes with me.

"No, Trish, probably not if they grew up in the city."

We walked without talking for ten or fifteen minutes, circling back to the van. Once we were cruising down the road again, Pat and I went back to scanning the sand and scrub for signs of ...what? I really wasn't sure.

Over the next half hour we spotted and retrieved a few more water jugs and an old jacket Glenn remembered from the last search. He said he guessed no one was coming back for it. As we began to take on some elevation in the foothills, the saguaro cacti appeared, standing like sentinels up and down the hilly desert, their prickly arms stretched upward to heaven. A Border Patrol truck passed our van every fifteen or twenty minutes. Glenn waved every time and usually the agents waved back.

Just as we reached the one-street town of Arivaca we saw a Border Patrol van parked on the left shoulder across the street from the library where Glenn had promised we'd take a pit stop, the library's bathroom being the last one before they drove into open desert.

But Glenn wasn't looking at the library. His eyes were on the Border Patrol van.

"They've got a bird." Glenn was already pulling their van over as he spoke. "That's one of the names they give to border jumpers, Trish. The guides are coyotes; their customers are birds."

The migrant sitting hunched forward on the tailgate was young and handcuffed. He looked like he was probably about my height and weighed maybe a hundred-forty pounds. He had on a black T-shirt, jeans rolled up at the cuffs, and leather sandals. His hair was the same glossy black as Carlos' hair, and his bangs fell over his eyes just the way Carlos's did. He looked like any other young man in his early twenties. He could have *been* any other young man in his early twenties, except that he was handcuffed. He didn't really look up as Glenn and Pat and I got out and walked over, but he saw us.

There were two agents; I could tell the taller agent was not happy to see us. He turned away and lit a cigarette. Glenn nodded to the other agent, then nodded toward the migrant.

"Does he need anything? We have water and medical supplies."

"No thank you, Sir."

The young agent who answered Glenn had hair the same dirty blond as my brother's hair and it was cut in a longish crew cut just the way Dennis had kept his the years he played JV football. I wondered if this guy had played football in high school. He sounded like my brother, too, with that inborn courteousness natural to the southern men I'd grown up around. This kid must be from Georgia—had to be.

"We have everything we need, Sir. He's asked to be taken in."

The agent nodded toward the emigrante, who still had not moved in his body or his spirit.

Yeah, he definitely had a south Georgia accen*t,* I decided. Maybe Valdosta.

Glenn shook the agent's hand and thanked him. We all trooped back to the van like ducklings and drove across the street for our bathroom break.

I barely gave Glenn a chance to dry his hands before I hit him with questions again.

"   Do you believe what the agent said? Do you think that boy really asked to be taken in?"

"Sure." Glenn gave one shoulder a shrug as we walked back to where the van was parked by thelibrary's small courtyard of benches and wildflowers and pottery wind chimes. He laid the flats of his hands against the side of the van and pushed back, to stretch his legs.

"They often give themselves up to Border Patrol or to us. A lot of them make it this far and then they see those mountains there," Glenn nodded toward the Sierrita Mountains, "and figure out pretty quickly they can't walk to Phoenix in one easy day's walk, the way the coyotes had told them, and they don't have enough water, enough energy, or enough hope to keep them going by foot over a couple of pretty tough mountain ranges. They decide to just go home."

I looked back across the street. The young migrant was stepping through the opened doors of the van with the friendly agent's hand on the young man's head to keep him from knocking his noggin.

Our drive through downtown Arivaca took all of four minutes. We passed a Catholic church, a post office, one old and very picturesque adobe house, a consignment shop of the sort run by aging hippies, a taco stand in old converted camper,and a small house or two before they turned west with the road, then a bit north, or at least I felt like we were heading north.

"Which way are we going, guys?"

I wanted to orient myself. Well, truth be told—I had spent most of my life wanting to orient myself. On family camping trips when I was little, Mama always kept a sharp eye out to make sure I successfully navigated the return trip from bathhouse to tent. I now blamed it on my literal brain: if I'd entered the bathhouse to the right, then it was logical (to me) that I should exit to the right. Either Mama or my disgusted brother would eventually find me happily meandering, perusing the camping lifestyles of my fellow temporary park dwellers.

Oh, Lord, please don't let Ruth be of the same bent as me. I slung my silent plea out to the cosmos.

"Sort of northwest." Pat answered me from the backseat. "We'll drive a ways, gain some elevation, then make a big loop south and back home. You know we're only eleven miles from the border here in Arivaca, don't you?"

"No, I had no idea."

"Yep, so it's likely that anyone who left on foot from Nogales in the past twenty-four hours or so would be walking somewhere within the loop we'll drive."

Pat wasn't kidding about gaining elevation. In less than an hour we were somewhere up around five thousand feet, according to Glenn. According to me, we were clinging by the van's toes to a high wire disguised as a dirt road surely not wide enough for the chassis to span without hanging off a bit on one side—only there *was* no side that I could see; there was only a rocky drop down to sand and cactus some hundred-million feet below us. Or so it seemed to slightly hysterical me, who was trying hard not to brake with my right-seat driver's foot while simultaneously testing with my right hand the strength of the bolts securing my door's armrest.

Almost on the very tip-top of one of those curvy stretches of so-called road, Glenn stopped the van.

"Want to take a picture, Trish?"

Oh, sure, because "Kodak Moment" was precisely what my brain had been thinking for the last mile or so.

"Right over there's one of the towers I was telling you about." Glenn continued, undaunted by my silent sarcasm. "It's part of what they call the Virtual Border. "

Just as he had said it would, the tall metal tower looked like it could fit right into a battle scene in one of the Star Trek movies. The saucer-like sensors at the top were the heads of aliens, watching. It was more than a little creepy and I was glad when we got back in the van to start down. Well, I was glad until we actually crested the rise to hang like the front car on a roller coaster for one eternal second, angled impossibly downward. I knew good and well the van had four-wheel drive, but it must also have been equipped with Tank Mode because we literally crawled and crept from rock to rock over foot-deep wash-outs the whole way down. Glenn navigated us safely to the bottom by feel and memory.

"Okay, Glenn." Pat at one point directed him, "right here's where if you balance the right front tire on that flat rock just ahead of you, you can skirt the left wheel along the edge of that wash."

Seriously? I was so impressed I almost forgot to keep clenching my guts and the door handle.

After several personal eternities, we were mercifully at the bottom, driving along the middle of a creek bed that would be dry until the summer rains came again.

It was just like being at the head of a holler in eastern Kentucky. The analogy relaxed me enough that I could finally release the door handle from a death grip and slowly let off on the imaginary brake pedal. Yep, see? There's a creek running through the middle, just like in any little holler in eastern Kentucky, with little clumps of trees and flowers alongside. The difference between here and Pine Mountain was that in the desert, creeks ran with sand and rocks instead of water, the trees were mesquite and ironwood rather than laurel, and the red flowers blooming like lights at the feet of the trees were poppies instead of tiny wild roses.

I was just about to ask the name of those flowers that were a patch of blue a little ways ahead of us—blue poppies?—when Pat yelled, "Gear. We've got gear off to the right."

Glenn threw the van into Park and was out before the engine had died completely. Pat was three steps ahead of him, the satellite phone in her hand. I half-fell out of the van and ran to catch up.

We saw Ruth's hair first. Her short spiky hair made a splay of dark slashes across the white sand under her head. She was curled on her right side; her back was curved right up against a barrel cactus, spine to spine.

"Aw, no. Ah, no, no, no."

Pat had begun to keen, or maybe it was me.

"Ella estaba enferma."

We all whirled around toward the voice. The blue splotch I'd seen was a backpack flung near the almost overgrown opening of an abandoned silver mine, and just inside the shade of the opening Ruth's companion had spoken from where she sat hugging her bent legs to her chest. Pat got to her first.

"Quien, doña? Who was sick? Ruth?"

Pat had her arm around the woman, resting their foreheads together.

"Sí," the woman continued in Spanish. "Yes, Ruth became very sick. She had her period, you know and felt weak. Then the heat made it worse. Always, she told me, she had trouble with the bleeding, but this time she was bleeding too much, too much. She asked the coyote if she could rest for a while, but he said if she couldn't keep up, he would leave her here and send someone for her. I knew he would send no one. They would not even give us more water. He left."

I turned from Ruth to look at the other woman as she talked, fiercely glad of a reason to look away from Ruth, and grateful for a reason to rage about some injustice less tangible than a young woman I liked, lying dead in the sand. "They left? Just left you here?"

Ruth's companion did not look up. What was the point?

"Sí, se fueron."

24
Cesar

Some people, they are born broken. Abuelo told this to me once and I believe it to be the truth. The place where a person is most broken cannot be seen on the outside for a long time, maybe, but the break, it is there, like a little crack in a bone or like the earthquake line under Mexico City. You know it is going to get more big one day. One day the person will step too hard on their leg that has the little bone crack and that crack will run up and down the whole bone, and split it into two. In the same way, the hot and wet days of July and Augustin some years will make the ground of Mexico so soft it will sink heavy into that crack under our country until the crack squirms and wiggles to get away. Then Mexico City, it will split apart just like the year my father died and Ruth, she was born.

"Any word, Cesar?"

I look up from my hands but I do not say nothing. My fingers, they are knotted together like I was praying. Maybe I was. The padre walks over to his desk and he looks at the office phone to see if the message light was blinking. It was not.

"I'll check back in a bit."

"Bueno, Padre."

I look back at my hands again. The phone stays quiet, but my mind keeps on to whisper to me about Ruth.

Ruth, she was born right over that crack while it shifted and then her Mama died. What is the first thing a baby will do when she is born? That baby roots for her mama. Ruth had no mama, so she had to root to a world that was cracking open. How can she not be broken inside?

All the time a baby is inside his mama's belly, he feels what the mama feels, even when the mama not know she is feeling. Then when that baby start to swim into this world, his mama must to swim with him; she got no choice. During this time between the worlds, the mama's body got more power than her spirit—I mean, she cannot say to herself to ignore this baby coming out of her and instead go to market that morning. No, she got no choice but to tie the strength of her spirit to the work of her body.

Ah, and what will happen when we look away from our spirit? It is in that moment that the devils take their chance to show us where we are weak. Always the devils watch for their chance to whisper to us about our little cracks, to let us not forget the places where we are broken.

When Ruth's mama went out of this life, she was working so hard to bring Ruth safe to this side that her mind could not think of nothing except to work very fast. Ruth swam into the air through the spirit of her mama while that spirit was going to God. It is for this reason that Death is the heritage for Ruth, even if she did not know this.

Probably Ruth did *not* know this. Most of us in our lives, we recognize our heritage never, but we cannot escape from it. I know this well. I was born to wander because my mother, she believed always in her spirit that my father would never stay with her or with her little baby; she knew this even while she was working to give life to me. The devils showed her the feet of my father always on the other side of our door at the same moment my feet came through her door into life, and so this become also my truth, and my heritage.

And what was the heritage of my brother, Carlos? While our mother push him through the canal, her mind had one thought at the center: that she would do anything, anything to keep our father with us. Ai, but if someone had told her later that was her sole thought then, she would have laughed—ai, no, I was thinking about how much it hurt to push this long boy out of me—but the truth of it was she thought then only of how to keep our father from leaving again. Because of this truth, Carlos was born open to anything, and this make him afraid of everything. People sometimes say he is weak; he is not. Carlos, he is a person with no gates, no doors, no locks. He got no way to choose to stay in or go out. Because of this, he carry a burden like God, but he is only a man, without the blessing of God's strength to help him to carry his burden.

All this talk in my head about Carlos made me jerk a quick look over at him in the other chair in the padre's office. He heard what I was just thinking? The last thing I need was for my brother to hear me speak his name in a same breath with the name of El Señor. I stare at Carlos, hard. He blows a little puff of air through his mouth and his legs twitch. Deep in the sleep. Good.

I should sleep, too. We walked all morning searching for the ladies. Unless Teacher brings to us news of them, this day might go on into the night. I stretch my arms straight out with my fingers tied together and I twist my hands to make the knuckles crack, trying to make comfortable for a nap, but my mind had not finished its journey.

By the time our mother gave to us Juan and Jose, she have no hope our father would ever be our father. She stop caring, so those little guys, they born with no care in them. They settle into happiness like it had no opposite, and that is where they have stayed.

Padre come back into the room. I look up at him and this time my mouth works itself.

"Padre, we still not hear nothing. You think they back soon?"

Padre set his coffee cup down on the papers on his desk. All his papers got rings of brown from where his coffee spill over. I should tell him some time that he don't need to spend his time to sign his name on nothing. If any people got a letter from Nogales that got a round brown stain on it, they know who send it before they open it. I know I am right about this, and I just meet him two days before. I believe when his mama was pushing him out (Ai, Dios forgive me for talk so plain about the mother of a padre) her one thought was about a cup of the coffee, por seguro. She thought: As soon as I get this boy out of me, I have myself a good cup of coffee.

"Don't know when they'll get back." The padre shook his head. "Depends on what they find." He drink a long drink from his cup. I want a long drink, too, but this not the time for that.

"Padre, it okay if I tell you about my dream last night?"

He smile at me. I think his mama smiled at him before she take that cup of coffee.

"Sure, Cesar, I mean—look at your brother over there. He's deep in dreamland, so maybe that's the place to be right now."

I shake my head, no.

"Carlos not dreaming, Padre. He running away."

I think about my dream for a moment before I begin the telling of it. This dream one of those dreams that will not leave when the morning come. It is not right for a dream to stay young while the day is going old. Dreams supposed to be memory by mid-day; they should not still breathe late into the evening. This one still breathing.

"I was inside a tunnel, Padre, but not like a tunnel where the road it goes over an arroyo."

I stop and grin at him. "You know, Padre, I mean those tunnels for water and emigrantes to run through? And not like the subway in Mexico City. This tunnel, it look like a hose for una aspirador—como se dice? Vacuum cleaner. Only this one big, gigante. I was crawl inside for a long way and every two, three minutes I have to go through wire in a big circle that hold up the cloth or what it was. I can see light outside and shadows of the people. All the time when I crawl from one wire circle to the next one, the tunnel it go tight around me, like someone pull the wire tight. I no could breathe every time the wire go tight, but every time I hear some person out there tell me to come on, keep crawl. I go past that tight place and I can breathe otra vez until I crawl to next place where the wire is."

The padre drink the rest of his coffee. He put the cup down on some papers that look like they maybe his homily for church next Sunday. Coffee drip down one side of the cup onto the top piece of paper. He did not see this. He look at me.

"You're still going through that tunnel, Cesar, that's why the dream won't fade. It's no dream; it's your life right now."

I would not ask Padre how he know what my life was. This was a man who know things, and this was a man who would not use the things he know, not even to speak of them, until a good purpose came.

"Okay, I know why the wire it keep tight—that when la migra catch us or we have to go back and try again. But who the voice that tell me to keep going? Maybe it my father because he never make it to where he want to be? Or maybe it my lazy brother over there?"

"It's you, Cesar."

That sound like a strange answer from a padre. I think maybe he would tell me it was the voice of God. That would be nice, to know God stay with me, God talk to me in my dreams.

"My voice, Padre? You not think maybe it the voice of God ?"

"How do you think God speaks, Cesar? You *are* His voice. So are we all."

Dios. I hang my head down low.

"Oh, then God sometime say very bad things, Padre."

He laugh. His laugh was loud and it was deep—the laugh of a man. It was the kind of laugh to make the sad people forget what they sad about. His laugh, it wake Carlos, and Carlos wake up smiling.

"Que pasó? What happen? They find the womens?"

Carlos stretch his shoulders up to his ears, still looking happy and like he had a good rest, but he froze in the middle of his stretch when he hear—when we all hear—Teacher's voice from the doorway:

"Yes."

Ai, Dios, that not a good *yes*. I do not want to, but I turn around and look at her. Teacher was wear her hair in a braid like my abuela always wear, but this braid come loose and a lot of curls hang sweaty by her face. My granny's braid look like that when she had worked all day in her garden and the little branches of the lemon trees had catch and pull at her hair while she was work in the heat of the afternoon.

Teacher was wear jeans and the shirt of a man over a T-shirt. The shirt was very dirty. Her face look red, like she not remember to keep on her hat in the desert.

All this I notice in a second, but it had no importance. It was her eyes that I look at. Her eyes, they were not there. Oh, sí her eyeballs and eyelashes and eyelids still sat on her face; that not what I mean. I mean that I could not find *Teacher* in her eyes. The life that was Teacher was die from those eyes, or it went away to some other place.

I did not see Padre move from his desk to the doorway, but he was there, with his arms around Teacher. My stupid brain work enough to tell me to get up. Give her your chair. Padre help Teacher to the chair as soon as I jump out of it and he help her to sit. Then he kneel on one knee in front of her like for the prayers, and he move his arms down from her shoulders, where he rested his hands on her lap and pulled her hands between the both of his. Even when he kneeling, he was so tall his head had almost the same high as Teacher. He leaned toward her so his cheek against her cheek. Both of them did not see how close they sit.

My brother still had not move. I know him well—he was hope if he did not move his body from where it was before Teacher came back, time would not move forward into this next moment. For sure, the next moment would be a bad moment to walk into.

Neither me nor my brother had not said nothing yet, and Padre had ask Teacher no questions. He was a wise man—why should he ask questions when the answers all sit in that chair behind dead eyes?

Ruth was dead, and maybe her friend, also. Teacher would say this in words when it was time, but the empty in her eyes had show this truth to me already. I only pray to God that all my loose thinking concerning the birth of Ruth had not been the open way for the broken places to come back to life and to take her life.

Teacher raised her head and shake all over, hard, like she had cold. She did this another time more, and then when she look at us, I see a little piece of Teacher come back into her eyes. Then I think to myself that the dead eyes had been more easy to look at than these eyes.

"Ruth's companion is okay." Teacher say to the room. "Her name is Alma," Carlos move at last.

"No, Teacher. No, no, no. You tell me no. You tell me Ruth okay, too."

He move right into try to argue away the truth. To argue was the only weapon my brother had.

Teacher pull her hands from between Padre's two big hands. She look down at his hands, pat them like to say thank you and they can go now. Padre stand, pull his desk chair around close to Teacher's chair, and sit in it. I squat on the floor by the arm of Teacher's chair the way my granddaddy used to squat by the fire in the evenings when he tell stories to us.

"Carlos." Teacher look at him with almost her real eyes. "I read one time that life is not lost by dying; it is lost minute by minute. I think Ruth believed in her heart that by staying in Mexico, she was losing her life minute by minute. I don't know her reasons for thinking this, but I am certain she felt the gamble she took was worth the risk. We should not dishonor her choice by rejecting it."

I nod.

"I am agree, Teacher, but tell us what happen. I want to know the rest of her history. I want to know so someone remember."

Teacher made a small, sad smile.

"We will remember, Cesar."

Then she tell us how they find Ruth all curl up on the sand and how her friend—Alma—how Alma tell them about how Ruth get sick, the Coyotes leave her, and Alma stay behind with Ruth. They got almost no water, Alma tell Teacher. The Coyotes would not give them no more water and would not let the others give no water for them. The desert was not yet so hot as June or July, but sometime when a person is feel weak already, it does not need to be too much hot for the heat sickness to take the person. It take Ruth, in just a few hours. Alma give all the water she had to Ruth, but the heat take her, all the same. Alma sit with Ruth until the spirit of Ruth was left, then she move into the shade of the old mine so her spirit would not also be give to the desert. That was where Teacher and the others find her.

"And Alma, Trish?" Padre spoke for the first time. "Is she with INS?"

Teacher nod, yes.

"We called Border Patrol as soon as we had Alma stabilized and gave them our location. They met us there within half an hour or so. While we were waiting, Alma told us 'the rest of her history'."

Teacher smile at me when she repeat my words.

"I asked Alma why they had left so suddenly, what had happened to make them change their plans and why they kept it a secret, rather than telling Rev. Freeman they were leaving. Here's what she told me."

Teacher pull a tiny recording machine from the pocket of her jeans.

"Aw, Trish," the padre roll his eyes and reach out to grab Teacher's hand, but not like before. "You know you weren't supposed to take anything like that on the search. You could have gotten yourself killed."

"Yeah, well, apparently it was someone else's turn to die today."

25
Cesar

Teacher put the recorder on her knee and turn it on. We all hear Alma's words speak to us.

"I had not so much hurry to jump as Ruth. I want to go to USA so I can have a good job. My cousin, la madrina de Ruth, she lucky because she a nurse, have good job. I not so lucky. I need USA for opportunity. Ruth and me, we pay la guida to take us the first time and that where we meet the two brothers. I think they are good men. I tell Ruth if we not make it this time, the brothers they get us to USA—maybe next time. I feel trust for them. Ruth, too, but Ruth have hole in her heart because she have no family. She have pain where the hole is. Pain make the mind work bad.

"After the padre let us stay the church that night, this guy call Ruth and say, I going in one hour but you got to pay me two thousand. Ruth say, Fine, and she all happy, tell me to don't worry about pack my stuff. She say she buy us new stuff in America. This your opportunity, Alma. That what she say. I take one bottle water and put in my pocket while she pull me out the door. We say the padre goodby."

I hear Teacher's voice:

"But, Alma, weren't you scared? I mean, before I left this morning to spend just one day riding around the desert in a van, I made all kinds of preparations. I could have set up camp with all the stuff I brought and I was still nervous. You and Ruth left Mexico for good, with strangers, and all you brought was one bottle of water?"

Alma's voice came back. She sound stronger, like she was the teacher, not Teacher.

"You know that everybody make a mistakes some time and that was the worst mistake I make is to let Ruth go. I didn't think. It was crazy. Ruth she all happy and, pues, maybe it work, who know? I know Ruth so young and so pretty to go without nobody to watch for her, so I grab the water and go with her.

"Then it was the worst dream of my life. This guy, he one of the Coyotes, he want to violate Ruth. I say him that it gonna be me and Ruth die first. This guy, he had, you know, bad things in his head. So when he see he not have Ruth without kill us, he look for chance to let us die without he kill us. I know that what he is thinking, so I keep my eyes on him, keep him talking.

"I ask him how many hours to Phoenix. Six, seven hours, maybe, he say me, and he shrug, like it was nothing. We could do that, no problem. I looked at my watch. Not yet five. The sun would not be at its most hot until maybe noon. Sure, why not?

"We hurry to keep up, turning when he turned and cut right through somebody's back yard where a dog started barking and pulling the chain tight trying to get at us. A light went on in the house, and then the next house, the same. Ha. We were the lights of morning. Each place we pass came awake.

"The next street run along the border, exactly. We cross this street, and I stop for a second to look down at the last sands of Mexico, mostly sand with little rocks mixed in that would hurt the feet without shoes. Clumps of desert grasses stiff and grey like the beards of old men stuck straight up from the ground. There are old men buried under this sand, I thought, and a shiver pass over me like water.

"The first shrine we see was near to one of the dirt roads the ranchers drive to where their cattle feeding. We cross those roads like rabbits, perch on the side of the road until it was clear of cars as far as we could see, and then: hop, hop—we were across and follow the path though the scrub.

"This shrine was white, and open in the front like half of a sea shell, a sea shell made from plaster. I think maybe how some man brought to this spot a bucket of the plaster he used in his work, to spread the wet plaster with his hands over a frame he shaped out of old wire. That was how it looked to me. I imagine him there in the sun, making smooth the plaster while in his mind he smooth the hair of a small boy.

"The shrine, it tall enough for a vase of red plastic flowers to fit inside the opening, and there were three bottles of beer around the vase: Dos Equis and Heineken. All this I saw as we walked past, but only when I look back once more did I notice the white skulls of cows in front of the shrine—three skulls as white as the Virgin's robes.

"Walk, walk, walk. The sun was no longer my friend. The ache down low in Ruth's back made her wish she could curl up with her knees hard against her belly, she told me. My mouth was dry and tasted of metal the way it does right after a tooth is filled. I looked at my watch: ten o'clock. Walk, walk.

"Then we see a clump of trees near to a cattle trough. Men were under the trees, maybe twenty men. The men watched us, but did not move from the shade. They not move at all. I ask them where they were going. One of the men gave a little cough, like he had not talked for a while and need to get his throat working. He cough again, harder, and spit on the ground near his hip. Ptoo.

"'Where am I going?' He shrug one shoulder. There was a rip in the plaid flannel shirt he was wearing; his shoulder poked through the rip. The old skin of his shoulder wrinkled when he shrug. 'This far and no farther.' I ask him why not.

"He say me because their guides were not of the cartel. Then the man guiding Ruth and me, he was filling his bottles at the cattle tank, but when he heard what the old man say he turned around so fast the bottle in his hand fell into the tank and floated away. He listened while the migrant man kept telling his history.

"The migrant say the cartel waiting for them when they stop to rest and fill their bottles. The cartel say no one but cartel is allow to carry los emigrantes across. They say they would be the guides now, but the men hve to pay them . The men say they got no money. What did the cartel man think? All their money, they paid to their guides. Pues, bien, the cartel then said to them– the migrants could carry drugs for them. The men say no, all they want is to get to Phoenix and get jobs. They don't want no part of drugs. Then el viejo stop his story to raise his head and look at me and Ruth for the first time. 'The cartel men laugh at us,' the old man say to me and Ruth. 'They laugh and say to find our own way to Phoenix.'"

Teacher's voice came again "But where were your guides? Did they leave?" Then Alma's voice answer back, more soft than before.

"That the same as what I asked. A man maybe my age pulled one knee up and rest his arm on the knee of his jeans. He look at me and say, 'Almost.' He jerk his arm up and point with one finger to the other side of the water tank, then he let his arm fall back down so that his hand hit the sand. Ruth and me walked around to see what he pointing to, while he keep talking.

"He say the cartel men forced their guides to go back to the border with them. They say they would drop the guides off at a checkpoint as a lesson to other guides who think they can do this work outside of the cartel. I ask the guy how is that a lesson, to let the men go at a border? I say los americanos maybe hold the men for a day or two, and then send them back to Mexico. So?

"But I walk to where he was pointing. Ruth, too. She get to the other side of tank before me. She reached back and grabbed my hand again, stopping so fast my nose bumped into her neck and my braid slap me a little on my face. She pushed with her hand over mine to shove me away from the tank, but I trip when she did this, and fall forward, grab hold of the side of the tank to keep from fall all the way to the sand. Ai, what I see there. Two hands lay on the sand, maybe ten inches from my nose. One hand had long, thin fingers and very smooth skin. The ring finger was missing from the other hand.

"These were the hands of the guides who had left, almost. These hands were the lesson."

I hear Teacher's voice make a little cry, like someone hurt her, then a man speak.

"She's over here. I think she's basically okay. We gave her water and..."

The tape stop. I look up at Teacher.

"That was Glenn." Teacher say to Padre. "I stopped recording there because after that, things got pretty hectic, just getting Alma into the Border Patrol van and convincing them not to handcuff her. Ruth had to be gotten ready for transport. There were papers to sign.

I gotta know. "Where they take Ruth, Teacher?" I think they'll hold her body at the detention center until they clear things with the Mexican government to return her to her family."

"But she don't got a family. That the whole reason she jump."

Teacher smile another real sad smile.

"She *doesn't have*, Cesar, not she *don't got*."

I knew Teacher was try to make things normal.

"She doesn't have no family, Teacher."

"Yes, well, since Alma's first cousin is Ruth's legal guardian, that makes Alma a relative by law, so she could claim Ruth's body."

Teacher wait for me to say what she knew I was say next,

"But Alma illegal, Teacher. That make her a relative out of the law and she can't claim nothing."

Teacher raise up her eyebrows. "Bit of a Catch 22, isn't it?"

I don't know what Teacher's words mean, but I understand.

"Ah, Teacher, your government it don't know what to do with us even when we dead."

My phone vibrate in my pocket. I take it out and look at it down low where the others could not see. It was my Ana.

"'Scuse me, Padre, Teacher. I be right back."

They think I need the bathroom. Carlos, too—he barely look at me when I left the room. Good. No reason to make more worry if there trouble at home. And I had a need to hear my Ana's voice.

We talk a few minutes, mostly about stuff a man and his woman talk about, stuff that sound like nothing to somebody else, but it everything. Ana ask me if we made it yet and I say her, *No, no, we're just waiting and haven't gone over yet.* Because if I tell her we tried two times already, she would say to come home. I tell her nothing about Ruth, but I tell her, "Remember the American teacher lady who taught me English when I was a kid? She's here and I've been talking to her." I would not lie to my Ana, so I give her the best half of the truth of my life here and hope she not ask for the other half.

I put my phone back in my pocket and start to go back into the padre's office, but then a bad thought walked into my head: when Carlos and me make it over the border and get jobs and a place to live, then it would come the time for Ana and Elena and Carlito to cross. I always know this, but not really, only in the way you know something before it stand in front of you and show you its face.

My Ana and Carlos's Elena would have to cross just the same like Ruth and Alma try to cross. And our wives would cross without us because we would need stay in the US and work to get the money for pay the coyotes. The coyotes charge more for womens because sometimes they can't walk so fast or so far like the men.

Dios, Cesar. I shake my head at myself. Do you want to become like your brother, always inviting trouble into your head before it think to come on its own? Your women will be fine. Just let trouble try to interfere with Elena. I love my sister-in-law, but she could make a coyote forget his plans to violate her just by her constant bitching at him.

I know I should feel shame for my thoughts, but I laugh, instead. Then I stop my smile before I walk back into the room with the people who hold Ruth's history.

26
Trish

When Cesar walked back into the office, I jumped up from my chair like it had just been electrified. Carlos jumped, too, and looked ready to run. Rev. Freeman raised one eyebrow and smiled at me.

"Trish?"

I knew what I needed. Mother Jones said to "Pray for the dead and fight like hell for the living." Alma was still living. Cesar and Carlos were still living.

"I need a shower, Rev. But first I'm going to finish my letter to my mama. And then I'll meet you guys in the kitchen where you can cook us a huge dinner. You cook; I'll clean."

"Amen," Rev. Freeman answered my prayer of petition.

The letter was still on the nightstand where I'd laid it; I picked up my pen with no intention of telling Mama what had been going on in my life. Mama wouldn't even want to hear all those details I planned to spare her. The information wasn't the point; the writing was the point.

Okay, I'm back again. Yeah, so, another day helping the Reverend take care of business. You'd like him, Mama. He's one of those preachers like Daddy was—he knows in his soul that being minister is both a vocation and an avocation, so there's just no point in being all high-and-mighty about the sacrifices you're called to make. It comes with the territory.

I can hear what you're thinking, Mama: "Hmmm... she's mentioned this man a lot. I wonder if there's a chance..." Don't even go there. It's not that I don't like him—I do. I like him, admire him, think he's funny, enjoy quite a lot just looking at him, and I have boundless admiration for the work he's doing. So what's the problem? No problem. Is he married? Nope. Never has been, as best I know. And no, he's not gay, Mama.

If I lived here instead of where I do, I might consider snuggling a bit closer, but I don't, so I won't. Which does not at all mean that we are not growing to love each other.

I've been thinking a good bit about love, especially since Cesar showed up. I knew as soon as I met that boy-- when he was a boy-- that he and I were meant to love each other. It was like we'd been waiting our whole lives up to that point not to find each other again, like we'd somehow become separated over a couple of incarnations until that day I walked through a little village by accident (or was it?) and he grinned at me. "There you are," his grin said to me. And for sure his grandfather recognized me, though that freaked me a little.

The problem is, what do you do with a love like that? It's not like you can come home from vacation and tell everyone you fell in love with a ten-year-old boy. They'd hear that as a perverted sort of love, which is not at all what I feel now and felt then for Cesar. He is my friend and I love him. He completes me and yet also pushes me to keep moving toward being a deeper person than I am now. I am apparently the same for him. Is that not love?

I know you've told me that you didn't want to have anything to do with Daddy when you first met him because he was "too good-looking, and good-looking men are always stuck on themselves." But then you decided to marry him when you realized you could not picture the rest of your life without him. I understand that. You know I've felt that way, too, but ended up having no choice but to imagine the rest of my life without my man.

Now I've grown to think of love as less restricted to proximity than I once believed it must be. I loved Cesar as a boy and even though I believed I would never again see him, our relationship has informed my life since then in no small way. Is this not love?

The good pastor and I need what we are for each other these weeks while I am here. Will we stay in touch when I leave? I have no doubt of it. If we never carry our relationship to a conventional level, won't our bond still be love? I have no doubt of it.

Sorry, Mama, to lay all this on you. Thank you for listening. But you would listen to anything I had to say, because I am the one saying it. This is, for sure, what love is.

Love, yes,

Trish

Writing to Mama was the balm that steadied me through my shower, all during which I thought of Ruth not being on the other side of the bathroom door.

Another phone was ringing as I headed down the hall toward the kitchen; it sounded like the Reverend's office phone. In the kitchen, Cesar was sitting at the long table with his sandals on the floor and his bare toes curled around the top chair rung. He looked so exactly like his ten-year-old self that my throat closed up.

"Hey, Teacher. You got two good men here to cook for you. What you want we cook?"

He grinned and waved a wooden spoon. Carlos still looked shell-shocked, but pretending all was well. I laid my hand on Carlos' shoulder for just a second, both for his sake and mine, and then nodded toward the pantry. We got busy rooting through the pantry shelves and the refrigerator to see what we had to work with.

"Trish?"

I pulled my head out from where I'd been leaning inside the refrigerator, and looked at him full-on. Uh, oh. His face was not the face of a man joining his friends in making a pleasant meal. He spoke to all three of us.

"I just got a call from Sister at the Casa. It's not going to be a quiet night. Some of the drug cartel guys are unhappy about so much American activity with deportees at the Casa." He paused and looked at me, "and so much activity here, for that matter—so they've been waving guns around on the street outside the Casa. We'll need to batten the hatches and stay close until we can see what's what tomorrow morning. Cesar and Carlos, you'll have to stay here again tonight. It would be too dangerous out there in your truck."

Oh, good—yet another thing not to write to Mama about.

"You don't got to worry about us, Padre." Cesar had walked over to where the pastor stood near the kitchen door and reached up to rest his hand on Rev. Freeman's shoulder. "Me and Carlos not gonna leave you and Teacher here alone. Hey." He grinned, and looked like Cesar again. "You gotta have some Mexicans here to do the dirty work, right?"

Rev, Freeman put his hand over Cesar's, gave it a quick squeeze, and then moved Cesar's hand down where he could grasp it between both of his for a moment.

"Por seguro, Cesar. And let's hope the dirtiest work you do for me this evening involves dishes and soap."

He shoved a dish rag into Cesar's hand.

"Nah, Padre, Not me. Teacher got to do the dishes, She say so."

I took the cloth from Cesar and sat at the table to watch my men cook. I loved watching other people cook, not just because I hated cooking, but because

I loved watching anyone do anything they obviously gloried in. The Rev and Carlos were deep into chopping peppers, onions, some leftover pork—two tall lean men chopping with the rhythms of pure pleasure. Carlos was as relaxed as I'd yet seen him. He and the pastor had synchronized their movements without being at all aware of it: gather, chop, sweep into a finished pile, chop again.

Cesar turned off the burner under the soup he'd been heating, and set down his spoon.

"Teacher?" He folded his arms and cocked his head in my direction. "You think there a reason you and me keep a history together?"

"I... I don't know, Cesar. Maybe it's just coincidence. But I guess I don't really believe that. I actually think we connect with certain people again and again because there's something that binds us together; we just don't always know what that something is."

Cesar unfolded his arms and pointed at me with his index finger, looking down his finger like it was the barrel of a gun.

"I think that something with you and me maybe is real bad luck. First you get the snake bite, then the earthquake, then my father die, then Ruth die, now we got a bunch of crazy drug guys wanna shot us. Teacher, you or me one is carrying a curse. We got to stay back from each other."

He was smiling while he said this to let me know he was joking, but I could see he wasn't just kidding; he was also asking.

"Or on the other hand..."

I knew I was heading into Pollyanna territory, but I'd been accused of straying there before. "Maybe it's that you and I need to be there to help each other when the bad luck comes. Maybe our friendship isn't about bad luck at all; maybe it's about the good luck of somehow always crossing paths when our hard times come, because there is a quality in each of us the other one does not have but needs to get by."

So, of course now my brain was screaming, "We get by with a little help from our friends..." To distract myself from the ear worm, I looked over at Rev (always a pleasant distraction), who had paused his meal prep in mid-chop when Cesar pointed his finger. The pastor was holding his knife still poised in the air. Oh, lay your weapons down, boys. First Cesar raises an air gun and now there's an actual knife being waved about. Lord, don't let number three be a real gun. I was trying to not let the air of possible trouble spook me into superstitious connections, but my mind wasn't listening to reasoning.

I knew the drug guys could easily make their way inside the walls of Nogales United Methodist Church, just as the sudden tension that night at the dance could have turned out to be some sort of gang domination over a community event instead of just a show-down between a small boy and his absent dad.

And how much scarier must Ruth's and Alma's time in the desert have been than this night ahead with its possibility of things going terribly wrong for us. At least we have walls that might slow down our attackers long enough for us to...

There my thinking dribbled to a stop because I had not a clue what our

Plan B might be. Rev. Freeman spoke up then, quietly and reassuringly. Reassuring nervous people was both his job description and his nature.

"You know, the cartel seldom breaks into buildings, especially not churches. If we were out on the street we'd be asking for trouble, but maybe not even there, at least not you and me, Trish. They avoid messing with Americans."

I was so delighted to hear this that I wanted details, lots of marvelous details.

"Why?"

"Well, like most people who make a life of illegal activity they try to keep from attracting the attention of those who could put a crimp in their lifestyle. Harming an American would greatly impair their ability to do what they want to do."

"What do they want to do?"

The pastor smiled and spread his open hands.

"Make a profit. They are a business; it's all about power and profit."

Somehow I did not find it comforting to think of the drug cartel as merely ill-mannered entrepreneurs. But the Rev's comment had at least broken the mood of imminent doom and I was hungry. If it proved to be absolutely necessary, I would panic again after supper.

It turned out not to be necessary. Out on the streets the evening passed quietly, oddly quietly. I heard none of the usual music from cafés or the chatter of families heading to those cafés for dinner at around the same hour I would have been getting ready for bed at home in Georgia. Not even a single car horn blared—a circumstance of note in a country where drivers use their car horns in the place of turn signals and brakes.

After our dinner and after I had washed the dishes as promised, Carlos settled on the sofa with a book borrowed from the pastor's study, the pastor himself went to his study to get a little paperwork done before bed, and Cesar and I sat by the fireplace to talk, or not talk. It made no difference to us.

The four of us had each gone to our place of comfort in the midst of grief, I realized as I looked over at Carlos holding his book like a shield. Carlos had a book, and Rev had gone to his office to re-set the balance between good and bad through the goodness of his work. So what about Cesar and me? Where was our place of comfort?

"Teacher, you tell me what your life is like in America?"

Of course. That was it: our place of comfort was in stories. That was how people like Cesar and me made sense of things—through telling life as a story.

"Deal. If you will then tell me about yours."

Cesar held out his hand to shake mine.

"Deal."

And so I talked about my teaching and the old farm I lived on and how close Mama and I had always been and how now that Mama was getting older, it was my turn to start being the one to do the looking after. I talked about my love of singing and my dogs and how I used my walks through my woods with the dogs as a time to sing whatever I pleased, as loudly as I pleased.

"That's one of the best parts of owning some woods, Cesar—you have a private place where you don't have to worry about looking foolish."

"I all the time look foolish, Teacher. Foolish is my talent."

I smiled at him. I knew good and well it was the sort of smile that would cause someone passing by and noticing my smile to startle and think, *Oh. She loves him.*

"No, Cesar. Your talent is for offering kindness in a way that does not make the other person feel indebted."

"Teacher, you a kind person, too. Why you never be married? You like the men, verdad?"

He Grouch Marx-ed his eyebrows when he asked about the men.

"Oh, yes, Cesar; I like the men."

I waggled my eyebrows back at him, clown to clown.

"So why you never marry one of the men?"

It was amazing how even though neither of us had said a word about my age, I was rapidly feeling as if my marriage market eligibility was about an hour away from expiration.

"Well, one time I came close."

With those words, the man I had come close with walked right back into my mind's eye, jingling the coins and the pocketknife he always kept in his right pants pocket, smiling at me, his coppery skin crinkling around the corners of his eyes the way it always had. He had been sixteen years older than me and even while he was still living I had mourned my missing out on those sixteen years.

I knew Cesar was waiting for the rest of the story, but was too much of a gentleman to rush me.

"He died, Cesar. Way too young, he died. We wasted a lot of time when we could have been together because I refused to date him for a long time after we met. Everyone had warned me not to get involved with him. They said he was a hound dog, and I guess he was, but not with me."

"He was a dog, Teacher?"

I grinned, and shook my head. My hair was almost dry from the shower and the curls moved loosely around my cheeks.

"A hound dog is an American expression for a man who is always running away from his woman and chasing someone else's woman. When the two of us got together, he was ready to stop running away and stay home with me, but God caught him before he made it there."

Oh, I had not intended to make Cesar sadder. And Carlos? I glanced quickly over toward Carlos to make sure hadn't heard my sad story. Whew. He was deeply into his book.

"And now it's your turn, my friend. Tell me of your family, Cesar. Your wife's name is Ana?"

"Si, Ana."

Cesar took a minute to enjoy the thought of Ana's face. When he looked up at me and started talking again, he had the look of a man who can never get over being awed by his own good fortune.

"My Ana, she love me too much."

I shook a schoolmarm finger in his direction.

"No, Cesar, you should say she loves you *very* much. When you use the word *too* like that in English, it becomes a negative statement. It means there is something negative about the way she loves you"

I could see Cesar thinking about his wife.

"Teacher, my Ana, she love me too much."

27
Cesar

My Ana had said to me that she was not going to sit at home any longer while I put myself into the danger again and again.

"If a bad thing is going to happen, then it will happen to you and me together, my husband. Listen to me: I am coming to Nogales. The next time you try to cross, we will both try to cross."

"And what of your sister?" I asked her. I put my back against the hallway wall and slid down to the floor, pulling my legs up and resting my elbows on my knees, bracing the phone against my jaw. This might take a while; I needed to get comfortable. "Is Elena to sit patiently at home with Carlito while you join with your own husband? I cannot believe she will allow this."

Allow this? I thought Ha. I knew my sister-in-law well enough to be certain as soon as Elena had heard of the plans Ana was making, she packed her suitcase and told their family it was all her own idea, not Ana's.

"Noooo...." Ana did not hurry to answer me, meaning I was right.

"No, well, actually, Elena and Carlito are coming, too." Ana's talking started to pick up speed, like an old car going downhill. "It makes sense, Cesar. We will all make it to the U.S. together, so you and Carlos will not have to leave the jobs you will find. You know your cousin told you he can find a job for you. We can go to North Carolina to your cousin and live with him for a time until we can find our own place."

I opened my mouth to remind her that my cousin had said *maybe* he could find a job for me, but Ana was not yet to the bottom of her hill.

"The money you and Carlos left for us goes too fast, even though we take great care with it. We cannot stop Carlito's toes from growing to the ends of his shoes. I know you cannot work for more money while you are waiting to cross, and the money you have must go to pay la guida. If we go together we can pay the guide once for all of us and then you and Carlos can get good U.S. jobs. You can work for three times the money anyone would pay you in Mexico and you can come home from your jobs at night to your wives and your children."

I grinned to myself as I sat there on the cool grey tile of the hallway floor listening to my Ana plan our future. Her love had already jumped us safely across the border and had us living in North Carolina where Carlos and me were working at jobs that paid a fat paycheck, while she and Elena watched over the children that God had not yet given us.

"And these little ones, mi Corazón—you have names for them yet?" I was still smiling as I asked her.

On Ana's end of the connection there a silence that was not a silence. Then she answered my question in a different voice, a softer voice.

"I was thinking if this one is a boy, you might want to call him for your father, to give your father back the future he lost while he was trying to give a future to another young one."

Ah. Dios. My brain leaned against the back wall of my skull and slid to its bony floor. *This one?*

But then, of course, I said to my wife many words that spoke of how the wonder of a son—my son—was a gift like none I ever would be able to give back to her, though I would try for all the rest of my life. I said to her yes, of course we would cross together as soon as possible and I would get that job with the fat paycheck so she and I and the boy in her belly could live the way my wife and son deserved to live. "Come to Nogales," I said to my Ana just before I said goodbye and that I loved her more than my own beating heart. I told her: "Take the money you have left and buy bus tickets for you and Elena and Carlito. I will meet you at the bus station tomorrow evening."

It was this conversation with my pregnant wife that was in my thoughts as I talked with Teacher. *My pregnant wife*: I could not yet say those words without feeling a shiver of worry yet also of happiness deeper than any well I had drawn water from as a boy. Oh, but then I looked at Teacher and I felt sad because the joy of having a child was a joy she had not known and would never know. She was too old.

No, not old. I stopped myself and looked away from Teacher very fast and then back at her out of the side of my eye, like I was not really looking at her at all, but at something very interesting just behind her. I wanted to see if she had heard me call her old in my head. It is always best not to meet the eyes of a woman while you are thinking thoughts you do not want that woman to know about. I believe women can see clearly into the minds of their men, and that some women can see in this way more easily than others. My Ana has sharp eyes to see into my thoughts, but I was as certain as the stars in the heavens that Teacher had the eyes of an eagle. I changed the direction of my thinking in case she was already looking there.

No, I thought, Teacher is not old at all, except in the unfair accounting of the years. This was true enough. Her mind was young and in looks she could rival a chica jovena. Ai, dios-not that I have ever looked at her in the way that men look at pretty women.

I turned my eyes up toward the ceiling, and beyond. I needed help out of this hole I was digging for myself. Ayudame, Señor. The Blessed Lord answered my cry by sending sleepiness to the Teacher. She yawned and her eyes closed a little way. Gracias, Señor.

"Cesar, I'm going to bed. Sleep well, and I will see you in the morning."

She did see me in the morning, and Carlos, too; I made sure of it. We all went to the kitchen for some breakfast at about the same time. Well, almost the same time. Teacher was already there when my brother and me came all sleepy and stupid down the hall wishing the coffee we smelled would come and meet us halfway. It met us at the kitchen door, in two cups Teacher was holding out while she smiled at us. Did all women wake up faster and happier than men, I wondered for the hundredth time?

"Good morning, mis amigos. Looks like the cartel guys decided to let us all sleep. The Reverend has already checked things out on the street and it seems quiet. *Praise God for that,* he said, and I have to agree with him."

Did she not praise God by herself? The coffee started to wake up my brain cells. Maybe she praised God through work instead of words. That was probably fine with God, I decided. Maybe He got tired of all the time hearing people talk, talk, talk. Maybe he wished more people would shut their mouths and do something. Teacher was always doing something and I never saw her do anything that was not good for somebody.

My brother and me had some things to do, too—although Carlos did not yet know about all of them. I wanted to wait until we left the church to tell him what Ana had said on the phone, because I did not want Teacher and the Father to know that our wives and Carlito were coming to Nogales this day. If they heard that our families were coming, they would understand *why* they were coming because Teacher and Father were both very smart. Also, they cared about me and Carlos. I would not give them reason to worry—that was the best gift of friendship I could give to them.

I finished my coffee and set the heavy white cup flat down on the table with a thud.

"Teacher, me and my lazy brother got to go check on our truck. We leave it out there with nobody watch it one more day and it gonna be a truck with no tires and no motor. Gracias for the coffee."

Teacher smiled at me from where she was sitting with her hands around her cup of tea like she was warming her fingers on this morning that was already getting hot outside. She always did that with her cup. Carlos sighed and rolled his eyes a little, but got up to go with me.

"Cesar?"

I stopped at the doorway and looked back at Teacher. I raised one eyebrow: *yes?*

"You are a good man."

Maldición. Her words told me I had not looked away from her eyes quickly enough last night. She had seen all my thoughts.

I walked down the hall and out through the front door of the church, but I stopped there for a moment while Carlos made noises of impatience as I looked around at the streets of Nogales where bad things could happen so quickly. But no

178

bad things will happen to us this day. I was sure of that all of a sudden. Teacher did not believe I pitied her as a woman with no babies, and she did not think I was a man who would be foolish with the safety of his family. She thought only that I was a good man. I raised my chin like a man who is sure of his own worth. How could anything bad happen to such a man?

"So we are to spend the day staring at cars driving by?"

I shook my head and slapped my arm up high around Carlos's shoulder. I smiled at him the way I used to smile when we were kids and I knew some secret.

"No, my brother; we are to spend this day preparing to greet our wives."

Carlos looked at me not with confusion but with happiness alone. It was not his strength to allow more than one feeling at a time to inhabit him. Because of Carlos I understood the ways of those like him who fight against a blackness always waiting to creep into their hearts and minds. That blackness, when it covered him, did so like the nights of our childhood that had no lights but the stars, and some nights not even the stars. I remember how the darkness then would not let me see even which brother was snoring next to me in our bed.

Also I remember the mornings, how the sun would come like a ball thrown against our window. One moment I would be lying blind in a world that was nothing more than the heaviness of flung legs and the sounds of unseen snorers, and in the next moment a deep yellow brightness would splash across my brothers' slackened mouths like a searchlight.

So it was with Carlos: I had watched him all our lives live too many days as if the nights of those days had forgotten to leave at the hour of morning. In times like those, he wore the blackness of his spirit like a winter coat, but then a morning would come when for no reason I could see, the coat would be gone and my brother would call me stupid, and I would grin like that stupid man because my brother was back. It was always one or the other: Carlos was here and happy, or he was gone to the devil's hole.

This morning, Carlos was here and happy. Our wives were coming to us.

"Good thing we took a shower at the church, eh, my dumb brother?"

Carlos slapped me across the back of my head as he spoke.

"You're still ugly, but at least you don't stink. I guess your Ana, she is used to seeing you ugly."

I slapped him back.

"My Ana, she is so beautiful her eyes can see only beauty, even when she looks at an ugly man like you, Carlos. Come, let us go find our ugly truck and see if it is still wearing tires. Then we have to find a place for our family to stay this night."

A little shadow of blackness passed over Carlos's eyes, like a small cloud blowing across a clear sky. He blinked. He did not want to let the dark into his soul on this day, but any problem like where to find beds for our wives might let it come in. I spoke quickly, to help him.

"I have an idea. Do you remember when we were searching all over town for Ruth and her friend?" And then I could have kicked my own butt for saying

Ruth's name, but Carlos was just nodding his head, waiting for my idea, so I keep talking.

"Remember we talked to the guy who runs the bus station and he told us about the little room he has at the back of the station where he sometimes lets los migrantes sleep? Maybe he would let us use that room for one night. There was just one bed, but Ana and Elena could sleep together, and you and me could make a bed on the floor with Carlito between us."

Ah, my brother was happy now, hearing his son's name and thinking about Carlito sleeping close to him this night. I had not yet told Carlos of my own son. That good news could wait until there was need of more good news.

"But, Cesar, why don't we just take the women and Carlito to the church? You know Father would say we could stay there, and think how happy it would make Teacher to meet Carlito."

"And think how much worry we would give to Teacher and Father when we leave tomorrow to cross. We cannot do that to them."

"Tomorrow?"

Carlos jerked his arm away from my shoulder and turned me with his hand to face him. A man pulling his racks of rebozos out on to the sidewalk for the day stopped and narrowed his eyes, waiting to see if we were going to be trouble for him.

I reached up and put my hand over Carlos's hand and spoke to him softly. "My brother."

The businessman relaxed: just something between hermanos. He knew all about such things.

"Come, let us move away from so many ears."

We walked down the sidewalk to where there were no businesses, only houses with one abuela sweeping the walk in front of her house. I nodded good morning to her, and began to tell Carlos some of what I had learned yesterday.

"I have not yet told you of the call that came from a guide who says he will take us across, but it must be soon. And after he called, Ana called. Ai, Carlos, I wish you had been there to hear her say she was coming with Elena and Carlito tonight. Eight-fifteen. Our women will be here at eight-fifteen."

I stopped talking for a minute so we could grin at each other like two idiots.

"We will meet them at the station and sleep there, too, if the manager agrees. Come, let us go tell this station manager why he must let us have the use of the room and then we will go check on our truck. We can talk there, where it is more private."

The man at the station talked tough, but he was a kind man in his heart. He had learned to act tough to keep away the street wolves who watched for weaknesses. Or maybe instead of wolves I should have said *the coyotes*. I grinned at my own joke. The station manager grinned back at me and shook my hand. I had just told him of Ana and the baby while Carlos was not listening, and the man thought I was smiling about that.

"Por seguro, mi amigo, your wife must rest here this night—and also her sister and the little one. Did you think I would tell you there was no room at this inn, eh?"

He elbowed me in my ribs. His joke was a clever one, verdad?

I laughed for the sake of his cleverness and then I thanked him and told him he was a good man. Perhaps if enough men in Nogales could be told of their goodness, it would become true.

The man had not spoken of payment, but already I was figuring the amount I had still hidden in my shoe, and how I could take a little from the total to repay this man for his generosity. I had eaten well at the church; I had no need for supper that night. That would save a bit.

Carlos and I kept quiet inside of our own thoughts for the rest of the walk to our truck. The truck was there, and gracias a dios, it still had all four tires. We opened both doors on the truck to let the hot air out and then we sat inside with the seats let back, resting. Carlos, of course, could not let such a peaceful silence go on forever, or for even fifteen minutes.

"Brother, you know this man who is going to take us over?"

"I know him a little. He is married with a friend of mine. He told me once whenever you need a favor, just call me. After we did not make it over the first time, I called him. He said he would see what he could do. He called me back yesterday and said he was going to take us. He has been a coyote for a long time, so he can do that."

Carlos nodded head.

"It will be okay, then. We are going to make it this time."

I nodded, too, but I would not tell my brother until the time came that the coyote also had said Carlito would have to make it first, by himself. When I asked the guy why, he told me any little black-haired kid looks like any other, so a kid can use some other kid's ID to cross over with fake parents who have legal ID. Carlito was a year and a half old so he could speak some words, but that was no problem, the guy said. They would give my nephew a little pill, make him seem like he just needed a nap. This way, the guy said to me, there are no problems for a little kid to make it over. No, not any problems. Then a day or two later, the women can cross.

And my brother and me can cross with our wives? The guy blew out a long breath on his end of the phone. Maybe, he said. When I asked the guy what is the reason for the *maybe,* he told me it depended on if I had the money. We charge 3000 for the women, only 1500 for the men. The women are slower, sometimes, and sometimes they need to ride. The men can walk.

Money. Again it all comes back to money. While we were at the church I had hidden in the bathroom to count the money in my shoe and count it again—so many times I started to worry I might wear it out before I could spend it. There was enough in my stash for Ana and Elena and Carlito, for sure. That was good. I wanted to get my Ana over soon because she was only going to get bigger and it would be harder for her to make it.

But there was not enough for Carlos and me to cross, both of us together. If we had to choose, it would be Carlos. I would not ask Carlos to let his wife and son go over without him. It had been hard enough for him to push the worry away when he knew they were safe at home in Jalisco with their mother and their sisters and their aunts and their cousins watching out for them. But to let them go to the U.S. alone? No. The darkness would come to Carlos's soul forever if I asked him to let them go alone.

I sighed and pictured again the stack of bills as I had seen them in my hands over and over at the church while I sat in the bathroom pretending to be taking care of nature. In my mind I could see the few bills that were left in my hand after I had counted out the money for everyone else. Half. There was only half the money for me to cross with my family. I had to know if this was going to be a problem.

"Carlos?"

"Hmmm?"

"Be right back. I need to visit a tree."

If I kept having to hide things from my brother he was going to think I had the bladder of an old man.

As soon as I thought I was far enough away so he could not hear, I called our connection. I talked to him and I told him the truth: we don't have too much money. But what if I pay maybe half for me? Then when I get over there and I can work at that fine job my Ana believes is waiting for me, I can pay him back a little every week. He said okay, that is fine.

Fine is how I felt later that evening when the bus pulled in with Ana and Elena and Carlito. The calendar said it had not been so very long since we had seen our wives, but it had been forever. I never realized when Ana was not with me how much of me was missing. I knew I was lonely for Ana, but it was not until I was holding her to my chest that I realized I had also been lonely for myself, because so much of me could not be separated from her.

The station manager was all happy for us. He kept looking at Ana and nudging me and winking. Carlos thought he had lost his mind.

"That one is not right, brother. We will need to lock the door to our room tonight."

I nodded *yes, yes.* I would have agreed to anything just then. I slipped the manager my supper money as I took the key from his hand.

The next morning came before I was ready to walk with it toward ten o'clock, which was the time our connection had told us to meet him. I opened my eyes, just the same, because this day must not catch me closing my eyes to anything. Little puffs of warm air were hitting against my shoulder. I looked: it was the breaths of Carlito sleeping in the curve of his father's arms. Sleep had taken away the little boy from his face and left the face of a baby, still, with his mouth working as a baby's will.

"Soon." The whispered word came from Ana, who was awake and leaning from the bed to where I lay on the floor. She reached down and took my hand and held it to her cheek.

"Soon, my husband, the little one beside you will be ours."

I shook my head *shhh, no,* tilting my head toward Carlos. He does not yet know. Ana smiled and nodded, I understand.

This, I thought, is why men marry. It is so we will have someone who does not need to hear words to know what we are saying. This is a marvelous thing, because we men are so often stupid with words.

I would have stayed in that moment longer, knowing that here was all I needed in the world—to be able to open my eyes and see the eyes of my Ana looking back at me, but of course no such moment can last. God is wise in this way. He knows we would never get up and do the work of the day if we were given the choice of staying in loving moments with our wives. Maybe this is why Teacher gets so much done, because she wakes up each day and stares into no one's eyes. I hoped right then that she and the man she had loved were given many such times before he left her. Surely God knew Teacher deserved a blessing like that.

"Papi?"

Carlito was pushing his little hand against Carlos' shoulder.

"Papi."

Ai, now it starts. There is no turning back to the peace of the new day once the little one is awake. We all rose and dressed and thanked the station manager again and again as we headed out the door to a café for food and coffee. The manager winked at me once again from the doorway and Carlos pulled his son close to his side.

Some might call me a coward for waiting to explain to my brother and our wives of the manner our crossing must take that day, but I prefer to call myself selfish, as that is at least a sin more manly than to be a coward. I wanted my family to have this time together, so I talked of small things and sipped my coffee slowly and watched Carlito play a game of toss the ball with another little boy.

The church bells rang the three-quarter hour. Nine-forty-five.

"Come, my family. Let us take a morning walk."

Ana looked at me, scared. Now?

Sí, mi corazón.

I picked up the backpack holding the water and other things Ana would need for her crossing, and Carlos did the same with his pack. We headed up the street two blocks to the border crossing building, falling in step with many other families crossing to the other Nogales for business or shopping. I saw the man who was our connection standing near the steel turnstiles, smoking a cigarette. I stopped, put my hand on Carlos's arm and waited for him to stop, too.

I let go of Ana's hand and squatted down to speak to Carlito.

"Sweetheart, you are lucky today. You will get to go first through the big gates, with Papi's friend."

I had not finished speaking before Carlito began to shake his head. "No, no." He held his papa's hand close to his face and looked away from me. It was good that he held tight to Carlos's hand because I believe my brother would have hit me. He had never hit me in anger, not even when we were niños. He kept his hand holding his son's hand and threw his words at me, instead.

"Bastardo. You knew of this."

It was not a question.

The connection was walking toward us. He had seen Carlos's face and he knew that two brothers fighting would make the guards notice us as more quickly than they might pay attention to two more poor Mexicans with their wives. He knew this would ruin everything and he would not get his pay.

"Mi primo. Como estás?"

The guy put his arm around Carlos's shoulder as soon as he reached us, and he kept talking like we were cousins who had not seen each other for a long time. He started leading us away from where Border Patrol might hear us and when we were far enough away, he switched from fake talk to telling us real low and fast what we were going to do. We stopped in front of a shop telling tourist crap, and Carlito let go of Carlos's hand to go look at some toy guitars.

"I got a birth certificate from some other kid, so your son can make it right now, easy. You are the papa, right?" He looked at Carlos. Carlos nodded, one nod only.

"Okay, Papi, you can walk with him to the crossing like you are his uncle. You hold his hand so he won't cry and we will take him across. Let's go."

Elena moved from where she had been holding onto Carlos's other arm. She looked like somebody had just shaken her to wake her from a long sleep. She stepped close to the guy and reached out her hand like to touch him, but she did not.

"By himself? But he is a baby."

The guy kind of shrugged one shoulder.

"That's why, señora. It is no problem for the babies to make it. He will go, easy, and tonight when it is dark, we will take the rest of you."

So the guy took Carlito and at first my little nephew walked because his father was with him, but then when Carlos turned to come back to us, Carlito cried, and pulled away from the guy. He started whining, real loud, "La guitarra. Quiero la guitarra."

The man turned to Carlos.

"Hey, you know what? I don't have money. I just have money for the taxi on the other side. Give me money because I have to buy the boy that toy guitar so he will shut up."

I handed the money to Carlos and he gave it to the man and the man just took Carlito and that little toy guitar across to Arizona.

All the rest of that day, Elena cried. I did not know it was possible for a person to cry so many hours. Carlos sat in the back of our truck under the shade of a big mesquite tree and held his wife, rocking her as he would have rocked his son. They did not speak to me and Ana did not *stop* speaking to me, all that long day. Her voice whispered on and on through the afternoon, giving to me the strength she should have saved for our babe.

I had betrayed two sons on this day: the son of my father and his own little son.

As soon as the sun began to slip behind the high walls of the church where Father and Teacher were probably cooking dinner (no, probably the Father was cooking and Teacher was promising to clean the dishes afterward), we picked up our backpacks again and left our truck again. The man had told us to meet him near the house where Carlos and me had crossed the last time, when la migra caught us. There would be a van there, the man said, to drive us a few miles west to where the wall stopped. We would cross over somewhere along the twenty-mile stretch between checkpoints, where the only border fence was made of posts and two strands of barbed wire that were easy to cut.

It was just like the first time we crossed, only this time four people from the family Ramirez would be crossing together, instead of two. And this time we would not have to hide under blankets because it was the dark of night and because we were so far from a patrolled crossing. They would just drive us across into the desert and from there we could walk to Phoenix.

The guides had already started loading the others into the van when we walked up. The van looked full, but one of the men waved his hand at us, impatient-like. Carlos crawled up into the open back of the van and put his hand down to help Elena up. The people inside moved as much as they could, but there was really not much room for them to move anywhere. I stood behind Ana and boosted her up because I did want her to strain; it might be bad for the baby. I handed the backpack to her and then I grabbed hold of the door frame to pull myself after her, but one of the coyotes jerked me back by my shirt.

"Too full. You go next trip."

He slammed the doors and slapped the doors with his hand to make sure the latch had caught. I could see Ana's face through the little back window. I smiled at her and gave her the OK sign with my thumb.

The driver started the engine, and the one who had told me to wait ran to the front to hop in, but he stopped, like he had just remembered that once he had been a good person. He turned back to me.

"It is because you paid only half; that is why you were the one to have to wait. But soon more people will be here to leave on the next van. That van will not have so many and you can go with it, for sure. Wait under those palo verdes over there. You will have just a little wait and then you can again be with your family, my friend."

And then they drove away.

28

Cesar

Thanks to God, Ana had the backpack. The phone was in there, and some food and water, and I had tied a blanket to the bottom of the pack. Ana told me she

185

brought some little bit of money with her from home and she sewed it inside her bra. She would be fine. Carlos had his pack, also, and some of our money from my shoe. Carlito had his guitar over in the United States and was waiting for us there. All of my family would be fine. For me, also, this was okay; just a couple of hours to rest like a rich man under those trees until I crossed, too, and then I will use some other guy's phone to call her, to find out where she waits for me. Everything would be fine.

And thanks to God it was me that got left back, not Carlos. This was what I was thinking after the van with my family inside got too far away for me to see the taillights. I walked over to the trees to sit and waited for my turn to go. Gracias a Dios it was not my genius brother who waited here alone because Carlos forgets things like how cold the desert is at night. I patted the blanket I had rolled up and tied with my belt, very tight, back at our truck. This night I would not suffer; only a few hours to take a short sleep under the trees until the man came back for me, and I had this blanket if the cold came down before he returned.

The sand under the trees was still warm. I wiggled my butt down into a hill of sand and leaned my back against one of the trees. I untied the loop of rope holding the blanket around my waist and shoved the blanket roll behind my neck. Ah. This was not so bad.

An owl spoke to me from some other tree far away from the one I was resting under. I looked out into the dark but of course I could not see him. Probably he sat on a branch of a tree farther down the wash, toward the open desert. Why are owls always far away? I had wondered this since I was a little kid getting my granny's water from our well in the last hours of night. In all my life, never had I seen an owl close by, and never had I heard one ask his question so early in the night as this one was asking. I shrugged. Ah, well. I was a traveling pilgrim and should expect to be questioned by all. I waited for Sr. Owl to ask again: *Who, who, whoooo?* I waited for him to finish and then I answered him true. One thing I had learned the first time I got caught crossing, was it is always bad to lie to the authorities, and the owl is the authority of nighttime. So I answered to him in truth, "This is me, Cesar Ramirez. I am a pilgrim who waits to be with his family again, that is all. I am in search of a good place where we can live."

Sr. Owl spoke no more. How could he? His next question could have been *why, why, why,* and this word is not in an owl's vocabulary. I smiled there in the dark by myself. I had answered his only question with a true fact, and now his job was done. Lucky bird. He had no need for reasons. Por seguro, he had no *interest* in reasons.

But there will be others who will ask why do you not stay to the home you have? Ai, Dios, if these people could open a little door to my heart and look inside, there they would look upon the casita of la famlia Ramirez as it stands in our village just ten minutes' walk up the mountain from Puerto Vallarta. I would say to such people, See? Here is my home and here would I stay until both my beards turned white, if only I could. It is this *if only* that is the reason I sit here now.

I squirmed a little where I was sitting. The warmth from the sun of the day was leaving from the sand and the night air was growing heavier as the cold came down from the wide dark of the desert sky. I unfolded the blanket and put it over my head and shoulders like a tent.

I pulled my legs up closer to my chest and I sighed. Talking to myself about my home had made me think of my father. I did not often think of him, but a man alone in a dark place will remember much he was sure he had put away the way a father puts his gun on a shelf too high for the little ones to reach.

My father. I sighed again, as if sighing might blow away the hurt of thinking of him. My father had left us, his sons and his wife, left us again and again because he knew that staying with us would cause his family harm. He left us because he loved us, hoping always this love would help him find a way to return. His deepest wish was always to stay home, even when he was leaving.

The night had grown too quiet. Was Sr. Owl still there? I looked out across the dark sand and waved my hand at the distance—one night owl calling another. I spoke very softly to my questioning compadre, "Please understand, Senor Owl, that this is the answer to why I am leaving Mexico. I am leaving my country because I love my country and would not stay here to grow more anger against her than I do now. I do not want to hate my country for what men have let her become."

Some words I had learned in school many years ago came into my head just then. Ah, Teacher, I thought—you would be proud of me for remembering words I was made to learn in school. I laughed, seeing how Teacher's face would look if she heard me say such a thing, how her eyes would grow wide and very green and she would... I slapped my hand over my mouth. Had I just laughed out loud? Fool. Carlos is right, you are his fool brother. Shut up, or the ones you do not want to find you this night will take you away from under your hiding tree where you can lie around talking with owls and American ladies and dead men.

But the words, Teacher (I whispered to her inside my head) the words are from your Shakespeare. I remember them exactly because my teacher would not give me a passing grade until I could hold in my heart three quotes from this man's plays, and also because—though I did not tell the teacher this—I liked the picture these words put into my head: it is wondrous to have a giant's strength, but tyrannous to use it like a giant. The boy with no father I was then thought it would be wondrous to possess the strength of a giant, or to have a strong giant in my life every day. *Wondrous* and *giant* were the words I carried with me from that classroom, but the word that walked with me now was *tyrannous*.

My government was tyrannous. It was like a monster so big it could not even see the people it stepped on, little people like my family. We worked hard; all the time we worked hard with our hands and our backs and our legs, but never would the government let someone of my family move into a job where we could work hard with our minds. And even if a man with a mind like my brother's mind wiggled into such a job, the boss could fire him as soon as he had thirty-five years, to hire a man younger who would not ask for so much money.

And the drugs. Ai, Dios. I had many times seen little boys with only six or seven years pulled into the gangs, and when I saw this, every time I could see Carlito's face on the faces of those niñitos. I would not let this happen to Carlito or to my own son. His face must be his own, not the face of a gang.

A shadow passed fast between me and the moon. Someone was coming. I pushed the blanket back from my head. Yes. There was a man walking toward me. I saw him in the way that in the night you try as quickly as you can to make sense of the shape moving like dark against dark, so you can quickly tell yourself this is nothing to fear.

"Señor? Eh, hombre? Are you there? We need to go. Let's go."
It was the man from the van who had told me to wait. I jumped to my feet and the blanket fell back from over my head. I grabbed a corner to hold it around my shoulders while I tried to run to him through the soft sand of the wash.

"I am here." I did not bother to quiet my speaking because he had not, but he shushed me like I had the age of Carlito.

"Shut up. You want la policia to hear?"

I knew he meant the Mexican police. Even the coyotes prefer to be in trouble with the Immigration over the Mexican police.

"Sorry, man." I whispered this time.

As soon as he saw I was following him, the man turned and started walking toward the river. Why were we going this way? Where was the van?

"Hey, mister—what is your name?"

He stopped and turned around so fast I almost ran into him.

"Why?" He asked me in way to tell me I would feel his fist in my face if I gave the wrong answer.

I shrugged one shoulder.

"Mi madre told me always to give people the honor of their names."

He stared at me through the darkness. It is not possible to look at a person in darkness, but it is possible to stare, because staring is done with the mind, not the eye.

"My name is Nicolas."

"And mine is Cesar. Nicolas, are we not going to the van?'

I asked him only *if*, not *why*, because the first price you pay for allowing someone else power over your life is that you give up the right to explanations.

"Nah, the van, it had problems."

He must have heard me stop breathing halfway through one breath because he shook his head and said, "Oh, the people all got crossed over okay, but then when I was driving back here the van started to drive bad."

I finished letting out the breath I had been holding and then I spoke to God before I spoke again to Nicolas. I gave to God a promise I would end my walk to America on my knees in church as soon as I was with my family on the other side. Before I ate a meal, before I kissed my wife, I would go down on both knees and give thanks to God for seeing my family safely over.

"So there is another car coming to take us across?"

Nicolas shook his head, *no.*

"Nobody but you left to cross. We are going to walk to a spot where we can wade the river and then I'll take you to meet some guys who will take you to where they left the others. You pay me when I leave you with those guys and you pay them when they get you to your family."

"Hey. Stop there."

A Mexican policeman was yelling at us, and another was running to cut us off before we could get to the river. Nicolas grabbed my arm.

"Let's go, let's go across."

I did what he said because he has the experience. If he was telling me to come with him, I decided, this must be the best way to go. I held my blanket up on top of my head and ran for the river, then I was running in the river and then just when I was thinking we were going to have to swim and that was going to be a tricky thing for me to do since I could not swim, Nicolas stopped running. He let go of my arm and started walking in that river like it was Sunday afternoon on the Malecon back home.

"It is okay, man. They are not going to come out here."

And he was right. The police were all just standing by the Mexican side of the river like they did not want to get their shoes wet, and they were yelling, "We will catch you. You will come back, and see what happens to you then."

The one good thing this Nicolas did for me was to lead me through at a place where the water never got deep enough to make me have to try to swim. I just kept holding my blanket on the top of my head and walking across that river like I was following Moses. We got to the other side and I was illegal again. It was starting to feel normal to be illegal.

Nicolas, he never stayed with me after that. He told me to wait right there, that he was just going to take a pee, but then he never came back. The Immigration came out from under some trees where they had been waiting for me. Nicolas, he knew they were there.

The Immigration men told me to lie down on the sand. The sand was cold. This was not fine sand like on the beach at Puerto Vallarta; this sand had bigger grains and the grains were hard, like tiny rocks. It felt slick, like some man's wife had slung the grease from her pans. The moon must have come out while I was wading the river because I could see the spine of a cactus shaped like a water barrel and it was just inches from my left eye. There was a tiny blue flower right next to my nose; it was folding its petals up tight for the night. I closed my eyes.

One man told me to put my hands on my back and he put the handcuffs on me. Then he pulled down my pants to check me for knives or guns. I could not do nothing because I was wearing the handcuffs and because they had the guns, not me. I felt somebody yank my pants back up; this man reached under my arms to help me stand up.

The guy who helped me up asked me in English, "Where are you going, man?"

I just shook my head. Where was my blanket? I was cold.

"How many of you are there?"

Again he asked me in English, so I answered him in English.

"Me, only."

As soon as I said this, another one of the Border Patrol guys pulled out his phone and called someone.

"We've got a..." Then he said some number that I knew was code for someone who understands English.

The guy near me asked again, "How many bears with you? How many chickens?"

I smiled at him, a little smile.

"No bears, no chickens, no owls. Me, only."

The "owl" was a joke between me and my owl friend.

They men opened the back doors of the Border Patrol van and led me over to put me inside. I stopped for a second before I lifted my foot up to the high step into the van while the man kept his hand under my armpit to help me balance. There was no one inside. Of course there was no one there. I did not really expect my Ana to be in there waiting for me and I did not want her to be in the van of la migra, but for a second I hoped she might be, just so I could know she was *somewhere*.

Blessed Virgin, where was my Ana?

The ride to the detention center was not very long, maybe twenty minutes. There were places all along the border where they took the migrants they caught, but I was not sure which one the guys were taking me to. There were no windows in the back of the van, and the Border Patrol guy who was riding in the back with me did not seem like the kind of guy to want to make conversation with a Mexican. I had nothing to do but think.

I did not tell you the whole truth last night, Sr. Owl. That was what I thought as we rode. I had said to the owl that I was leaving Mexico because I did not want to grow to hate my country, and that was true, but I did not mention that I also was doing this so my family would not starve. This was the part of the truth that was so basic I sometimes forgot it might not be understood by people who are not from Mexico. My owl friend, he was a Mexican owl and so he knows about hunger. It is why he calls out his question all the night. Who are you? Are you food for me and my family? I told him I was not, so then he had no more interest in me.

But I had been the promise of food for the family of that man Nicolas until the Immigration got me. A bigger bird than him caught me, so he had to go look in another place for his food.

The hunting had been good for the Americans, I saw when they led me into the detention center, a small building with only two holding cells and one already crowded with men. They put me in the other one with four men and three beds. The whole building stunk like a soccer team after a hard game.

One of the sweaty men in my cell looked about the same age of me; the other three were younger, almost too young to be called men. They were trying hard to not look scared. I stopped at the door to the cell and flung my arms out to the sides.

"You are lucky, hombres. Cesar is here to improve your lives."

Nobody moved, but they were ready to.

Pues, well, if they thought I was a crazy man, it would stop them from worrying about what would happen to them later. They could now worry about what would happen to them today, with a crazy man sharing their cell.

I would not make them share their food, though. No more peanut butter crackers for this Mexican. The first time la migra caught me, I ate peanut butter crackers enough for two lifetimes. It would be the same here. No man here would starve, but they did not cook meals for us because we were not prisoners; we were only deportees. Peanut butter crackers were good enough to keep us alive. Not for me. I would trim half a kilo from my belly by the time I was sent through court and back to Mexico on Monday.

One of the young guys leaning against the back wall slid down to a squat; he wrapped his arms around his knees and stared at the cement floor, rocking just a little.

I would go to court on Monday with these men and we would all be deported. Then I would jump again.

29
Trish

I was in my bed and almost asleep when I realized Cesar hadn't told me the story of his life. He'd mentioned his wife and then when he saw me yawning, he'd said it was time for him to go to bed, too. Well, I was not about to let him get away with that. Tomorrow, I'd hold him to his promise. I turned to my left side and became one with my pillow.

I slept like the dead. Oh, Lordy, no—that was a lousy word choice. Okay: I'd slept the sleep of the innocent, as Mama would say, with that sort of slow rising into consciousness that at first gave me no memory of yesterday's dark moments. I lay perfectly still and waited for the significance of this particular day to come back to me from where it had lain all night like a trap or a treasure.

It didn't take long. Oh, right. A sweet young woman died in the desert, and we could have all been gunned down by the cartel last night.

But evidently there would be no lily for me on this day. I was so stoked by not having been murdered while I slept that I decided I'd rush through my shower, write a quick note to Mama and then get some coffee started for the guys.

Dear Mama,

I won't lie to you—things have gone south down here south of the border. The good news is that my old student Cesar and his brother Carlos have reappeared in my life. The bad news is that they are here in Nogales because (the Rev and I believe) they're trying to jump the border. The good news is that

Cesar is still so inherently a gentleman that the reason we were reunited is because he was bringing two young women to the church so they'd have a safe place to stay. The bad news is that the women disappeared the next day. The good news is that they've been found. The bad news is that one of them is being deported on Monday.

There was no way in hell I was going to tell my mama in a letter that Ruth had been murdered. No other name for it but murder.

The good news is that a storm kept Cesar and Carlos here in the church last night. That seems fitting, somehow. The good news is that I'll probably beat this letter home. The bad news is that I'll be leaving behind two guys I love. And Carlos, too.

This is not the kindest letter I could have written to you, Mama, but it is the truest.

Me

My hair was still dripping when I dashed barefoot down the hall to the kitchen to get the coffee perking, though they'd likely regret my impulse because a person who doesn't drink coffee should not be trusted to make it.

The pot had just stopped brewing when I heard footsteps in the hall, so I filled two mugs full and met Cesar and Carlos at the kitchen door.

"Morning, guys. Want some breakfast?"

"Nah, Teacher, we gotta check on our truck. We been lucky nobody bother it, but we don't want waste no more luck when we need save the luck for other stuff more important."

"Well, that makes sense." I said while I watched them chug their coffee. Carlos gave me a nod and Cesar flung a grin my way as they left by the kitchen door, leaving me alone and for once wishing I wasn't.

"And what are your plans, Ms. Morning Person?"

The good pastor had followed the smell of coffee into the kitchen, so I poured a new mugful and slid it the length of the wooden table to him like I was sliding a cold can of beer down a bar. Didn't spill a drop.

"What do you need me to do, Rev?"

"No, Trish."

He shook his head back and forth as he shot his right arm toward me with his hand out and the palm up, exactly like Diana Ross cueing the opening of "Stop in the Name of Love."

" Don't think about what anyone needs from you today. You've been through a lot the past day or two. You pick your agenda for today. It's Friday; maybe you should start your weekend early, do some shopping, read a book."

"What I'd like to do is find out what's going on with Alma. Do you know where she is? Is there anything I can do to help her?"

Rev. Freeman dropped his hand back to his mug.

"I do know where she is, but there's nothing you can do to help, at least not until Monday, and even then you can likely offer only moral support through your presence."

"My presence where?"

He let out a loud sigh of air through his nose and settled back in his chair. He pulled his coffee close to his chest, resting his elbow on the arm of the chair.

"Okay, here's the process. When Border Patrol picks up anyone without the right papers on the U.S. side of the border, or when someone gets turned over to them by one of the humanitarian groups the way the Shepherds gave Alma over, the migrant gets taken to a holding center. Since Alma was picked up toward the end of the week, she'll be held there until Monday. On Monday afternoon, she'll be taken to court with fifty or sixty or so other deportees. They will all be advised of their status and their rights and will be asked to plead guilty or not guilty. Almost always, the deportees have decided in advance what their plea will be and almost always their choice is to plead guilty.

Then they're led from the court room and processed out of the U.S. in various ways. In Alma's case, seeing as she's from Mexico City, she'll probably be brought back here to Nogales…"

I interrupted him, "Brought back from where? Where will she go to court? Phoenix?"

"No, no, sorry—Tucson. She'll be taken to the Federal Courthouse in downtown Tucson, a block or two from the capitol building. So, anyway, then they'll bring her back here to Nogales and process her through the Border offices. She'll be given half her bus fare home, and then told she's free to go."

He'd been watching me while he explained all this. I knew my eyes tended to darken from a cheerful green to a dangerous brown when I get angry or indignant—people had told me so often enough.

"So she is to be given the means to ride *halfway* home? Then what? She should walk across that last mountain range or two?"

"Don't shoot the messenger, Trish. I'm just giving you the facts."

He smiled and put his hand over mine. His hands were always warm, I'd noticed, and he never wore rings that might feel cold or hard when he touched someone who was frightened.

"Where the facts stop, that's where our work starts. You know this, remember? One good thing they do at the Casa is to escort people like Alma down the street to the center that distributes grant monies and donations as matching funds for bus tickets, and then they take them to the bus station to help them buy their tickets. I told you all this when you were worried I might be spending my own money on bus tickets."

"Right. Sorry. Brain's a little addled today."

I backed off, reminding myself the Reverend was not the enemy.

He patted my hand, then sat back and went on.

"The guy who manages the bus station is a good man; he always works to find the best deal on a ticket, and I happen to know he often lets migrants sleep for a night or two in a little back room while they work out what they are going to do next."

I gave him one brisk nod. I knew now what I was going to do next.

"I'll go to the Casa today."

Alma would not be there yet, of course, but someone else equally discouraged and worried and out of options would be, and it might help me to help them. I glanced at my watch. Eight-thirty. Just enough time to wash the dishes, brush my teeth and get some shoes on before I walked the three blocks to the Casa. That day's guests would be finishing their breakfast when I got there and I could just fall in with the other volunteers to help with clothing and first aid.

But Rev. Freeman interrupted my Daily Planner updating.

"That's fine, Trish; they always need help and your reason for being here is to help people, but you need to stop and write on one of those Post-it notes in your head: "Do something for Trish." I want you to take some time this weekend for yourself. You can't ladle soup from an empty pot. What do you do at home to feed your soul?"

I gave him a grin of mystery. "I buy violets."

He grinned back. "'…and with the dole, buy violets to feed my soul.' I'll bet you don't buy them—you probably grow them."

"Yep."

All of a sudden the smile fell from his face..

"You know, Trish,"he spoke more slowly than before. "sometimes working to make things better for other people is not a virtue. You need to make certain you aren't doing good works as a way of keeping people at arm's length. So long as you are giving, you aren't open to receiving, and so long as you don't have to accept, you can keep yourself to yourself alone. I'm asking you again: what do you do at home to feed your soul?"

I was carefully truthful with my answer.

"I walk in the woods or work in my garden."

The Rev lifted his head high enough to see city sidewalks through the kitchen window.

"Not exactly an option here. What else?

"I write."

He leaned forward and spoke to me like he was quoting scripture.

"Then write. These people need you to write. Tell their stories, Trish. Pearl Buck said, 'Stories are for the people.' Not *of* the people, but for the people. People like Alma and Cesar and Carlos are too busy surviving to record their own stories. You can serve them best, you can honor them best, by writing their stories."

Then he laid his hand on mine again and left it there for a moment. I knew this was his way of praying with me, because he respected that I was a person who had little use for spoken prayers.

Rev. Freeman picked up his coffee and went to his office to start his day's work. I went back to my room to brush my teeth and put on my sandals. I was out the door and walking to the Casa not even ten minutes after he'd given me my assignment for the weekend.

There were fewer people finishing their breakfasts at the Casa than earlier in the week.

"It's usually like this," one of that day's volunteers told me. "The numbers are biggest mid-week after a weekend's worth of migrants have been picked up. They have their afternoon in court on Monday and by Friday most of them have left here and are on their way home or somewhere else."

Because there weren't so many needing help, I was able to spend a nice space of time with one man who had lost his shoes in the desert. We rooted through the piles of shoes and boots the Shepherds had brought in, until we finally found a box printed with the size I guessed he would wear. Trying to match Mexican bodies with American sizing was generally a matter of guesswork or trial and error for the volunteers and the migrants. One clever trick this man told me about was to cut a piece of string the circumference of his waist and use that to measure the waists of the jeans lying in sorted piles on tables where breakfast had been served a half hour before.

I found a box marked 81/2.

"Here, I hope these fit. They're really good boots, and they're new."

The young man took them out of the box as gingerly as if they were wired with explosives. He put both boots on and laced them very slowly. After he tied each bow, he tucked the loops underneath the boot tongue. Then he leaned forward on the step he was using as a seat and rested his forearms on his legs for a few long minutes, staring at his boots while I stared at him. He reached down to his right boot, untied the maker's tag from a shoelace eyelet, and almost reverentially tucked the tag into the pocket of his shirt.

He looked up at me.

"These my first new boots."

Ever. He means his first new boots, *ever*. Dear God in Heaven.

What a long strange mission trip this had been. I looked back at the young man's shirt pocket with the boot tag tucked away there. This is what the Rev wants me to write about. Just this.

Back in my little room at the church, my feet propped on a pillow and my laptop balanced atop my lap, I wrote my way through Friday evening and Saturday morning. A little after noon on Saturday, I saved what I'd written to my blue flash drive with peace signs on it, and then I slipped the inch-long memory stick into the pocket of my jeans just in case the church burned down while I was eating lunch.

While I was fixing myself a plate of cheese and bread and fruit, my guy meandered into my thoughts, his hands in his pockets and a slant-wise grin on his face like he'd just come home from work and intended to let me know dinner could wait awhile. I sure wished I'd told Cesar more about him. They both had the same kind of quick and quirky wit; they would have liked each other.

I stopped mid-chew. Where exactly was Cesar? We hadn't heard a word from him or Carlos since Friday morning. I swallowed and headed down the hall to Rev. Freeman's office.

"Hey Rev? I'm going for a walk, okay? Do you need me for anything?"

"Sure do. I need you to let me come with you on your walk. I've been too long sitting, too long thinking. I need a change."

I tilted my head, "And so you chose walking with me as an activity that would allow you to cease thinking? Thanks a heap."

He smiled gently at me as he shut down the computer on his desk and stood up.

"You are a restful person, Trish."

It was an afternoon made for walking—not too hot, and the rains of summer nearly past. It was one of those days when I truly believed I could walk forever.

"Padre. Buenos dias."

A man leaning against the doorframe of the bus station entrance was yelling hello.

The Rev waved back and kept his hand out, ready to shake hands the way men do when they have known each other long and like each other well.

"Señor Pineda. Buenos tardes."

He rested his left hand over the right hand of the bus station manager, to hold the handshake in place a minute longer. The man was almost as tall as Rev. Freeman, but lean to the rev's solidness. I'd met Sr. Pineda the first day I volunteered at the Casa and knew already he was a kind man. He gave Rev. Freeman's hand a quick squeeze and then broke the handclasp to greet me.

"Como estás, bonita? You have no more customers for me from la Casa yesterday?"

I shook my head, no, smiling at him.

"No, it was fairly quiet yesterday, and that is a good thing."

"Sí, very good. I am always happy when I can to help, but it better when no one need our help, no es la verdád? Last night I have one family want to stay in the little room, and no other persons after the family they left this morning early."

"Oh, you had a family here last night? They weren't sent over from the Casa, were they?"

The manager shrugged. "No se. I not know where the brothers come, but their wives arrived on the bus at the evening, and the little one with them. The niñito need a bed for the night and also the wife of the brother who was no so tall, she need a place to rest because she carry their baby inside her, he tell me."

I always found it interesting the way people described other people: *the brother who was not so tall*. And so was the other brother a giant, I wondered?

"Señor, how tall *was* the brother who was the father of the little boy?"

"Oh, no so tall, but only that the two brothers very different; I would not think they be brothers. In looks, they not the same, but also the tall one look like he carry a lotta troubles, while the other brother all the time make jokes."

The station manager gave a little shrug.

"They both good men, I know this. I tell them they can stay in the little room two days, three, but they left on this morning early. The brother who make the jokes give me some money. I think he should not give the money because he need it for the baby, but I no give him insult to say I not take the money."

A tall brother and a short brother? One somber and the other a clown, but a generous clown? Sweet Jesus.

The Rev's hand closed over my shoulder in a squeeze meant to shut me up before I spoke foolishly. I mumbled a couple of semi-polite words to Sr. Pineda while the men shook hands again in a warm goodbye.

"I know what you're thinking, Trish," my most reverend friend whispered toward my left ear as soon as we were out of Sr. Pineda's hearing. " and I agree, but whatever Cesar and Carlos are doing is none of our business and we have no right to make it Sr. Pineda's business. There's not a thing we can do about it, anyway. We're talking about two grown men making decisions for themselves and their families, and they certainly don't have to clear their decisions with us first."

I stopped walking long enough to let out a sigh shudder through my shoulders and neck.

"But their wives are here. And Carlito. Wouldn't you think they would have brought their families to meet us? Wouldn't you think they would at least have told us their families were coming, so we could be excited for them? And didn't you hear him say that Cesar's wife is pregnant? I didn't know that. I don't think Cesar knew that. And, yes, I am whining. There are times when whining is entirely justified."

"I agree."

"I'm not at heart a whiner. You know that, don't you?"

"I do." He kept walking while I got the whines out of my system.

One block, two blocks nearer the border wall, and there next to the wall was an old truck the rev seemed to be steering me towards. Well, not really all that old, I could tell when we got closer, just coated with what must have been a week or more of traffic dust, except for where the door handles were clear of dust and, oddly, so was most of the pickup's open bed. Rev. Freeman stopped next to the driver's door window, swiped a small circle of the glass clear of dust with the back of his hand and peered into the cab.

"Their backpacks aren't in there."

"This is Cesar's truck?"

"Uh huh."

"They're gone, aren't they?"

"Uh huh."

I didn't get much writing done the rest of that weekend. I knew from hard experience I can't write when I'm grieving. The Rev, bless his heart, got caught in the Hav-A-Hart trap of proximity to me and my useless raging. Despite Sunday being his most demanding work day of the week, he gave a me wave of his hand as soon as services were over and I followed him down the hall toward the kitchen.

"There's some leftover soup in the fridge, Trish. Warm it up while I make us a couple of sandwiches."

Suddenly I was starving. I worked my way through one bowl of soup and half a sandwich before I hit him with my first question.

"Where do you think they are?"

"You know where I think they are, Trish, because you think the same thing. You just haven't admitted it to yourself yet. They are either already on the other side of the border, or they are somewhere getting ready to cross."

I set my sandwich down.

"I hate that. I hate that we didn't know. Why didn't they tell us? Don't they trust us?"

He reached across the table to cup his hand against my cheek for just a second, the way Daddy used to do. I leaned into his hand, the way I needed to.

"They trust us, Trish. But much more than that, they care about us. They wanted to keep us from worrying—it was the only way they had to thank us for our friendship."

"Then there's nothing we can do."

Rev picked up his spoon again.

"For Cesar and Carlos and their families, no, there's not much tangible that we can do right now. For my part, I'll chat with God a bit later today. But, remember, Alma still needs our support. She'll be coming through court tomorrow afternoon and then they'll bring her back here to Nogales. I want you to go to Federal Court tomorrow to be a presence for her."

"Yessir, I can do that." I gave him a military nod. "But how am I going to get to Tucson? I don't have a car or a Mexican driver's license."

"Yes, I know. I'll call Joy. She'll be coming with The Shepherds to work at the Casa in the morning. If I give her a heads-up to make arrangements, she can bring her own car and you can meet her there. One of the volunteers will drive the Shepherds' van back home when they're finished and Joy will take you to Tucson."

He ate the rest of his soup and I finished my sandwich.

30
Trish

"Hey, hon."

I looked up from the pile of women's jeans I'd been sorting by size.

"Trish, you up there?"

I was right; I thought I'd heard Joy talking somewhere. "Right here, Joy."

"Come down and help us unload these clothes. As soon as we get things set up for the morning, you and I can hit the road."

Every single one of the locals who were volunteering at the Casa that day were making their way over to where Joy was emptying the Shepherds' carts of their piles of donated clothes and first aid supplies. They adored her. I leaned against a porch post so I could watch the dozen or so men, mostly, who were bustling around Joy ten steps below me. And well they should. She couldn't possibly weigh even a hundred pounds—and ten pounds of that was raw optimism—but she strode unflustered through bureaucratic battlefields in their behalf. That woman down there was a spiky-haired little ninja who had sure earned her army of supporters.

"Trish, honey. Need a hand here."

Joy never broke stride while she rang my tardy bell, tossing a small box of bandages to a weary-looking woman with long braids coiled around and around on top of her head exactly the same way my grandmamma had worn her waist-length white hair. I stopped wool-gathering and stepped lively down to the street.

"On my way, Cap'n."

I stopped halfway back down the steps to pass along a load of clothes being handed up, and to send a plea to the universe: *please let me see Cesar again before I leave.*

"And, Rev, that *was* a prayer." I said out loud without intending to.

"Cómo?"

A young Mexican woman bringing up an armload of underwear stopped to speak politely to the *americana* talking to herself. I smiled at the woman and shook my head—*it wasn't important*—then I took the woman's bundle of socks and scivvies from her and carried it over to a table.

We got the carts emptied within fifteen minutes, but another fifteen passed before we could get on our way. One person—and then one more— needed a word with Joy.

Finally, though, tall Me and tiny Her, walked back down the steps to the sidewalk, pulling two empty metal carts side by side toward the border gates. We kept to the pedestrian lane, falling in line with families and businessmen going to the Arizona Nogales for the day, weaving our way along with them through revolving steel-barred gateways while we fished our IDs from our pockets. The guards all knew Joy, so they just grunted or nodded for her to *go on, go on through*. They looked more suspiciously at me and my passport while I squelched an itch to make light social jokes. Airport Security and Border Patrol do not joke.

We sweated uphill three-quarters of a mile to the only parking lot where the Shepherds were allowed to leave their vehicles, heaving the first cart and then the second into the back of the big white van. Joy slammed the double doors and gave the right-hand door one slap of her hand to make sure the latch had caught. She waved her remote toward her car parked on the far side of the van and clicked twice. We got in and headed out of the lot, north on Highway 19.

"This is the road I came in on two weeks ago, Joy."

"Um hum. You flew into Phoenix, right?"

"Yep, but I was too keyed up then to notice much except that to my Georgia eyes it looked pretty barren, in an exotic sort of way."

"And how does it look to you now, hon?"

"Exposed."

We passed the tiny community of Rio Rico and then the artsy village of Tubac with its cluster of galleries right by the highway and a sprawling compound of pricey houses all of the same cream-colored adobe as their high-walled enclosure. Green Valley was the largest town along the route.

"Right over there to the left, Trish." Joy waved a hand to a low mission-style church planted all around with bright beds of flowers. "There's our church. That's the home of the Samaritans."

When her church had faded from sight, I turned back around to the front window's view of nothing but desert spreading toward rolling hills in the not-far distance. All along each of the washes we drove over, clumps of Palo Verde trees bloomed as sunnily yellow as the forsythia in my front yard must be blooming by now . Joy glanced past me to see what I was looking at.

"They're gorgeous, aren't they, hon? I don't know which is prettier —the spring wildflowers, or the Palo Verdes in bloom. But I'd probably vote for the trees because of what they do: Palo Verdes are nurse plants to other smaller plants like the mesquites and barrel cactus. Palo Verdes grow where there's water, so the smaller plants settle in under the trees for water and for the shade they find there."

Judging by the next look she zinged my way, I was meant to take a lesson from what was she was saying.

"Those trees serve exactly the same purpose for migrants out in the desert, Trish. Many desert travelers have survived the heat by sheltering in the washes under the Palo Verdes until nighttime."

But Cesar and his family were city folks. Would they know to watch for havens like these? I didn't ask.

The nearer we got to Tucson, saguaro cacti filled the desert like armies of tall green humanoids gathering for an attack. Or maybe more like sentries with their arms spread wide in warning to migrants trying to cross the Saguaran Desert.

I was finally beginning to admit to myself that Cesar and Carlos and their families really were out there somewhere among those cacti. The Rev. was right; the guys had found a chance to get their families over and they took it. They left without a word because contacting us could only have muddied the waters.

Maybe even real waters. Where did they cross? Did they have to wade the river? And how the heck could they have gotten a toddler across without the little guy pitching a loud fit the way toddlers do?

"Joy?"

"Hmmm?"

Traffic was getting heavier as we neared downtown where highways 19 and 10 merged.

"How do the families who cross keep their babies quiet? You said they shelter under groves of trees during the day and walk by night. I'm guessing they try to sleep most of the day, but how do they convince a toddler to go along with that? Or even before that, when they are crossing over the actual border, how do they stop a baby from crying?"

Joy glanced at her side view mirror and changed lanes before she answered.

"They drug them, Trish. Sorry, but it's true. They give the babies a mild sedative or sometimes even just a swallow or two of something like Benadryl, to make them sleep. A baby that's sleeping doesn't cry."

A baby when it's sleeping, has no crying. What Joy was saying made perfect sense, but things that make sense aren't necessarily comforting.

"Joy, I wish you hadn't told me that."

She shrugged and looked rueful. I wasn't sure I had ever before seen anyone look rueful.But then my brain handed me another song and I had to laugh. I gave her right shoulder a tap.

"Okay, Joy, apparently you can take the woman out of Georgia, but you can't take REM songs out of the Georgia girl. Here's what just popped into my head: 'If wishes were trees, the trees would be falling. Listen to reason; reason is calling.'"

Joy raised her eyebrows at me and smiled."Well, now you'll have a chance to see for yourself what happens when wishes and reason collide. There's the Pima County Federal Courthouse."

I got out as soon as she'd park, eyeing the courthouse's polished metal walls while I rolled the kinks from my neck. Whose bright idea had it been to make the courthouse look like a medical research lab? There was absolutely nothing warm or welcoming about it; even those tall expanses of window were tinted to keep out the Arizona sunshine. Maybe that was the point.

Joy was slinging one strap of a small backpack over her left shoulder and already walking away from me toward stores and galleries and restaurants a couple ofblocks away.

"Leave your cell phone in the trunk, Trish. You can't take it in with you and you don't want to have to leave it in the open basket by the scanners. I'm going to run some errands while you're in court, but I'll be back before you're finished. I'll meet you in front of the courthouse."

She was leaving me?

"Oh. Okay. Thanks for bringing me. See you."

Mama would have been proud of me for thanking Joy instead of clinging to her backpack and whimpering for her to come with me. Of course, I didn't *have* to go in. I stopped with my hand on the front door's metal pull bar and rested in the comfort of this truth. I could turn and run to catch up with Joy if I chose to. If she thought I was being a weenie, she wouldn't say so. She'd keep her opinions to herself and put me to work helping her with her errands, which in all likelihood-- this was just dawning on me-- involved running legal interference for some other migrant.

"Permiso."

A young Mexican woman with a baby in a stroller was trying to slip past me. My ethical calisthenics were causing me to block the doorway to people without the luxury of choices.

Lord in Heaven, Trish. Just go in there.

I yanked the glass door open with a satisfyingly dramatic grunt, tossed my purse into the plastic bucket that zipped it along a conveyer belt to be scanned and walked through the body scanner not too fast and not too slow, just right.

"Third floor." a guard boomed at me as I grabbed my purse and asked where I needed to go.

The wooden courtroom door in front of me when I exited the elevator was as massive as the courthouse entry doors had been; I had to use both hands. I tried not to make eye contact with anyone while I scanned the room for some obvious sign of where I should sit in the cavernous white room laid out in four sections of wooden pews turned so that each section faced a space of open floor in front of the judge's bench. If not for the microphones and translator headsets planted like drive-in movie speakers across the middle of that space, the center of the courtroom would have looked for all the world like a dance floor with an MC platform.

I stepped all the way into the deeply refrigerated room and rested my hand on the scrolled back of the nearest bench. It was the last one in a row of five that together could have seated thirty or forty people, but all but the first bench were empty. A white couple probably in their sixties were sitting there with their heads bent together, almost touching over notepads opened on their laps. They seemed so at home there that I slid onto the bench behind them, close enough for comfort but separate enough to deny them if they turned out to be fruitcakes.

Then the smell hit me. The whole courtroom stank of sweat, a thick rankness from people who'd trudged three days in desert heat.   I thought back to two nights before, when Cesar and I had sat up late talking in the well-scrubbed rooms of the Methodist church. Sometime in the wee hours of that night, he'd admitted to me that he and Carlos had tried once already to jump the border, but they'd been picked up by Border Patrol.

"The worse thing, Teacher, is they call us bad names for what we can't do nothing about. They call us *skunk* and *stinky*. How we supposed to take a shower in the desert?"

Then being Cesar, he'd eased back on his criticism a little, wanting despite himself to be fair.

"Ah, not all the men. Some of them okay, treat us good. I guess there good policia and bad policia, right, Teacher? "

"Sure thing, Cesar."

He grinned, remembering when I'd taught him that expression, but then he turned serious again.

"I wish Americans know there good Mexicans and bad Mexicans."

I shook my head hard, trying to shake Cesar out of my mind because it was Alma I was there for, not Cesar.

"Steve, Marcos, hi. Thanks for being here."

Some lawyer-looking types were claiming the pew across from me by laying their briefcases on the seat. A Latina, tall and slim and stylish in a dark grey suit, greeted the two guys—one American and one not— before she reached over the back of the bench in front of her to put her hand on the shoulder of a woman sitting there. The woman's long thick braid swung against the wooden bench with a soft *whomp* as she turned partway around to see who had touched her, and when she saw, she smiled up at the lady like she had only just that moment remembered how to smile.

I guessed the Latina was some sort of advocate for any female migrants who'd been picked up There were only five women, all on that front row. The woman with the braid sat nearest me; next to her, a girl who couldn't have been eighteen was picking at a loose thread on her orange sleeve; and the short woman right in the middle was Alma.

I couldn't tell if she'd noticed me or not. Should I wave? Go up and speak? *Could* I get out of my seat and walk up there to let her know I was here? Courtroom etiquette was not my strong suit, never having been in a courtroom. The one and only time I'd been called for jury duty, the whole mess had been settled by lawyers in some inner sanctum while my fellow would-be jurors and I were sentenced to watch Fox news in a waiting room. All I'd gotten out of that experience was a thank-you speech on the importance of showing up to do one's civic duty, and a thirty-dollar check a month later.

So I truly had no idea if it was fine for me to step across the aisle to let Alma know I was there for her, or if the legions of toned guards and way-too somber Border Patrol agents lining the walls of the courtroom would immediately toss my disorderly self from the courtroom. Even if no one gave two hoots whether I spoke to a woman about to be booted back to Mexico, would my hand on Alma's shoulder help or humiliate her? Hesitation seemed the better part of good judgment, so I kept to my seat, waiting to see what would happen next.

While I waited, I studied the four Border Patrol agents lining the wall just on the other side of my pew. Three of the guys looked like every young Marine I'd ever seen: high-and-tight haircuts, granite-block shoulders, and legs that carried the muscular memory of playing quarterback in high school. Any emotions this group might have been feeling were locked away behind a rigid ethical code and good manners. These three were guys who might not share my politics, but they'd be polite.

The fourth agent, though, was the sort of person I instantly knew I would hate. My reaction to him put me in mind of the punch line to an old joke about God speaking to Job: "No, no particular reason why I put all those curses on you, Job. There's just something about you that pisses me off." Something about that agent made me ready for any excuse to be pissed off.

"All rise."

And we did.

The judge was a black woman with a face like your favorite aunt. She was maybe forty years old. The bailiff announced her to all present as the Honorable, and we were given permission to sit.

She addressed the defendants.

"All of you should have access to translator head phones. Does everyone see them? Is there anyone who does not have one? "

She paused, peering for a long moment over the top of her glasses at the rows of men and the one row of women, then at the lawyers, and last, at the teeny amen corner of visitors where I was sitting. We all felt firmly put in our places.

"If your headphones stop working at any time, I want you to stand."

Another pause, another sweep around the room over the top of her glasses, checking for comprehension. I was starting to decide I liked this lady.

"If you have any problems at all, stand, and we'll stop everything until you get a set that works."

I looked out of the corner of one eye to where the men were seated, the way I used to watch Saturday afternoon horror movies when I was little, not brave enough to commit myself to seeing the whole of whatever was there. I could tell that the men were all handcuffed. Were the women? Was Alma?

The judge was speaking again her voice as rich as sorghum. I sure hoped this lady sang contralto in some church choir because it would be a pity and a shame to waste that voice on legal speech alone. I could just hear the honorable judge offering up to a swaying congregation the swoop and rise of "When I was sinking down, sinking down, sinking down....what wondrous love is this?"

The judge looked around once more, nodding her head at the rows of migrants, looking each person in the eye the way I'd not been willing to do.

"Okay. Next I'm going to advise you of your rights. I know you have each been told of your rights by your attorney before you come in here today. I know your attorney has discussed your rights and your options with you. If this is not the case, let me know now."

And then she waited. I was becoming more and more and impressed by how this lady combined mandated legal process with... kindness. Yep, kindness was exactly what I was feeling from her. Her careful pacing of the proceedings was rooted in an intention to reach across the body of legal thoroughness to embrace its other side, benevolence.

"You have the right to a lawyer and to meet with a lawyer."

I should be writing this down. I rooted around in my purse, fishing out a hotel notepad and the free pen from my school's most recent in-service training day.

"You have the right to hear the charges against you and to hear what your options are."

Options? Huh. I had no idea Alma would have options.

"You have the right to remain silent."

I looked at Alma and the three ladies on the row with her: nothing but stoic silence there. Way to uphold your rights, ladies.

The judge led us by example into a moment of reflection on what we had heard so far. She sat there as if she and we had all the time in the world. You are one classy lady. I winged my silent compliment toward the front of the courtroom.

She moved to the next step in the proceedings:

"If you plead guilty to the charges against you, you will be asked a series of questions."

I jerked forward in my seat. We were moving from the rights to the charges already? That was one quick trip.

"I will address you as a group first." she explained to the migrants, "and tell you what your maximum penalty could be. Then I will call you up individually and ask you the questions."

The judge looked around the room, waited for a full minute—which is a much longer span of time than you'd think—and then she spoke again.

"For a guilty plea, you could receive up to six months in prison and a fine of up to $10,000."

I counseled myself not to snort.

Oh, no problem, because Alma has a spare $10,000 in her back-pack. Oops, no wait, she no longer even has a backpack because she had to leave her belongings behind in the desert when she and her dead companion were picked up. *Stop it.* I was being self-serving. This wasn't about me.

"In order to prove guilt, the court must determine that you have no legal authority in the United States, that you came from Mexico, and that you came through an illegal port of entry."

This was Alma's crime? She had walked from one square foot of desert to a different square foot.

"If you plead guilty, you will give up your right to a trial. If you plead guilty you will have a criminal offense on your record, permanently."

She was doing her utmost to wield her power fairly, but the judicial cards were stacked against her.

"Finally, in return for a guilty plea to the petty charge of illegal entry, the government will dismiss the felony charge.'

Yes. I snatched hold of the positive within so much negative as soon as the judge spoke it. Gotta love the U.S. legal system. I might disagree with the idea that these migrants should be charged at all, but at least I lived under a system that had been designed to give the best possible shot at guarding against punishment which was grossly out of line with the action that had brought the charge. The system didn't always work, but the intent was there.

The judge set down the papers she'd been reading from. Apparently, her "finally" had marked a point of transition in the proceedings. A couple of guards moved to where Alma and the other women were sitting. The guards escorted Alma and her seat mates to the front where they stood facing the judge and a microphone for each of them. Their arms hung at the front of their blue prison uniforms. Their hands were cuffed. Lord God.

Alma was the second woman led to the microphone. Each woman was asked the same questions and each gave the same answers.

"Do you understand the charges against you, and the maximum penalty?"

"Sí."

"Do you understand your right to a trial?"

"Sí."

"Are you willing to give up your right to a trial?"

"Sí."

"Of what country are you affiliated?"

"de Mexico."

"On April 12, did you enter into southern Arizona from Mexico?"

"Sí."

"On the plea of illegal entry, do you plead guilty or not guilty?"

"Culpable."

Alma gave her plea and a guard led her out through a door, stage right. I let out a whoosh of held breath. That was that.

I'd see Alma at the Casa tomorrow and tell her I'd been in court with her. It would be my last chance to work at the Casa before I flew home on Wednesday. I checked my watch. Two-thirty. Joy wasn't picking me up until three-thirty, so I had time to walk around downtown Tucson for a bit.

I grabbed my purse and stood to slip out the door just as the first group of men was being led to the front. There were seven of them, handcuffed, but also shackled together at their ankles. I'd had no idea. My brain would not provide me with a single snide comment to make about this sight. There *are* no words to say about tired, sad men in shackles.

I turned away, and in turning, saw Cesar at the end of that line of bound men. I was pretty sure he hadn't seen me, but his words had.

Teacher, you think there a reason you and me keep a history together?

Looking at my boy up there in shackles, all I could think was yes. Yes, I do, Cesar. I didn't have a clue right then what that reason might be, but maybe it didn't matter. Sometimes the history itself is enough.

There was a hand on my shoulder. I turned around, away from Cesar, to see who had touched me, even though I already knew.

"Rev? What are you doing here? Where's Joy?"

He smiled and squeezed my shoulder, then dropped his hand so he could hold it out to me.

"James, Trish. My name is James. Carlos called me. He made it over with the wives and his little boy, but they picked up Cesar. I knew the timing was right for Cesar to be brought to court today."

He gave a little shrug of his shoulder and another smile, kind of a sideways smile.

"I thought you might want me to be here."

I took his hand.

He gave me a little tug toward the door.

"Let's go home and wait for Cesar."

CPSIA information can be obtained
at www.ICGtesting.com
Printed in the USA
FFOW04n0818030217
31972FF